W9-CMF-749

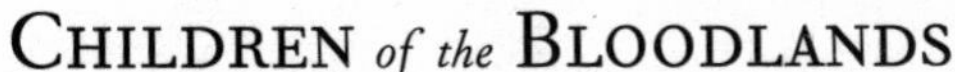
CHILDREN of the BLOODLANDS

S.M. BEIKO

CHILDREN OF THE BLOODLANDS

THE REALMS OF ANCIENT
BOOK II

Published by ECW Press
665 Gerrard Street East, Toronto, ON M4M 1Y2
416-694-3348 / info@ecwpress.com

Editor for the press: Jen Hale
Cover design: Erik Mohr
Interior illustration: S.M. Beiko
Author photo: Teri Hoffard Photography

Library and Archives Canada
Cataloguing in Publication

Beiko, Samantha, author
Children of the Bloodlands / S.M. Beiko.

(The realms of ancient ; book 2)
Issued in print and electronic formats.
ISBN 978-1-77041-358-0 (hardcover).
Also issued as: 978-1-77305-229-8 (ePUB),
ISBN 978-1-77305-230-4 (PDF)

I. Title.

PS8603.E428444C55 2018 jC813'.6
C2018-902526-3 C2018-902527-1

The publication of *Children of the Bloodlands* has been generously supported by the Canada Council for the Arts, which last year invested $153 million to bring the arts to Canadians throughout the country. *Nous remercions le Conseil des arts du Canada de son soutien. L'an dernier, le Conseil a investi 153 millions de dollars pour mettre de l'art dans la vie des Canadiennes et des Canadiens de tout le pays.* We also acknowledge the support of the Ontario Arts Council (OAC), an agency of the Government of Ontario, which last year funded 1,737 individual artists and 1,095 organizations in 223 communities across Ontario for a total of $52.1 million, and the contribution of the Government of Ontario through the Ontario Book Publishing Tax Credit and the Ontario Media Development Corporation.

Canada Council for the Arts Conseil des Arts du Canada

PRINTED AND BOUND IN CANADA
PRINTING: FRIESENS 5 4 3 2 1

For the families who made us,
and the ones we choose along the way

THE ONE TRUE CHILD

The ONE TRUE CHILD

NORTHERN SCOTLAND

Stop crying and be braver, Albert had said. But now his mouth wasn't moving. The skin of his forehead was as split as the crack in the world they had found, but his forehead was leaking red, leaking too quickly and too much. Saskia had crouched stiff and numb more than an hour, pressing her whole body weight into the wound to make the red stop.

Stop crying!

But she couldn't. Not in the dark, in the cold, as she made slow progress through the woods. She thought about all the things Albert had said, the things that led to this.

She exhaled a shaking breath, dragging the heavy sack through the crunchy leaves. The rope burned her small hands. Albert wouldn't say a thing anymore.

It had been their secret — his and Saskia's. What they'd found down in the woods at the bottom of the scrabby glen that day, months ago, just after Saskia had turned eight. Papa had been home, rare occasion that it was. She understood that they needed money to pay the bills and that Papa needed to work as much as he did, but sometimes she resented the long road that kept him from them for weeks and weeks. And there was also the invisible road inside of them that divided their hearts. The road paved black when Mum had died.

On that brighter day, the day after her birthday, Papa took them for a walk. He wasn't as strong as she remembered him being. He seemed bowed as a croggled tree. His knees weren't in good shape, and he was not young. Albert was fifteen, but their parents had had them late in life. Saskia didn't mind; this is how she thought all parents were. Old and grown and wiser than she ever could be.

But she could see age in Papa's stiff walk, the hours and days of driving taking its toll. It made her feel sick. "Go on ahead, ye wee gomeral," he'd said, sitting on the crest of a hill. "I can see ye from here."

But they'd gone too far into the woods, and Saskia knew Papa couldn't see them anymore. Albert always had to go far, as far as he could, to make it count. Saskia only ever wanted to be near him. She wanted his protection, and she wanted to protect him, too. But above all, she wanted to show she could be brave.

Albert stopped at a massive split in the rock of the munro — it was as if a big axe had cut it in half. The sun shone into it, revealing the barest crack in the world.

Albert climbed down to investigate. Saskia didn't protest, but she wanted to.

"There's something down here," he said, frowning into the small crater. "You've got small hands. C'mon."

Saskia twisted her shirt in those small hands and picked her way down. She and Albert bent, heads touching, and she put her hand in —

"Sss!" Saskia pulled her hand back, shaking it.

"What?" Albert grabbed her hand, alarmed, and they both stared at the cut, the blood trickling around Saskia's wrist and dripping into the crack.

The ground shook, and Saskia screamed. Albert grabbed her hand, pulled her up the hill, and they took off in a blur back the way they'd come.

Papa was close to laying an egg because of how long they'd been gone. Albert was too breathless to explain the cut on Saskia's hand, to waylay Papa's anger as he wrapped it up too tightly in his handkerchief, making Saskia wince as he dragged them both home in furious silence. "Where did you get a knife?" Papa asked gruffly, not believing either of them when they said there was no knife. Just a crack in the ground whose darkness haunted them all the way home.

Albert stayed up most of the night thinking about that crack. "I had a dream about it," he said. "We have to go back." It didn't matter what Saskia felt about it — she would go where Albert went, and that he'd said *we* meant he wanted her there, meant she had to. They rushed out when Aunt Millie had fallen asleep in her chair in front of the telly. They knew they'd have more than a chance the minute the whisky bottle clattered onto the sideboard. It was summer — what little they have of it in the north — and out here, children could do as they pleased. They could chase the massive herds of deer, they could scrabble up and down rocks. They could get into trouble. It wasn't like in the cities or bigger towns like Durness or Thurso. So much desolate freedom here. Saskia knew it'd have to end sometime, but she didn't suspect it would be this soon.

They went back to the crack, and it was so much wider. The ground around it was black. "Probably that earthquake," Albert guessed, but Saskia didn't remember there being earthquakes in the Highlands.

Then there was a bang, loud like thunder, and Saskia jumped and ran, ran fast and far without looking back until she realized she was running alone. She twisted and screamed, "Albie!" But he hadn't followed. She couldn't leave him behind, knew he'd never do such a thing to her, so she turned around, and he was just as she'd left him, standing there above the crack, mouth open, frozen in awe.

The grey amorphous thing crawled out of the world and into the air. A column of ash. A straight cloud of smoke. It opened a mouth and words came out. "I am the Gardener," it said. "Thank you for raising me."

The voice was soothing, calm and clear. Saskia was shaking all over, but she wouldn't leave Albert. And when she looked down at her hand, with the big scratchy bandage, she knew this was all her fault.

❧

There was no road in the woods. Saskia was following the brook, which crept along an impassable munro. *What's inside the mountains?* Albert had asked whenever Aunt Millie took them driving for a change of scenery. *The sharp, dead peaks have many secrets*, she'd say, but Aunt Millie wasn't prone to fairy stories. Or tales of monsters.

But they'd found themselves in a monster story anyway.

Saskia stumbled, pitched, and slid on her knees. She'd dropped the rope, but when she whirled around, the sack was still there. She'd wrapped Albert in his Ninja Turtles bed-sheet, but it was faded from years of washing. It seemed to glow in the dark.

She whimpered when she noticed the dark patches showing through. She clenched her bloody hands and stood on shaking feet.

Her hands stung even worse now, as if the cut were still fresh. Picking the rope back up and continuing on was so much harder than starting out. Why did she have to be such a cry-baby? Why couldn't she be like Albert? Why did she have to do this alone? There wasn't much she really understood — not in the way grown-ups did — but she knew that if she didn't do this, she'd lose her brother forever. She would be in the biggest trouble of her life. And not with Papa or Aunt Millie. What waited for her in the dark woods scared her most.

She could tell she was getting close, though. The humming in the ground thrummed through her tired legs into her bones. So she kept going.

❧

Urka told Albert and Saskia that they were special. That it had come from a land plagued with ruin, and that she and Albert were the key to saving the three rulers of this faraway place who were imprisoned there forever.

These three rulers, according to Urka, had a precious child, and it had been sent to the Uplands — that's what it called Earth — to get help. To find a family. And Saskia and Albert were the family they were waiting for.

Every day that they snuck out to visit it, Urka got bigger and the forest around it got smaller. It said that eating the trees was the only way to get its strength up after the long journey, and that the trees here weren't like the trees back in its home. "But soon that will change," Urka promised. "Soon this world will be covered in the trees I know."

Saskia tried to look Urka in its eyes, all six of them, to try to see if it was telling the truth, the way she did when Albert told her a fib to get a rise out of her. But it hurt to look into those eyes — like looking too long at the sun. She should have known then.

Albert asked, right at the start, if Urka could grant wishes. Urka was quiet a long time as its ash body hardened to stone, grew huge in the shadow of the mountain that hid it. It said yes, a horrible bone-grating affirmation, then praised Albert for his cleverness. Saskia scrunched her nose and questioned *how*, especially because Urka could barely move a few feet from the crack it had crawled out of and seemed weak despite how many trees and dead things it had shoved into the big mouth in its growing belly. That was when the eyes fell on Saskia, and she turned away. That was when Urka saw she doubted. That was her second mistake.

In the deep, dark woods, she finally collapsed. The moon shone through the cleft in the rock, shone onto the place where the crack had opened into a valley and devoured the light. Her head pounded and she was impossibly hungry.

"Child," came the voice, like the metal hangers in her closet grating on the rusty bar Papa said he'd replace but never did. Saskia shrank and instinctively covered the sheet-covered lump of Albert with her body. "Child," it said again. "At long last."

❧

Albert became loyal to Urka the minute its smoke-column head came out of the ground. Albert trusted it and everything it said. "It's a proper quest," he said, almost to himself, nodding and walking with a determined spring all the way home. "I knew I was destined for it. I knew it."

Papa had always given Albert a hard time for not being more into sports, for not getting better grades. Papa was a hard person with high expectations. But Saskia always saw that it hurt Albert, even when he pressed his mouth closed and said, "Right," after each critical blow. Saskia thought if she did her best, it would be good enough for both of them, but it never was.

And Urka bestowed easy praise. It was grateful that Albert tended to it. The bigger its body got, the bigger its promises became. Promises of great power, of rewards, of wishes granted. They gathered bigger and bigger bundles of wood, stole the axe from the garden shed. "I don't think we're supposed to do this," Saskia had warned. Cutting down the trees here seemed like a crime, but Albert told her to stop whining. That this didn't happen to every kid, and they should be grateful.

Then Urka spoke of their mother.

"Do you miss her?" it asked. Albert flushed in the way he always did when he was about to cry, but his jaw compressed and he nodded. Urka seemed only to speak to Albert now, almost wary of Saskia. She missed their mother, too, though she barely remembered her.

"My masters can bring her back." Urka's biggest promise of all. "They can bring back anyone you have ever lost."

"How?" Saskia asked. Her doubt was sharp still, and her words echoed loud off the split mountain.

Urka smiled, feeding a massive tree trunk into its belly. That was the first time Saskia had noticed the dark flames there. "With a power I can give to you. A power you have earned."

Albert was desperate. He demanded that power, like it was Christmas and he wanted lordship over Saskia's new toys. She thought he'd been changing more into a grown-up before this, but when they'd met Urka, Albert's eyes shone with a petulance she'd never seen. A willingness to do anything blindly for what he was owed. "Give it to me!" he barked. Urka was more than happy to deliver.

Something black and cobweb-wispy floated out from the horrible furnace inside Urka's belly into the daylight. Saskia screamed when it touched Albert. To her shame, she went totally numb, unable to stop it, because she knew it was bad, knew she could never abide it on her skin, knew she wasn't brave enough. But moments after it touched Albert's hand, it vanished.

Albert jerked. "What did you do? It's gone! I don't feel any different!"

Urka bowed its head. "Patience," it said, and Albert looked insulted. "Soon all our family's dreams will come true."

Albert got reckless after that. He pushed his mates too hard. He didn't play fair. He hit his best mate Roger right across the mouth and broke the skin, all because Roger said Albert was acting funny. No one said anything after that. No one said much to Albert in the days before Aunt Millie said the same, reaming him out for hitting Roger. Albert was scratching his neck, the place where the black splotch had appeared the night before.

"What's happened to Ava's sweet boy?" Millie muttered, resurrecting their dead mother. "Imagine what she'd think to see ye now."

Saskia yelled, tried hard to wrench Albert's hands away from Aunt Millie's throat the minute they shot there. Saskia clawed and scraped at him like an animal, but he swept his sister aside like tissue paper, and she crashed over the table, taking a lamp with her. She looked over her scabby knees to see Albert pull away from Aunt Millie gently, like he'd planted a kiss on her neck with his hands, and Saskia saw that she was still breathing, clutching the arms of her chair like the room was spinning.

A collar of black webbing spread over her pasty neck. Her feet hammered against the chair like she was trying to run away but couldn't get up. Then her shoes burst, and horrible black tendrils — roots — stabbed through the carpet and the hardwood, and as Albert slipped out of the house smiling, Saskia screamed and screamed.

"Come closer, child," Urka spoke to Saskia now, out of shadow, reaching her with smoke tendrils. "The time has come to reclaim what has been lost. Do not be afraid." But Saskia knew better.

"The time has come," Urka said again. "Bring the boy to the Gardener. Urka will make it better. My masters will be your new fathers and mother. They will heal all."

"How?" asked Saskia. "What will you do with him?" She hadn't realized she was crying so hard, tears and snot mixing, drowning her, falling onto the blackening face of her brother, who could have been sleeping but for the blood. She dared not ask, "Can you really bring him back?" in case Urka changed its mind.

"Oh my sweet child of earth and ash," Urka said, and Saskia felt something in her hair — something hard and sharp, that must have been Urka's hand trying to soothe her. It clenched her scalp. "Give the boy to me, and I will show you."

When Saskia had stopped screaming and retching in the living room, she was afraid to move. She stared at Aunt Millie, who had become some kind of horrible tree, her feet roots throbbing and churning the floor, her hands and arms stretched above her head, branches reaching into the ceiling, searching for a way out through the cracking drywall.

Albert had killed Aunt Millie. Or had turned her into a monster. Either way, he had done this. Air still rasped out of the place Millie's mouth had been. Her eyes were covered in hard black bark. She looked like she was trapped in a nightmare.

Albert had not returned, and Saskia was afraid to go after him, afraid to move and wake up the thing occupying Aunt Millie's chair. But she wanted to be brave, even now, so she went outside shakily. It was morning, grey and overcast. Looking out onto the glen, there weren't many places Albert could be, but Saskia zeroed in on the middle distance where the woods dipped down towards the brook and the cradle of hills. She knew Albert was there, but she wasn't about to go. She would wait. She would scream and cry and beg and she would get Albert far away from here, from the monster they'd woken in the woods, and to a hospital in a city. Because surely he was sick. Surely a doctor could help.

Saskia sat on the wooden step, knees drawn up, head buried in her arms, until it was dark. She heard a stick break and whipped her head up. Albert stood very close by. He looked much older, and grave. But more than that — even in the darkness, Saskia could see the black creeping up the collar of his T-shirt, the tips of his fingers. He stared at her like he couldn't believe she was there.

"Urka said it could bring Mum back," he said. His voice was distant and more childlike than ever. It was a reason, but even Albert didn't sound like he believed it.

"Aunt Millie . . ." Saskia started. But she was so tired. She wanted her mum, too, wanted Papa more than anything, but she and Albert were alone now. The roots of the tree that had once been Aunt Millie had ripped out the phone line. The nearest neighbour was a car ride away. They were trapped.

"Roger is a believer now, too," Albert said quietly. "It's

starting. Soon all our dreams will come true. We will be a proper family. You'll see."

He reached for Saskia, but she was lightning fast, on her feet, off the stairs, and away from him, a bit down the hill. Albert didn't reach for her again. "You're so selfish," he said. "Stop crying." And then he went into the house for the last time.

Saskia shouldn't have followed. But she was too young to stop and think. "A-Albie," she sobbed, in the living room. "We have to . . . to call someone. We can't —"

He twisted and lunged so suddenly Saskia barely had a breath to get out of the way. Albert smashed into the sideboard, glass and wood exploding with strength that had never been his. Saskia stumbled deeper into the house, towards their shared bedroom, blinded by tears and terror. But when Albert struck out again, like a venomous snake, something turned to rock in Saskia's stomach.

"Stop it!" she shouted, as if it were just a game and she'd had enough.

And she met the blow of her brother's whole body, turning him aside with a powerful shove. Slowly, as if underwater, Albert's shoe caught the carpet, his eyes his own, only for a second, before his head struck the bedpost, and the light left those frightened eyes forever.

Be brave, Saskia thought again. She unwrapped Albert all the way and did so gingerly, afraid that she would catch the black sickness that had twisted her dark-haired brother so. But she would do anything Urka said if it meant bringing him back.

If it meant untangling the thing that had wrapped itself so firmly around his heart. Or erasing her own horrible mistake.

She stood back and turned. Urka had grown enormous, like it was carved from the munro it had split in half. It spread its arms; at the end of them, the two axes it had for hands twisted and changed into claws. It gathered Albert up and fed him into its belly furnace. Albert did not burn but glowed like a coal. Saskia held herself in a tight hug, because there was no one else to hold her, to tell her it would be okay. Because she knew she could never go home again.

"You must believe," Urka said, straining its horrible hands to the sky and then to the ground, its rocky body growing and humming and glowing ever brighter. "Will you help my masters rise to their rightful place? Will you devote yourself to your fathers? Your mother?" A flicker in the furnace. "*To their one true child?*"

Saskia was not stupid, no matter how many times Albert had told her she was. Saskia was bright and selfless and knew deep down she was a good person. But she would have done every terrible thing she was afraid of to bring Albert back. So she took that goodness and locked it tightly away, hoping, maybe one day, it might save her.

"Yes," she said. "Yes."

Deep within Urka's furnace, she saw Albert's eyes open, and a black tendril from her brother reached for her and made her part of it.

Part I

Tremor

A Burning Shade

August 9, 1996

Dear Roan,

I always write these letters with the intention of sending them to you, but they have turned into a kind of diary instead. A place where I can put so much down, even when it seems there isn't enough paper in the world. I always feel more compelled to share things with you than the people who are closest to me. My partner. My own daughter. But you are distant, still almost like a dream. And now more distant still.

You have been marked.

I had to put the pen down after writing it. Because now it's been made true. The Moth Queen picked you — you — after everything I've given to this gods-damned Family.

I've been in this world long enough to see unfairness. I've given my life to correcting some of it. And yet still fate, the gods — call them what you will — they still come for my blood. No one is safe.

I didn't want this stone. I didn't want the responsibility. After a while, though, it seemed like I was the only person who could handle it. I enjoyed being the hero. But it's been thirty long years of it. If I can't save my own family, then what good am I to this world?

I'm about to do something. I don't know if I'll succeed. It's something I have to do alone — not as though I'm not used to that road. But I can't stand by any longer. The Narrative, the balance. It isn't real. The rules I lived by are broken.

You've been marked. I will come back for you. I've told Ravenna to wait. But she's my daughter, after all. She may do something rash. And I won't be here to stop her.

Roan . . . I don't know you yet. I saw you only the one time, and you were so small and fragile, Ravenna let me hold you for just a few minutes. I knew that what Deon said was true, all those years ago. You will do great things. You are meant to be in this world. And I will see to it that Zabor doesn't pluck you from it.

I'm going away to a place I can't describe. Ruo said she'd send you some postcards, to make it seem like I've gone on a globetrotting adventure. If I do succeed, you'll grow up knowing the truth. Or, if I fail, you won't be around long enough to feel the sting of being abandoned by a grandmother you never knew.

I suppose the last place I'll see with these waking eyes is Edinburgh. I've been everywhere, lived and passed through ancient cities and bustling metropolises and vacant spaces that are empty on the map. The house in Winnipeg . . . I thought, maybe, I could really live there, be near Ravenna, rebuild what broke between us. I kept the house and all the things I collected over the years in it, shipping them there like a tithe to be paid, preparing a den I'd never inhabit. Wishful thinking. Maybe one day it can be yours. Maybe one day you can have the life that slipped away from me.

But we had a life here, too, in Scotland. Ruo, Ravenna, and me. The window boxes have been empty for a long time. I've told Ruo that it isn't worth it, keeping vigil over me as I journey to do the impossible. Time might be different there; I could come back tomorrow, or a hundred years could go by and everyone I love could be gone and it will all be too late. But Ruo has already given up so much for me. She said she might as well give up the rest.

Someday maybe we will come back here together. Someday maybe I will let go of all those possibilities of peace. Today is not that day.

Dear Roan. I'll see you soon.

Love, Cecelia

I folded the letter up, carefully. I'd taken it out and reread it, along with the others, so many times that I could recite it by heart. This was her last letter. Something shifted in me when I read it, the stone itself reacting. Edinburgh. I knew I still had to be here, knew that I would find answers here for the journey Cecelia had sent me on before I lost her. I tucked the letter in my jacket, which I hung on the hook inside my locker at the back of the restaurant. I turned away from the change room door, fastening my work shirt's buttons over the heavy, burning burden lodged in my skin.

The Dragon Opal.

Cecelia had managed to separate herself from it, hide the stone beneath her summoning chamber, and come back to the world as a fox named Sil. To guide me. To save me. She really had given everything up for me. But why? So I could carry this mysterious rock that kept me up at night, that made me think I was going crazy? To what end?

I sighed. Three months of nothing. She'd used a name in the letter — Ruo, a name she'd never mentioned before as Sil or in any of the other letters. Whoever that person was, they'd been with Cecelia before she went on a quest that lasted more than fourteen years in order to save me from death itself. And maybe that person had some answers for me.

But I wouldn't get them tonight. I fastened my pocketed apron around my waist, tucking in my order pad and pen as I passed the kitchen. Tonight I was on the dinner rush.

I had been dead — twice — and this was infinitely worse.

Stepping out onto the dining floor always made my chest clench as though I was pulling away from a blow. I usually started the night surveying the chaos from the host booth, where other servers girded their loins for dealing with complaints or customers' thoughtless barbs. Or grappled with the heavy reality that *this* is where your choices had led you.

But I didn't have time for an existential crisis. Not right now. Table Five was leering at me over a watered-down Jim Beam. A full-scale inappropriate jaw-tightening look that, especially because he was probably twenty years older than me, spoke volumes: You are meat. Bring it here.

I rolled my eyes and turned away. It wasn't worth

indulging the fantasy of "accidentally" burning the place to the ground. I needed the money.

Nabbing a job on the Royal Mile seemed easy at the time, three months ago. Following the bare trail of Cecelia's past here, I figured the Dragon Opal would steer me in the right direction the minute my red-eye touched down. I didn't think I'd still be here, with little to nothing to show for it, except a worryingly-close-to-expiring youth visa and barely a pound to scratch together for French fries — er, chips.

I didn't think the stone would have its own agenda. But I should've known better.

The night droned on. Drink order, appetizers, mains, dessert. Clear the tables, wipe them down. Rinse and repeat. There wasn't anything wrong with serving; it was actually a nice break from being hunted and fighting bad guys. But I wasn't a patient person at the best of times. I was trying to lie low, trying to figure out where Cecelia had lived, if she'd had any friends. But fourteen years was a long time to be gone. A lot could have changed.

I blinked and found I'd arrived at the kitchen staff access counter on autopilot, pulling orders for tables six through seven. Couples taking up whole booths in the rush, ordering the cheapest fare. Despite the virtually revolving door of starving tourists coming in, looking to cram burgers and chips and guzzle beer after their castle and brewery tours, I could read the crowd easily: I'd be lucky if I got tipped more than ten percent tonight.

My chest tightened again. I resisted the urge to scratch at the skin under my standard-issue uniform, to pay it any notice. It wasn't long ago I was doing the same with a bad eye, which got too much attention as it was.

Today had been an okay day, though. I was going to keep it that way.

I had to admit, I still loved seeing people's faces light up as their food arrived, but I usually didn't linger. I was tired, bone-tired — that never changed — but I was mostly tired of people asking the same goddamn —

"Oh wow! Your eyes are different colours!" the blond at seven squealed. "Are those contacts?"

Tonight, I decided to play coy. "Yep! Thought I'd mix things up a bit. Can I get you folks anything else?"

"Are you from America, then?" the blond's beefy date sputtered around widely cut chips, the house special. His accent suggested England. Manchester, as rough as it came.

"Canada," I said through a fleeting smile, before retreating stiffly with their empty pint glasses.

And the night went on. My feet ached. There were no moments to myself, not really. Not even in the bathroom, with female co-workers hammering on the stall door that *Roan oh my god Six is having a meltdown about her scallops* because I seemed to be the only one capable of handling these things with a level head. If only they knew that this was small potatoes to what I'd faced.

Lather. Rinse. Repeat.

The hair on the back of my neck prickled, and I felt my throat flush. I turned and saw Table Five raise his empty glass. He was still here? Hadn't I seen him two hours ago? I didn't move, and another server swept in to take his order. Five didn't seem to mind, and I turned away before I could get a *proper* look at him with my good eye.

No time for any of that.

I held onto this job with a death grip. No matter how banal

it was, or how being here meant I wasn't *out there*, doing the investigating I'd come here to do, I'd do it. I'd keep quiet and keep my head down as long as I could. I wanted to do this the right way. There would be answers in Edinburgh. There had to be. And it kept an ocean between me and the home I couldn't go back to. At least, not now.

I sneezed. "Bless," Athika said, though it came out as more of a sigh as she scratched in the depths of her massive afro-hawk with a pen.

"Thanks," I grunted back. A bitter exchange of service-industry exhaustion.

"So do you know that creep, or what?" Athika squinted, tapping an order into the touch screen till. "He's been undressing you with his eyes all night."

I felt hot despite the high-powered AC. Hotter than usual, I mean. I whipped around and sure enough, there was Table Five, except now he had downgraded to the bar. To a better seat in the house.

The flames were close under my skin, but my words were cold. "No," I replied to Athika, trying for indifference, but I could feel the menace rising. Feel it straining out of control. I didn't want to do this, but I knew I had to.

I left the till station and went around to the other side of the restaurant to the dining lounge, which still allowed me a clear view of the bar through a decorative glass wall. I let my vision fall in and out of focus like a flexing lens, and then — *click*. My amber eye lit up the restaurant around me.

I tested it on the crowd. Mostly Mundanes tonight, but there were Denizens all the same. I hadn't noticed my heart rate ratcheting up, but seeing them — the gauzy impressions of Rabbits, Foxes, and the odd Owl hovering over their human visages — loosened the tension in my fists. My gaze lingered on the Foxes. My own Family, my tribe, and I thought of Sil, as I always did in these situations. Her voice was clear: *Focus, pup, or you'll get burned.*

I straightened. *Focus.* I swung my spirit eye onto Table Five, hunched over the bar. His leathery, pockmarked face. His twitchy, bony hands on his glass. He was scanning the restaurant, too, wriggling in his seat, maybe trying to see where I had gone. He actually wasn't as old as I'd first thought — maybe in his twenties? — but he was in rough shape, hair thinning, skin bad. Sick. He was turned away from me, and I couldn't get a clear impression . . . but then his eyes met mine. Black. Red rimmed, but the edges were glowing.

I staggered, grabbing my chest and coming down hard on one knee. *No, not now.* I crouched behind a recently vacated table that was still covered in abandoned plates and half-eaten food, and I tried to focus on the patterns in the hardwood planks underneath me. I shut my eyes, both the spirit and the human one, and mutter under my breath to try to find purchase for calm — *the Veil. The Den. The Warren. The Glen. The Roost. The Abyss. The Bloodlands . . .*

What had been like a prayer suddenly felt like a hex. I wanted to pull my hand away from the stone, embedded in my skin and bones and exposed like a geode, but I couldn't. Usually when I named the realms of Ancient, it brought me some clarity. Some ice to the rising heat inside me. But I hadn't added the Bloodlands to that list, not ever. I had avoided all thought of it except when I walked there in my nightmares . . .

"You okay?" came Ben's concerned voice, as he hovered over me. I scrambled to my feet, afraid he'd try to help me and get burned for his generosity.

"Fine, fine," I muttered, adjusting my shirt, which was damp with sweat where I'd bunched it in my fist. I didn't bother offering an explanation — just willed my legs to walk and wove back to the other side of the restaurant.

I wasn't afraid when I looked at Five again. I should have been but, probably to my detriment, my first impulse was anger. Anger that this *thing* had the nerve to come after me in public, with innocent people around. Anger that I couldn't escape my enemies no matter how far I ran or how much I gave up. I poured that fury into sharpening my gaze, turning the power on my spirit eye up to eleven. Five followed me with his black eyes. The din of the diners and boozers and wailing tourists fell.

He wasn't a Denizen. I didn't know *what* he was, but it wasn't human. It couldn't be. Not with how he seemed to look inside me, seemed to know what my jolly name tag hid behind it. But maybe this was it. Maybe this was my break in the Mysterious Case of Cecelia's Extremely Vague and Overly Threatening Prophecy. All this time I'd refused to ask the stone for help, had done everything I could not to let it get inside my head like Eli's stone had.

I didn't think. I should have tried to lure him outside, behind the restaurant, to some dark place. I should have played the weak, unassuming teenager role. But I couldn't. Not after all this time.

I was being reckless. I could hear a whisper reminding me to focus, but it hissed and died in the simmering coals of my heart as I came around the bar.

"Have you been served tonight?" I asked Five casually, noticing his now-empty glass. His black eyes shimmered in the bar lights, which cast his face in ghoulish shadows.

"Not nearly as well as you could serve me." He grinned back. His teeth were yellow. His hair was wiry like a terrier's. A rough twenties, he was all skin and bone. He wore a corduroy vest and worn shoes. His voice was sandpaper.

"Allow me." I was definitely not a bartender. I was also not legally allowed to serve alcohol on this continent. But I doled out a generous glass of whisky and slid it to him. "On the house."

Five was still smiling. I still didn't know his name, but it didn't seem to matter. That he was at table *five* was telling enough and probably some kind of ironic destiny.

He didn't touch the drink.

"Can I get you anything else? Or is it just me you want?"

The smile deepened. Widened. Like an open sore. "The mongrel is perceptive."

My ear twitched, as if it were trying to swivel to pick out a familiar sound, as a real fox's ear might.

This was my opening. "Do you want to take this outside?"

"Oh no," said Five, as though grateful for the gesture. "No, this is just fine." He surveyed the room full of witnesses and potential victims, though the dinner rush had since ended. Still enough people and servers left behind to get hurt all the same.

So I did as a Fox would — I talked and waited.

"Well, I'll be outside," I said, hands flat on the glass bar counter. "And what happens there is up to you." I turned. The bladeless hilt of my garnet sword was strapped to my ankle, though I hadn't been able to use it since fighting Zabor. That didn't matter. I was aching for this. The fight was cinematic in my head despite the mounting number of holes in my plan.

But I didn't get farther than a step before a hand snapped out and wrenched me back by the forearm. It held fast. The stench of burning flesh flooded my already keyed-up senses. *His* burning flesh.

And yet he still smiled.

Only a few people turned — probably the Denizens. The rest went about their eating and drinking. I looked around wildly, and I tried to thrash away, the man's skin blackening steadily from his fingertips up along his arm.

"Troublesome mongrel," he said again in his terribly familiar voice. "I have come to give you a warning, targe stealer. Fox traitor. I have left the garden to bring you good tidings."

I watched his arm cook between us. I wanted to throw up. "Urka?"

"My masters are eager. They tire of our beloved ashes. They wish to make this a world for their own children. They extend gratitude for helping them."

I pulled, but the grip was iron. No one was moving to rescue me. I felt myself getting hotter. I knew I could burn him alive if he didn't let go, but I had to know. "Helping them with what?"

Urka's human face shimmered as his clothes caught fire, the synthetics fusing and melting to its skin. "For helping them send their beloved child past the Veil and into your realm. For it could not have happened without you."

The black eyes were earnest. I remembered Urka's stone axe hands, the furnace in its belly. I stopped resisting.

"The children are coming," Urka said. "They are coming for you."

My chest tightened, and in my moment of terror, the

stone perceived its chance. The fire inside me escalated into an inferno, left my skin, and poured out like hot gas. Urka's gaping yellowed grin peeled away as its very human body stretched, blackened, hardened. Then the grip seized, throwing me backward into the ten-foot-high decorative shelf of alcohol behind me.

I didn't have time to stop myself. The Dragon Opal wouldn't let me. I was a powder keg, and the minute I connected and the glass and liquid rained down, I knew the inferno was no longer just inside me. The restaurant lit up like Hogmanay.

It was dark when I got back to my flat. I barely remembered the journey — my brain only flickering on when I shut the door with my body. I jolted like I'd woken from a bad dream, terrified as I looked around. Everything seemed so normal, so safe. What little I'd brought with me from Canada in a small backpack — clothing, books — scattered around the partially furnished flat. Jackets. Shoes. The testament of my solitude. Of a yesterday when things hadn't gone so completely to shit.

It definitely didn't look like the flat of a murderer.

I lifted my trembling hands, which were black with ash and soot. Had it happened? Had I really burned down Fingal's Pint with everyone in it? All I remembered was my heart getting too hot to breathe, my skin coming apart in cinders. A yellowed smile. *The children are coming for you.*

I crumpled to the ground, breath catching. The stone had saved me — had done its job to protect its precious host. And had made me into the type of monster I had given everything to destroy, to come here to stop.

Urka. I clenched my fists, remembering the last time I'd seen that wretched thing, down in the Bloodlands. It was the last thing in this world and however many others that had seen my mother, after she'd disappeared. After the man I thought was my father had been punished in the aftermath with his life.

I suddenly felt utterly spent, like I had no room to feel anything else. I had lost control. I had let it happen. My terror and rage had cost me.

I had no one to call for advice. No mother or grandmother who could console me, who could teach me, who could help me. I was on my own. I had to be. But I wasn't truly alone. I touched the stone in my breastbone, ran my fingers over its raw curves. It felt quiet now, only giving off a glowing warmth. It was spent, too. But the whispering, insistent voice it always used, however quiet, floated to the surface.

The voices of the thousands that had come before me, boring deep into my synapses. I shut my eyes and let them in.

TRIBUNAL *by* AIR

Eli was not a nervous person. Even before the Moonstone, he was fairly self-assured. He stepped into things because he sought them out, and if they didn't go as he planned, then he'd try again from another angle. A survivalist's approach.

But even now, on a private plane headed towards a Grand Council that would weigh in on his actions in Winnipeg the past season, his heart and mind were in turmoil. He had gone against the stone's influence in the end, and yet it had had such a hold on him for so long, it had resulted in the deaths of innocent Mundanes and Denizens alike. A year ago he would have been immune to this excruciating brand of soul-searching. The ego alone from his own tremendous power would have prevented it, and he wouldn't dare be dwelling on his best-forgotten origins with a mad mother or the bitterness of a father he barely knew only claiming him after she'd died. Empathy, however late coming, was already tedious.

It was a lot to bear at once, yet despite it all, he had some modicum of peace, one thing he'd managed to win back for himself: he could finally push the voices away. He could try to rebuild himself separate from the Moonstone.

Eli glanced about the plane, carrying at least a dozen aides and Owls in addition to Eli and Solomon. Satisfied no one was watching, he pushed his sleeve up, bringing his arm into the light shining through the porthole window. The scar was white now, coiled around his flesh with the indentation of the thin gold chain that had bit into it months ago, down deep in that strange underworld. He'd looked at it often, wondering if it would fade away entirely or if he'd have it for life.

And he wondered if *hers* looked the same. If she looked down at it, too. Roan Harken.

He pulled his sleeve back down with a huff of frustration, fighting to refasten the cuff buttons. Any clarity of mind he had now, he owed to her. Pigheaded, ridiculous, amateur Roan Harken, who had stumbled blindly into a power greater than anything her dim-witted existence, up till now, could have ever quantified. And yet . . . With her stupidity came a clear conscience. Something Eli couldn't say he'd *ever* had, even before his own Calamity Stone. But he despised that she was out there playing the hero. Last year, throughout the ordeal of Zabor, she never once suggested that it was something she had to do on her own. Yet no one had heard much from her, much to his chagrin, since she climbed into a plane not unlike this one and shut everyone out. Including him.

Eli grimaced out the window, bright sun cascading over

the tops of the clouds the plane skated over. *Roan*. The colour of ashy dust on a horse's coat. Usually an animal too strong for its own good, gentle but easily led, headstrong and terrible when it got out of control.

Roan.

The next Paramount of the Foxes . . . the thought was a bitter, laughable one. Her? Already she had no idea what she'd gotten into, taking that stone. Accepting it. What it had already cost her, and what it would, very soon, if the Conclave of Fire had anything to say about it . . .

Eli felt the plane jutter slightly. He tensed, meeting Solomon's eyes in the seat facing him.

"Just turbulence," Solomon said in the soft reassuring voice of a mentor, and Eli slammed the door shut on his mind. With newfound clarity came carelessness, and his father was nearly as perceptive as he. It didn't help that Owls' power allowed them to send tendrils of thought into weaker minds, and lately Eli would let those thoughts in without thinking.

But closing off meant that the only way to ascertain someone's feelings was *to talk*. Tedious.

"Are you all right?" Solomon asked. He had the decency to look unconcerned, even in his stiff posture, his body not yet accustomed to the new artificial leg from the knee down. He hadn't fared well in the battle against Zabor, and yet he'd done all he could. Eli wasn't shocked that he'd survived but that he'd been injured at all, knowing his power. Once, it crossed his mind that Solomon taking himself out of the deciding moment of the fight had been intentional, perhaps — a visceral changing of the guard to make way for the son he trusted would show up despite his shame.

Eli glanced back out the window. "I'm uneasy."

"About the tribunal?" Solomon looked surprised.

Much had changed but not Eli's ego. "*Tch.* I called the thing. And if I know anything it's this Family. They haven't had qualms about my actions for years as long as it protected their interests and the Narrative's. No. Something else." He looked his father in the eye. "You feel it, too."

Solomon exhaled through his nose. Eli had spent enough time with the man to concede a resemblance between them, but the line was thin. He'd always felt that he took after his mother, though his memories of her were like sharp splinters. And Eli still resented Solomon too much to probe. Eli was just another ritually conceived Denizen, born to a woman who had known the location of the hidden Moonstone. Yet when she refused to claim it for the Family, the Stone itself destroyed her mind. Eli wouldn't soon forget that Solomon only became interested in him when, after being granted his mother's fatal legacy of the Tradewind Moonstone's location, Eli had next been chosen by it.

"Things have changed because of that Fox," Solomon admitted, drawing Eli back from the edge of old furies. "Zabor may be gone, but I fear she won't be gone for long. She went almost too gently into her good night."

Considering that a good part of Winnipeg's downtown core had been decimated in the wake of Zabor's rising and that many Mundanes and Denizens had been killed . . . Eli didn't really consider that "gently." And the psychological cleanup the Owls had to perform on Winnipeg's Mundane population had been taxing, to say the least.

But he wasn't an idiot. "So you think it was planned? That she wanted to return to the Bloodlands?" Not a day went by when Eli didn't think of that place — the ruin and the utter void of it. The horrors that dug their roots deep there. The place had nearly claimed him and Roan, too, for their efforts in retrieving the targe that would put Zabor back in that miserable hellscape. It hadn't been an easy feat, but it was something countless generations before him had shied from attempting. Maybe there had been a reason.

Now Solomon looked out into the wide sky. Creatures of air that they were, the vault gave Owls some peace. "I think there's more yet to come. More that we don't know." Solomon sucked on his teeth, grip tightening on the gold-topped cherry wood cane he relied on. "The passing of the Dragon Opal isn't a good sign, either."

Eli's heart squeezed. Yes, there would be an outcry from the Fox Family soon if there hadn't been already. Because without fanfare, ritual, or blessing, Roan had been given a greater burden than the one she'd originally been cursed with by Death herself. Perhaps this was the Moth Queen's true intention, after all: that an uninitiated girl, who had had no concept of Ancient and its universal machinations, would be given one of the most powerful artefacts of their world . . . Eli rubbed his chest. He knew that following her like a watchful dog wouldn't have helped, that spitting warnings and oaths and trying to show her how to control a Calamity Stone would have been rejected. But he could have offered her more. Could have at least extended himself to her as a . . .

Instead he let her leave alone. Allowed her to be isolated in a strange country, with nothing and no one to guide her. Because that had done him good, hadn't it?

The plane lurched again — this time, the wing took a noticeable dip as though it was banking. It righted itself even more suddenly, yet the air and sky outside did not change.

Eli could feel it in the wind. "That's not turbulence."

Suddenly, an announcement from the cockpit came through. "Whatever this is, it's not showing whatsoever on our radar. We've lost connection with air traffic control. We're flying dead, sir. GPS is still connected. We've just passed the Bering Sea . . . I'm going to have to divert towards Magadan airport. It's the closest, sir."

"Russia?" Eli quipped, but the plane took another dive, and Solomon signalled for his aide.

"Tell the pilot to take us wherever he thinks is wise. We need to get out of the air." When the aide scurried off, he looked hard at Eli. "And away from the water."

Eli nodded tightly. He undid his seat belt and went up to the cockpit. "I have to see it for myself," was all Eli said to Solomon's unspoken concern, as he crossed the aisle with a meaningful glance to his father. After everything, he hadn't forgotten waking on his return from the Bloodlands and seeing the look on Solomon's face. He'd given Eli the same look just now. Bald fear and regret.

The pilot and co-pilot acknowledged Eli as he dismissed the aide. "I swear, sir, this is the first time we've seen *that* since we left Montreal."

That was a swirling column of black punching through the golden cloud and rosy clear sky only a few miles ahead. It was sending massive tendrils towards the plane, rocking it whenever one made contact, then vanishing in a black flash.

Eli let the Moonstone in completely, let its influence permeate his flesh and his mind. Then he opened his mind into the void they were heading to.

A faceless face. Burning. A terrible sound and smell — familiar, something he remembered from . . .

"Urka," Eli muttered, recognizing the fume for what it was. His mind was haunted with the screams of trees.

"We need to descend *now*," Eli commanded. "If you come up against any more rough air, I'll help level you out." A warning light and a sharp buzzer came on suddenly.

"Shit," the pilot said, then, "Brace yourself!"

The next blast of air smashed into the plane and sent a violent tremor through every soul aboard. For a moment, they were dead in the air, then Eli felt his stomach drop.

They only free-fell for seconds, but it felt like a prelude to a blackout. He felt his molecules reshaping, flesh flexing, as he focused the power of the stone in his breastbone, felt his mind grasping the air currents outside of the plane, and he released his own terrible torrent back towards whatever was attacking them.

Such a retaliation took a lot out of him. Eli came back to himself seconds later, jolting at the touch of a calm hand. It was the aide. "Sir?" she asked shakily. "Do you need help?"

He batted her hand and good intentions away, staggering to his feet. "What's happened?"

The aide led him back to his father. "We've levelled out. We're descending. But there's a com coming through. It's from Soon Yin."

Solomon was bent over an iPad, but the picture and sound coming through were breaking up. "Park, I'm sorry, I can't —"

"—urn around!" This time the voice was clear. "You must go back! Do not come here. They're . . . they're all —"

The sound did not cut out; in fact, it was clearer, because they could hear heavy breathing. Park Soon Yin, the Owl magistrate for Korea, was calling them from his cellphone, from somewhere dark, somewhere hidden. He was so far away, he could not telepath the warning, but verbalizing it could soon cost him.

Eli reached over his father's shoulder. "Park, where are you? What's happened?"

The shadowed, haunted face of the magistrate swung into view. The picture was clear enough now to see the moisture on his face. Sweat or tears, Eli couldn't tell.

"It was children. It was all children. They had the Serenity Emerald. The Rabbits —"

The signal cut out then, and the plane banked.

Eli staggered backward into the seat across the aisle. The iPad clattered, and the aides and other Owls they were travelling with let out a collective cry.

"We need to change the flight plan," Eli grunted. Against the pull of the sudden gravitational change, he yanked himself towards a window, which was pointed up. He looked over the wing, saw that it was coated with black muck. And the sludge seemed to be crawling, expanding. Hunting.

Eli felt the change of the Therion, even before he registered allowing it. Fight and flight. The bones in his back flexed and separated, making room. His focus sharpened. Everything seemed to become tighter.

"No," he heard Solomon say, as Eli clenched his taloned fist and found purchase in the aisle with the heavy black claws of his feet. "You can't —"

"It's no longer a matter of that," Eli said. He sent a warning into the minds of everyone on board to *hold on*, for their fear had opened them to reception. Once he felt they were all buckled down, Eli wrenched the emergency hatch open, slid out, and slammed it shut again.

They were breaking through the cloud cover now, but the shock of being 20,000 feet in the air was enough to send Eli reeling, even in his elevated state of power. He had flown high in the years of testing himself, but never this high.

The cold was a lance. The rush of the wind was a thousand razors. But this was the power from which he'd come, and when he braced, feeling feathers penetrate his flesh and protect him from his mother element, he relaxed into the current and let go of the plane.

The wind filled his wings and he banked and tumbled underneath the jet, pulling away quickly from its turbulence. When he came up and righted over it, he saw that the column of black they'd observed from above the cloud line was coming back towards them, shooting barbs of the same sludge that spread over the right wing.

The column was gaining, but in the meantime Eli sent a frost-sharp torrent at the black matter on the plane. That shattered it, seeming to stop it from advancing and growing, and the plane was able to pull up and back into a controlled descent.

When they finally cleared the blinding, stabbing cloud, all that spread below them was the wide and hungry sea.

"Shit," Eli said.

He soared ahead, pulling the air current around him like a blanket and letting it shoot him farther and faster than the heavy plane could manage. His Owl eyes could see sharply; land wasn't far, but with a quick shoulder check, Eli confirmed that they'd never make it before that column of destruction caught them first.

Leave them, too many voices suggested. *Find safety. You*

must protect the Moonstone. The Emerald approaches. They can never be brought together.

Eli jerked, nearly crumpling. *The Emerald, here?* Park had mentioned it in that fleeting moment. Had said it was *there*, in Seoul. How could it suddenly be *here*, over Russia?

Leave them, the Moonstone screamed again. Eli shook off his surprise and confusion, mastered himself again. The Moonstone and its occupants had such an elegant way of saying *Let them die for the greater good*. But Eli had learned autonomy, which they'd all have to get used to.

"No" was all he said, out loud and into the screaming void of sky, as he pulled up higher and landed softly on the plane. He dug his talons into the steel body for purchase, squared his back, and sent his mind into the terrified passengers within: "Whatever is causing this is coming too fast. The plane won't make landfall, let alone an airport in time. We're going to have to do this together."

Eli scowled. He knew that the power of the Moonstone alone would be hard-pressed to take control of and smoothly land even a small aircraft without casualty . . . but he felt Solomon's mind reach out to his and offer the mental equivalent of a squeeze. Pride. Allowing the other Owls to help would make them all more determined to survive.

Eli didn't have to ask twice. He opened up everything inside of him like an aperture, spreading tethers of gold psychic light to the passengers. They grasped onto the lifelines and tugged.

Eli lifted himself from clinging to the plane, arms akimbo, fingers twitching. He pulled the air back to him, around the plane, buffeting and cocooning it in a manufactured hurricane. To master the wind itself, to pull it out of its self-contained current, was seen to some as another tenet that must never be broken. But even the ancestors in the stone, though they cried and moaned before, were silent now, focusing the power of Ancient, always given with a price.

"I call upon the element that breathes life into the others, from the tempest to the breezes in the lowlands. Phyr, mother of wisdom, I charge your power to my name and your Moonstone."

Eli felt a warmth in his chest, one that he had felt months ago, in an airport in a small Canadian city, fingers wanting to reach out but never able to.

He thought of Roan.

"Wind!" he howled above the gale and ripped the very element from her place, pulling it inside him.

It was a tricky thing, bearing people and metal and trying not to come apart, carrying these burdens past the sea and to whatever land his failing eyes could find. Eli felt like he was being alternately crushed and ripped into pieces as he slowed the plane into his control while still guiding it safely to land. Too many smells and sensations assaulted him — the sea salt, the resin of nearing trees, and something like tar, like burned bodies and souls, nipping at his heels.

His chest was heavy. His heart *hurt*. And suddenly, something latched on to one of his great wings and burned like a brand.

Eli screamed and let go of the plane.

❧

What woke Eli was not the gentle hand of a well-meaning

aide this time, but the tensing of his whole body, pre-retch. He rolled over painfully, sputtering, pulling air back into his lungs as if he'd been drowning. But his fingers dug deep into soil and sand. Earth. They'd made it.

A burst of flame exploded nearby, and he covered his head, cinders and bark and tree branches showering down.

Maybe not.

He staggered to his feet, which were partway human again, but long razor claws dug into the ground when he stumbled. His clothes were torn, one arm still half-feathered, and when he tripped, pain stabbed through his scapula. He was still partially the owl Therion, one wing broken and hanging behind him. The stone seemed silent, and for a moment Eli was both excited and afraid that it might be silent forever, but it hummed at the edges. With a small jolt, Eli was able to grunt his way back to human form, shedding the wings and feathers and righting himself as best he could.

He was in the woods, but ahead was a new clearing — made by the plane. Its nose was crumpled, its underside crushed from the impact of the landing, but otherwise it looked intact. The emergency hatch and slide had been deployed, but when Eli came around, he couldn't see anyone else, couldn't find any other waking minds when he cast for them. And if the explosion hadn't come from the plane —

Eli turned. Not more than two feet away from him was a child. Her clothes were covered in ash, her skin mottled with black and almost cracked, like brimstone, red shimmering below the surface.

"Will you meet my family?" she asked, pointing to the trees.

Eli stepped back. The air was sick with the reek of sulphur.

From the woods emerged more children, faces blank, eyes glowing. Their skin and faces ash-smeared wrecks.

Eli. He jerked. The voice was inside his mind. He'd left it open and did not dare shut it now, because it was Solomon. He couldn't see him, couldn't find him. There were only the trees, branches stretching to the sky, like arms . . .

Eli, the urgent voice said, and he knew it was coming from the trees. *Run.*

Behind the children coalesced the dark column that had ripped them out of the air. It was a solid murk, each tendril it sent ahead a leg to pull itself up, crab-like. And it did — into a body, with features that hardened the longer Eli stared. It was seven feet tall, eyes obscured by an inverted triangle of shining black bone. The smile beneath was unforgivable.

And sure enough, embedded in its shoulder was the gleaming, corrupted green of the Rabbits' Calamity Stone — the Serenity Emerald.

Then the Moonstone screamed, and Eli knew he should have listened to it when he'd had the chance.

Ashes *to* Ashes

Cecelia was already undoing her coat as she stalked through the club's side door, squeezing through the tight hall that connected the stage door's poky corridor to an even narrower stairwell to the change room. *Nothing like a rat maze to start off the day*. As she passed through the main hair and makeup room, she threw the coat onto a sofa, like it was an afterthought, because living in the moment, everything was. Had to be.

"Watch it!" someone barked, and Cecelia waved her hand, feeling the kinetic heat ripple from her elbow to her fingertip. *Whatever*.

Once in the dressing room, behind a closed door, every little motion was a muscle-memory dance number. One-two-one — powder, blush, mascara. A sweep of a brush into a gaudy palette worn down to a scant ring with plastic backing showing through. Eyes cat sharp and blazing under the three-out-of-seven mirror lights — the rest having sat dead in their sockets since she moved to Toronto three blissful months ago. Who cared? There was light enough, the brush feathering over her décolletage till she tossed the brush, too, and unpinned her wild rib-length mane. Backcomb, spray, set, pat.

There was a meditative quality to preparing for a show, and the method of it made her thoughts lapse back to years of training: the repetition, the steadying of the heart, the lessons and the worshipping all in servitude to a godhead she neither respected nor believed in. Should she ever have the misfortune to cross it, she'd laugh in its face.

Heels on, ostrich-and-silk robe slung over her bustier. Singed feathers littered the floor as she crossed the room, checked herself. *Goddammit.* She'd have to take a trip to Kensington Market, see if she could find another robe at that consignment boutique. But more than that, she needed to be more careful. Even when you controlled your own pyrotechnic show, everything was a delicate liability — especially the glamour.

"Thanks, Charlie," Cecelia muttered as the stage boy, nervous but obliging, handed her a glass with the usual vodka soda, once she'd made it back up to the main floor and backstage. True, she'd only just woken up an hour ago at the crack of sunset, and adding alcohol to a natural belly fire wasn't going to do her any good . . . but she'd earned it after the recent dreams. If she kept count — and for what little peace of mind life afforded her now, she didn't — she couldn't remember the last time she'd *really* slept. Not since Chartrand's little runaround. Not since giving the Conclave the middle finger. Not since she pushed away a lineage that put her in the path of a power she'd never wanted in the first place.

And not since she'd left Ruo behind with barely a word.

Cecelia lit a passing showgirl's cigarette with her fingertip but flicked it out a second later in case the girl was looking a little too closely. But they never did. Cecelia smiled at her, like a big cat at a slow bird. She knew better. She was careful around Mundanes . . . even if she took to a stage five times a week to light herself on fire in front of a roaring crowd of them. She was the one in control. And no one could take that away from her now.

She staggered slightly and caught herself on the wall, holding her stomach like the dreams were there, held tightly under the satin, trying to claw their way out. *A torrential sea. A crack in the world. The face that is hers and not hers. And the dark at the bottom of that crack. So dark it blinds . . .*

"Cece," the stage manager, Louis, barked in her face. Her eyes narrowed at him, and he looked like he immediately regretted it.

"What is it?" Cecelia went to take another pull on the cocktail, but the glass was empty and probably had been for a while. She shoved it at him. "I'm here on time, aren't I? You can't threaten to fire me over anything today."

She glanced towards the stage they flanked now, from the wings. Kitty was still swaggering through her number. Tables were starting to fill. Kitty resented the fact she was there just to warm everyone up for Cecelia, but she worked the stage every night like it'd be her last. And it could be. There really was no need to "warm" anything up when the inferno could do it all herself.

"You, uh, got a visitor." Louis thumbed behind him, wiping his sweating brow as he fumbled with Cecelia's empty glass. At least he didn't ask very many questions. His confident stride petered out pretty quickly once he realized Cecelia was a broad who bit back. She had little respect for Louis, but he was still the reason she was able to live this free life, with all its dull caveats.

When Cecelia turned, the corner of her lip twitched, but she didn't betray herself with a smile. She inhaled, steeling herself, as if her tight corset and peignoir could be the heaviest armour. And like the warrior she once was, she headed into the charge. "Ruo," she said thickly, folding her arms over her bust. "Never thought I'd see you in a place like this."

Ruo had made a show of meeting Cecelia's gaze, but she couldn't hold it for long before her expression broke. "I could say the same about you."

Despite their parting, Cecelia took the risk and opened her arms. It was the barest hesitation, but Ruo leapt into them with much more impact than Cecelia anticipated. She was half a foot shorter than Cecelia on any given day, but Cecelia's six-inch heels made Ruo look Lilliputian in comparison. Cecelia had to keep herself from squeezing *too hard*.

"You hadn't written in a while. I was worried." Ruo pulled away, reflexively tucking her short hair behind an ear, even though Cecelia knew it never stayed put. Much like Ruo, who was still looking about, hesitant and nervous. "Now I see why you didn't."

"Oh relax. Haven't you heard it's the '60s?" Cecelia waved her off, hands on her hips. "And wasn't it you who encouraged me to do something that was a bit more *expressive*?"

The twins, Gretchen and Hilda, wearing only tassels and matching grins, passed by like it was cued, and Ruo's face darkened several shades, which even Cecelia could perceive in the pot light's shadows.

"I didn't mean *burlesque*," she hissed back, squeezing close to Cecelia to accommodate the backup dancers that had just taken over what little space there was back here. "How can this be better than —"

"*Anything* is better than the Conclave." Cecelia draped her arm around Ruo, pulling her closer, lowering her voice, arching a perfectly drawn brow. "You wouldn't be here on their behalf, would you?"

Ruo looked away.

Cecelia sighed, a vice-grip locked on Ruo's wrist as she dragged her deeper backstage, behind the curtain concealing the furthest wing. She deposited her onto a prop fainting couch.

"Hey!" Ruo protested, but Cecelia loomed over her, her index finger, now aflame, the only thing lighting her dangerous face as she leaned in.

"You know what you mean to me." Though she smiled, the words were cold. "But don't think I wouldn't burn you or anyone else who tries to take me back to that gods-forsaken den of iniquity." She snapped her fingers and the flame made a pop, which in turn made Ruo jump. "This club is far cleaner than the dirty dealings I had to put up with from the Foxes who claimed to be as saintly as even you. For three months I haven't *once* thought the words *Ancient* or *Five Families*, and I will be damned if I have to hear them from you. For whatever reason."

A sudden rush of emotion brought Cecelia back to her feet, a few steps back. She sucked back the stone in her throat.

But she started at Ruo's sardonic chuckle, her slow clap. "What a performance," Ruo said, leaning back, hands behind her head. "You were always so good at the dramatic pity party. Is it intermission yet? Do I get my line?"

Cecelia unclenched her fist when she realized her long nails were biting into the flesh. Her mouth twitched. "It's nice to see you still don't take crap from anyone. Least of all me."

"I thought that's why we broke up?" Ruo teased. "You just couldn't handle someone saying *no* to you. Let alone calling you on your *crap*."

Cecelia parked herself on the chaise's arm, leaning her head back with closed eyes as the live band's brass section hit a crescendo. "I don't remember us *actually* breaking up, though . . ." She couldn't help the dig, even after —

"Chartrand's dead," Ruo said suddenly, and Cecelia's eyes flashed open.

"What?"

Ruo's grin remained, this time accompanied with blatant bitterness. "I can see you're busy, though. Fan-dancing through life like you weren't next in line."

The stage lights flickered over Ruo's face, and Cecelia had to look away. She was telling the truth. And worse, she hadn't come gladly with the news. Because Ruo was still the best of either of them, the best Fox she'd known, really, and Cecelia had willingly left her behind.

"If *he'd* been fan-dancing through life he'd still be around to live it." Cecelia's chest buzzed with too many feelings. She needed to get herself under control, or else she'd end up burning down the stage and everyone on it.

Cecelia clutched her abdomen, feeling sicker. "No," she said, getting up immediately. "I can't get dragged into this again."

She started to leave but Ruo grabbed her, fierce and determined despite the height difference. Despite the words and memories that hung between them, it was the deed with Chartrand and the Conclave that had driven the last wedge. No matter how close they were in the moment, some divides couldn't be crossed again.

"All they're asking," she said carefully, "is that you consider attending the Arbitration. Chartrand was training a young boy. He's the most likely to be chosen by the Opal. There's no obligation on you."

It was Cecelia's turn at a bitter smile. "Even Chartrand would think that was a fool's errand, sending a child into a spiritual war zone."

Suddenly there was Louis, panting with his clipboard under one arm and mopping his sweaty bald pate. "C'mon, Bettincourt! You're killin' me here. Get up there."

"Oh hold your damn horses, Kitty's still picking up the rhinestones from her pasties." Cecelia whirled, all bright eyes and confidence as she pulled Ruo in, tipped her head back, and kissed her. It was just like it had been, just for that moment — even though the past was *long* past and probably wouldn't come back anytime soon.

Cecelia pulled away, Ruo's face stunned. "I'll go. I'll watch. Whoever they get to fill that idiot's shoes will need to pass muster." She cupped Ruo's chin thoughtfully before stepping back. "Leave it to the best idiot to judge the next in line, right?"

Cecelia turned back to the stage, crossing to her mark when the curtain came back together and her intro was played. She looked behind her, and there was Ruo, watching and still breathless. The beat thrummed high in her veins, the flame building. She hadn't yet moved but the heat was intense inside of her.

She smiled at Ruo. *Don't worry*. And even though her former lover smiled back and nodded, they both weren't fooling anyone.

The curtain pulled back, and Cecelia swept into step with the luscious refrain. Men catcalled and whistled. She wasn't afraid of them. She wasn't afraid of anything. This was where she felt the most alive, the most free. Here, on this stage, with the ghost of Ruo pressed against her as it had been many times before this. Cecelia already knew what she would do, bitter that the steps were already laid out for her, beaten into her. She would go to the Conclave of Fire. She would resist taking Chartrand's place, but the Stone was always the last word. Even though she railed against it, it had to be true: the stone had probably already chosen her, and it had shown her as much in those nightmares of fire and darkness.

As she spun, her peignoir catching in well-practiced fire and burning out again, Cecelia soaked up the cheers and the kinetic energy in the air. Because she knew, as she felt the fire flash around her, this was the last time she'd ever be free.

I gasped like I'd had my head held under water, staggering and falling on my hands and knees to pavement. *Pavement*? I blinked blearily around, the world swimming back into focus as my lungs pulled for purchase. I was outside, on the sidewalk. I had come down on a crowded sidewalk, pedestrians swerving to avoid me as I staggered weakly to my feet. Probably afraid the crazy was catching. Didn't blame them.

The vision. What the hell was *that*? After the disaster at

Fingal's Pint, I'd gone back to my flat. Closed my eyes for a second, and suddenly I was . . . elsewhere. Else*when*. A vivid dream where I was both inside and outside at once. A woman named Ruo, the name from the letter that brought me here. I'd let the stone in . . . was it showing me some kind of memory?

I touched my mouth, tried to master my racing heart. Was it showing me *Cecelia's* memory?

Fresh pain shot from my spirit eye into my head like the optic nerve was bristling with thorns. When it cleared, and I looked around again, stepping around a corner, I realized where I was now. I was on the Royal Mile. I was standing outside of where Fingal's Pint used to be. I didn't remember getting here. I just remembered —

A flash. A fire. Table five. A man disintegrating as he held on, warning —

"Roan?"

I whipped my head to my name, body flushing cold. There was Athika, decidedly not burned to a cinder, and next to her was Ben, and they stared at me like *I* was the ghost.

"Jesus," Ben said, "I was gonna say you look terrible, but I guess anything is better than dead."

The grin I managed was more like a twitch. "I could say the same for you." The words felt weird on my tongue, like I'd just heard them, said them, and I tried to shake the vision away. "How . . . ?"

Athika suddenly surged forward, crushing me close in a hug that I couldn't even try to match. When I coughed, Ben pulled us apart, saying, "Well, if she wasn't dead before, she is now."

"How did you get out?" Athika ignored him, still holding

tight to me like I was her lifeline. "And . . . are you sick or something? You're burning hot."

I'd grown used to Athika's fussing since moving to Edinburgh — she reminded me of Phae, and I hated that I seemed to exude a *please take care of me* pheromone, even if it was met with the best of intentions, so I tried backing away. She held on.

"I . . . I don't know. It all happened so fast. I think I was, um, blasted out onto the sidewalk. I woke up in a hospital, but they let me leave . . ." The lie came almost too easily, and I didn't wait to see if they'd bought it, averting my eyes to the wreckage.

Ben followed my gaze, nodding. "That's what all the survivors seem to be saying. Everyone made it out, and when they couldn't find you in there, we thought . . . well. We thought you were the only unlucky one not to make it."

I froze. "What? You mean no one . . . ?" I let the word *died* hang in the air, because it seemed too good to be true. An answer to my desperate misery, a clearing of my ledger. "Wait. How did *you* guys get out?"

I scrutinized them both more carefully. They didn't *look* injured in the usual ways — maybe a bit of emotional scarring — but if either of them had been anywhere near the blast that was so painfully painted in my mind's eye whenever I closed my actual eyes . . . there was just no way.

Athika's grip seemed to flex. Ben moved closer.

"Miracles do happen," he smiled, but it wasn't the same friendly grin I'd gotten used to these past months. I didn't know why, but the smile seemed more like a threat. "We're just glad you're okay."

"Yeah. I'm okay." I broke Athika's grip with a swift jerk

back that I played off as moving closer to the building's remains. Fire trucks were still surrounding the restaurant and the surrounding buildings. A definite crowd had gathered while emergency crew diverted the foot traffic and incensed cabbies around the cordoned-off square that I'd incinerated. That was still on me. I raised my hand to touch my chest but forced it back down. *No. Not me. Something else trying to use me.* And I wouldn't let it.

"They still don't know what caused it," Athika was saying behind me. I could feel her and Ben's eyes boring into the back of my head. "Do you have any ideas? Do you remember seeing anything?"

I made an effort to search the crowd so I wouldn't have to meet their eyes. Something was wrong. They couldn't know. Could they? Out of the corner of my eye I caught a flash of Ben, and something pulsing at his neck, just where the collar of his shirt started. Something black, like a stain of ash. Except it was moving, branching out. Growing.

I winced again, this time overcome with the image of the man at the bar, holding tight to me, his arm blackening . . .

"I've gotta go," I managed as I spun away from them, from Athika's red-shining eyes and outstretched fingers, the tips of which seemed to be going dark.

I shoved my way through the crowd, feeling sick. I needed to talk to someone, anyone.

"Easy there," said someone in front of me; I was moving so fast I'd ricocheted off him.

I apologized. His hazel eyes were too kind for me to deserve. "Best be careful," he said, his accent thick. "Trouble's about, girlie."

"Uh. Right." I moved away from him, from the rest of the

crowd, but even when I was across the street and around the corner I felt eyes following me — maybe the man's, maybe Ben's and Athika's. Maybe eyes that no one else could feel but me.

And as the whispers from the Opal grew more urgent, I felt more alone than I ever had.

He watched her go. He knew she felt it. It took more than he cared to admit not to go after her now. *Patience*, hissed the thing inside. *Soon*.

He turned up the street, went the other way. When he passed the entrance to the Edinburgh rail station, he kept going. He hadn't been down there since his prison cell had smashed open under heavy axe hands; the six earnest, gleaming eyes wide with triumph as he was pulled out to freedom.

He hadn't felt fresh air in seventeen years, and the rush of those trains had been enough for his wind-starved skin. Down in that underground, he'd heard their song.

Patience, he told himself firmly, smiling, until he wasn't in the street at all.

FAR *from* SEA

"Where are you going, Nattiq?"

Natti zipped up her hoodie and took another breath through her nose as she tried for patience. "The zoo, Aunty."

Aunty's cough was ragged and wet, like an overflowing ditch at spring's first melt. It was getting worse, and so was her memory. "Right, right, the zoo," she said, as if she suddenly remembered the last ten times Natti had told her. "What you going there for? Don't you live in enough of a zoo already?" She laughed, but again it was overtaken by painful hacking, and Natti forgot her impatience.

"Here." She hurried to one side of Aunty's old La-Z-Boy, handing her a glass of water and a pill. "It's for the job interview, remember? They're looking for fall camp counsellors."

As Aunty drank, Natti thought about her chances, which were slim. A high school dropout with a GED, her only work experience flipping burgers at various fast food places up and down Portage Avenue. But she needed a change, to move up. She wanted to do something with real purpose, and while avoiding deep fryer splashback helped pay the bills, her dignity was slipping.

And at the rate Aunty was going, Natti needed something more flexible to help out at home.

"Miriam is going to look in on you later, okay?" Natti was making for the door, worried she would miss her bus. It was a long ride and two transfers from Point Douglas to Charleswood, and she was grateful for the kindness of neighbours who had taken care of Natti more times than she could remember.

"I don't need Miriam or *anyone* fussing over me." Aunty scowled, bringing a hand to her temple. "It's just the water . . . the waters have changed. And I can't seem to remember . . ."

Natti had heard this all before; ever since Zabor was sent back to the hole from whence she'd come, Aunty had changed. Startled in the night, talking in her sleep. Even in waking, she sounded like she was moving slowly through a dream, the details of which slipped through her fingers with every need of reassurance.

"And Aivik?" she yawned, the combination of the water and the Aspirin maybe, hopefully, calming her — though still doing nothing for her memory.

"He's on a long haul, Aunty. He drives a truck now." Natti checked the oven's clock and felt rising panic. "Miriam will be by soon; I've got to go." Then she was out the door in a flash, even though cardio really wasn't her strong suit.

She had to chase the bus and bank on a red light, but she still made it, panting and already sweating once she got on. It was fine; she'd have almost an hour's journey to collect herself as she held on to the safety bar near the front of the #45. She'd have to transfer soon, and there was no point sitting.

Underneath the hoodie she was wearing her best shirt — which really wasn't much to write home about — and under her breath she rehearsed the things she'd memorized from a library internet search on job interviews. True, she'd done them in the past. But this was important. A job with fewer hours and higher pay seemed like a dream. And maybe, just maybe, it could lead her to taking a few classes at the U of W here and there. It might change things. But she had to get it first.

Her transfer came up quickly, and she was on the #21, settling into a seat near the back as the bus filled, stop after stop. Natti watched the city flick by and realized that, even though so much had changed in only half a year, the people didn't register it too much. True, everyone had been deeply affected by the flood. There were places in the city still being rebuilt, families grieving lives and homes lost to the deluge. But the city didn't fold up; it kept going because it had to. People blamed it on ill luck and temperamental elements — *A neat trick on the Owls' part*, Natti thought — and threw themselves into routine to distract themselves from what they all must have felt: that something unreal had happened. Something otherworldly. And it'd all happened so fast, even though the monster had been lurking there for hundreds of years before it was gone again.

The bus passed by the U of W, and Natti watched the students filtering in and out of the grand castle-looking collegiate in the centre of the campus. As usual, she envied them. She tried to slot herself into their places but came up short with the visual. How could she belong there now? Her powers, and those of the Families she'd grown up being taught about, had always seemed like an inconsequential, additional sense. Something she'd fit in to a regular life. But now she'd seen a couple battlefields, had come out on the other side, and found that she *liked* it. Liked having a warrior's purpose, even if it seemed like comic-book trash on the surface. She'd been a hero for once. She'd been a part of saving the day so this city could hold on to normality.

But the next day, after the flood waters had receded, she was still just Nattiq Fontaine, dropout from the North End, not knowing if her mother was still alive, living in the house of a woman who probably wasn't related to, let alone an actual aunty. Meanwhile the students at the university she idolized complained about having to take Indigenous Studies to graduate, thanks to new legislation.

The entire *world* was different and only Natti noticed.

The bus chugged along, avoiding potholes and the never-ending construction set up to fix them. Halfway there now; she combed her hair with her fingers, undid and retied her ponytail. *This is as good as it gets.* At least the zoo was near the river. No matter what, those dirty brown waters led to some sea, somewhere, even if here it was filled to the brim with a city's refuse and rejects. And any path to the sea, however far or indirect, gave her a bit of peace.

Despite what Aunty was hearing or seeing, the river felt quiet to Natti as she got off the bus at Overdale, crossed Portage, and headed into the park. She stopped for a second on the stone bridge, filled now with joggers and parents pulling kids in bike trailers. The wind whipped off the water and teased her hair into her eyes. She shut them; there was a hum there, a definite absence. The river hunters had been silenced, too, and for that one breath Natti remembered the one river hunter she'd called Brother. One she wouldn't see again in this world, though she hoped he'd made it to the next.

She kept moving. No, the river wouldn't make a sound now that its queen was gone. Yet there *had* been something in an undercurrent. Not a threat, but a warning. That the absence was either short-lived or not as empty as it appeared.

❧

It took every nerve in Natti's body to turn around and put her back to the interview, to this entire day. *I thought your name was Nat.* The counsellor, Rachel, had frowned at her. Maybe Natti already knew even trying this was a stupid idea.

She stormed off down the path, cheeks hot as she bit back tears. The same old song and dance — an excuse about the position already being filled, the brush-off about her volunteer experience, her track record. All it took was one look, usually. Why did she bother getting her hopes up?

It seemed a cheap consolation prize that in her need to escape the failed interview as fast as possible, the counsellor had left Natti in the zoo, free to wander the exhibits without having to pay the entry fee. Even though minutes ago she would've said anything to work here, as a cloud passed over the sun, Natti realized what a sad place the zoo was. Coming from a culture that viewed animals and the earth itself as sacred from which power came — even though her Seal roots seemed more distant since Aunty's illness — Mundane places like this never sat well with her.

She found herself at the North American birds exhibit,

then the boreal forest enclosure. She wondered how many Denizens came here and didn't feel like freeing their Family's namesakes. Owls fluttered in their enclosures and foxes roamed in their pens, coats and plumage dull, eyes fixed on nothing. Natti scoffed; maybe this is where all Denizens deserved to end up. Someone else's pretty cage.

She wandered deeper, feeling that strange hum again, that pull, that she'd felt when crossing the bridge into the park. The river wasn't far off and, without turning her head to look, she knew it was on her right side, just beyond a service road and a steep bank. But it wasn't the river humming her forward, and she stopped herself as she read the sign beside the inukshuk that made her heart catch — *Gateway to the Arctic: Journey to Churchill.*

Natti felt a chill up her spine, which was a welcome relief to the heat of her rage and shame, and joining the crowd of squealing babies and stressed-out parents longing for summer to be over, Natti went inside.

She allowed herself the barest moment of childlike reverence, entering the space that was dark as a cave of ice, water rippling around her on all sides and above her head. It was like her best dreams, the ones where Aunty showed her spirit impressions of the Abyss, the sacred place of the Seal Family and the kingdom ruled by its dark fighting Empress, Ryk. Natti never thought she'd see something like this in Winnipeg, of all places, and it calmed her fury, even beyond the rubbernecking tweens whipping out their phones to take selfies instead of enjoying the moment.

Then two white and hulking shapes moved across the ice-glass ceiling above them and the hum Natti felt turned into a roar.

The polar bear exhibit, she knew, had become local tourism's most recent crown jewel. It was no wonder; despite their huge country with all its natural wonders, many people — Natti included — might spend their entire lives here, and even this glimpse into the natural magic of the world offered a respite from that reality. The sun struck the water and Natti felt herself calm as she was pressed closer to the glass by the crowd.

At first, the bears paddled with a hypnotic cadence as if the people weren't there at all, as if the water suspended above them and the people in the open air below inhabited two different realms. And they very well did. No matter how trapped Natti felt now by circumstance, at least she had some freedom — unlike the bears.

The minute she thought it, her heart lurched, and the humming felt like a wave crashing on a distant icy shore. No, not a shore — a glacier with a beating blue heart — and the image was so stark and sudden she was only broken out of it when the crowd jostled around her to get a better look at the bears . . .

. . . two of which had stopped swimming right in front of Natti and seemed to be staring at her, and only her, through the divide of the glass.

One bear swam tentatively forward, paws and nose pressed into the glass. Natti felt like her feet had been frozen in the same ice she'd just seen, and someone said, "Whoa, look what they're doing!" and the crowd squeezed closer. Unable to move, all Natti could do was stare helplessly into the black eyes of the creatures in front of her, which, she noticed, seemed to be growing more agitated as the crowd pressed.

Something else was stirring in Natti — the same fury, the same aggravation, of being rejected only minutes ago. Her fist tightened as people told her to *move* or phones came out in front of her as if she weren't there, trying to angle for the best shot of the bears swimming in aggravated circles before the swooning audience.

Natti tried to find her voice — *stop pushing. Stand back.* But everything was frozen — legs, mouth. But not her mind, not when she saw that crest of ice again as the two bears came back to the glass, paws pressing uselessly, and Natti heard it.

Please, came two voices that nudged gently against her thoughts. *Help us*.

The crowd was overwhelming. She felt like she was going to be trampled, crushed. And in a surge, she felt that glacier turn over, revealing a power so blue and enormous that all she could do was ride the wave it sent through her, and she opened her eyes to the sound of the crowd screaming for the exits.

At first, she didn't know what was happening. There was a lightening sensation of floating above it all, but that wasn't Natti — that was the tank's water, which had surged and lifted completely out of the glass-bottomed enclosure the polar bears called home. The bears themselves burst out of the water for higher ground, narrowly avoiding the deluge as it came back down onto the glass, which exploded outward in a tidal crush.

Screams echoed and faded as the exhibit collapsed around Natti with a sound like an aquatic thunderclap. When she finally opened her eyes, as if in a dream, she realized that her hands were out, and that the water surrounded her in a delicate orb. Inside the water with her, swam the bears.

Natti couldn't help herself, opening her mouth to release

precious air as fear began to grip her. Then one of the bears swam forward and pressed its forehead to hers just as she considered the possibility she would be eaten alive.

Thank you, came the thought, the words, in that strange watery tone that Aunty had sang to her so often. *We knew you would come.*

What? Natti sent the thought back, less as a word, and more a general outcry of surprise. Too many questions roiled through her: They had been expecting her? Why?

The second bear swam forward, jerking its head to the side as if to say *hurry*. The motion was brief, but Natti could see clearly this bear was agitated beyond the situation; it had a dark ring around the coat at its throat, and Natti could feel it wasn't natural.

A siren blared outside their protective bubble. The crowd had long scattered, but others would come soon to assess the damage. To lay blame. And they wouldn't believe what they saw even when it was right in front of them.

We must get to the water. We can feel it near. Will you help us further, Sea Daughter? Now that calm inner voice was one of urgent panic, and Natti felt like someone had tied a ribbon around her ribs and yanked sharply. Why her?

Without thinking she went through the familiar movements, guiding her hands, heart racing. She knew that now was not the time to be afraid. The water shifted and carried them like a great serpent out through the rubble in a flash, across the access road, and deposited them into the fast-tracking brown of the Assiniboine River. Guided by the current and the desperation of the hunted, Natti and the bears dove deeper and headed east, towards the Red River, and the only place she could think to hide them all.

Aivik parked his car on the street. He'd have to get his buddy to check the engine belt before he left for the next haul. Not like it mattered — he always parked his little Toyota at the depot after trading off his semi, and he'd be parking it again for the next trip out to Fort Mac. But he wanted the peace of mind; the car was the first thing he'd managed to save up for, his little point of pride, and having that "check engine" light come on didn't sit well with him. At the best of times, Aivik didn't like surprises.

Takeout bags swung heavily from both his hands — he was hoping to hearten Natti and Aunty with more than just his early return from his first successful drive. Now that he was older, Aivik was doing his best to take charge and help out, despite his absence, and he knew Natti had her hands full with Aunty's flagging health. A little something from Neechi Commons always perked them all up.

It was warm out despite the shifting clouds, but when Aivik reached the crumbling steps of Aunty's house, he flagged. Had he really felt a chill in the air? His hand paused at the latch when he looked down and saw water seeping out from under the poorly sealed storm door. *Errant water in the house of a Seal never bodes well*, Aunty used to say.

"Natti, what —" Aivik started, frustrated that on his first haul he'd come back to another roof leak or a burst pipe or something else he'd have to fix on his off time.

But there wasn't really much he could fix about the two soaking polar bears with their hungry eyes on him as he burst into the living room, dropping the takeout bags when he jerked his arms up defensively.

Natti was holding up her hands, too, pulling the water out of the carpet as she popped up from behind the shaggy beasts. "Look, Aiv, it's not —"

"Hope you brought enough for our guests," Aunty said, tone familiarly wry above her rising cough. "Or something stronger than *water*."

Hollow Spirit

Eli feels the wind. In his hair. In his lungs. Impossibly, he breathes. Then he realizes he is *the wind. That it passes right through him, in and out, like a needle and fine thread. Like a red ribbon connecting everything — thoughts and body . . . though he's not sure if his body is a factor any longer.*

He is standing in a spiral of white pebbles, which makes a path to a shrine of tokens left behind by tourists, wanderers, those rare few people who still believe in magic. Playing cards and coins and paper clips. He bends down and sees the remnants of a gold tooth lodged in the dirt. He tries to extract it, but his fingers — what he thinks are still his fingers — pass right through.

You cannot touch a memory, *he thinks*. If that's what this is, anyway.

He stretches back up, feels the wind tugging him around in a slow waltz. He knows the place, even though it is shrouded in mist and damp and almost two decades' worth of time he seems to have lost between then and now.

The Fairy Glen.

He grew up not far from here, in a croft, he remembers. There was a woman there, spitting and wailing. She had a terrible secret, one that she passed down to Eli before he was even ready. He was like a boy trapped in a fairy story with the ending ripped out. In his tower he waited, but he never felt ready to leave.

When the wind spins him around again, he is facing a boy who stares at him as if he can see him. Or through him. Eli doesn't wave, and even though the boy is moving towards him, he moves around him entirely.

Eli remembers something else vague, about children. Children with desolate eyes and crimson smiles, children with coals beneath their skin. They followed a creature — a man — a creature that had once been a man, and where there had been screaming people, suddenly there were trees . . .

Eli shakes his head, and the wind whispers. He follows the boy up the hill.

On the hill is a well-worn switchback. A child's mountain pass. The boy has come here many times before, but Eli thinks — knows — he's come here now because the boy has followed someone here. Someone who will be at the top of the hill. Eli's heart quickens and sickens, like a child's does as they prepare for the jump-scare and hide behind their hands, tensing. Something inevitable waits at the top of that hill. The ending that Eli isn't sure he wants to see.

The boy stops and looks over his shoulder, right at Eli. Not through him, this time. His eyes ask, Do we have to? *And Eli doesn't know what to say, even as the wind sifts the boy's hair, his clear eyes that are his own wincing with the cold.* Let's just go home. Under the covers. Someone else will save us. Save her.

They turn as one to the sound of errant sheep bleating below them, and from up here they perceive the tourist shrines more clearly. Even though they haven't come very far, Eli realizes they are high enough up now that, if they fell, they could get hurt.

The boy continues going up, closer to harm, and Eli has no choice but to follow.

They come to a dark pass in the rock. The boy wriggles through like the path was made for him, and then there is a climb. Eli watches the boy struggle, all skinny arms and wheeling legs. Eli knows that, looking down at his hands, made of the same silver fog of winter breath, he couldn't help the boy up even if he wanted to. Eli truly is a ghost. And knowing any physical limitations are gone, he lets go of gravity's hold and floats to the surface of the rock, just as the boy emerges.

The boy is not alone. A figure stand stands on the precipice of the caer — the castle, *she had called it, in her lucid moments when she held him while the nightmares readied for the next salvo. Those moments when he could believe it would all be all right.*

Her arms are out, as though they could be wings. She is trembling.

"Go home, Eli," she says. His heart catches; her voice is clear. For once her mind is knowing. "You have to go home now."

Eli the ghost almost opens his mouth to answer, but the little boy does instead. "You have to come, too." He is twisting his shirt in his hands. The wind calls through the pointed hills beckoning.

The woman turns. Her hair is a wild, furious tangle, but her eyes, Eli's own eyes, are serene. "My brave boy," she says. "I know what you dreamed of. I know the stone is calling for you.

But you have to promise Mommy you won't go after it. No matter what anyone asks. Please promise."

Little Eli nods. He is being brave. He is always so much braver in this dream when Eli watches it, over and over, though he knows that the boy is raw with terror. She is so close to the edge. "Okay," he says. "Let's go home now."

"My darling," she whispers, and it is not her voice, but the thousands that came before. The ones that have tried to wrap their silvery tendrils around Eli's heart since a girl he once hated helped him cast them out. The voices that ruined everything. "Don't you want Mommy to stop hurting?"

"Please." But there is no boy anymore. Only Eli. Reaching, as she backs nearer to the edge. He is close enough to count the lines around her mouth, carved from too many nights screaming, crying. She touched the Moonstone, and it hurt her. It had chosen the little boy when he was still inside her, and the stone would not be refused.

She turns her back on him again. He rushes to her, feeling that perhaps this time, in this dream, he will be able to pull her back to safety. He'll take her down the hill to the fisher's croft and make her up some fresh broth, and put her to bed, and he will read the only book there — Island Birds *— until the pages crinkle with his drying tears, and all will be as it was, because desolation is better than nothing at all.*

But, as always, his hand is too late, and he feels her dark hair just missing his grip as she leaps, turns over, face finally at peace as she shuts her eyes and lets the air take her back to the earth.

Eli woke still screaming, full of a pain he couldn't quantify. His arms, his wings, were twisted around him, and he could still hear the wind . . . but he couldn't move, like he'd been encased in glass. One eye looked out into the dismal world in front of him. A smouldering plane wreck. And trees, black trees, reaching and reaching, as he was, to the darkening overcast sky. Trees whose minds, he knew, were trapped in nightmares like the ones he'd just barely surfaced from.

Trees that were once Owls, and one that maybe was his father. And now him, too.

Eli screamed, but in the dead forest, there was no one to hear but the wind.

❧

Phae barely shifted, even when a blast of wind cracked the trees around her in the fading crepuscular dusk. It wasn't uncommon for a summer windstorm to rise out of nowhere in Manitoba, and both she, and her subjects in the field past her hiding spot, were accustomed to the temperamental prairie elements. To the changing world around them.

She raised the DSLR to her eye, adjusted the lens and the shutter, popped off a few shots. Focus. Another batch. She scrolled through the display. Sunset, she felt, even after only a few months dabbling with photography, was one of the best kinds of light, especially now at the start of autumn. She came upon a shot she was particularly proud of, and with that same surge of pride came disappointment, because there wasn't anyone she could really show it to right now. Not her parents, who still resented her for taking the year off rather than going directly to university and the med school track she'd been preparing for. Not Barton, who was more preoccupied than she'd ever seen him, training endlessly with his new running blades and throwing himself into his still-new powers.

And not Roan, who, even though her image and voice had been so close on their recent FaceTime call, was the farthest away of them all.

"There you are!" Phae had said into her phone, trying to put on the cheer. "I'm out in the shed for some privacy. I put in a new router so the connection should be better . . . Where are you?" She mentally calculated what time it could be with the six-hour time difference — afternoon, judging by the background in Roan's screen, which seemed to be a restaurant of some kind.

"Oh, I'm in a café . . . just needed to get out of the flat." Her voice was lowered, and she looked around a bit anxiously. She looked like she hadn't slept.

Phae immediately cottoned on. "I tried calling you yesterday as soon as I saw the news. That . . . that was the restaurant you worked in, wasn't it?" The minute she'd seen the flames and the words *freak explosion in Royal Mile pub* all over her Facebook feed, she knew right away. "Was it . . . ?"

"I don't know what it was. Honestly." Roan exhaled like the breath she'd been holding was a painful one. "I came here for answers, and after months of nothing, I'm suddenly knee-deep in way too much *something*." She got up, seemed to move to a quieter corner with her cellphone. "I couldn't help it, Phae. There was this guy . . . he seemed to know who I was. *What* I was. But there was something wrong with him. He gave me this warning . . . I have no idea what it meant. For a second I could've sworn it was Urka's voice — it's stupid and bizarre, I know. But what about our lives is normal anymore, really?"

Phae nodded, consciously loosening her jaw at the mention of Urka. Things had happened so fast when Roan came back out from *hell* just last spring, and the images she'd painted would certainly haunt Phae's nightmares for a while yet. There was no telling what it was doing to Roan, who rubbed her face now, that same pain evident in the crease between her mismatched eyes. All Phae wanted to do was push herself through her iPhone and do something to erase that — even if she had to use the powers she'd been secretly resenting lately.

"It's not just Fingal's Pint that's been weird," Roan went on, lowering her voice. "I'm . . . seeing things. Not just visions, like what I usually see with the spirit eye. I'm seeing . . . memories. I think the stone is showing me Cecelia's memories. And they're vivid, like I'm *in* them. Then I'm pushed out, and I wake up in places I don't remember being. But I feel like I have to keep watching, keep letting the stone show me. Like Cecelia is trying to tell me something."

Phae frowned. "Or the stone is trying to control you, Roan, the same way that Eli's did. You need to be careful." She didn't want to call it wishful thinking, that Roan's grandmother was trying to communicate with her from beyond the grave. Phae knew a raw wound when she saw one.

Roan's smirk, however weak, was followed by the same old sardonic tone. "I know you're dying to encase me in bubble wrap, Phae, but I do still know how to take care of myself."

"Hardly." She smiled, but it was brief. "The guy who confronted you, the one with the warning. What was weird about him? I mean, aside from the usual. Weird can encompass too many factors."

Roan glanced around, brought the phone closer, and made her voice quieter. "That other thing on the news. *You know,* the Cinder Plague?"

Roan was right to whisper *that* in a public place. The Cinder Plague had become more widespread than SARS, with twice as much panic as the news spread the word faster than the disease itself. Roan could get kicked out of the café for even mentioning it.

"*Sinusitis erysipelas*? You mean he *had* it? Did he touch you?"

"Yes. Well, no. Look, he touched me, but I'm fine, see?" She showed her hands. "No black gunk, no sudden fever. Again, *fine* is a relative term. But like you said before, Denizens don't seem to be affected. Just, you know, regular people who don't have a supernatural immunity."

Still, Phae felt her heart speeding up. "Did he —"

"Yeah, he *definitely* exploded right in front of me, and that's when the rest of the restaurant followed suit."

The worst part of some of these isolated cases was that those with already-compromised immune systems seemed to literally combust. Incidents had been isolated, and some had speculated that the illness was caused by some biological weapon rather than just a skin fungus. Researchers and governments were already hastening to manufacture a cure, but what was most sinister was that its origin remained vague, though it was striking Western countries and not the usual developing countries. And cases seemed to be popping up more and more in Scotland, of all places, since Roan appeared there.

"It can't be a coincidence," Roan said, voicing Phae's greatest worry. "I show up here, this freak virus pops up, some guy with it issues me a warning before making me blow up my restaurant . . . and I saw some of my co-workers after. No one died, Phae. But I thought one of them, Ben . . . I thought he had . . ." She winced, neck tensing as she bent forwards like she was about to throw up.

Phae leaned in as close to her phone as possible. "Roan? Roan, are you okay?"

" — fine," she heard, when Roan's face was back in the picture, and though Roan had tried to hide it, Phae had seen her clutch her chest before quickly dropping her hand. Roan sighed raggedly. "I'm just tired. It's all been a lot. But I guess I asked for this, didn't I? I wanted action. Now I've got it."

Phae let that sink in a bit before she said, "Roan . . . you don't have to do this alone, you know. You went out there by yourself. I'm sure you've kept your aunt and uncle at arm's length. We're all stronger together, remember? We should be there with you. It's obviously getting too much —"

"Phae," Roan cut her off, voice wavering but hard. "I can't chance it. Not if I'm going off like an atom bomb. I'm trying to stay in control. I can't let what happened to Eli happen to me. I could hurt someone. I don't want it to be you." Phae knew that was as much as she was going to get on the subject. "Speaking of which . . . where is Mr. Know-It-All-Before-You-Know-It?"

Phae's mouth twitched. "Geez, you must have it bad if you can't say his name."

"Oh knock it off, will you? Eli and I don't have . . . a thing. Anything! I don't hear from him and I don't want to." Roan had told Phae about how he'd shown up at the airport. She'd thought the gesture was sweet and didn't mind letting Roan know every chance she got.

"Maybe if you did talk to him, at least he knows what you're going through." But Phae didn't know if he'd be back anytime soon to chat. "He's gone off to Korea, I think. To face the consequences of . . . what's been happening with his own stone."

"It's not his *fault*, though." For someone she didn't seem to care about, Roan was quick to defend Eli. Phae didn't point it out. "The stone changes you. It's, like, got a mind of its own. Several minds. And they're all fighting for control. It's like the stone knows what's best. It has its own plan." She looked away, biting the inside of her cheek. "Anyway. Don't worry about me. You've all got your own lives to worry about. Like if you're gonna do university or not."

"If only I could take Supernatural Anxiety as a major . . ." Phae muttered. "At least it would be something to get my father off my back."

"Hey," Roan said, "it's your life. Not theirs. You take as much time as you need, okay? I know you. You won't be down and out long. Purpose is your middle name."

Phae stuck out her tongue. "You know it's Lakshmi."

Roan's face fell. "I'm sorry, Phae. It's my fault. I dragged you into all this . . . stuff."

Stuff, like *weird*, didn't exactly cover it, but Phae had just shrugged, remembering that field in the snow what seemed like years ago, when she'd made a choice to save a stranger, who had become an ally, who had become a boyfriend, and now was something she couldn't qualify. It was the same field she sat at the edge of now, as the deer she'd been photographing scattered back into the brush with the tangle of her thoughts.

"It was still my choice," Phae said to no one.

"What was?"

Phae startled to her feet — luckily her camera strap had been around her neck, otherwise she'd have destroyed what she'd traded a whole year's tuition for.

"Sorry." Barton held his hands up. "I'll be less stealthy next time. And by stealthy I mean I'll trip over more logs and get stuck in more bog puddles, since my actual approach only scared every deer in the forest . . . except you." He lifted one of his running blades to show her the mud and debris he'd tracked with him.

"You didn't have to come all the way in here!" Phae admonished as she led them back out to the main path through drier ground. "I thought you were supposed to be taking better care of your *equipment*." She took his arm, even though he hadn't asked, and steadied him.

"Ah well, if I'd broken anything, it's not like I don't have a world-class demon-slaying healer for a girlfriend." He leaned down to kiss her, but at the last second she turned her head, and it landed perfunctorily on her jaw.

Barton pulled away, still holding her by the arm. "You okay?" he asked. He'd been asking that a lot. Phae forced a smile up at him — she was still getting used to how tall he was, since he used his wheelchair less and less.

"Fine. Just lost in thought again." She took his hand when he offered it as they walked back down the path towards the forest's entrance, but she stared at the ground. "How was the meeting?"

It was Barton's turn to go a bit quiet before he replied. "Complicated."

"What's wrong? Did something happen?"

He seemed to be searching the sky for the words, and when he slowed his pace, Phae knew it wasn't because of any discomfort in his legs. "Yeah. A lot of somethings." He'd grown used to the blades already — had been running with them, barely taking them off . . . a boon of the sports scholarship he'd graduated with. No, he'd told her there was no pain in his legs now. Said they were a part of him. But there was still something she saw flicker in his eyes.

"I'm going away for a while. I dunno how long. And . . . well, I wanted to ask if you'd come with me."

They'd stopped altogether, and Barton was still holding her hand. She extracted it gently. "I'll need a bit more than that to go on, *karagosh*."

He grinned at her pet name, but the smile faded quickly. "It's the Rabbit Paramount. It's what Arnas came over to talk to me about. My parents already knew something was going on with the higher-ups, now that they're more involved with the Family again, but official word has just come down. He's . . . well . . . they don't know *where* the current Rabbit Paramount is. But they do know that his stone is missing. The Serenity Emerald."

Phae's chest tightened. The first person she thought of was Roan. "What does that mean, *it's missing*? Did someone take it? And how could they — I thought the stone-bearer and their Calamity stone couldn't be separated?" What Phae didn't know about this bizarre world of Ancient could fill a library.

"No one knows much. Or else, no one's saying much." Barton shrugged, then staggered as a fresh blast of wind nearly knocked them off the path. "You spoke to Roan recently, though, didn't you?"

Phae nodded. "Just a couple days ago. She seemed . . . she was alive." Phae had told Barton about the explosion. He'd already said, after it happened, that the Fox Family would probably be looking into it, according to Arnas — but since the Families didn't seem to cross lines to speak, it was tough to know what they would do about it.

"Par for the course." Barton zipped up his track jacket against the cooling evening air. "And has she heard from Eli?"

"Why?" Phae knew where this was going, though she'd just asked Roan the same question on their call. "I don't think so. He was going to Korea, I thought?"

"He was." A dark look passed over his face. "But he's missing now, too."

So. It was as she feared. "Someone's targeting the Paramounts. And the stones." They walked for a bit in silence until they reached the parking lot and Phae's car. The two got into her sedan, buckled up, and headed towards Wolesley.

"Do they have any idea who it is? Or what? Or *why*?"

"No," Barton said. "This is all happening too fast. Everyone's already saying that the Cinder Plague might be something darkling-derived, since it popped up so quickly after we got rid of Zabor . . ." He smirked. "Things were simpler, back then."

"Right." Phae didn't say what she really thought about times past she'd never get back. "So what does this have to do with us going away together?"

"Well . . ." Barton was playing with the door lock, so Phae

figured it was something she would already have a hard time going along with. "A gathering's been called. There hasn't been one in a long time, apparently. It's a meeting of the Rabbit, Owl, and Fox Families. The Seal Family hasn't mentioned if it'll come. And there are no human representatives of the Deer Family, really. Can't exactly trap a bunch and not expect a democratic stampede." She caught him looking at her meaningfully from the corner of her eye, but she pretended to be focused on the road.

"And where is this meeting? When?" Phae knew there had to be a catch, that he was trying to get her to go back out into the Denizen world since she was so useless in this one. She felt like she'd always be straddling a line between them.

"A place called Magadan. In Russia. In a few days." Barton said it all quickly, like it'd make it seem less than seven thousand miles away. "It's around the place Eli's plane disappeared. It's not just a meeting to talk. They want to form a coalition. To fight."

This time, Phae did look at him. "To fight? Fight *what*?" She felt the panic rising, remembering their last battlefield and what had been lost there. "Do they think this is something to do with Zabor?"

"Like I said, no one knows. But they want to be ready. If something is out hunting the Calamity Stones, it can't be good." His mouth quirked. "I'd be less concerned if they were called the Fuzzy Bunny Stones, but apparently they're dangerous if in the wrong hands."

"Anything is. Even a fuzzy bunny." They were on Academy already, making good time towards the Maryland Bridge. Maybe *too* good.

"Hey, you know it's only fifty here, right?"

Phae checked her speedometer and took her foot off the gas. Even her subconscious wanted this conversation to be over.

"You want to go halfway across the world to join up with the magical army corps to fight an enemy you can't name?" Phae didn't mean for it to come out bitter and sharp, but she didn't retract. "And you think I'd want to come with you? To do what, exactly?"

"Phae . . ." Barton said gently. "I know things have been tough lately. And that your parents haven't exactly made it any easier." His hand tentatively moved to her knee. "You could use a break. To go away. And I thought, maybe, this might show you that you *do* have purpose. Even if you seem to think you don't."

It was a good thing they were both belted in when Phae slammed on the brakes at the Wolesley intersection — the light had suddenly turned red and brought with it a wave of pedestrians who were nearly bludgeoned by the hood of her car.

"It's okay," Barton was saying, trying to bring her back down. "Phae?"

But Phae's hands gripped the steering wheel, lighting up with flickers of blue and white. Her hair had crackled instantly into a crown of antlers too big for the driver's side to accommodate. When the pedestrians had continued on unharmed, she knew they'd all been too preoccupied to notice they'd been saved by the shield she'd automatically generated.

"No," she said, taking the left sharply and heading mercifully closer to Barton's house. "No, it's not okay. I can't just . . . I can't go with you. It's not my place. I need more information first. And there are things here I need . . . to do."

"Like what?" Barton seemed to feed off her agitation. "You picked up this photography thing on a whim — and the Phae I know barely knows the meaning of the word *impulsive*. I get that this whole thing reads like some *great power great responsibility* thing, and you're trying to find your place in it all. But we're both in the same boat here. I wasn't raised in the thick of this stuff like other Denizens and neither were you."

He still hadn't broken through by the time they'd parked in front of his house, and when his voice softened, Phae knew it was his last attempt. "We were both given *gifts*, Phae. Gifts that other people would kill for. And if we can help, especially after what happened here, with Zabor, why don't you want to try? You wouldn't have to be alone. I wouldn't let you —"

"But I *do* want to be alone!" Phae's voice, more a high shriek, pinged in their ears in the silence that followed. She didn't know who was more surprised — Barton or herself.

"I see," he replied flatly. "Well. I'm sorry I interrupted you, I guess."

She didn't even turn her head when he got out. But she rolled down the window after he tapped a knuckle on the glass, and she met his gaze, her own misery reflected behind his glasses.

"Just think about it, okay?" he said, trying to smile. Forcing it, like she had. "Even if you don't come . . . I don't want to leave like this."

Phae exhaled, the numbness passing. "Neither do I."

Barton's mouth stiffened into a line as he patted the car door, turned, and went into his house.

Phae wanted to get far away from here, and as quickly as possible. Russia suddenly felt like a solid destination to do just that, but only if Barton wouldn't be there. Or the black hole promise of more monsters and bad guys to go up against — a fight that Phae didn't have in her to join. Not now, anyway.

She drove off. Had she always felt this anxious, deep down? Had she been burying it under a manufactured calm, protected by her scholastic achievements and the career path she'd chosen before she'd left kindergarten? You'd think the blinding heroics of last spring would have given her the same confidence boost it had to Barton, but to him this was all a comic book dream come true. Now Phae was the one who couldn't move forward, let alone change. Power hadn't made her feel stronger; instead it had done the exact opposite by exposing her weakness.

Just think about it. What was there to think about? Even if she was armed with all the information, which either wasn't forthcoming or didn't exist yet, given that Denizens on the elder level were scrambling — what would be the tipping point for her to jump into any kind of fray?

Roan had asked Phae to come to Edinburgh, even if the invitation was half-hearted. Phae knew Roan wanted to keep everyone away, just in case. But even with that request she'd felt more of a pull than she had from Barton just now.

Phae's phone went off in the cup holder, and she pulled over immediately after glancing down, seeing who it was.

"Oh good, you picked up for once. Hope it isn't a bad time?"

Phae closed her eyes, summoning hard-won patience. "Best not get into it."

"Right, I won't. You know I don't like sharing." She was thankful for Natti — always down to brass tacks. "If you're not wallowing as usual, can you come to my place? Like —" There was a grunt as Natti seemed to drop the phone, then pick it up again. "Sorry. Yeah. Right now."

"Is it Aunty? Is she okay?" She'd been hearing from Natti with more frequency these days because of Aunty's condition, which Phae couldn't do much about — and even the gruff Natti, who had trouble asking for help at the best of times, was grateful.

"Actually, she's fine. But she's not happy. And neither are the, uh, guests we've got." The sound of something ripping, loud, near her ear and — what was that? A roar?

"Do you have the nature channel on?" Phae frowned.

"Something like that," Natti clattered. "Look, it's kind of an emergency. I know you don't have anything else better to do. I'll owe you. Well. I'll owe you *more*."

Phae was already shifting back into drive. "On my way."

Wolesley, and all of Barton's unanswered questions, faded in the rear-view as she headed north towards Portage, Roan's words from their last conversation playing over the anxieties she pushed to the back of her mind: *Purpose is your middle name*.

The Stonebearer's Burden

I was so engrossed in saying goodbye to Phae that I didn't notice the woman come in and head straight for me. She grabbed me before I could pull away.

"I know it's you!" she spat in my face. Her breath was bitter and I recoiled when I got a clear look at her face, which was a knot of scars and burns, the eyes milky white, yet her teeth were in remarkable shape. "I could hear you, even out in the street, the noise . . . You thought you could come back without trying to find me? After everything? You thought —"

I ripped my arm away and the woman staggered, shielding herself. I hadn't noticed the arc of flame I'd generated until I saw it flash in those dead eyes. She was rail-thin, bent, wearing clothes that looked like they'd seen the battered side of a donation bin in the rain.

I straightened my hoodie; after just talking about the

Cinder Plague, I felt a sudden need for a scalding shower. "I . . . I think you're confused." I had to relax, push down the panic. Not everyone was out to get me — but after Table Five, I wasn't taking chances. Even on a homeless derelict.

I stepped around her and met all the eyes turned on us in the café. I thrust my hand into my pocket and pulled out a five-pound note to save face. "Here, maybe get yourself something hot to eat?"

But she didn't take the bill — just stared past me. Through me. Like she'd just been shaken out of sleepwalking. I knew she must be blind. I shoved the money into her hand and she recoiled again. The initial fury she'd met me with was now dull confusion.

I turned to go, nearly made it to the door, before she said, "Cecelia? It is you, isn't it? I heard —"

By the time I'd turned, the café manager had come around the counter and between us. "You can't be in here —" But the rest had been drowned out by the woman's incoherent shrieks as she backed into the corner booth I'd just vacated, someone at a nearby table snickering and pointing their phone at her.

I was out on the sidewalk and booking it back to my flat before I could watch the outcome. It was too much. Before I returned to the flat, I bought some blackout curtains. Might as well go full hermit.

Why did I think going back out had been a *good* idea? It seemed like everyone, everywhere, was having a bad time of it. Cinder Plague, terrorist attacks, children disappearing, the environment tanking . . . Maybe not leaving the flat for a while would give me the illusion of safety — just like Phae's reassurances. But right now, nowhere was really safe, was it?

It was a couple days after the woman in the café. I got out of the bed and moved to the edge of the dark curtains, peering outside. My window looked out onto Lauriston Place, which connected, eventually, to the Meadows down the Middle Walk, near the Old Medical School. The sidewalks and roads were always a bustle of activity, but now it seemed like the shadows were deeper, even in the daylight. Were strangers looking up at my building, watching me watch them? I felt like a kid staring into a dark closet, the clothes on their hangers growing more monstrous with each passing breath.

I closed the curtains and turned back to the room, pacing and chewing my nails down. *The children are coming for you.* I'd replayed it in my mind so many times, like a broken goddamn record, that it sounded like a hopscotch chant. A hostile playground charm. I hadn't seen too many kids around since the explosion, though I'd kept my spirit eye out. The only young people dogging me were Ben and Athika, leaving well-meaning messages that brought me back, again and again, to the black marks I'd seen on them, marks so much like the ones on Table Five. Marks reminiscent of the hideous pile of ash they all should have been. I was relieved no one had been hurt, but . . . they should've been. And that made me all the warier.

The Cinder Plague had started with kids, hadn't it? I pulled my finger out of my mouth, watched it bleed freely from the nail bed I'd pierced. *The children are coming for you.*

I know it's you! The blind woman — she'd used Cecelia's name. She'd have to have known her, from some time before, maybe when she'd lived here. I snatched up the letter, reread it despite knowing it by heart. The letters had, at first, been the only clues to what Cecelia had been up to before sending her body, and all its baggage, back to Winnipeg. To where she had been when her own daughter was defying the tenets that sent Denizen children to slaughter-by-darkling and had died herself trying to find a way to stop it.

I was still thinking about that woman, though, days later . . . how had she mistaken me for Cecelia? It had all happened so fast, and I hadn't consciously turned my spirit eye on. Had she been a Denizen? Had she *heard* the stone somehow, like I did? What the hell was going on?

My chest tensed up, as if the clockworks of my heart and lungs had suddenly seized. I fell forward, catching myself on my bed. The voices surged. I covered my ears, but I knew it wouldn't help; the voices were *inside* of me, tangling with my own thoughts, rattling the cage.

"Stop it!" I begged through gritted teeth.

The children are coming . . .

You thought you could leave me behind?

Even with my spirit eye closed, there was no escaping the rush of images, either; I couldn't close anything off. Extrasensory pinpricks jolted out of my pores like sparks. Seeing jumbled fragments of memories that *weren't* mine. A waking manifest nightmare I had no say in backing out of — terrible and frightening and too much.

"No!" I screamed, lurching and knocking into my coffee table, which I picked up without thinking and smashed into the wall. Then the lamp. Then I upturned the sofa, strength surging through me. "Get out of my head!" The heat was rising, and I felt myself expanding with it like a rippling cloud of ozone. I threw more furniture into the walls to redirect the sensations, if only temporarily. Was my neighbour banging on the wall, telling me to keep it down? I was close to cratering those walls, so soon whatever noise I was making would be incidental to the damage I knew I was capable of. Maybe this time I'd take the whole building down and the tenants wouldn't be so lucky.

The voices only got louder, battering back against me and bringing me to my knees. "Please," I tried, and in the roar, just as I was about to give in, to let the fire consume, I heard it — like an afterthought. Like a question.

Roan.

I latched onto it. Focused. The tidal wave of screaming and rage in too many languages with too many demands still roiled, but I took a deep breath. Took control, turned them down. And they faded around that one keystone, my name, and suddenly it was quiet.

Roan.

I opened my eyes. I was standing. The flat was gone. The space was dark and mercifully silent. I looked down. The floor was black granite with silver marbled veins, becoming clearer the longer I stared. Flashing underneath me were three concentric gold circles.

I looked up.

Cecelia stood before me. Not the shrunken woman in the hospital bed I'd known. Not the little fox or the warrior. It was the formidable and almost *too* beautiful younger version I'd only lately seen in this waking dream world I suddenly had access to. She stared at me, her eyes keen and knowing.

There was only one name I could call her. The only name I trusted.

"Sil?"

She smiled. The darkness faded into light, and the summoning chamber was gone, and Cecelia wasn't smiling at me.

I shifted to a layer behind this world, to what I knew immediately must be her memory, and saw the woman named Ruo coming down some pillar-lined steps towards her.

"You clean up nicely," Ruo remarked, and Cecelia gave a mock bow. The two of them were dressed smartly and in matching gear — a black double-breasted tunic belted over red and gold trousers, collars high and crisp. Ruo's black hair was a tidy frame around her neat features, while Cecelia's flowed down her shoulders to the small of her back. Ruo's eyes flicked to Cecelia's feet. "Are you immune to wearing sensible shoes?"

Cecelia ran a finger around her tight collar and winced. "I always hated this getup. We aren't acolytes anymore. I won't get a dress code slip for mules. Unless you're giving them out now."

Ruo sighed. "Well, if the Conclave wasn't expecting you before, now they'll hear you coming from a mile away." They'd started the long trek across the black marble court towards the Dragon Grounds, and they definitely drew stares from the young trainees and council masters alike. Ruo openly admired Cecelia's squared shoulders, her defiant stare ahead, as she tried to keep up with the taller woman's determined strides.

"Let them look," Cecelia replied to Ruo's unspoken anxiety, though her cynical tone seemed thinner than usual. "I know what they're thinking. And I don't care."

"And what exactly is that?" Ruo shot back under her breath. "There might be too many rumours to name them all."

"I know they're all expecting me to put myself forward for the stone. I'm looking forward to soaking up their shock and disappointment." Cecelia corrected her scowl — on the flight here, she knew that her greatest weapon was coaxing her features into placid apathy. To show the Conclave she didn't care one way or another who the next Paramount was, and that she was only here to pay her respects to her deceased master — and whatever else he'd been: former confidant, bitter political adversary, one-time bedmate. "They think I had some kind of attachment to Chartrand and that it would put me higher in the pecking order. But coming all the way here to deny them is worth much more."

They'd avoided talking about it any further on the long flight, through too many time zones before landing in Aleppo, but anything could happen today, and there may not be another chance. So even though it was painful, Ruo finally brought it up. "But you slept with him, anyway. Surely you knew there'd be talk."

Cecelia stopped. They were at the edge of the outdoor sanctum, the Middle Eastern sun punishing, but she turned her face towards it regardless, soaking up the light, the original fire, as any Fox may have.

"I was curious, honestly. And Chartrand was weak, for all his power and bluster and proselytizing. I wanted to show him I didn't fear him. That I was *more* than him. It made me feel strong — and it's the '60s, for gods' sake. Surely a woman can do as she pleases." She took a breath. "I didn't love him. You know me."

"Do I," Ruo said dryly.

Cecelia blew out her cheeks. "Anyway . . . people thought we were going to marry, or something. That it was some likely outcome for the benefit of our bloodlines. Yeesh. If our dalliance had yielded anything, I would have gotten rid of it. Me with a kid! The idea of bringing a child into this kind of world . . . having tremendous power, hiding it from the rest of society for 'their own good,' maintaining balance from the shadows in a world consumed by greed and destruction, all for a silent, thankless god? No thank you."

"Here we go." Ruo laughed, and she started walking ahead, Cecelia catching up with hurried strides.

"What?"

"You complained about Chartrand's proselytizing, but ranting in general was always your favourite pastime."

"Because he was *insufferable*. Both he and the Conclave think they can control us all under the guise of the greater good . . . we talk about the Owls being high and mighty, but the Foxes are no different." Cecelia sighed raggedly. "This Family doesn't own me. Or you. That's the message I wanted to send by leaving."

"Yet here you are." Ruo had lowered her voice as they stood out of the way of a group of acolytes being guided down the great staircase, bearing fire in the palms of their hands. Cecelia peered down the steps, hewn from the shifting sandy earth, that descended into the canyon's chamber, lit by shadow and flame. It mimicked the Den of Deon, the astral place where their power came from and returned. The more Cecelia saw the Fox Family and their intentions for what they were, the more she thought of their sacred meeting grounds as less a temple, and more a tomb.

She had last been here with Chartrand and, so sure of herself as usual, she'd pledged it would be her last time stepping foot here. The sun would be at its zenith shortly, and her pledge to cut all Family ties would soon be sorely tested. Chartrand had laughed in her face then, and she'd pounded him across the mouth for it — but he was probably still laughing now, from beyond the grave, as she stood on the precipice once more, word broken for Ruo's sake more than anyone's.

Cecelia looked aside when Ruo twined her fingers in hers. "It's really too bad that you need a man to make a baby," Ruo said finally. "I wouldn't have minded being a mother. If I could have shared the title with you, I mean. For all your blockheadedness."

Surprised, Cecelia smiled warmly. "It's a brave new world," she said as they started their descent. "And after this, I intend to enjoy every opportunity it affords."

The crowd down in the great hall was thick, low chatter filling the close space like a beehive. Cecelia made sure to remain as close to the back wall of the temple's topmost tier, and Ruo stuck to her side. The room dipped like an amphitheatre anyway, with a recessed bowl surrounded by graded levels, so wherever one stood the view was without compromise. The flame of the bowl burned low but visibly, and in the heart of the white-hot hearth was the Dragon Opal.

"I have to admit," Cecelia murmured, "the stone really looks better without Chartrand hanging off it."

Ruo elbowed her, cutting her eyes to the increasing number of critical stares shot towards them.

Cecelia turned her nose up but obediently hushed, looking back down to the bowl. The sunlight streaming through the skylight moved closer to the bowl with each passing second. The three gold circles incised in the black marble orbited the flames heavily — flames that would have appeared only when Chartrand died and would come to rest within the stone forever once his replacement was chosen.

Chartrand had been Paramount for twenty-five years,

and this was the first Arbitration Cecelia had ever witnessed. Despite her spiritual skepticism, there was something kinetic in the air, an excitement beyond the grief of losing such a strong leader — flawed though he was. Even with the advantage of Denizen longevity and his own stamina, his death had been a shock — and due to natural causes. A heart attack in his sleep. A disappointing end for any warrior, especially the leader of a Family whose chief obligation was to fight to the last.

But the Arbitration meant opportunity for a new beginning with a new kind of leader. Perhaps the stone would choose someone young, someone not so tied to the old ways, someone with a fire fit for the modern view. *Someone like me*, she couldn't help but think, but she shoved that aside, suddenly paranoid the stone could somehow hear her. Instead she looked for the next most likely candidate in the crowd. It wasn't hard to find him, for he was surrounded by a handful of masters and a slew of his peers. They clasped him by the shoulder, shaking him as if in preemptive congratulations. But he only stared back at Cecelia with those hazel eyes, face impassive. For an eight-year-old, he had a gravity she never would have. It made her slightly ill to imagine someone so young willing to give up his life for that kind of duty.

Cecelia smiled, nodded. Looked away again. She was itching to get this over with. Whoever was chosen would have a hell of a time of it. Access to power and influence to support your ideals was one thing. But if she'd learned anything from Chartrand — from the Families in general — it was that power corrupts, no matter how good your intentions. And the responsibilities attached to the Dragon Opal, to any Calamity Stone, were too enormous to consider. The majority of the acolytes and masters here considered being chosen a great honour. But it was a curse. Cecelia was going to sink her teeth into the normality the Mundanes took for granted and hang on for dear life.

She took hold of Ruo's arm then and pulled her closer, maybe squeezing a little too hard. No one was going to take her hard-won peace from her. Least of all that damn stone.

Then the three Fox elders entered the bowl, and the golden circles stilled underneath each of them. The crowd hushed, and though Cecelia had a rudimentary idea of how the ritual went, she didn't have to wonder after the details for long.

"Sons and Daughters of Deon," came the voice of the woman in the front, whose circle was directly at the lip of the bowl that bore the stone. "We honour now the latent flame of Paramount Chartrand Lavereux, and his devotion to his phrase in the Narrative. We place our grief upon his name and consign his fire to the Opal."

The other two elders raised their hands, embers coming off their arms as they performed the rite, and the bowl's flames rose in kind, seeping into the stone as it called Chartrand's light to its core. The heart of the stone shone, and there was a sound like a gasp — though no one in the chamber had made a sound.

The second elder spoke: "The light of Deon shines on all Denizens, though it was the very flame taken from the sun that shines within her Fox kin."

Then the third: "One Fox's flame is but a pinprick in the heat of Ancient's furnace. Let now the heart of Deon wake and turn on they who is worthy to bear it in this waking plane."

The sun touched the stone, then, above and below it

consuming the bowl, the stage, and the elders, was a twisting golden inferno whose heat touched them all with its corona.

Cecelia had steeled herself for this, as bands of light shockwaved through the temple, but everything inside her seized as the brightest flame, like a whiplash, came straight for her and Ruo. Cecelia immediately let her lover go, spun, and smashed the blade of light aside with her own fire.

When she touched back down a breath later, balancing on her less-than-sensible shoes, another band of light struck out.

"*No*," she snarled, her fury unbearable as she lurched aside, turning the flame as it cracked into a pillar. The shocked acolytes nearby scattered.

It was the third band that lashed out only an instant later that wrapped firmly around her extended forearm, nearly yanking her off her feet. She planted them and pulled back.

"Submit to the fire!" rang a voice from the lower bowl, and she knew it had been the first elder. "You cannot be unchosen!"

"The hell I can't." Cecelia managed to smirk, overconfident even now despite straining against the flame's pull. She kicked her focus up and brought her other arm cracking down on the cable of light, shattering it with a kickback that made her shoulder feel it'd been hit by a cannonball.

Cecelia knew without having to look up that all eyes were on her, but she didn't bother meeting any of them. She pointed down at the stone, heaving, as if it had come alive to challenge her.

"I refuse to take any part in this!" she roared. "I bear no loyalty to any Family of Ancient that blindly follows rules and rituals that suit no one but those in power. That drive a wedge between us and the rest of humankind. You have no power over *me*!"

"Insolent girl," the second elder admonished. "The stone's choice is absolute!"

Cecelia was as incredulous as they were, and she barked a laugh. "You'd want someone as a leader who wants nothing to do with you? You've just proven my damn point!" This time she whirled and addressed the temple, voice rising. "Tell me, *brothers and sisters*. Surely there are those among us here today who would not follow me, stone or otherwise. Who feel that they are more worthy of that miserable relic. Please. I insist. Step forward and claim your due, because I don't want it. And I never will."

Cecelia's eyes landed directly on the young boy as they had before — there was something different in him now. An eagerness. She saw his feet shift. She knew that the hunger Chartrand had instilled in him, that brazen confidence of boys who know they can be great, was probably like a flaming itch beneath his flesh. He glanced quickly between her and the stone.

They all did, even Cecelia, for the Dragon Opal was rotating, speeding up to a blinding hum.

And though the light did not fade, it grew into a massive figure, a kneeling one, that rose to its full incredible height, flaming tails a shivering halo behind her, bristling mane brushing the skylight, as if the sun itself had become a woman.

Not just a woman — but Deon herself.

No one moved. No one breathed. Some fell to their knees in shocked reverence. But Cecelia knew this, too, was a kind of test. And she stood her ground.

"*Not lightly do I cross the Veil*," came a voice like a house fire, "*but to have my gift refused three times warrants my coming.*" Her enormous head surveyed the chamber, the fox snout of spark and hair, and the human mouth beneath curled in a hungry grin. "*But it is so like a Fox to question a command. Even that of her Matriarch.*"

The eyes burned to look at. The eyes of the sun. But Cecelia found her legs taking her down the steps to the bowl, to the warrior queen she had been taught had given her so much, yet she'd said Her name in vain too many times to recall. She stopped at the god's feet, which were like a fox's hindquarters, the legs clothed in the hides of the darkling beasts of the original wilds she had slain in all the myths Cecelia told herself she didn't believe. Deon was large enough that Cecelia could clearly make out the pictures incised in the dried hides — the constantly moving record of the Narrative's greatest battles.

She craned her neck up to keep meeting that unforgiving stare and said the words she never thought she'd have to use. "First matriarch of the Family that bears my blood, Your gift may be mighty, but it is not for me to have."

Cecelia was close enough now to see that Deon's grin bore many sharp, cunning teeth. "*And even without the authority I seek to grant you, you think that is your decision still to make?*"

Cecelia swallowed. Surely the mother of all Foxes could see reason. "There are others, Deon. Others who might do you credit in bearing your image, your power. Who would lead by your example as I . . . cannot."

The eyes of blinding gold narrowed. "*And what of my example do you not hold with, daughter?*"

Cecelia knew better than to go back on the offensive. She was already on thin ice, so she chose her words carefully. "There is such a thing as too much power. And Denizens are no better than humans, despite what they may think." Cecelia cut a quick glance to the elders standing close by, their faces nearly apoplectic with rage and terror. "The world has changed since you and your sisters ruled and shaped the land. There are old tenets that are no longer relevant in the twentieth century. Approaches and ideologies that need to change. Many may think we need to follow the old ways to keep balance, to follow Ancient's order, but there is still disorder and chaos despite that. We may be made in Ancient's image, but we are flawed creatures. I know my limitations and I accept them. And so I could not do you proud."

Cecelia had been taught much about these old gods, and she knew that the root of fearing them came from their ability to know what was in their Denizens' hearts. She desperately wanted to turn around, to find Ruo in the crowd, to draw strength from her. But now she bricked up the true reasons for refusing, smothered them before they could give her away. If she bore the stone, she would say goodbye to any life she could have with Ruo. To her own ideals for a just world.

She didn't know how much longer she could hold Deon's gaze, though, and she knew it would be easy work for Deon to incinerate Cecelia where she stood.

"*I assure you, daughter,*" Deon finally murmured after deliberating, "*that even my sisters and I bear our flaws. And with that admission, perhaps you are right. Perhaps what my Opal heart saw in you is not fit for the gift.*"

Cecelia felt her eyes widen and fought to keep her mouth closed. Her heart sped up. Had she heard mocking in Deon's words? But the god swept Her mighty hand in an arc, and from the flames that made Her she grasped the enormous bone hilt of Her garnet blade.

"But that leaves my stone inert, which it cannot be as long as the wheel turns. There is little that would please me better than to punish you for your selfish ambition in refusing me. But you are all just children. And children crave nothing so much as a game."

Cecelia heard someone nearby mutter, "A game?"

The blade arced back above Deon's head, flashing caustically as it drew down the blaring desert sun. "*Your Matriarch will oversee a Sun Trial, and your elders will choose the champions they feel are up to the extraordinary gift I offer. Perhaps those who might be more grateful for the chance to serve Ancient than you clearly are.*"

Cecelia took one step backward, eager to bow out now that her scrutiny was over, but the great dark blade came down like a guillotine, and the tip rested threateningly at her breast.

"*And you will be* my *champion, dear daughter. For I do not suffer a challenge lightly. And I fear neither do you. You will participate in the trial, and you will do so to the extent of the gifts I have already given you. Give me any less than that, and it is your flame that will gutter this day with no promise of the Den afterward.*"

Cecelia gritted her teeth, fists squeezing tighter. God or not, the screen of her anger made her believe she could fight Deon here and now and damn the consequences. Even if there'd be no room in the afterlife for her.

Deon brought the blade down and rested it at Cecelia's abdomen, speaking kindly. "*If you would not fight for me, then do so in the name of the other life you carry. At least show fealty to her.*"

"What?" Cecelia couldn't help it, and she twisted, looking for Ruo, whose hands were cupping her mouth as she looked on from the amphitheatre's shadows.

"*The trial will begin at sunrise next. And when the stone looks kindly upon any of you, know that its word is mine. And it is final.*"

A screeching gasp filled the room as if the fire had consumed every last bit of oxygen, and Deon was gone in the fizzle. The stone remained, though it dimmed and returned to rest in the now flameless bowl.

But something else clattered at Cecelia's feet, something she hadn't earned but would be made to use regardless.

"Pick it up," said the elder just behind her, her mouth a grim line. "You can only say no to a god so many times."

For once in her life, Cecelia didn't argue. She bent and grasped the bladeless hilt of Deon's sword, and as Cecelia held it in front of her, a geyser of flame ribboned outward, and there was the bruise-purple garnet blade, deadly and heavy.

Her other hand came up to her stomach, aware now of the tiny fluttering spark beneath it. *Her*.

She looked up to find Ruo again, but she was gone.

I heard the sound then — the distinct crackle and sigh of a fire extinguishing. When I opened my eyes, the memory had faded, and so had the flames. Flames *I'd* conjured. And in my shaking hand was the same hilt Cecelia had only just picked up. This hilt was cracked down the centre and still stained with the dried, dark blood that had been Zabor's. I had brought it here with me, all the way from Winnipeg, but

I couldn't get it to generate a new blade. I thought it was broken beyond repair, like me. Until now.

I watched the crack under my hand fill with red light like a newly lit forge, saw it fuse together, and leave behind the barest scar. The flame I'd heard extinguish must have been the sword, because a fresh purple blade shone in front of me in the moonlight.

That's when I panicked, checking my surroundings for the first time, because I wasn't in the flat. I was in a park . . . no, the Middle Walk to the Meadows. It was nighttime now, the sky clearer than it had any business being.

And I wasn't alone.

The little barefoot girl standing on the path in front of me mustn't have been more than eight or nine. Her clothes looked slightly ragged and faded, like she had been living rough for months. Her hair was short-cropped, her small eyes dark and blank. As dark as the creeping black stains on her pale skin, enflamed at the edges with an eerie glow, like she was burning from the inside.

"Please," she said. "I can't find my family."

I held the sword in front of me, needing both hands because I was shaking so badly. "Stay away from me," I warned, though she hadn't moved at all.

"*Please*," she said again, this time in a low hiss. For a second, I was almost convinced the plea was genuine.

I jerked aside as I caught sight of more of them, seeming to materialize out of the dark. Different skin colours, different ages. But still the black marks, the red underlighting sunken cheekbones and hollow mouths.

"Please," said the teenaged boy on my right, but he was

smiling sickly, and I could see the ashy marks covering his arms as he reached.

I twisted, more boys and girls and teens hopping the chainlink fence and ringing me in a defiant circle. My jaw tensed at the sound of their crackling laughter.

"Don't be scared," said a familiar voice, and I turned back to the first little girl. Standing behind her, with a hand on the girl's arm, was Athika. Ben stood beside her.

I felt my stomach flip and shook my head, sweat beading off it. "It's not you," I said out loud, more for myself than them. "You're infected. I just . . . need to get you help." But I knew, just as they did, that no help was coming.

"Don't be scared," Ben repeated. And the circle started to close. "We know you've lost your family, too. But you can join ours."

The beading sweat hissed away as I felt myself getting hotter, saw my hands and the blade in them sparking. "Don't come near me!" Now my arm spit arcing flames. My chest hurt so much, and I knew the terror was because of the stone. The stone that was alive and awake — the stone I couldn't control.

"We wouldn't have found this family if it weren't for you," Athika was saying. Were all their eyes, at once so black, now glowing as red as my sword had? "You saved us by destroying us. We can show you. Show you what it was all for."

The images before me wavered — just the kids at first, then the deeper darkness my spirit eye could perceive, and the voice beneath the one belonging to my former friend, whom I'd condemned just by knowing her. It was that other voice that shook me loose — the voice of that demon in a hellscape I couldn't ever leave.

"This isn't the Bloodlands, you overgrown pet rock," I seethed. "It's me you want. Let them go, Urka."

The true face beneath Athika's, Ben's, the little girl's, all of them, shone through with its sickening grin and six triangular eyes. "All of my masters' children are sacred. And you will help them meet their makers."

Something clicked inside me — a great furnace, a gold inferno like the one I'd seen in Cecelia's memory. "I'll show you a maker," I said, and the fire took me.

But this time, I took hold of it, too. I sharpened myself as I had on that battlefield with Zabor, and I felt my body changing around my own insistence for justice. The kids staggered back, shielding their eyes as I grew before them, and I saw my own light reflected back at me.

I looked down at my hands — broad, claw-tipped, still clutching the blade. My feet felt different, like they'd been stretched, all my weight on the balls of them. And I felt the pressure and heat behind me spinning right up my spine: a wheel of nine tails.

I was the fox warrior now. And I was in control.

Whatever apprehension these creatures had seemed to dissipate as quickly as they'd shown it. They hissed, snarled, and snapped, mouths wide with rows of barbed teeth, but the first one to burst towards me was Ben. The impact of his body against my raised arm made me stagger, and though I'd burned him on impact — cratering his side in an explosion of ash — this wasn't Table Five. The ash reconstituted around my arm, pinning him to me as his clawing fists rained down.

I pivoted, lifting him off the ground, and threw him into three more preteens coming in for the next charge. One caught the other on the face, and his skull shattered, but with one bitter look back at me I watched the ashy flesh and bone knit back and solidify with only the faintest cracks remaining.

The garnet blade pulsed. "No," I said under my breath. I wasn't here to kill anyone. These weren't river hunters. They still *looked* human, and maybe they could be human again. I defended, blocked, threw them aside. Leapt and spun, avoiding their desperate reach. Whatever the plague was, it was an infection. They were victims. I just needed to get out of here, but the more I deflected, the more came after me.

Pain like a bullet cleanly exiting my eye socket brought me down suddenly. I looked at my hands, still clutching the blade, but they weren't mine. They were Cecelia's, nails long and red, and the night-stained grass of the Meadows was now the sandy terrain of the desert at sunrise.

My body was pulled up out of my own accord, as those fighting me — still children, yes, but healthy, well trained, and, I recognized immediately, Foxes — came back around for another go.

I — Cecelia — parried and shook them off, flipped into the air by the blast of fire kicking up under my heels. We were in an arena, under the glow of the morning sky. *The Sun Trial.* Cecelia's thoughts grabbed hold of mine. I was back in the stone's memory. But I was also in the Meadows —

Then the boy, whom I'd recognized from the crowd of Foxes at the stone choosing, was suddenly a wiry girl, and it was night again, and I crossed my arms in front of myself to smash her off me.

She had been reaching for the stone.

"My masters don't need you," said a young boy, who had latched onto my leg with his teeth. I kicked him off in one smooth movement. But the voice carried to the girl who yanked back on my flaming tails, despite her hands being incinerated for her effort. "Give us the stone. We will set you *free*."

With a yowl I turned on her, smashing her to the ground with the butt of my blade, sending my leg in a spinning kick to the tightening knot of bodies that rushed me with the next breath.

With the *crack* of impact, it was sunrise in the desert once more, and I stood over the boy, getting back to his feet, his small arm rocketing towards me like a guided missile. The other challengers had fallen — it was just us now.

I turned the blow aside, but they kept coming. I knew — Cecelia knew — we could have come down on him and ended this, but there was this war inside. *I have to lose. If I'm given the stone, I'm trapped here forever. If I don't, then that's it for me. And for this child inside me.* My own thoughts twined around hers like a briar. *I can't kill them. But I can't keep holding back. I can't let them take the stone. I can save them all.* The sun seemed to be climbing quickly, like it was Deon's eye, watching the both of us eagerly beyond time. *I've been given a choice but I have none.* Our thoughts were the same. And with each blow, the world changed. A fist, the desert; a kick, the Meadows. On and on, blow for blow.

I couldn't keep this up much longer. Neither could Cecelia. We had to do something. For my part, I knew the stone, felt it *wanting* to intervene, to end this here and now. For Cecelia's part, I could feel her embracing the inevitable. For a moment she'd thought that maybe, just maybe, the boy could best her. He was Chartrand's second pick, after all. But he was young, and angry, and flagging.

"Fight back!" the children and the boy and the stone

screamed, and they all came at me as one, hands reaching for the prize lodged in the centre of my chest.

The blade flourished and came down in an electrifying wave of heat, and the world was filled with light and fire — so much fire — and I collapsed in a heap.

The desert was gone. The powerful armour of the fox warrior's body gone. And so were the children, though the shadows hissed and burned and glowed as they receded. Not from me — for once I'd managed to keep the stone in check, and the garnet blade had only come down on the now empty pavement of the Meadows path. But standing in front of me, his back to me, was a man, his arm aflame and body rigid. Flanking him were others, similarly poised and ready, dressed in the black and red and gold uniform I'd only just seen through a window into the past.

They were Foxes.

The children, as they retreated, snapped at the air, but they didn't come any closer, because in the man's flaming hand was Ben, held by the throat, and he was bucking and snarling like a spitting rabid dog.

"No!" I rushed forward, but the man's hand had squeezed, and there was nothing left of Ben but a pile of disparate ash, unable to become anything but dirt.

I let out my last breath and let the night swallow me.

Part II

Quake

The ICE *and the* INUA

"Have you ever seen these before?"

Eli knew that the tree, and the stone, had swallowed him into another dream. Why it was choosing these particular memories, forcing him to relive them, he didn't know. And by his own estimation, time was running out. He wouldn't have enough time to understand.

He was a boy again but grave and old inside, struggling with these two co-existing states. He looked up at the man standing over him — Solomon, the man his mother's cousin had called before her body was cold in the ground. The man called to quench the inconsolable storm Eli had conjured that day, wreaking havoc on the island and the sea. Apparently Eli had great power. Apparently that made him useful.

Apparently Solomon was his father — but he had left his mother to die, and for that Eli would never forgive him.

"No," Eli said. His current knowledge waged war against

his past, and he knew the picture well that Solomon was pointing to in the old book, here in the Archives, the vast sanctum of knowledge the Owls kept.

"These are the Calamity Stones," Solomon lectured, and he paced behind Eli's chair. "They are the physical embodiments of the First Matriarchs of the Five Families. They can be borne only by the Paramounts of each Family, for they are conduits of great power. They are the gods' souls, the core of their powers, and those Denizens who are chosen to bear them can tap into that strength. That influence. Contained within are the spiritual memories of each Paramount that has come before . . ."

Eli studied the drawing as he had as a boy — this time with a peculiar sense he was looking for something deeper. He touched the page, reading each stone's label, "The Dragon Opal. The Tradewind Moonstone. The Serenity Emerald. The Abyssal Sapphire. The Horned Quartz."

Solomon had come back around from the other side of the room. He nodded. "To be chosen by one of these stones is a great honour. And also a great burden. Once the stone has chosen its bearer, that person becomes the leader of the Family. And that person and the stone cannot be separated. Until death."

Eli's eyes flicked up to Solomon's. He seemed to be waiting for something, so he asked the burning question. "And where is *this* Family's Paramount? Why don't *we* have a stone?"

The corner of Solomon's mouth twitched, perhaps in delight that Eli had called this Family, the Owls, his for the first time. Before this, his only family was his mother. They looked out for each other. To learn now that he had another family, a different kind — one that raised him up for the powers he thought he'd pretended to have to make his dark life seem more palatable — had been hard enough to navigate as a boy. Now at twenty-five, he still wasn't sure where he belonged.

Solomon avoided the question and asked instead, "Do you know what the Owl Family's key duty is to this realm?"

However much Eli didn't trust the man, he wanted to impress him. "Maintain order. Maintain the Narrative."

"And above all else?"

"Keep all Denizens' powers a secret, so that regular people don't know about us. Or fear us."

"Or worse," Solomon added, but he didn't elaborate. "To accomplish this task, Phyr, our Matriarch, gave the Owls the ability to change people's very thoughts. To take away a criminal Denizen's power. We are Her justice in this world. It is a privilege and a challenge. The Tradewind Moonstone has not chosen a Paramount in some time, because to take on such a power would take a truly great mind. Some have said it was too much power. Some say we need a Paramount, now more than ever."

Solomon had paced the full circuit again and was now standing behind Eli's chair. "The stone has hidden itself, waiting to be found by the one most worthy. Perhaps one day we will go looking for it, you and I."

Eli just stared at the drawing of the stones, and the longer he stared the more they seemed to glow. "And what happens if all the stones are brought together?"

Solomon's hand came around Eli, turning the page to an image of three massive shadows with gnashing, snarling faces. A dark moon above them, blotting out the sun. "Then it could open the door between this world and another. A dark world. And so the stones, and the Families, remain divided. They each have their own duties to perform in this world. If the Brilliant Dark were ever to open into our realm, it would change everything. For better or worse, we don't yet know." Solomon shut the book. "Luckily, the fifth keystone is not in this realm. Fia would never give up the Horned Quartz. So the gods keep us safe."

Eli twisted in his chair. Solomon was staring out the window of the tower now, to the great peaks of the mountain range beyond.

"Solomon?" Eli asked. He was a man now, but he was still as frightened. "Can you tell me what's going to happen?"

Eli watched as Solomon's skin crackled black. As the flesh blew away, mere ashes on the wind, his glowing eyes were sad. "Only you can know that now, my boy." Then his father and the memory were gone.

❧

"So this is . . . highly illegal. And if I try to list all the reasons why, I'm sure I'll miss more than half." Phae pressed her back to the fridge, never taking her eyes off the two hulking polar bears who were, mercifully, preoccupied with the massive piles of fish that Natti had made Phae pick up on the way. Watching them consume the fish instead of her, she was grateful she'd erred on the side of buying the majority of the seafood aisle.

"Yeah well. I didn't have time for the law. That's a job for the Owls, who will probably be here soon, if not the useless Mundane police." Natti watched the bears warily, too, but more out of the corner of her eye from her place at the chipped Formica kitchen table. Now she looked up at Phae. "You wanna sit?"

"I don't want to make any sudden moves, thanks." Phae folded her arms but still didn't look away.

Aunty was still in her recliner, which was only about ten inches away from the smorgasbord. Out of everyone, she seemed the least concerned. She coughed heavily, and one bear — the one that Natti had identified as the injured one — looked up at her and sniffed.

Aunty finally sucked in a breath. "They ain't interested in eating us. If it was people flesh they wanted, they woulda snacked on their damn zookeepers."

The bears smacked their lips, the strongest of the pair watching them with open curiosity. The bear with the dark stain around its throat ate more slowly, as if swallowing each morsel took its entire concentration.

"Okay so . . . again I'm really not too sure why I'm here. Or why they're here." Phae used her eyes to point; she had been taking special note of those jaws as they worked on salmon flesh and bone.

Even Natti seemed a bit unsure. "They were chattier before I busted them out. I was hoping they'd give me more to go on by now, and I figured the food would help loosen their tongues . . ."

"They *spoke* to you?" Phae blurted, though at this point, and after everything, why should she be surprised? Sil, though gone, was not yet a distant memory.

Natti shrugged. "Sort of. It was in my head. In the water. They needed help. I just went with my gut. We both know I'm not a thinker."

"Hey, you said it . . ." Aivik muttered from the corner,

nursing coffee from an old plastic Blue Bombers tumbler. "So what are these guys? Some kind of Therion? But they're, like, not seals. Don't polar bears *eat* seals?"

"Sometimes," came a deep voice like thunder from the living room, "but there are tastier meats as the sea is wide."

Natti got carefully to her feet; Aivik stayed put, but Phae didn't know what to do. The room fell silent.

Aunty let out a low, rumbling laugh. "Good thing for us, then. Though for Phae, not so much. Most of the Families take Deer for prey at the best of times." She raised her hand towards the bear nearest her, and he sniffed it.

"Grandmother —" he nodded after his assessment "— I see what ails you is the same blackness that takes my brother in its fist."

Aunty broke into another cough and so couldn't answer right away, but Natti had begun a tentative approach. "What do you mean, blackness?"

The bear turned his impassive eyes on her, dark as the subarctic night when the sun has fled for weeks. The chill she felt was not a natural one, and in that brief glance she inhabited a vast and unforgiving tundra.

The eyes flicked past her, and Natti followed them. Phae straightened.

"You brought a Deer. Canny to have summoned a Healer. We were wise to have waited for you. Though Maujaq was getting closer to sinking to the bottom of his tank and never emerging as the days wore on."

Phae joined Natti warily. "Your brother . . ." Her eyes cut to the silent polar bear, Maujaq, who had turned away from not only his food but their conversation, nipping at his arm. "He's ill?"

"In his spirit." The first bear dipped its head. "The hurt is deep. And if he founders, I cannot make it back. We must return together or not at all. I will be trapped here for all time, however much longer that might be." The bear rolled its mighty shoulders, getting up and moving suddenly to the other bear, cuffing with his snout.

"Up now," he said, not unkindly. "Help has finally come."

Maujaq served them all a dangerous look. "Humans will not help us. We must make this journey on our own." This bear's voice was the sharp edge of an icy shore, unforgiving and pitiless. The grimace became a snarl. "It is because of *them* we are here in the first place, Siku!" The bear spat and stood up on its hind feet, its head brushing the ceiling. Natti brought an arm across Phae, but the first bear's mighty paw came down and so did Maujaq.

"If I can bring you low with half the effort, we will not make it far." Maujaq's teeth were still exposed but not for challenging his brother. Phae could feel it across the room — a pain like it was in the air, prickling her skin. Siku nudged him back to sitting. "This is not our world," he said, "and we have relied on humans to survive. We must do it a while longer." The bear's head came back around to Phae and Natti. "Will you look at my brother, Healer? Will you help him?"

Phae's jaw tightened. "I'm not sure if I can. But I'll try." And she came forward, each step a prayer not to be eaten.

"Don't you recognize them, Nattiq?" Aunty pulled her recliner back to its upright position, stretching her neck. "Or maybe all that soft zoo living has made their chosen bodies impenetrable to the truth."

Maujaq sneered. "Be careful, Grandmother. You are still

a Seal. And when the ice breaks up, one of you could feed us for a week."

The first bear was in front of Natti scarily quick, its head towering over hers even though it was on all fours.

"You're Inua, aren't you?" Natti guessed.

There was a flashing cloud of silver sparks, and Siku turned back towards Phae and his brother before he might answer. Phae's hair curved off her neck, weaving into antlers as the power took hold, her hands hovering over the dark stain in Maujaq's yellowed fur.

Her eyes were white, turned inward. "This pain, this injury . . . it's . . . familiar." Her brow knotted. "It's deep inside. In the blood. Coming to the surface. Like a parasite." Maujaq shut his eyes, the menace in them extinguished when Phae sank her hands into the fur, into the black. Her elbows juddered, antlers crackling. She grunted and pushed, and Maujaq convulsed.

"You're hurting him!" Siku cried, and on impulse Natti reached out to his powerful flank.

His head twisted back around, lips peeled over a black and sandy maw as big as her head, but she held fast. "Wait," she said.

In a moment it was over. Both Phae and Maujaq pulled away from one another, breathing hard. Natti went to her friend, pulled her up and away from both bears as Siku came forward to nuzzle his now relaxed brother.

The black stain remained.

"It did not work. You did not heal him," Siku murmured, disappointment mingling with anger.

"No." Maujaq lifted his head, rose, shook himself. "But I feel as if I can face tomorrow, Siku. I feel restored . . . for now." He turned to Phae, bowed. "Thank you, Healer. I know these things are not so simple."

Natti steadied Phae, but Phae pushed her off. "I'm fine," she lied, still looking at the bears. "You two. You're not really bears, are you. You're . . . like Sil. Some kind of spirit inside an animal's body. But you're not human, either."

"We are Inua," Siku confirmed. "Spirits of this Earth. These bodies were given to us from the great glacier so that we may walk here on behalf of the Abyss. We are messengers."

"Messengers?" Natti interjected. "Wait. Back at the zoo, you told me you knew I would come. Are you saying you have a message for . . . me?"

Siku bowed his head. "It is why we have been sent to this world, this strange land of stone and glass that moves too quickly. Our watch was a long one. And now we can make the journey back. Now that we have found you."

"Back up." This time Aivik decided to join in. "You two are from the *zoo*? Weren't you guys, like, brought here from Churchill? Separated from your mother as cubs, or something; taken into captivity. For conservation." The entire room seemed to stare at him. "What? I read the news! You've been here a few years. But now you're suddenly Ryk's messenger boys? You're, like, a city-owned science project."

The bears turned to Aivik as one, twin pairs of eyes as severe as the underside of an iceberg.

Aivik sat back down and closed his mouth.

"Yes. We came from the north together. And this was our purpose." Siku looked between Phae and Natti. "You are to come back with us. To unleash the Sapphire. To bring the Empress up."

"The world is as sick as me," Maujaq said, nodding. "But the Empress. She will defend it with her sisters. She will help cleanse the black water with her own, before the world is plunged in shadow."

"Great," Natti said. "It'd be a dull life if animals weren't dropping in to deliver apocalypse missions and prophecies."

"Who's the Empress?" Phae looked between Natti and Aunty. "And the Sapphire?"

"He means Ryk," Aunty croaked. "First Matriarch of the Seals. The Abyssal Sapphire is her Calamity Stone. It is kept beneath the sea except in times of war. Like the Deer, we don't keep a Paramount because we Seals know that kind of power can't be carried around lightly. If these boys are here to bring it up out of the ice, then it ain't good." Aunty's own gaze seemed to go inward as she clutched her housecoat tight at the thigh. "The water *has* changed. It's gone dark. The water and the world."

Siku scented the air, as if that darkness was in the room with them. "There isn't much time."

"There never is, is there?" Natti started pacing, looking like a caged bear herself. "Zabor wasn't the end of this. Just the beginning."

Phae shook her head, looking to Maujaq. "When I was trying to heal you, it felt like when the river hunters infected Barton. This illness, this virus, I could hear it. It's *alive*."

"A plague of ash," Siku growled low. "It comes from below."

Natti whirled. "You mean the Cinder Plague? The one from the news?" She met Aunty's eyes, dull in the already poor living room lamplight. "I thought Denizens were immune. I thought we were *safe*."

"It is a sickness that evolves," Maujaq sighed, seeming less restless now, more alert, focused like his brother but still with the edge. "I feel it growing, trying to find its way to the heart of me. It grows stronger as its master does."

"And who's this master?" Aivik asked.

"The child of the Bloodlands," Siku said. "It has risen. And so we must go north, with you. As it was foretold."

Siku was in front of Natti now, stopping her in what had become a frantic back-and-forth over the worn carpet. "But why *me*? I don't —"

"Not just you," Siku corrected, rising back on his legs to mimic her stance, spreading his paw. "All of you."

Aunty did not cough this time, but her breath rattled in her chest as she struggled to get up. Aivik went to help her, but she batted him off. "Leave it," she muttered. "It's about time we got outta Dodge. And sitting around here ain't doing anything for me." Aunty was getting more cogent the longer the bears were here. "When an Inua comes to your door and summons you, you go. Still waters run deep, but you never go against a tsunami."

"Whatever *that* means!" Aivik threw up his hands. "I have a job, you know! Not to mention how we're gonna go anywhere with *TWO POLAR BEARS*."

"Calm down." Natti waved him off. "You'll blow a gasket." She folded her arms, surveying the brothers. "You still didn't answer me: why us?"

As Natti looked deeper into Siku's eyes, she realized they were not black — they were the blue of midnight, and clear, and fathomless; the longer she looked, she thought she saw, shimmering at the bottom, the crest of the northern lights that she'd only seen in photographs. And the glacier and the sea she had seen when they'd begged her help. A glacier with a glowing core, and a sea cracked wide.

"We are only messengers," Maujaq said. "We were sent from the Abyss to take you back to it. Back to our Matriarch. And we cannot go home without you."

"And where is home?" Phae was still trying to process all this, her hair gently sparking as she rubbed the feeling back into her fingers.

"North," the bears said together, as if that covered it.

"God . . ." Aivik sighed, burying his face in his hands.

"Where ice meets sea," Siku said. "There are Seals there waiting to call the glacier up. To open the Abyss, to commit a Paramount to the cause. The child of the Bloodlands is already moving. It seeks to open its own gateway, to unleash its sires back upon this world. The world will crack, the sea will rise. We feel it as you do. It is the sacred duty of all to protect this fragile world with what power there is left in it. You have already proven you are capable of it." At this, Siku bowed its head. "You did not suffer Zabor lightly. She and her siblings cannot attain purchase here, as they have attempted to since the Narrative began."

Aunty already had her coat on and a bursting carpet bag at her feet. "Well? Let's get a move on."

Voices raised in protest fought for a foothold, and Phae raised her hands up, the loudest of them all. "I can't do this!"

"Oh c'mon, girlie, you heard the bears." Aunty flapped her arm, thumbing at Maujaq, who seemed bemused. "This one might not make it if you're not there to fix him up."

But Natti came forward in her defense. "We can't go dragging Phae into this. It sounds like Seal business," she qualified. "And Phae has a family here, Aunty. And a boyfriend. She can't just —"

"Barton's leaving, too," Phae blurted. "The Rabbits . . . Something took the Serenity Emerald. And the same thing is after Eli's stone. And maybe Roan's." Her face flushed at Natti's open mouth. "Well! Barton only told me like an hour ago, and then you called! He's going to a Rabbit gathering, in Russia. There's a coalition forming. It seems like all the Families are preparing to fight."

Aunty's fists were up, and she seemed thirty years younger. "About time."

Natti looked between them. "So this is really happening. Again. But we'll all be scattered on the map this time." She raised an eyebrow at Phae. "Lemme guess. Barton asked you to go with him, and you turned him down."

Phae flushed deeper. "I . . ." Then the words finally found their way out of her. "It didn't seem like my place. Neither does this. But honestly, I don't know where my place is anymore. The Deer Family is different. There's none of . . . this." The bears, Aivik, Natti, and Aunty were all part of something, a deeper bond. And Phae felt like she'd always be on the other side of the force field. "I don't have anyone to turn to. I don't know what to do."

Then a soft, enormous head was underneath her hand, pressing. Phae startled but didn't jump away. Maujaq was being gentle, but he could still tear her apart if the mood shifted.

"Our mother will know," he said, and Phae's heart twisted, wanting to believe. "She will help you find your way. Can you help us with ours?"

Phae let out a breath. She'd already taken an enormous leap of faith last winter, when Roan had begged her to. That's where all of this started. But what if Roan needed her, too? And Barton? Or Eli? Too many tethers, too many choices ahead, with the darkness, like a mouth, closing in . . .

"Okay, okay, hero party —" Aivik said. "Logistics, people. Two giant bears. The four of us. Heading to some place up north. How? I mean, this is all fine and whatever, but I've got a long haul to Alberta tomorrow and —"

"That's it!" Natti jabbed a finger at her brother. "Your haul. We all ride in your truck in, like, the transport trailer. Big enough, no windows. Fastest way to get across the country without being noticed."

Aivik was caving. "But . . . my Alberta job . . ."

"Alberta?" Siku scented the air, as if he could geolocate with his nose.

"It's to the northwest. Is it the Fort McMurray run again?" Natti asked.

Aivik nodded. "Yeah. It'll take me a couple days, but the border to the Northwest Territories isn't far from there, if that's where these two need to go. And if I make the run business as usual, then no one will ask questions about me using the truck." His shoulders fell. Phae could tell he really wanted this job to work out. "But after that, no guarantees."

Natti slapped him hard on the bicep, and despite the fact that he was twice her size, he winced. "Good. It's settled."

"Is it?" Phae asked wryly.

"You can come or you can stay." Natti squeezed her friend's arm. "But I feel this in my bones. This is our part to play in whatever's happening, just like before. And maybe you can find your part, too."

She left the room to start packing. Phae and Aivik exchanged a glance, and he shrugged before following his sister.

Phae decided she had to be like Natti. *Don't think. Go with your gut.* Whatever was in her gut she couldn't tell, but the familiar twisting that had kept her up at night seemed to be letting go, inch by inch, the dread falling away into a darker sea.

A wave was coming, and she could ride it or drown.

❧

Aivik shifted the huge rig into park, one elbow slung out the window. He'd slept as much as the others, which was to say very little.

Natti saw another man in coveralls approach Aivik's truck from the receiving dock, and they exchanged words. The sun wasn't yet up and the truck doors were slammed and locked by the dock team that scurried off to prep the next load. If Aivik got out of the truck to reopen the doors, it'd look suspect. He glanced to where they were hiding but quickly looked back to the man in coveralls. He was doing his best to appear convincing, to Natti's eyes, anyway.

"Too bad Eli had to get himself in a plane crash," Natti muttered. "Brain hacking would come in handy about now."

"Yes," Phae said through her teeth, "you've mentioned that about twenty-six times now." They'd considered calling on Seneca, their only real ally in the Owl Family in Winnipeg since what happened last spring, but with two technically stolen bears on their hands, and Seneca having ties to the police, they didn't want to chance it.

"Still valid," Natti grunted.

They'd been waiting on the other side of the parking lot for the past twenty minutes. Getting the bears here had been the hardest part and had to be achieved mostly on foot. There was no way Siku and Maujaq would fit into Aivik's crummy sedan, and no one could sleep much anyway, so they'd hit the streets. Besides, the transport industrial park was only a few miles away from Point Douglas. But now it was time for the moonshot.

Natti glanced up at the sky. Still overcast, and there was moisture in the air. It'd have to be enough. Her fingers twitched. The man in coveralls moved away from Aivik's truck, went to the back of it, and shouted over some nearby crewmen to open the rear door. Then he left. Good. He'd fallen for the last-minute inventory request. A foreman would come around in less than five minutes to see Aivik off post-inspection. They had to run.

"Now!" Natti barked, and a pulse twitched down her wrists as she reeled every humid droplet out of the air around them, thickening the mist into a raincloud that could cloak them. The bears bolted, Siku carrying Aunty and Natti on his back, Maujaq carrying Phae. They reached the truck just as the man Aivik had spoken to was coming back around. The bears scrambled inside, and Natti jumped off and yanked the door shut behind her. She couldn't bolt it from the inside, but she hoped it would hold until Aivik could secure it when they made it to a truck stop. *If* they made it.

The truck screeched and rumbled beneath them as Aivik threw it into gear, edging the massive trailer out of the lot. Natti staggered in the dark, catching a sharp edge on her hip but holding on. There was shouting over the roar of the engine and the crunching of gravel — the inspector, maybe, the guy in the coveralls?

Then from closer by, they heard Aivik shouting, "It's all good!"

Then the speed increased beneath them, like they'd actually hit the road, and after a few minutes like this in the silence of the trailer, braking and going, she figured they were winding through the city towards the Trans-Canada. Natti finally let the tension in her body go.

A white light glimmered; Natti squinted, holding on to boxes and crates. It was Phae, letting her power flow and flicker like a lightning bug night light. Phae held out her hand and Natti took it, for both reassurance and help coming down to the dirty trailer floor without smashing her face as the truck navigated too many service road potholes. In the ring of Phae's light, Natti watched the bears move to a far corner, Siku pressing into Maujaq protectively as he gingerly put Aunty down between them.

Natti and Phae looked at each other, still trying to catch their breath. They settled on some crates, adjusting somewhat to the jostling impact of the road under the sixteen-wheeler. They'd have to. The road beneath and ahead was a long one, and now they had nothing but time to consider the consequences at the end of it.

The CONCLAVE *of* FIRE

Eli had fought for what had probably been days. He should have died of thirst or starvation by now. But he could feel it — the hard fingers of the tree wrapped firmly around the Moonstone, piercing it like a needle. The tree had made Eli a part of it. It fed off his terrors, his nightmares. It tapped into the stone's power, too, and as long as the tree lived, so would Eli.

The bark of the tree was his flesh now. The roots his bones, tethering him to the earth. That in itself was a nightmare for a child of the sky.

He had seen these trees in the Bloodlands, for surely that's what Eli and the rest of the Owls who had miserably followed him here had become. Hope trees. *Nothing tortures more than a hope*. It was as if Eli were there again — and maybe he was, since the stone wasn't differentiating between reality and his own memories. He saw that great hulking demon Urka and its axe-hands that slashed the bleeding flesh of the tree, dug around in its remains, and replanted it so it could hope anew for salvation.

But that tree, back then, had been the soul of something. Something punished. And now it was Eli's turn. In sore silence, the only kind he had, he admitted his soul more than deserved the lashing it was enduring.

All he had was time. Why had no one yet come? The debris had been masked by the thick, twisting grove made by the attack's victims. But surely the Owl Council, whatever remained of them, knew they had disappeared?

He hoped, though he didn't dare pray. And with each passing day of disappointment, his prison grew stronger.

But why hadn't they taken the stone? They'd obviously managed it with the Rabbit Paramount, for there had been no mistaking the Serenity Emerald glinting on the enemy's shoulder like a trophy. Separating a Paramount from their stone was a feat in itself, one that this enemy's small army hadn't been able to achieve with Eli. Not yet, anyway. Maybe he'd been left here in cold storage, and once the cavalry recouped, they'd return for their prize.

Eli never liked being someone else's sure thing.

But he was reaching his limits far too quickly as each day passed. Exhausted and in pain, he was unable to figure out why this was happening or repress his terror that it could be happening elsewhere to other unsuspecting people. They had to be warned. *She* had to be warned. If Eli couldn't escape these creatures and the devastating shadow that led them . . . when they came for Roan's stone, she wouldn't have a chance.

Eli tried to scream, but the tree squeezed, and the nightmares took hold.

A scream woke me, like a knife in the kidney, and I twisted with the force of it.

I was probably most surprised to find it was me screaming, and it *really* surprised the man sitting on the edge of the bed I was firmly tucked into.

"Good lord," he said, leaping to his feet, hands up. "You've a right pair of lungs, don't ye?"

My legs were drawn up and I clutched the sheet to me, but as I woke fully I saw I was still dressed, still whole. I kicked the twisted blankets away, unzipped my hoodie, and thrust my hand against my chest.

I don't know if I was more relieved or disappointed to find that the Dragon Opal was still there, as much a part of my skin and bones as it had ever been, glowing warm as an uneven geode at my sternum.

"So it's true," said the man, whom I'd almost completely forgotten about. "It chose ye."

I flicked and narrowed my eyes at him, zipping back up. "And who the hell are you?" I slid off the bed, keeping it between us as I pressed up against the wall. I tried not to let on that my legs felt like soup or that I was fighting not to vomit. I straightened my spine. "And where the hell am I?"

His mouth, an impassive line, broke into a charming grin. "God," he whispered, shaking his head, "yer so like her."

"Quit dodging my damn question." Regardless, I searched his face — hard to tell the age, but late forties at least judging by the crinkles at the corners of his mouth. I didn't recognize him, though, not from any of Cecelia's memories or from any of my own. Could he have known Cecelia? Or even Ravenna? But when my spirit eye decided to boot back up, one thing at least was clear. Beyond those hazel eyes, the dark hair, and the curious scar that cut a line from his left eyebrow down to the cheek, the man was a Fox.

"Didn't mean to dodge. Name's Killian," he said, offering a mock bow that only set my hackles higher. "And yer in a compound in Glencoe belonging to the Conclave of Fire. The leading force of the Fox Family. Who will be pleased to see you and the stone are in fightin' fettle."

A shiver went down my back. *The Conclave of Fire*. I'd heard the name before but in someone else's life. To have it made real here and now made me wonder if I was still somehow trapped inside the stone's memory.

"That's supposed to reassure ye," Killian said, his voice even. I tried master my face as Cecelia would. I was probably still giving him massive, obvious stink eye, but I wasn't sure yet if he deserved any less.

"Well, it doesn't." Cecelia's memories, though biased, had already taught me not to trust the Conclave, or at least to take their measure with a grain of salt. I looked around. The room, filled with rows of beds and lit with enough torches to insinuate daylight without windows, was spartan and stone-hewn, the air close. It reminded me of Cecelia's summoning chamber underneath her house in Winnipeg, and I felt certain we were underground. "And what? They sent you to interrogate me, good-cop style? Or do I have a hall pass to take a pee before the tribunal starts?"

"Oh." He suddenly seemed at a loss, rubbing the back of his neck. "The lav's at the other end of the infirmary . . ."

"I was joking." My mouth quirked.

"Oh," he said again, but he seemed amused if not relieved. "Right, well. Yer no' a prisoner here. Quite the contrary. Yer —"

"A guest?" I finished for him, crossing my arms. "Which is totally political doublespeak for *prisoner*."

He sighed. "Then we better get a move on so I can prove yer otherwise." And instead of taking the semantics any further, he pushed the door open and swept his arm out. "After you."

I hesitated, but I figured that, if anything went wrong, at least the stone had my back. It'd protect its own interests, at the very least, and I was attached to it. So I followed.

It wasn't some narrow corridor he led me to; I'd expected the place I was taken to be a Gulag, like a bunker, or at least something close to. But directly outside of the infirmary's door was a set of stairs, suspended above an enormous open cavern, and if I staggered I would've slipped off the edge into the shadows cast by the flickering light below.

The man, Killian, turned smartly and caught me by the elbow — he'd finally noticed I was off balance. "Careful," he said, but the warning didn't damage his cheerfulness. "Wouldn't want to lose the Paramount just as we've found her."

If there was anything that would make me dizzier, it was being called that. "I'm not the Paramount." I yanked my arm out of his grip, willing my body to be rigid, to be strong.

I looked away from him and back down into the cavern, noting crossing tunnels and arenas and suspended pathways not only beneath us but above as well. The place was massive, crawling with activity, deep down under the earth.

I couldn't keep the awe out of my voice as I followed Killian closely as we stepped onto a wider landing, heading for more steps, still descending. "What is this place?"

Light glinted and heat flared all around us. What I assumed were students, of a range of ages and ethnicities, went through regimented exercises as we passed, fists and flames striking the air, pulling back, again and again, led by three supervising masters. Some couldn't help themselves, looking up when we went by, pointing. Whispering. Even the teachers who scolded them watched me with bald curiosity, and I quickly looked away.

"This place is many things. A training ground. A stronghold. One of many. All of the Families have these sorts of keeps in key places around the world. This one is only about three hundred years old — the original one was in Ben Nevis, y'see, but it seemed a better bet to move when it became a protected site. Too many hikers."

I frowned. "Ben Nevis? The mountain?" I looked closer at the rock-hewn stairs, the high-climbing walls of the cavern. He *did* say the place was in Glencoe. "Are we . . . are we *inside* a mountain right now?" I was tempted to make a *Lord of the Rings* reference, but I didn't want to look *that* giddy.

"That we are," Killian chirped, because, to him, this was all rote. "It's a Fox thing, liking the underground. Like a den, y'know? 'A wise Fox prepares in the dark to better command the light.'" I could feel him surveying me expectantly. I had drawn up beside him, trying to match pace, keeping an eye on him while ignoring the much louder remarks as we went by.

When I openly shrugged, he chuckled. "It's the Family motto," he replied in his bright brogue. He must have been born in the Highlands. "Ye better brush up on yer Fox knowledge before meeting Mala. Thought I'd give you the express course on our way."

"Mala?" I forced myself out of my awestruck reverie at

the general surroundings. I had to admit, as we passed glowing antechambers full of fiery fighters, underneath columns and through tunnels covered in arcane symbols and sigils, I felt a growing excitement. I didn't know that I'd been missing something like this, a secret world just on the outskirts of the one I'd been brought up in. A world to which, maybe, I belonged.

"She's sort of the de facto leader 'round here. She's keen to meet ye. Probably not too keen that ye technically outrank her, but she's a canny woman. She won't want to make an enemy of you. Least not before tea." Killian's grin was sardonic at best.

"You and me both are strangers in a strange land," he went on, and I looked at him anew. "Haven't been anywhere near the Conclave in decades, myself. So I'm also on thin ice, so to speak. Best we interlopers stick together, aye?"

I was curious what he meant, but I figured I had bigger problems. The place was extraordinary, and being among Denizen family had felt like too much of a relief up front. I had to be careful. I hadn't known about this place for a reason.

But if Killian was *like* me, then he wasn't close to these Conclave people, either, and he was right. I needed to be ready. He seemed like he wanted to chat, and I let him. "So do you have any idea why they brought me here?"

Killian's mouth twisted. "Och, that one's a bit too obvious, eh? But I suppose there's much ye weren't privy to. Extremely long and drawn-out story short, the Dragon Opal has been *missing* for a number of years. And so has its Paramount — yer granny, y'ken? Yikes, really never thought of someone as formidable as Cecelia as a *grandmother*, but there it is. Everything happened so quickly with the Zabor incident in Canada, and some deemed it better to stand by and watch rather than intervening, hoping the stone would reveal itself. Evidentially ye made off with it a little too quickly to track. Though it was a lucky thing you came to the very place where the Conclave had gathered now that there's this new threat of those boggy kiddies running 'round. Very lucky indeed . . ." I caught him glancing down at me again, this time with his own sort of reverence.

It was getting on my nerves. "Why do you keep looking at me like that?"

Killian grinned. "I'll let you sort it out. Same reason they're all looking." He jerked his head, and some of the knots of fighting instruction had ceased, small bunches coming closer, getting bolder.

If it was the exhaustion from the attack talking, or just my own shrinking will, it was painful to look at them, the growing adoring crowd. Bile churned in my stomach, and the skin around the stone itched. That feeling of belonging was short-lived. I wasn't like them. Most of these kids had been brought up knowing they were different, that they had power, and they were special because of it. Ancient's world was in their programming. Mine had been badly rewritten and had one too many bugs.

I raised my voice. "I already told you. I'm not the Paramount. I'm not . . . your leader or anyone's leader. I'm just me. And I aim to keep it that way."

Killian just shrugged. "Good luck with that. You've been picked, girlie. Whether they like it or not. Whether *you* do."

We finally arrived at what had to be our destination. An amphitheatre, set low at the basin of the cave, ringed with graded levels. I had seen this place before, or else something like it — in a place on the outskirts of Aleppo, forty some years in the past. Suddenly there was a flash, and the powerful form of Deon was at the centre of the bowl, towering over me, lowering her blade —

"Easy now." Killian had me by both arms, and I couldn't stop myself from cringing. He put me upright and let go just as quickly, rubbing the back of his neck. "Listen. Whatever has happened, ye've had a rough go of it. Believe me, I know what it is to make your way through alone." When I looked up at him, his casual joking air was gone, replaced entirely by a fierce determination to make me *see*. "But ye aren't alone. We're called Family for a reason. For better or worse, we are tied by the same element that drives us. And we are stronger together. Remember that."

I was expecting him to reach over and squeeze me, or some other overly affectionate gesture, but he just stood straight and waited. His words lit something else in me I hadn't known I was missing, and I tightened the corners of my stinging eyes so they wouldn't betray me.

"And don't let them get to ye. They'll certainly try." And when he turned aside, body angled at the bowl beneath us but unmoving, I knew he would be right behind me. But I had to choose to go first.

Waiting below, seated around the empty bowl in a semicircle, were five people. They were all Foxes, which I could tell from their colours alone — tunics and trousers and cloaks in that unifying scheme of black, red, and gold. Some of the gathering I recognized from the barest of glances when those cinder kids had attacked me. The woman in the centre of the five I did not. Her tunic was bright red, offset by her olive skin and piercing grey eyes. She stood when I stopped before them, and Killian moved to the side.

"Hello, Roan," said the woman. "I trust you are feeling better after such a long period of rest?"

I reflexively looked at Killian, who was staring straight ahead as if I'd disappeared. "How long was I out?"

"Three days," croaked the man closest to me. He looked to be in his seventies, but his back was rigid with the discipline age afforded him. He leaned forward on a plain walking stick, despite being seated.

"Didn't realize I was on some kind of blackout schedule," I snapped. I heard Killian clear his throat aggressively.

"My name is Mala," the woman went on, hands folded in front of her. So this was the Conclave's leader. She made no move to be as friendly with me as Killian had been, and she ignored him entirely as she introduced the others. "These are our acting Council members. Akilah Fante . . ." the Black woman with the elaborate hair wrap nodded ". . . Jacob Reinhardt . . ." the ginger-haired man's icy eyes narrowed at me ". . . and Edward Kilduggan." The elderly man with the walking stick worked what remained of his teeth in a grimace. "We welcome you to our sanctuary. You are safe here."

"The stone," Edward barked, stamping his stick. "Let us see the *stone*."

Mala cleared her throat. "Now, there's no need —"

"Edward is right; we need to test its provenance before we go any further," Akilah cut in. She smiled to me encouragingly, and it put me off in such a tense and hostile space.

But it also made me realize that this was their world and the stone was as much theirs as mine. I wasn't about to let them rip my shirt off so I unzipped my hoodie as a show of good faith.

"That's it . . . that's *it*!" cried the woman beside Mala, whose name she had not yet given, leaping to her feet but tripping over them. Mala caught her smartly by the arm.

"It's all right, Ruo. We know."

A knife went through me. Because the woman Mala steadied was the same one who had come after me in the café, shouting about Cecelia. And the name rang in my ears like an explosion had gone off too close by.

How could I have seen it through that mask of scars covering her face? But the stone and my spirit eye layered on the neat features of the woman Cecelia had obviously loved decades ago. And now . . . she was shaking and frail, and Killian came forward to relieve Mala, helping Ruo sit again.

"It was Ruo who told us where you were," Mala said. "She had mistaken you for Cecelia. But we already knew the truth. And I am sorry for your loss. We all are."

A general note of assent from the peanut gallery, reluctantly given.

"She went down fighting." Akilah Fante nodded. "An honourable death."

I scoffed, Cecelia's old grievances seeping out through me unbidden. "And I'm sure you made her feel *honoured* when she was alive and kicking."

Their reverent grief clicked over to defensiveness just as quickly. "The apple doesn't fall far, it'd seem," drawled Jacob. "You are Cecelia's granddaughter, sure enough. And you have the Dragon Opal. Yet from what we know, you were raised a Mundane, with no knowledge of your lineage or ties to Ancient until a bare few months ago. You may have managed to seal a darkling, but you have defied every law we have and taken what was not yours to begin with."

I blinked at him. Then I looked at the rest of the gathering. "So?"

"*So*, she says!" Edward slapped his thigh. "The gods are laughing at us still."

"Hey, if you're all so sore about me and this stone, you are more than welcome to take it off my hands. I didn't *steal* it. It was just there. And suddenly it was *here*. And . . . I don't think we're compatible. So if you think I'm going to fight you on that, I'm not."

The glance the four of them exchanged was almost too obvious. My heart was hammering, manic with hope.

"The stone has its own mind," Mala said evenly. "Whatever we wish of it, you two cannot be parted now."

And we're stuck with you, I mentally finished for her. That was it then. I loosened my fists at my sides. Suddenly it was Eli's voice in my head — *it will destroy you.*

Nothing for it. "Well then. What am I here for?"

Mala straightened. "War is coming," she said. "And we must prepare by rallying around the Paramount."

I felt my skin prickle again. "Will you stop calling me that? I'm *not* the Paramount. I'm not Cecelia." I zipped myself back up, all the way to my throat. "I can't lead you. I've got my own problems."

"Our problems are the same," Mala answered wearily, pacing slowly around the bowl in front of her counterparts. "The attack you suffered. It is not the first in which we have intervened. There have been others, too many. And some we were too late to stop. An enemy has risen that we do not recognize. And it is after the Calamity Stones."

My skin around the stone itched again, pulsed warmer. As if the stone knew we were discussing it and sensed it was in danger.

"We were lucky to have found you when we did. If not for Killian, we aren't certain what would have happened." She turned towards him and I saw him leaning against a huge pillar, still staring straight ahead, pretending he was invisible and accepting no praise. "We are also grateful to see him after his own long absence." That time, the corner of Killian's mouth twitched; so he really was under scrutiny as well.

Then Mala looked between us. "I know the attack happened quite quickly, but it was Killian who saved your life three nights ago."

I froze. Suddenly I was back there. And there was the man who, standing in front of me, had squeezed away Ben's life like it was nothing. I wasn't about to thank him for it, and when he did look up at me, I turned away.

I had to press on, like that carefully won trust hadn't just been totalled. "These *kids* are after the Calamity Stones? The Paramounts of the other Families —"

"Whatever the creature is that has brought this plague with it, we know it has the Serenity Emerald, the stone belonging to the Rabbits. The Owl Paramount is missing, too, but according to their Council — what's left of it, anyway — the creature doesn't have the Moonstone."

"Eli is *missing*?" I barked, and Edward jumped.

"Indeed." Mala quirked an eyebrow. "Though I heard he tried to kill you enough times that he should warrant less concern."

I bit the inside of my cheek. "I guess," I admitted, "but without him, we wouldn't have stopped Zabor."

"The girl trusts an Owl, no less. *This* is what we have for a leader now . . ." Edward stomped his cane, shaking his head.

I couldn't stand this. "I already told you —"

"And what of the Stonebreakers?" Akilah asked the rest of the gathering. "That shadow cult has been quiet. *Too* quiet." She laid the barest glance in Killian's direction. "What if they have brought this creature here, and what if they rally around it?"

Mala held up her hand. "We are being vigilant." She could probably see the confusion on my face and addressed me directly. "The Stonebreakers were Denizens who believed the Calamity Stones must be destroyed rather than used. Indeed, we thought those from that extremist coalition had given up their schemes almost twenty years ago. Many of them have been imprisoned. Our intelligence has not uncovered a connection yet. One enemy at a time."

"Enough." Jacob slapped his open palm onto his thigh. "The Opal is safe. If this creature, this *Seela* as it calls itself, comes here with its army of brats, or if the Stonebreakers have planned all of this, it does not matter. We will be ready."

Mala looked as if she sensed an incoming insurrection. "Jacob —"

"Ready, huh?" I bit back at him, and he glowered at me. "So far you've dragged me down here against my will and just slammed me with more unanswered questions than you've addressed." I looked back to Mala.

She nodded, eyes narrowed. "You're right, Roan. There is much we must speak of. Perhaps we should do so now, in confidence." She tilted her head at the gathering. "You will excuse us, elders." And she opened her arm towards me, inviting, and turned aside.

The others stood at being dismissed, Akilah moving to Ruo's side to help her stand, and without thinking I went to them first.

"Cecelia?" Ruo's head perked, blind eyes searching.

I took her hand impulsively. "No, it's . . . my name is Roan. I'm Cecelia's granddaughter. Do you remember me? We met in Edinburgh a few days ago in a café."

Her face, already pale save for the angry red in the creases of her ruined face, softened. "Oh." She bent her head down to our joined hands, clasped her other one over it. "She's dead, isn't she?"

Being in Cecelia's memories lately had numbed me from that reality. Kept it at bay. Hadn't I only just seen her? How could she *really* be gone? So when I said yes, it felt like a lie, and the residue of that must have travelled through our hands, because Ruo jerked away from me like I'd bitten her.

"It's all right," the headscarfed woman put her massive arm around Ruo, led her away. "She needs rest." And they were already out of reach before I could try again.

"Roan?" Mala called.

I whirled. Right. Time for answers. I shot that icy-eyed twit Jacob one last scrutinizing look as he passed me. Killian was nearby, too, but he didn't look as if he was going anywhere. He shot me a thumbs-up, but I looked away quickly. I didn't know if I even wanted his support.

I followed Mala through a passage into an antechamber, and the door mercifully shut everything out behind us. We were alone.

"The Paramount of this Family has been most neglectful in her duties." Her back was to me, and she spoke instead to the wall, which was hung with an enormous tapestry faded by time. I recognized the style — in Cecelia's memory, Deon had something like it incised in the leather bracers and armour covering her body. But this depicted something else. Three massive dark shapes hulking ominously in the sky, a split sea, and a drowning world — above it, a black orb.

"The rules. The training. The preparation. Cecelia always went her own way about things."

I thought of Cecelia, her overwhelming need to reject the stone, and that she'd spent her entire life serving its will and leaving us behind because of it. "She did her best."

"Her best wasn't enough." Mala spun to face me, her face hard. "Do you know how long she was gone? Fourteen years. She and the stone. She put us all in jeopardy so she could avenge her daughter. So she could save *you*." For a second I thought she was blaming me, but there was admiration there. "Impulsive and heroic to the bitter end."

I lowered my head, looked at my hands. I swore I'd felt her small fox body there, only for a second, on a battlefield that was far too late. I clenched my fists. "*She did her best*."

Mala didn't argue that time. "Indeed." She sat heavily on the recessed bench underneath the tapestry and held out her hand again. "Please."

I hesitated, but where else would I go? I crossed the room and joined her but put enough space between us on the bench to fit another person. "And in those fourteen years," I ventured, "you were the leader here in her absence?"

Mala smiled. "I've done *my* best here." She reached out a hand again, as someone would on meeting, and I felt a warmth from her that I could trust, so I took it gingerly. Her grip was firm but comforting. "I do so admire you, Roan.

What you have accomplished. What you have sacrificed. It can't have been easy, doing so much for a world you knew nothing about." She squeezed a little too hard, then released. "I envy your naïveté. You acted without being bound by the laws or tenets the rest of us are. But such a tether runs out eventually. There are rules. Rules that have protected us in this world for centuries. Rules that exist to protect not only Denizens but those without Ancient's connection. The Families once worked together towards a common purpose, a common peace, but we are all divided, as you can see. And a crisis does not make it any easier to unite."

I was on a leash, that much was clear. Mala turned her body aside, bringing a leg underneath her as she eyed the tapestry critically. "The world is in pain. And Ancient still sleeps. I cannot say for certain what this new enemy wants. But it only rose because Zabor was sent back to her siblings. And just like us, the darklings are stronger together."

She was the third person to say that to me. I stared at her; that time, the accusation was definitely there. Table Five's chilling and bizarre warning rang in my head — *our mother thanks you for helping her . . .*

"What . . . you mean the thing causing the plague, trying to collect the stones . . . this wouldn't have happened if Zabor hadn't —"

"There is no good and evil in our world, Roan. But there is destruction, the kind that can be held back by inches or succumbed to entirely." Mala was still staring at the tapestry like it was asking a question she couldn't answer. "Keeping Zabor sated was, true, only a temporary solution to a greater problem. I fear that sending her back to the Bloodlands was a part of her plan, however good your intentions were. If I were in your position, to see it through a lens unclouded by the laws of Ancient . . . I may have done the same."

I leapt to my feet; after everything I'd given up last spring, I couldn't believe that I'd been wrong all along. "But you . . . Zabor was *killing Denizen children*. Every year. You would've kept that up, what, until there were none left?"

Mala sighed. "It's more complicated than that."

"You're just as bad as the Owls." I couldn't stomach any of this, and I paced to the other side of the room. "So all of you were content to let that go on? For the greater good? Is that why I'm here — for a dressing down?"

After a drawn-out silence, Mala spoke. "What you did was honourable. A brave and courageous thing. I will not fault you that. Nor will I belittle the sacrifices made for it. What matters now is that something else rose from the Bloodlands after Zabor returned there. The children that follow it — they call it Seela. It calls itself the child of the darklings. The plague it brought here affects only humans, those not born with but hungry for power." Now she stood. "Seela cannot succeed, Roan. To bring the stones together is a disaster we can't even fathom." She pointed to the tapestry. "This is an ending we cannot rewrite, but it is only one possible outcome. If Seela brings the stones together, it would have the power to unmake the world. It wants nothing more than to be reunited with its parents. To make this world a Bloodland it can rule."

My fists were crack-tight and sparks spat off me. I saw wariness rise in her. "What am I supposed to say to that? What exactly do you want from me?"

Her eyes fell from my face to my chest. "The stone has a mind of its own. Surely you know that by now."

I cooled down at that. "So?"

"So it chose you. For a reason. These things are not done lightly. Some say that you took the stone, that you did not earn it. But in the end, we know you were chosen as a conduit. You have a power and a will to fight. You have what it takes to lead."

I bunched the fabric of my hoodie above my sternum, tired of listening. *You aren't alone*, Killian had said. Mala was asking for my help. But I needed some of my own, too.

"You really can't take it from me, can you?" My voice was small.

She shook her head sadly. "It is a bond that can be broken only by death. We are not so desperate yet."

Hardly comforting. I thought of Fingal's Pint, the havoc I could wreak. "But I don't know how to control it. There was . . . an accident —"

"We know, Roan. But we can show you how to control it. A tremendous power is within your reach, a chance to join us in the fight that is certainly coming. You could be a part of this. But we have to trust each other."

That was a long shot. I needed time to think. "This has all been a lot to take in at once."

Mala was quiet. "Of course." She crossed the room back to the hidden door that would lead once more into the meeting space. "I'll have Killian show you to a private place where you can rest." As she ushered me through the door, her smile did not reach her eyes. She knew as well as I that this wasn't going to be easy.

When I met Killian again at the bowl, now devoid of the squabbling Council members, he bounced to his feet. "Right. Rest, is it? I'll take you to the sleeping corridor, so you —"

"No." I had made sure Mala was well beyond earshot and turned down a distant tunnel before I answered. "The woman who was here. She had scars . . ." I swallowed. "Her name is Ruo. Where did they take her?"

Killian hesitated. "She's back up in the infirmary. But I don't think —"

"Think what you like," I said, brushing past him, remembering all too well Ben's throat in his hand before Killian murdered him. "I can find my own way."

He didn't try to catch up with me, and I didn't look anywhere else but ahead.

The place seemed a bit more deserted now as I climbed the steps, carefully retracing the path I'd walked to get here. I assumed there was some kind of communal meal in which everyone participated, which allowed me now to move a bit more freely without the thousand-stare judgefest. It made me realize that I had no idea of the time and couldn't remember when I last ate (or felt like it) but most of all I felt lost without seeing the sun —

I stopped dead, the edges of my vision and the world peeling back, because I was suddenly back in that memory — the one where Cecelia was on a sandy arena ground, locked in combat, and the sun I'd missed only a second ago was beating down on the back of my neck.

I stayed still, calmed the blood roaring in my head. All I needed to do was watch. The stone was showing me this for a reason.

"Get up." Cecelia stood over the boy, blade at his throat. She sounded exhausted. "Get up and return to your master. It should have been you. But I guess . . . it is what it is."

The boy got to his weary, trembling feet, and Cecelia

grabbed him before he could tip over. "It was an honour to submit to you," he mumbled as if it were practised, before returning to a cluster of onlookers that had come down to the arena now that it was over. That it was decided.

Four acolytes came out, bearing a brazier. In it sat the stone, and in the shining sunlight came Deon Herself bearing the stone up, moving towards Cecelia like a glittering mirage.

Her grin was the worst to stomach. "*Dear daughter*," the goddess said. "*It is time*."

Cecelia was a hard woman. She had become that way mostly to survive. But even now, in her twenties, and after having survived much, this was one thing she knew she couldn't. She felt scoured inside. She wouldn't look at the god or the proffered gem.

"Please," she tried one last time. "Please don't give it to me."

A clawed hand found her chin, tipped it up. "*You spoke of a need for reform. I do not dwell in your world but through you, and so those choices are up to you. But you will be great, if only you allow yourself to be. There is more ahead for you and this stone than your present regret. Keep this stone safe. Use it wisely. Prepare your blood, because it is for her you must keep this stone — and the world you occupy — safe from darkness*."

"Her? You mean this child —"

"*Not this one. Further still*," Deon said. And Cecelia opened her hands, the stone warm in her cupped palms.

The memory peeled back again, and it was just my hands outstretched before me — empty but still warm. *Further still*, Deon had said. Had she meant me? Everything she had said to Cecelia stirred my heart, as if she'd been talking to me and not just my grandmother.

There was one person who hadn't been in that crowd, either revelling in Cecelia's triumph or consoling her in her misery. One who might have answers for me, though her mind seemed splintered beyond use. The urgency to see her now threw me into motion, and I bolted for the infirmary.

The Scars Beneath

Barton sighed, thumbing through his phone as he waited on the train platform. He didn't know what he was expecting — a call, a text. There really hadn't been a point to getting that roaming package, had there?

"Listen," his dad had said, too many time zones ago, back at the Winnipeg airport where his parents were seeing him off, "I'm sure Phae is fine. And you have to admit . . . Alberta is just a tiny bit closer than Magadan for a finding-yourself road trip."

Barton had shifted his duffel back onto his shoulder, glancing between the NEXUS special entrance, where he could be scanned with his prostheses, and the exit back into the airport parking lot. Only days ago, Phae had refused to join him. Had backed away from him and the bond they'd built. Natti had spirited her away on some other side quest.

I'm sorry, she'd texted. *I know what you're thinking. But maybe this is where I can figure things out.*

On the road. With some prophetic polar bears instead of her boyfriend. He didn't even know if they were broken up or not . . .

Barton dropped his eyes from his dad's openly concerned face. "I do kind of wish you guys were coming."

He should've kept that to himself. His mother was already having a hard time not crying. "This will be good for you," his dad went on. "For the both of you. You've got a lot to figure out. Time apart never hurt anyone. And remember you've got your whole life ahead of you. So much to look forward to."

His mother took his face in her hands, and he let her. Things had been tough since coming to terms with the power they had kept from him all his life. But they had done it to protect him and had made inroads back to strengthening their insular family.

"I am so proud of you," she'd said, this time letting the tears go. "You make this Family proud." And this time he knew she meant the Rabbits, too.

A train on the opposite track blew by, its horn blast smacking Barton back into the present. Maybe his dad was right. So much had happened since last year, maybe too much to process. It'd be good for him. As the train passed, the ground rumbling beneath him, Barton knelt carefully and put his hand to the platform, shut his eyes. Felt the earth stretching and groaning beneath the weight of the train, the station itself. Felt further still, past the roots of concrete and rebar into the bones that kept the world turning. It calmed him, that subtle tectonic energy coming back up into his arm. He was a part of something now that he'd always known he was meant for. Phae would be fine. So would he.

"Barton Allen?"

He raised his head to the woman above him and gingerly got back up. She didn't offer to help, seeming to know he didn't want it. "And you're Kita?" She matched the description he'd been given before arrival — shaved head, big hoop earrings, almost as tall as him.

"That I am." She nodded, flashing a bright smile that contrasted well with her loam-coloured skin. "You are from Kenya, yes?"

"Canada," he corrected. "My parents are from Kenya, though. And you?" He hazarded a guess from her accent. "South Africa?"

"That's right," Kita said, adjusting her own pack. She seemed built like a soldier. "Parents are from Somalia. We didn't go as far as yours." She looked him up and down. "I have heard the stories of you and your friends. Sealing a darkling. That is a feat. And you — you opened a Bloodgate on your own. After being severed."

Her bluntness caught him off guard, but she wasn't wrong. "Yep."

"Hm." Kita turned back to the platform, looked down the tunnel. A light was gradually drawing closer. "I am glad you've come. We will need all the help we can get. And it would not hurt to have the best on our side."

Barton straightened his spine as their train rushed by them, standing steady. Wherever this train went, it was down another tunnel, cutting through the Earth — *his* Earth. Steady beneath him, whatever happened.

❧

Of course I got lost. Typical. *Start out cocky and you end up paying for it.* The admonishment was almost in Sil's voice, too, but I was already being hard enough on myself without needing her to remind me.

I'd ended up in an open space, flanked by pillars and flickering flame on platforms of varying heights. Targets? Another of the stone's many problems was that I felt an itching sense of déjà vu, though I knew I'd never been here before.

I stood in the centre of the space. There was a skylight, high above, filtering in sunlight. I shut my eyes and tried to let that light inside me, to remember that no matter what, it was that light I followed. I felt a rare moment of calm. Lately I'd been driven by one impulse — to run away rather than towards anything. Especially this legacy I'd had dumped in my lap. Talking with Mala hadn't exactly assuaged the myriad worries crushing me, but there had been a kernel of hope there — that now I could belong somewhere, with people, with a Family. Maybe this was a start of a course correction. Maybe things would be okay. Maybe they could show me how to be a better me, one who wasn't impulsive and who could, for once, accept help when I so desperately needed it.

My head snapped in the direction of the oncoming voices and footsteps hurrying across the stone floor and into the chamber. I reacted too late to run off, so I looked like an idiot in the spotlight instead, a group of kindergarten-age kids in what looked like oversized training gi, staring at me agog. They were led by an aged but alert female master. And someone I still hadn't quite figured out: Killian.

"Speak o' the devil." He smiled. I closed my mouth and

tried to relax my body — I'd automatically fallen into a defensive stance.

"Whoa, is that really her?" said a gap-toothed girl in the front of the group, breaking away and rushing towards me.

"Felicia," the master snapped, and the girl pulled up short of me but didn't look away.

"Err. Hi?" Awkward wave, hand dropping.

Killian sidled up, though he kept his distance. "Don't crowd the poor girl. She's been through enough without yer caterwauling," he said to the gathering, then he turned to me, face wry as the student hurried back to join the group. "This is the junior class. Wee trainees just getting their start. Ye have a bit in common, I expect."

I resisted spewing a retort that wasn't remotely kid-friendly. "Thanks." I glanced from the awestruck kids to their teacher then bowed my head. "I'm sorry for interrupting your lesson." I turned to go.

"There's no need to rush off!" the master reached towards me, coming forward. "In fact, it would be nice for you to stay. If you so choose."

I stiffened. The woman, wiry but strong, had a shy look on her aged face that belied her obvious years of experience. A reverence I'd never get used to or feel I'd earned.

I rubbed the back of my neck. "I mean . . . sure, I can watch?"

"Excellent." She turned smartly on her heel, and the kids froze. "Now I expect you all to pay extra attention. Be mindful of your behaviour and focus — especially in the presence of your Paramount."

I could see the kids grow redder with anxiety, and I interjected, "I'm not —"

Killian grabbed my elbow and steered me to the sidelines. "Och, now, just button it. They need to learn discipline whatever ye think yer not."

The children went into formation, and the master went through the lesson. It looked a simple one — a lesson about control, about calling up the fire, which some seemed to be struggling with.

My eyes darted away from the training circle to the far edge of the great hall. There were men and women wearing the red, gold, and black tunic I'd seen Cecelia wear in the stone's memory. Their faces were impassive, and they didn't wear weapons, but they were alert, scanning.

They all seemed to be watching me, too.

"Guards," Killian whispered, before nudging me in the ribs. "Ignore them, pay attention to this."

I frowned, glancing back to the lesson, the kids. "Why are there so many of them?" I'd counted almost twenty in this hall alone. Sure I'd seen a few in my super-lost wanderings, and given what was happening, security was a given. But twenty guards for a kindergarten class?

Killian didn't look at me directly. He only smiled, with a hint of a sneer. "Can't be too careful with outsiders about."

I blinked. Did he mean me? Or *him*?

". . . of the Five Families, ours is an element that has a mind of its own," the mentor was saying. "Sometimes you will need an outside spark to get going, and that's all right. Soon you will be able to call the flame to you obediently — but it has to trust you first."

I surveyed the group, trying to ignore the guard presence. They were all so young and here they were learning something I'd barely been able to grasp only six months ago, give or take. Sil really did have her work cut out with me, and I was surprised she hadn't given up on me sooner.

"I'm sorry," Killian whispered to me. He'd been quiet as we watched, the children moving through stances and tai-chi-esque drills. I raised an eyebrow but didn't answer.

"That boy, in the park," he qualified. "I know ye knew him. He was yer friend. I'd seen ye with him before, outside that restaurant. That's where I first saw ye, y'ken."

I tried to conjure the memory from when I'd seen Ben and Athika at the Pint's smouldering ruins, when I'd already surmised something had been wrong. I'd bumped into a man I'd just as soon forgotten in my haste to get away.

I turned back to the kids, folding my arms tighter. "I see."

"Ye don't, I don't think." I heard him sigh heavily. "It's a terrible place to be, having to take a life, even if it's to save another. I think ye've been spared that so far, maybe, but it will only get harder. Ye will have to make the call sooner or later, though, especially with the responsibility ye have now."

"A responsibility I didn't ask for," I seethed, but I wasn't about to get into it here. I felt I owed it to these kids' teacher to provide an example of self-control, something I needed badly to learn.

"All the same," Killian went on. "It wasna out of malice what I did. Your friend was too far gone. I've seen it before."

I thought of the first time I'd met Ben. We'd had a nice conversation about nerdy things and had clicked right away. He had an easy, friendly demeanour. But now my last memory of him was his twisted face, his tarry gnarled body, his need to kill me.

"I think I knew it," I said. "I wouldn't have been able to do . . . what you did. I'm grateful for the good intentions, but

I can't directly thank you for it." That's as far as I was going to go with gratitude.

"Aye. I'll take it." Killian's good humour was returning to his tone. "How was your tête-à-tête with Mala?"

I snorted. "Oh, about the same as that little tribunal. Scrutiny. Judgment. Disappointment that it's me she's got to answer to. I don't blame her. I don't blame any of them. Bad shit is going down and I wouldn't want me leading the charge, either."

"Give yerself a wee bit more credit than that," Killian said quietly. "Ye've done much for these people without asking anything in return. It's them that owes ye."

"I wonder —" The teacher stopped and lifted a hand towards me, beckoning. "Might you be willing to demonstrate, Mistress Harken?"

I felt my body flush with the panic of being put on the spot. "Uh. Demonstrate?"

The woman bowed. "It has been some time since I myself have witnessed the Deon avatar shown by a Paramount. I'm sure the children would be thrilled to see it."

My pulse thundered in my ears as the kids stared back at me, eyes wide. So trusting and naïve. What if I blasted this entire place to kingdom come? They wouldn't thank me for it, and my dwindling sense of personal pride wouldn't, either.

But I pushed down my fear, decided that if I was going to control this stone, it was now or never. "Okay."

The master ushered the children back as I stepped into the band of sunlight filtering from the faraway cavern ceiling. The warmth wasn't just on my skin. It was underneath it. I shut my eyes and levelled my breathing, pushing my awareness gently into the stone's as I had done before. But this time it wasn't a matter of crisis. I wanted to take careful stock of how to go about this when I was present, in control. Something that I hadn't been so many times recently.

The voices came, tentative at first, then a rush over my synapses, demanding and furious. I winced, trying to search beneath them for that word that had brought me back from the brink, spoken by my only connection to all of this.

"Roan," Cecelia said. It was like an embrace, and I fell into it, and I felt the flames effusing out of me, shaping me, pulling me as I grew. Beyond it all, I heard a collective gasp of the children learning as I had that while fire could tear anything asunder, it could also light the way.

Killian and I parted ways at the sleeping quarters a little bit later. "I could go with ye to see Ruo," he'd offered after the demonstration.

The lie formed quickly — that I wanted to go rest on my own before I saw her, and he demurred, showing me to a room similar to the one I woke up in. It didn't matter if he believed I was going to stay there or not, he accepted that I wanted to be alone. Wherever I ended up.

I waited for the sounds of his footsteps to diminish down the cavern hall before leaping to my feet. It was time to find Ruo. To find the answers I'd been looking for in Edinburgh in the first place.

I thought about the young learners as I passed further groups of trainees and acolytes, and this time I didn't break eye contact with them. I met their gazes full on, nodding, feeling a strange and sudden sense of belonging. Renewed purpose, maybe. I could do this. Everything was going to be okay.

It was my second attempt at finding the infirmary now — the only place safe for her, for herself and others. I figured that she'd be rested by now, after the Council meeting so many hours ago. Even though I sincerely doubted what she could offer in terms of intel. Blind and maybe senile. Yet she had remembered Cecelia, had heard the stone. I'd probably need its help, after all.

The compound was an anthill, and the tunnels and close corridors still looked nearly identical. Luckily, after Barton had been attacked, Sil had taught me about keen hunting senses I could use to find him. I'd use them now to find Ruo.

Ruo had reached out to touch me. The recollection of it slammed through me like a car impact, and I felt it again now as I paced through the mountain, felt her body inexplicably crash into mine — or the ghost of it — and I staggered around a corner.

Not ten feet away from me there was an open door, and I heard something heavy hurtle to the ground and smash.

"Be still!" someone grunted, and I soon found myself standing in the doorway, watching a man in a plain grey uniform holding his hands away from Ruo, who was crouched in the corner gripping a ceramic shard in front of her like a knife.

"Keep away from me," she hissed. "You took my *things*. I want them back. I want to go *home*."

I was at the man's side in three paces. "Can I help?"

Ruo backed further into her corner, jabbing her shard outward. "Who else is there? Don't come near me! Don't stick me again!"

The man in grey took a step back and took me with him.

"It's dementia. She's very confused. We can't release her, either — she's . . . she's homeless." He seemed apologetic. "She needs sedation. She's a danger to herself." I noticed then he had a needle primed and ready, likely to sedate her given her hysterics. I realized Ruo must be in her seventies if she was around Cecelia's age . . . but she was still as fierce as if she were mine.

I took a tentative step forward, hands up, even though I knew she couldn't see them. "Ruo? Do you remember me? We spoke at the Council meeting earlier." The milky eyes shifted towards the approximate source of my voice. "It's Roan. I've come to visit you."

"Visit me? No one visits me. Everyone just leaves. *Leaves*." The scars at the corners of her eyes hemmed them in bitterly. My heart stung.

"Do you want to sit with me awhile? Just the two of us. The needle is gone now. I think the nurse finally gave up." I shot the man in the grey scrubs a look, and as quietly as possible he backed off. Ruo still hadn't dropped the shard, which I realized had been picked up from a pile of what had recently been a huge stoneware bowl, now shattered in a pool of water.

Ruo's mouth twitched a smile. "They always give up. They always leave."

Then the smile fell, and I saw her nostrils flare, like a dog air-scenting. "What's that? That warmth. And a voice . . . I could have sworn . . ."

I looked down and saw the stone doing something I hadn't yet experienced. It was pulsing beneath my shirt, like a beacon. The voices were rising but in the merest whisper. When I glanced back up, Ruo's arm had slackened and her eyes were distant, like someone was speaking to her.

When she took a step forward, hands sweeping in front of her, I stiffened, but she caught the edge of the nearest bed, guided herself onto it, and sat perfectly still, save for her hands running over the shard protectively. She was nodding, but the voices from the stone were fading now, then gone.

Had it been speaking *to* her?

I carefully lowered myself beside her. I didn't know how far I would get, but I had to try. "Ruo? Do you remember Cecelia? Do you remember the last time you saw her?"

Before coming to find me, Cecelia had been gone from the world for fourteen years. Ruo may very well be the last living person to have spoken to her before Cecelia went down the Ancient rabbit hole.

Ruo's breath whistled through her nose, the creases at her mouth flexing. A cloud passed over her face as I studied it. The burns told part of the tale, as if something had come at her, like an iron baseball bat wreathed in fire. The band stretched from one temple to another, making a mask, and I thought, *Like a fox's face*.

My spirit eye showed nothing. She had been a Fox once, I knew that from the memories. But like Barton, there was only the ghostly impression of Denizen there. Her connection to Ancient had been severed.

Then Ruo smiled. "You remind me of my daughter," she said. "We raised her all over the world. Had to, because of Cecelia's position. But we lived here for the longest stretch, in Edinburgh. We had a flat." She spoke as if she were still there. She couldn't have known or understood we were almost on the other side of the country now, and maybe miles beneath it.

"She didn't mind, though. Moving around. As long as there was somewhere she could plant flowers. Ravenna liked to plant things. She used to say her true love would be someone who could make anything grow. Cecelia was terrible at gardening. She didn't like things that took patience. Didn't like setting down roots. It's a good thing we had only the one child."

At first I thought she was descending back into delusion, but she dropped one thread and picked up another one. "I haven't seen Ravenna in so long. She went to Canada, you know. Too cold for me."

I felt a chill like the spring wind off the Assiniboine at Omand's Creek. Though I was still here in the infirmary with Ruo, I could picture it clearly. The life Cecelia had wanted for the two of them. Two women raising a child in the '60s . . . they'd been brave. But no matter how low Ruo had been brought now, that love was still there.

"Did you know Ravenna had a daughter, too?" I asked, swallowing. "She named her Roan." Though I'd already introduced myself to her, it felt like we were communicating in a different dimension, and she didn't seem bothered by connecting them. I wanted her to stay calm.

Ruo nodded. "Ravenna liked horses. I can see that." She tilted her head. "I think . . . Cecelia did something. She wanted to help Roan and Ravenna. It's hard to . . . remember."

"She did it. She did help them." I couldn't speak for my mother, since now I'd never know what had happened to her when she fell into the Bloodlands. But when I felt the stone pulse again, I felt more a conduit than ever before. "I think Cecelia wanted me to meet you. I guess it might make you my second grandmother."

Ruo had reached up with such a quiet grace, so innocent, that I couldn't stop her before her hand was laid protectively over the stone. The pulse rose to meet her, stayed aglow, but didn't do anything further. It wasn't threatened. I felt the warmth spread through my synapses, and I wondered if Ruo could feel it, too.

Her smile now seemed like it held more than just wistful remembrance — more a touch of bitter irony. "She shouldn't have gone, that night. The Stonebreakers were radicalizing. It was a trap. And Cecelia knew it. But she went anyway, to confront them. She was always trying to make them see reason, Denizens and the extremists. And if they didn't, she negotiated with her fists." Ruo's jaw worked behind her sunken cheeks, and she clenched the stone with a claw. I suddenly felt a rush of cold and realized with sudden terror that I couldn't move. The room was flashing, but I couldn't shut my eyes. There was a reel clicking over inside me, flooding me with images and voices.

"She was always so rash. I didn't want her taking unnecessary risks. So I went with her. The Stonebreakers were meeting in the South Bridge Vaults. Cecelia wanted to smoke them out. A show of force. But I could tell she needed to understand them, too. There was a fight — there always is. We cut through them easily enough, but the leader was an Owl. They had been planning to test a theory, to see what would happen if they separated a Paramount from their stone. They tried it on her. But I got in the way of the two of them. And that's the last time I *saw* Cecelia."

I had been there just now, watching for myself, paralyzed — underneath the city, fighting in close quarters, the flash of fire and air and then, suddenly, sharp iron fingers inside my mind, my insides, teasing out what made me *me*. The man, the Owl, was taking the core of me, the fire itself. The stone fought back, but this Owl was strong, his grip, though caustic, was intense.

Then I saw Ruo rush him from behind, put an arm around his neck, and jerk him back. He twisted and that grip smashed into her, pulled back, and put her between the Owl and Cecelia, just as the Opal lashed out with a sickening surge of flame that scraped over Ruo's face. The Owl had hit Ruo with what had been intended for Cecelia — a blast that ripped her Denizenship and her power from her in one fell swoop. And with Ruo's own fire taken from her, so too was her imperviousness to it, and Cecelia's own attack had been turned on her lover.

The vaults slipped away and the light of the infirmary came back by pinpricks. I was holding Ruo's limp wrist in my grip like a drowning sailor to passing debris. Her face was still impassive, yet the smile lingered.

"I know it was an accident," Ruo said quietly. "But Cecelia always had to do things her way. Whatever it cost the rest of us." I dropped her hand, afraid I might burn her further than Cecelia had.

"So warm," Ruo muttered, voice growing heavier, arms slowly coming up around herself to rub a chill away. "I'd forgotten what it felt like."

The feeling was still only just coming back into my body — a completely new sensation, like this body wasn't mine. A feeling that brought up almost too much dread for things to come.

Cecelia had lived in Edinburgh, had had a life here with Ruo and Ravenna — a *family*. A family divided, if Ravenna had come to Canada and left them both behind, and with what limited memory served and Cecelia's letters, it was because of some schism — whether it was marrying my stepfather, Aaron Harken, or otherwise. But fourteen years ago Cecelia had gone on a solitary journey and so followed Ravenna to Canada eventually (well, her comatose body did), yet here was Ruo at the end of her life. Alone, her vision taken from her when trying to protect the woman she loved, trapped in the mire of her mind, cut off from her powersake . . .

At the core of that abandonment was Cecelia. The clearest culprit. The loudest voice haunting the stone she'd saddled me with was yet still an unreliable narrator.

No one visits me. Everyone just leaves.

"There she is," said a voice at the door, and Ruo jerked towards it. I felt stiff and semi-cogent, so I saw the smile break across her face before I saw Killian passing me and taking Ruo's outstretched hands.

"Are ye behaving, girlie, or are they giving ye the fun meds?" Killian sat on the bed next to the one we occupied, holding Ruo's hands tenderly across the divide. "Och, yer cold as death. Too bad the Conclave doesna keep whisky."

His eyes flicked to me, and I got up, moved to stand by the edge of the bed as I felt the stab of something cold beneath the Opal. A sort of kinship for his kindness towards me mingled with irritated suspicion. I'd gone out of my way to ditch him, and yet here he was anyway, *again*. Had he done as I had — waited around . . . then followed me?

"This is my granddaughter, Killian," Ruo smiled. "She came to visit me."

Killian looked genuinely surprised, even though he must have known Ruo couldn't see his expression. "Oh, aye? Verra nice." He nodded at me. "She's the spitting image of

Cecelia. But can't say for sure whose eyes she got — they're two different colours."

I felt my face flush under his appraisal, then felt agitated that it had. But then I grasped the admission. "*You* knew Cecelia?"

He didn't answer directly but didn't disappoint. "I grew up with yer mother."

At that moment the floor was suddenly no longer under me — it rippled and met my back in the wake of a massive thunderclap. Ruo shrieked, but Killian held onto her, keeping her on the bed.

"Christ," he said when the fissure subsided. "The hell's that?"

The nurse who had originally tried to sedate Ruo burst back into the infirmary, gasping. "Get up!" he shouted. "We have to evacuate!"

"What's going on?" I pulled myself back up using the bedframe, but the ground was still vibrating under my feet. Then a concussive horn blast sounded. A warning.

"The cavern, it's —" Then the floor gave way beneath us entirely, and the beds and our bodies followed the crumbling stone as it fell away. I watched it all like we were trapped in a transparent mire, every flickering neuron leading back to the stone, which flared outward its own shockwave. I shut my eyes and let it.

When I opened them again, sound and fury was abating. The representation of my body on this plane was no longer mine, the fox warrior's body wrapped around me as armour. I lifted my heavy head and dragged the nine tails up to follow, sweeping debris from it with a crack. My arms were tight to me, the fire ebbing back inside me for the next round. When

I winged them stiffly open, Killian coughed from under my left, but Ruo, in my right, was unconscious, a red mark forming on her brow where a falling rock had smashed it. It had all happened so fast, I'd barely registered catching them both and cleaving them close to me. At least Ruo was still breathing. I held onto her, but I let Killian go.

Both he and Ruo were covered in dust, which showered on us as the compound throbbed like a heartbeat. Sound came back into my field of awareness — that distant warning horn, screams from every corner of the once-bustling hive — and my vision, which made everything appear abrasive and enflamed, went back to something human as the rest of me did, shrinking down until I was holding Ruo in human arms.

Killian crawled back to my side. "Thank you," he croaked, then he took Ruo from me and I collapsed backward onto my hands. "What in bloody Christ is going on 'round here?"

We were lucky — the beautiful order of the Conclave's sanctuary had been gutted, now looking like an alien planet of plinths and shattered stone and collapsed pillars. The impact seemed to have taken out only our immediate area, but the hysteria carried through the caves as another distant quake came rippling towards us. Aftershock? Or the fist reeling back to finish the one-two?

I got to my feet, looked around. "I doubt it was an actual earthquake. That'd be too easy." And it didn't seem likely that the clever Foxes would fill a barracks with young trainees on a fault line. I thought about those fragile children from this morning's lesson and felt sick. "I don't smell explosives, either. It couldn't have been a bomb. There's no smoke . . ."

"We'll puzzle it out later." Killian had Ruo in his arms; he was stronger than he looked, and more decisive. "We need to find Mala, get Ruo out with the rest for the evacuation. And if it is an attack, then we've got to get you to the front line." His smile was grave. "Ah, I bet you thought I'd say, *Let's get you to safety*, but if yer Cecelia's granddaughter, I know I'd be wasting my time."

Another shower of dust came down on us, but I slashed my arm down and lit it up, staying close to his side as he led the way.

We came out into the clear moments after, the system of stairs leading down to the bowl sanctum now shattered like pottery. Killian held Ruo tight, picking down each step carefully, but another tremor stabbed through and he slipped. I grabbed him hard, going rigid as the stone falling around us, and he didn't fall or drop Ruo's dead weight.

We made it to the landing, and the dust cleared, showing figures rushing, voices closer. "Roan!" someone called from the next set of stairs down. The speaker's eyes were wide, mouth forming a warning I couldn't hear over the emergency horn.

"It's Mala," I said, and I surged forward to go down to her, but behind me Killian cried, "*Wait*!" and a boulder broke free of the landing above, knifing through the remaining stairs to the bowl as if they were made of butter. One more step and I would've been taken down with it. There was a black pit at my feet now where the steps had been.

The Opal perceived the oncoming threat, and I grew as the heat inside me did, the blade in my hand a dark arc over my head as it cleaved through the next bombardment of rubble, and the next. I'd transformed again quicker this time, and through the fox warrior's eyes I watched the rocks vanish into that dark oblivion below. I'd have to carry Killian and Ruo over that chasm, hoping we didn't get crushed while I tried it.

"We have to go another way!" Killian shouted above the din, and I spun at the sound of his voice. He took off down a corridor and I rushed after, letting the fox warrior's power stream through me.

I stayed close, the fiery glow of my body lighting the way through the dark. Many of the torches that normally kept the space lit had been thrown from their moorings as the world beneath us cracked and groaned.

"It's the Serenity Emerald," Killian grunted, face blood-red from the exertion. "Has to be. Yer right, this wasn't an explosion of any kind. I'll bet ye anything it's that Seela shite leading that army of brats." Killian staggered, catching himself on the wall.

I swung around to him, reaching, but yanked away to avoid burning Ruo. "It's all right," he smirked, sweat cutting down his jawline. "Just an old man out of shape. Need to catch my breath." He looked to my hand, which was Deon's hand. "Can't say I've ever had a god come to my aid, so at least I can die having that pleasure."

"I'm not a god. And we aren't going to die," I replied, the voice remote in my ears and far too mighty for how I felt inside. "I can carry her awhile if you lead."

"Better not." Killian straightened again, adjusted Ruo's body in his grip. "There's nothing to protect her from ye if things go sideways. Which they just may." Though Ruo's face was slack with unconsciousness, those burn scars were an expression all their own. I put as much distance between us as I could in the narrow tunnel, which seemed to stretch into dark infinity.

We climbed uphill for a while in silence. Seela. I couldn't picture the monster that apparently led an army of burning, snapping children to do its bidding. With the Emerald, the stone of the Rabbits who could control rock and earth, it wouldn't be a long shot that it could split a mountain in half. To get to me. More people put in danger, more lives lost. What could I have done to stop it?

The stone can only be separated in death. I could've given my life so someone who knew what they were doing could take over. I wondered if it was too late.

Killian stopped to rest only once more, and I kept the fox warrior up as a shield. The tremors and the screams alike seemed to be fading the farther we went, and with one last check behind us, I felt like we might be in the clear. "Where are we going? What about the others?"

"There are many vents like this scattered throughout the compound. The damage seemed to be centred on the infirmary and outward. Sleeping quarters and the dining hall are on the opposite end, which is where everyone most likely was congregated. We saw Mala around the main way in and out. Once we're out, we'll double back on the surface and hook back up with them."

I could do nothing but trust him. The grade of the tunnel tilted steeper, with only the strain in my legs to tell me. Judging by how far underground the Conclave's compound was, we might be climbing awhile.

The fox warrior form was difficult to hold, and now that the silence and the darkness was close and low, I knew I couldn't hold it for too much longer. I shut my eyes, went deep down inward. The sensations led me to a visualization of hundreds of searing flaming cables, and with each breath

I undid one. I went through them piece by piece, the light dimming by inches, and releasing the last one, I felt the fox warrior return to the stone that kept Her power in check, allowing it, at least, to rest.

I emptied my lungs but kept my arm alight, and I saw Killian turn his head and catch me in his periphery.

"Aye, good idea." He nodded, smile flickering in my torchlight. "At least ye didna pass out this time. I'm gallant, but I can't carry ye both." His breathing was even but laboured, as he walked and spoke. "Yer learning quickly how to work in tandem with the stone. Nothing like a crisis to test ye. Well done."

It was true; transforming back had taken energy resources — as much as keeping the transformation in place. "I feel useless," I deflected. "You're doing all the work."

"No worries. I'm glad to put as much distance between here and back there as we can. For more than the obvious reasons."

Another tremor, but it felt more like a truck going by than a tectonic shift. Anxious mind going a mile a minute, I remembered the hall full of wary guards. "You got something against the Conclave, too?"

"Hm? What do ye mean, 'too'?"

My head was spinning; I had to put a hard divide between Cecelia's memories and perspectives and my own. They'd started twisting together. "Cecelia. She didn't like them, either."

"Aye, an understatement, but aye." I couldn't see his face, but there was a smile in his words. "Let's just say Cecelia and I were of the same mind on a lot of things. We kept our distance from the Conclave. Having the stone never means having absolute control. The Conclave didn't like her approach to conflict resolution, and she didn't much like being told what to do." Killian grunted, but it was because, thankfully, the climb was levelling off. "It's the same with all these Families, ye ken. With a lot of the old power structures of civilizations. They give all the power to one person, but they try to sway that person with an assault of perspectives. It's meant to keep the power in check, keep it balanced and honest, but it's too many voices, too many contradicting vendettas. Ye lose yer own voice and will in it, until there's nothing left of ye and yer the slave to the whims of a council or the legacy that came before ye. And if the Conclave couldna have a say in how the stone was used . . . then surely it wasna being used for the good of all. Whatever that was at the time."

Too many voices. The stone was silent now, but for how long until it pushed me out of the way again? "Yeah. This stone is like a mini Conclave I get to carry around 24/7. The voices . . . screaming over one another. Sometimes I can't shut them out. This is one of the rare times I've been able to make it do what *I* wanted. And the Conclave acts like I wanted this. It's . . . it's driving me insane."

I realized I could see the back of Killian's sweat-drenched head nodding. There was a bit of light ahead, and I lowered the flame of my stiff arm.

"I canna imagine what yer going through. But yer no' wrong. The Conclave wants to control ye. It's how it's always been. Yer a loose cannon. They canna have that, not after Cecelia going rogue for so long. They know yer suffering. But they want ye to think it's for a noble cause. *For the Narrative*. Always that bloody thing."

I knew all too well what people would do for the Narrative — the story we were writing with each step and choice. "I remember when I thought the Narrative was just a legendary origin story."

"Aye, it's that. The Narrative is *forever*. It is the beginning, the middle, the end. Ancient's great blueprint that Denizens must follow, protecting life itself even as our powers fade with each season. All to guard a dying world populated by the selfish and greedy that its verra creator has forgotten." His bitterness was so thick, I was surprised he didn't spit.

"I still can't see *why* the Conclave isn't your biggest fan, really . . ." I said. Killian laughed. "But that doesn't explain why you bothered coming back after keeping your distance for so long."

With the next step, a cool breeze moved through my dishevelled hair and across my face. It felt so good that I stopped short. We were outside, and Killian stiffly knelt and placed Ruo on the ground like she was made of glass. He collapsed beside her, star-fishing his sore body and shutting his eyes with the bliss of the spent. Ruo seemed so peaceful, too, burned face relaxed in the light of the waxing half moon above us.

We were in the woods. Behind us was a shrub-shrouded rockface; we'd emerged from a cleft in the stone, what could have literally been the backdoor of a mountain.

"I came back here for *you*." Killian stared up at the stars. "I told ye. I ken well what it is to be alone. Soon as this thing started hunting stone-bearing Paramounts . . . well. I wanted to see ye safe. For Cecelia's sake. Mostly I wanted to find ye before the Conclave did. But beggars can't be choosers."

Ruo shivered in her sleep. Killian sat up immediately,

digging his finger in the earth and etching the triple ring pattern I'd seen in so much Denizen iconography. He twisted his hand over it, and a fire flashed above the arcane symbol, undulating and alive in the air without any fuel. His fingers stretched, and the fire did, too.

I crouched down across from him. "Shouldn't we keep moving?" I also questioned the intelligence of lighting a beacon to our whereabouts considering we had been fleeing an enemy attack, but the woods around us were alive only with the sound of night birds and crickets.

"We'll get going soon," he said. "Let's get her warmed up, though. It will be a long night, and I'm no' a spring chicken."

He lifted a knee up and rested his arm across it. He kept complaining about being old, but he didn't look it. His dark hair and engaging eyes certainly lent to this illusion of youth, but in the fire I saw the lines about those eyes and his mouth, that scar running from brow to chin. His cheeks and jaw were lean, shaded with the beard growth of a few days, but now that I could appraise him closely, there were shadows there, ones I recognized from staring into my own bathroom mirror. The shadows of too many sleepless nights.

"You grew up with my mother," I said abruptly, and Killian's keen eyes flicked up. "What was she like?"

His face tightened. I hadn't edited the grief out of my tone — I was too exhausted. "Canny. Clever. Intense. Beautiful." He looked away from me. "Aye. I spent time wi' her. Even though she moved around a lot. *Lots* of time. When training breaks for the both of us allowed it, of course." He looked away suddenly, as if he'd been caught out.

A tingle of understanding. He'd been close to Ravenna. Maybe more than friends. The things this man knew, this man I'd only just met, outstripped what I knew about my own bloodline by miles.

"They were incredible women, Roan, yer granny and yer mother. Gifted. Strong-minded. But conflicted about where their hearts truly stood. I hope ye didna mind me saying, but yer so much of both of them. Beyond looks."

My pulse picked up. I needed more. "And . . . and my father? I mean. My biological father. I know now that Aaron . . . that she remarried . . ."

I watched his face change, eyebrows shifting his hairline in bemusement as I stumbled over my desperation to learn something, anything, about the strangers who made me. "Everything I know about my family is all snippets and secrets and it seems like anyone who knew them died before I could learn more or hasn't been in their right mind for a long time to paint an accurate picture." *Or I didn't bother asking before it was too late*. Ruo hadn't moved, but her eyelids fluttered like she was dreaming, upper lip curling at whatever she saw.

"So ye didna know anything about your father." Killian was moving his hand over the flame and back again, fingers twining through it and casting odd shadows on his face. "No one told ye anything about him?"

I shrugged. "Up until a few months ago, I thought Aaron Harken was my father. As if I needed another plot twist in all of this . . ."

A crease appeared over the bridge of his nose. "Do ye remember the Stonebreakers? The radicalized group that Mala mentioned earlier?"

I nodded slowly. "It was a confrontation with them that left Ruo . . ." I trailed off. I don't think it bore repeating, nor telling him how I knew. I wanted to keep that close for a while longer. I didn't even know if I could trust Killian, but I felt I had already started.

"Mm. They believed the stones would be better off destroyed, and wi' them every Denizen's connection to Ancient. Without Ancient's influence, and wi' the Narrative itself cast aside, they saw a world whose ending wasna governed by divine plan. The Families were so divided as it was, that some of these Stonebreakers saw it as a way to unify. Those in power disagreed. The extremists were deemed a threat, though they were only founded on the notion of open dialogue about the rights to such power, about keeping it from the rest of the unsuspecting world. To be a Stonebreaker was to forfeit yer Denizenship.

"Cecelia was no ardent worshipper of Ancient or its laws, but she kenned there was a balance. She fought the battles when need be, defended the vulnerable, pushed for reform, and tried to make this a more just system. But she saw the cracks even before the Opal chose her. True, the Stonebreakers were extremists, but she wanted to understand their perspective.

"Ravenna was adept, and she loved the stories we grew up on. She saw her mother as a great hero fighting evil at every turn. But Ravenna was less about fighting and more about scholarship, about using her words and a well-crafted argument. She and Cecelia always clashed about the old ways in the modern world, about the privilege of power and using it scrupulously. Rare was it that Ravenna wasna over in my back garden, crying about some argument they'd had or Cecelia's need to control every part of her daughter's life. Ravenna loved being a Fox, didna understand why her own mother, the Paramount of all Foxes, could be so embittered towards the Family and the world.

"Then there was yer father. Ravenna thought he hung the moon. He wanted to give her everything, but he was of a mind with Cecelia — one of her best students, in fact — and he wanted nothing more than to shape a balanced world that he could feel secure in sharing his life with Ravenna. Raising a family with her.

"He fell into like-minded circles verra easily. He had a silver tongue. It didna take long before he was allowed into the fold of the Stonebreakers. They were a convincing lot. He kept it secret from Ravenna, and Cecelia, too. But yer da was young and rash, and the Stonebreakers' ideologies shifted around this time: they still wanted to destroy the Calamity Stones, but they felt they needed the backing of greater powers. So they turned to the darklings. They thought if they took the stones, used them to release the darklings and gain their support . . . well. It spiralled out of control. They were mobilizing to wake Zabor, even. But they got caught. Yer father included.

"Ravenna felt betrayed. She couldna stomach he'd turned on everything she held dear, that he'd be willing to do terrible things for the 'right' reasons. So she cut him out of her life, went to Canada, and stayed put. Cecelia had kept a house there for years since it was a bit o' a demonic hotspot, what with Zabor there, and to yer da, it may have well been the other side of the universe. Because he was put into a Denizen prison with the rest of the extremists, and the movement was quenched."

The fire between us straightened like a rod, flipping backward on itself as it retracted into Killian's arm, his pores reeling it back in with a crackle. He dusted off his hands and got to his feet. It was a beautiful trick, but the charm of it was tainted by him ramming his boot into the ground, scraping away any evidence of the three circles he'd drawn there.

My father, imprisoned. Was he still there? Was he still alive? "What happened after that?" I struggled up stiffly, still hungry for details. He'd already bent down, scooping up Ruo as if she weighed nothing, his former fatigue seemingly gone. "Did he ever try to contact Ravenna? Did he know about . . . me?"

"No." The answer was quick and sharp. "No, he didna know about ye. C'mon. Best keep moving."

And so we did, walking farther into the moon-brightened woods. Behind us, I swore I heard spitting and snarling, but when I turned to look, it was only a night bird, calling as it should. Then nothing at all.

A Chosen Daughter

"Firenze, Kita," the burly man nodded, going down his list. "And Allen, Barton. Yes, we've been expecting both of you." The man visibly sized up Barton from his running blades to the crown of his fade. "The debriefing has already started, but you can catch the rest of it if you slip in quietly."

Kita nodded, unceremoniously dropping her pack and adding it to a mountain of them in the loading dock where they'd ended up. Barton simply followed suit, happy to lose the load and crack his neck. It'd been a long trek from the stockyards at the end of the train's line to the industrial park and the very derelict-looking warehouse at the pier. People came and went from the loading bay, taking packs and loading them for a run to the camp at the bottom of the hill.

Kita had told him they'd only just set this place up, but it was already a hive of activity. She said it was mostly the militarized arm of the Rabbit Family that had started it, and more Rabbits and Foxes had turned up as the week went on to strengthen the growing coalition. The Coalition proper, and the ensuing camp, began as soon as the Serenity Emerald, and the Paramount, went missing.

"Now that your Owl friend is missing, too," said Kita, "this seemed the best place to set up. I'll show you why afterward."

They came to a steel door with a push bar, and Kita led them in, releasing it gently as they came into the back of a huge factory, its massive machinery rusted still and filled with thousands of old shoes. The windows were blacked out and fluorescent lights cast an acidic buzzing shine on the gathering, men and women standing or leaning on empty conveyor belts and giant steel tubs on castors. One man was talking in the factory's most open space near the centre, and Kita and Barton nudged their way closer to get a better view.

". . . unprecedented, to say the least." The man was in his forties, Chinese, wearing the same pressed green linen that everyone seemed to be wearing — the Rabbit colour.

"Commander Zhou," Kita whispered. "He runs this unit now. The former commander has gone off to lead the search for the missing Rabbit Paramount in Mongolia, but they doubt it is a recovery mission anymore."

Barton turned his full attention back to Commander Zhou. ". . . we are tracking the seismic data at the crash site and have just received word from Mala of the Conclave of Fire that after a direct conflict with Seela's infected servants, they have recovered their Paramount, and the Dragon Opal, safely in Scotland . . ."

Relief washed through him and Barton's hand twitched

for his phone to text Phae, but he returned his hand to his side. "He means Roan," Barton said, nudging Kita.

The speaker turned when Barton spoke, causing him to freeze like his powersake. "Barton Allen." The man nodded. "Welcome. You've come a long way to aid the cause, and we are grateful." He bowed and, uncertain how to reply, Barton responded with an awkward dipping of his chin. "Barton, as you all know, was one of the five who sealed Zabor in Winnipeg. Heen herself restored his formerly severed connection to Ancient, and he was able to open a Bloodgate soon after."

Barton had been accustomed to stares of pity or open scrutiny, but this was different — the room hushed and swelled with admiration, and he stood straighter.

The commander nodded smartly and surveyed the crowd, which Barton realized were all stiff and trim with an air of discipline. Fighters. Those who had trained maybe their whole lives in their Family's power. He may have just been given a strong accolade, but he had a lot of catching up to do.

"This is all the intel we have so far. The Conclave of Fire in Glencoe will be dispatching a force soon, and as soon as what remains of the de facto Council of the Owls arrives from Korea, we will send a team to Rathgar's crash site to ascertain if there were any survivors. Or any further risk. You are dismissed." The bodies began to disperse, the noise of the crowd carrying with them as they pushed for the doors. The commander came straight for Barton and Kita, hand outstretched.

Barton took it, squeezing hard. "Thank you for coming," the commander said, and his tone of hardened leadership flicked over to open fatigue. "Before Kita shows you to your bunk, I wanted to show you the site monitoring team."

"Certainly, sir," Barton replied, trying to keep alert as Zhou turned and led them through a doorway at the back of the factory through a screen of thick plastic flaps. On the other side were twenty monitors, with a team of at least that many at their own laptops, watching feeds or scrolling through walls of code.

The screens fluttered through the same image over and again, some of them moving in slow circles and focusing in and out on the rough landscape. "Drones," Zhou said, answering Barton's unspoken question. "We got quite a few down there without any interference. But they aren't picking up anything, movement-wise."

Barton went closer to the screen, squinting, pushing his glasses up the bridge of his nose. He'd never seen a scene like it: a small jet plane with a crumpled underbelly sat in a grove of twisted black trees. The emergency slide had been deployed from the plane but had since deflated, a sickening yellow against the overcast and the ashy tint to the rough landscape. He checked another feed from the drone flying the farthest up and saw that the grove was contained just around the plane, as if it had popped up overnight to hide the crash.

"What . . . how did it land so perfectly in these trees?"

"It didn't." Zhou frowned. He was standing over an unoccupied laptop, clicking and typing swiftly. The screen nearest them flickered and zoomed in on one of the trees.

Twisted in the bark was a face.

"Gods," Kita murmured.

"We have never seen anything like this," Zhou went on, tapping further. "We believe this is the work of the stonehunter and its cinder army." Zhou brought in another drone, zooming in on yet more trees, their faces gnarled in silent screams of agony, branches seeming to stretch by millimetres the longer they watched. Barton didn't say it out loud, but he wondered if Phae could get a solid long-exposure shot with this horror show.

Barton clenched his jaw. "Are these the people from the plane? The Owls?"

Zhou nodded. "And we believe somewhere amongst them is Eli Rathgar. And the Moonstone."

Barton moved closer to the monitors, nearly pressing his face against the glass to see if he recognized anything in the horribly transformed victims surrounding the deserted plane. They all looked, miserably, the same.

He turned to the Commander. "Where is this site? You said it was close?"

"Just outside of Magadan proper. A few miles off the coast. There's nothing out there anyway, and for discretion's sake the Owls are trying to keep it off the Mundane radar."

Barton was tense with the need to move. "I'd like to accompany the party that does the initial recon of the site, sir."

Zhou nodded again. "Of course. I'd expect nothing less. We are in a holding pattern until we hear from the incoming Owl Council. Or if anything on this front changes." With a few keystrokes, the top two rows of screens logged an ongoing seismograph reading. "We haven't had any hits yet, but we figured the site might end up telling us something on its own. We've never seen anything like this before. And if the geography changes, we'll need to know. In case this happens again, and so we can try to prevent it. Or at the very least minimize the damage."

Damage — military speak for casualties. Deaths. Because that's what was coming. If Eli was down there, in this body orchard . . . Surely he wasn't. There was no way he could be . . . A cold dread filled Barton's stomach as he imagined entire cities afflicted with whatever had hit these Owls — streets and cars pierced with black roots that had once been flesh and bone, the doomed victims forever reaching towards a pitiless sky.

The Commander hit a few more keys, and the monitors resumed their continuous feeds. "At any rate, you two have had a long journey. Best get some sleep." Then Zhou himself took his leave, maybe to find his own bunk, and whatever oblivion it could afford before the next march.

"After looking at this," Barton said, still staring at the ominous black shapes around the motionless plane, "I don't think I'll be sleeping for a while."

A couple hours later, we found the house.

"No lights on," I noted. The door was wide open and clapping in the breeze.

We decided to take our chances. Ruo had woken by now, and though stiff she moved obediently wherever my hand guided her. She'd been quiet, too, and I believed, however fleetingly, that we weren't being pursued and had lost whatever had come after us and the Conclave. For now.

The house sat at the top of a hill and was raised on stilts, the underside hemmed in by cedar lattice. There was a shed close by, and when we reached to the rise, I saw a road down the other side, endless empty country stretching black around it. Where did the road lead? Where the hell were we? Everything had happened so fast since the confrontation in the Meadows. And Glencoe was pretty much on the other side of Scotland, if I remembered correctly. I had no idea if I even had my cellphone when I was brought to the Conclave, and we weren't exactly rigged out with any tech aside from our hands and the will to keep one foot in front of the other. But at least there was a road: one we could follow to maybe find the Conclave and figure out what was really going on.

Ruo and I waited at the bottom of the house's stairs while Killian went up to check the inside. He held a flame in front of him, disappearing through the door.

"Is he gone?"

I startled at Ruo's voice, clear and urgent in the cold mountain air.

"Killian's just going to see if —"

"You have to go," Ruo urged. "It's not safe."

A lump formed in my throat. What did she know that I didn't? "Ruo —"

Her hand was shaking in mine, but it went suddenly still when Killian reappeared at the top of the porch steps.

"It's deserted. Well . . . guess that's a relative term. You'll see soon enough. But it's out of the wind, and we can rest here for the night."

I narrowed my eyes, let them fall back on Ruo. But she was staring at the ground, almost catatonic. What had she been trying to tell me? "And what about the Conclave?"

"Better to seek them in the daylight," Killian said, staring over my head and into the trees at the bottom of the hill. "Don't like the feel of those woods in the dark. And maybe we'll find some food here."

Food. Shelter. Quiet. Could we risk taking a breather? I knew that it didn't matter if we could risk it or not, because with Ruo our progress was already slow, undermined. It was taking a toll on us both to watch out for her, carrying her most of the way. And we couldn't go on forever.

But I felt something and I whirled to face the woods, as if hungry eyes were watching us from those trees. I gripped Ruo's hand tighter. If something came after us now, I'd be no use to either of them if I was dead on my feet. And I was in no rush to run into either those cinder kids or the Conclave, for that matter.

Killian helped me bring Ruo up the stairs and inside. He tried to shut the door behind him but realized it was broken. He managed to tie it shut with a dusty blanket he'd nabbed from a sofa just within the entry of the house.

I jerked Ruo back from going any farther in, for the thing that sat decaying in the living room was something I didn't expect to see in my waking world.

"Fuck," I blurted. "What the hell is that thing doing here?"

Killian bent down, hands on his knees as he peered sickeningly closely at the twisted black hulk that stabbed the floor and the ceiling with its gnarled . . . branches? Roots? But they'd been limbs once. There was a gaping hole in the centre of it, like a knot, and I imagined it had been a mouth. And though the bark looked tough as wrought iron, I knew if I dug my fingernail in there hard enough, it would bleed.

"Ye've seen one of these things before?" Killian straightened up. "It's what those children do. They spread this sickness and turn unsuspecting folk into these abominations. Still stumped as to whether or not there's a cure for either the kids or their victims." Then he closed his eyes in shame. "*Stumped*. Sorry. Poor choice of words."

"They're called hope trees." I guided Ruo into another recliner near the spare kitchen, tried to make her comfortable in the mouldering cushions. "A staple of the Bloodlands. And the sick SOB who runs the place."

"Urka the Gardener," Killian nodded. "Aye. Forgot ye've actually been there and went toe to toe with the vermin itself."

"Which means Mala was right. Whatever this Seela thing is, it's trying to turn the world into its own Bloodlands." I looked the black charred hunk over; my spirit eye showed a flicker of what lay beneath, its soul departed but the residue clear, though faint. "And if it was one of those kids that did this, they fled and didn't come back. The news said the virus broke out in the Highlands, right?"

Killian didn't answer, busy now tearing through the cupboards, but they'd already been raided, long ago, and the sound of skittering claws and the desperate squeaks of rodents proved there wouldn't be enough for three starving adults.

"Damn." Killian smiled, and it threw me off. "Well. At least it's dry, aye?" He took one last survey of the room and Ruo and I in it. "Right. I saw there was a shed 'round the side. Maybe there's something in there or something I can make a snare with."

"A snare?" I gaped at him.

"Aye, a snare! We're Foxes. Natural hunters. And if I come back empty-handed, ye'll both probably be asleep by then, and no harm in my grandstanding. And at least there might be a well where I can get us some water." He scratched the back of his neck. "Ye'll be all right? I won't be gone but a few minutes."

I couldn't help but smile back, trying to be reassuring. Killian had gotten us a long way under the mountains and out of the black forest, and I doubt I could've gone far without his encouragement. "We'll be fine."

And with that he nodded, strode to the door, and let himself back out into the night.

The second he left, Ruo bent over herself, coughing so violently I was afraid she was going to choke. I had no idea what to do. "Hey, just breathe, okay?" I tried to sound calm, but I felt nothing like it. "Ruo? C'mon, sit up, I'll see if I can find that well Killian was —"

When the coughing subsided and Ruo slumped back, I froze, watching her throat swallow what air it could. I hesitantly lit my hand in the dark living room, bringing it closer to her neck, and the huge black stain there I hadn't noticed before.

I felt the weight of the dead hope tree tingling at my back when Ruo's eyes opened, seeming to glow red at the edges. But how? How had she become infected between the shakeup at the Conclave and now? There hadn't been any of those kids out in the woods, none that had come anywhere near us if there were. Killian had carried her the entire way here, out of the mountain . . .

"I . . ." Ruo lifted her hands to her face. "I can see." She glanced at me, at the dark room around us, even stood up and brushed past me as she went to the open doorway. Her breath caught and she went still again.

I moved behind her but not too close. "Ruo . . . you need to come back inside."

Even from here, I saw her ragged cheeks glistening. "I'd forgotten so many tiny details. The tops of trees." As she turned towards me, I saw her milky eyes had cleared, and though fathomlessly black, they were wide behind the curtain of tears. "You look . . . so much like both of them."

My eyes stung, and I couldn't help myself. I surged forward, and she took my hands and pressed them to her mouth.

"Gods," Ruo muttered, looking at my hands in hers. The longer she stared at them, the blacker hers became. "I can feel the heat. Inside of me. But it's nothing like Deon's. It's in my blood, like an infection." She backed towards the door, clasping her fingers over her eyes. "I begged every day for my sight to come back, just once more. For my mind. And it has but . . . not like this."

Then her hands dropped. She was silhouetted by the open sky behind her, the rolling hills, and moonlight touched them, as if we were nearing the pre-dawn gloaming.

Her skin glowed like a deep mine fire raged beneath it. "You have to go," she said. "Before he comes back. Or before . . ." Her finger pointed, and I whirled to face the horrible creature growing behind me.

The tree had moved.

"You're late," came a voice from outside.

I turned again to face the doorway and dashed past Ruo to the porch, stopped short. At the bottom of the stairs stood Mala, flanked at her back by six Foxes poised to fight.

Between us and them stood Killian.

"Late?" Mala replied, her keen eyes lighting on me. "I think you knew it was only a matter of time, otherwise you wouldn't have stopped. You *wanted* to be found."

After a drawn pause, I saw Killian shrug, and he half

turned so I could see his face. "Well, ye've found us. Now what?"

Mala's hand snapped up to her chest, cupped. It erupted with a flare. "I'm going to do what I should have done when you came crawling out of the woodwork. Put you back into a cell where you belong. Roan." Her eyes still hadn't left Killian. "Come down. It's all right now."

I put myself in front of Ruo. "I dunno how evident it is, but I have no idea what is going on." I took Ruo's hand and felt her squeeze it back. Whatever the plague was, it hadn't taken her fully yet. "Ruo needs help. She's been infected with the Cinder Plague. Whatever grudge match you two have going on, I'm not going anywhere until you help her."

I saw the corner of Mala's mouth pull back. "If she's been tainted, then she is one of them. Come down now before she tries to take the stone."

"*Get out of here*," Ruo hissed, pulling urgently on my hand. "None of them matter. Only you."

"Roan," Mala tried again, her own voice matching Ruo's rising panic. "Please. Come back with us. Whatever Killian has told you about the Conclave, it's not true. He's been lying to us all since he brought you to us."

She was really not helping her case. "What are you talking about?"

Killian took one step forward, and the six fighters behind Mala lunged in kind, hands and arms primed and lit with sacred fire.

Killian laughed, and the sound carried up the hill to Ruo and me. "Ye think ye can scare *me*? It's ye who should be afraid. She doesna need me to tell her what's in front of her. What the Conclave plans to do if she doesna play by yer rules." Killian shot me a look. "Remember when they said ye canna separate a Paramount from the stone? There is the one way. Believe me, they've already considered doing it."

Mala had said as much herself. *It is a bond that can only be broken by death. We are not so desperate yet.* But maybe they were now, after what had just happened at the Conclave.

"Roan, *please*," Mala begged. "This man . . . he's dangerous. He's a liar. He's a *Stonebreaker*." The fighters were getting restless, and Mala signalled them to stand down. "I don't want to fight you. There were many injured and killed in the quake. We need our Paramount. Seela is close. And *he* —" she levelled her accusation at Killian's mocking grin directly "— brought that monster and its army to our temple."

"And who's to say it wasn't *ye* that did it?" Killian shot back. "Ye've never been beneath sacrificing yer own Family to twist things to your way. I may be a Stonebreaker, but I would never betray kin. And I won't allow ye to twist Roan to your ends." Suddenly Killian snapped his arms out, and they were wreathed in dancing embers. Sparks flicked from his hair.

I was frozen in place. Who could I trust? I'd only just met both of them, but they both had agendas. Just like the stone itself. By the look in Mala's eyes, I didn't think she was beneath cutting me down to take the stone and perpetuate the Fox Family's version of *the greater good*. But Killian had just admitted he was a Stonebreaker — an extremist who believed the stones were better off destroyed. And Ruo's warning rang between my temples.

I couldn't believe it, but . . . for better or worse, after all the grief the Dragon Opal had caused me so far, I agreed with him.

Mala seemed resigned now, and she looked back up at me with a cutting glare. Because she could see that she'd lost. "So be it." And the six fighters vaulted over her, piling onto Killian without mercy.

He met their blows with blunt efficiency, weaving and crossing, matching strike for strike as they tore into him, broke his line of defense. It was all happening too fast, the cold hillside scorching under their brutal dance.

Mala crossed the hill to the bottom of the stairs, the battle raging around her while she sidestepped it carefully. I pressed Ruo back into the house and blocked the doorway with my body.

"There's no sense protecting her," Mala said tensely. "She is one of them now. One of Seela's followers. She will try to kill you."

"And what are *you* gonna try?" I hazarded. "If you're not going to help her, stay away from her. And me." Mala was moving up the stairs, and the stone strobed a warning beneath my sweat-soaked clothes.

"I'm not here to harm you. Killian was imprisoned for as many years as you've been *alive*. When he escaped, he came to us. We granted him temporary clemency in return for finding you. And he did. Now that clemency is spent. We need our Paramount."

So the guards, the wariness. They'd been for Killian. Imprisoned? Something else flickered in the periphery of my memory, but I had to focus on Mala. She'd taken one more step but stopped, staring openly at the Opal between us. I could feel the intensity of its heat, feel my clothes burning away as it boiled from its shimmering green and crimson core. In its light, I saw the expression of Mala's utter defeat transform into something like desire. I thought she was strong, but all she saw before her was power.

Then there was a howl as Ruo pitched herself from behind me, knocking Mala down the stairs and collapsing on top of her, snapping and clawing at her face. But Mala *was* strong, and she released a burst of flame, Ruo heaving off her with a scream.

I swerved, launching from the porch and heading for the fray that had been on the cusp of crushing Killian, who was crumpled to the ground and wheezing for air. I landed over him, brought my arm up, and smashed into the oncoming blow of the icy-eyed man I recognized from the Conclave.

"Stand aside, *child*," Jacob Reinhardt snarled, straining with his full body weight on me. "This man is a traitor to our Family. To Ancient itself."

"Yeah, well. Not like Ancient really cares either way right now." I pushed my other arm behind me, felt for the hilt in my back pocket. He'd seen, but I was faster, and just as his opposing strike came down, I countered again with the flashing garnet blade, and he staggered and fell with the blow.

I felt Killian at my back just as two of Mala's guards recovered, heading back for us. They came down hard, and they were fast, better trained. We all shared at least the same kinetic thread of mania, along with the exhaustion of trekking all night with little rest or hope for it. I didn't want to hurt them, felt myself fighting both their advances and the stone's need to devour everything with its power. *Just let me in*, I felt it urge. *Let me end this for you*. No. We'd beat them back, we'd tire them out and try to outlast them. But I couldn't—

"Stop this now!" Mala cried over the din, and her fighters pulled back, bloodied and breathing raggedly. Killian stood behind me, and I heard the air rattling out of him, knew he was clutching his ribs. I rubbed my mouth and spat blood, but I didn't break Mala's glare.

She had Ruo in her arms, her forearm throttled around the old woman's char-coloured throat. Ruo bucked, gasping and shying away from the flame pressed dangerously close to her face.

I let the garnet blade clatter to the ground. "No," I heard myself say. "Fine. I'll go with you. Don't hurt her. Please." The stone was no longer hot in my breast. It was ice cold with dread. For a second I imagined Cecelia was standing near me, her face wide with the same panic. The stone was silent.

Mala shook her head, but it was her low laugh that took me off guard. "Just like her. Heroic to a fault."

Rough arms seized me, shoving me to my knees. With the grunting and thrashing I heard behind me, I knew they'd grabbed hold of Killian, too.

Mala's knowing smile widened. "Perhaps it's best we didn't get to teaching you how to control the Opal after all. Now you'll come quietly. But you need to *see*, Roan. To see what your need for justice and your altruistic pity nearly cost you. Cost this Family."

Mala threw Ruo to the ground, and she was still an old woman, fragile and vulnerable and a clattering body of bones. I struggled against the hands holding me back, but no matter what I did, I was Roan Harken Nobody from Winnipeg again. I couldn't call the fire to me.

"Stop it!" I screamed. "Leave her alone!"

Mala stood over Ruo, and in the moonlight I saw Ruo's

skin turning blacker, the coal-glow guttering. She raised her heavy head and looked right at me.

She smiled. Nodded. "Our granddaughter," she said. "My last hope." And just as Mala brought that flaming hand down on Ruo, the ground trembled.

"Bloody hell?" said the man holding me, who seemed so sure of his victory only moments before.

Then Ruo's head cracked backward at a sickening angle, and from her mouth surged an impossibly huge spear of black, impaling Mala straight through the neck and up through her skull, killing her instantly.

The rest happened too quickly to react: the ground crumbling, the Fox fighters slammed backward by rock and the very hill that seemed such sure footing before. Ruo blackened to ash and continued to grow outward, upward, arms now branches, feet now roots, spreading and creaking as the world fell down around us.

I fell on my hands and rolled, saw Killian there, his hands moving in time with each concussive blast of rock sending his attackers back. Like he was conducting a symphony. Like he was *churning the earth himself.*

He saw me. His mouth curled.

No.

Then I was in the air, too fast to stop myself as the rocks at the bottom of the hill rushed up to meet my head.

The tree didn't want him awake. It took so much more joy out of seeing him suffer, helpless, in these dreams. This time, Eli was walking barefoot along the frigid beach, pebbled with sea-smoothed stones as big as his hands. He looked down at them; they were his hands as he was now, not those of the young boy's. He smoothed them over his face. It felt so real.

When he dropped them back to his sides, his mother was there. The surf ebbed around their feet. She didn't seem to either notice or mind. She had turned, pointing out to the wide and treacherous water, where the horizon line stretched to boundlessness, mist shrouding rocks that had killed and would kill ships full of unsuspecting men.

But the sea and the sky were red. And at the edge of his mother's quaking finger, Eli saw a maelstrom. A gap in the water, a crater. A fissure rocketed out from either end of it, and a thunderbolt like a sword came down from the bloody heavens, cleaving the earth.

The sea ran into the crack, which grew wider with every pulse of his heart. Now Eli was standing on a cliff, overlooking the raging sea and the crack that split it in two. Not two feet away from Eli was Roan Harken.

She was different than the last time he'd seen her. She seemed thinner, like she was wasting from the inside. Despite the apocalypse raging around them, her arms were folded comfortably as she stared down into the abyss.

"Harken?"

Her head whipped up, those mismatched eyes widening when she saw Eli. "Eli? What are you doing here? I thought you were missing?"

He tilted his head. "What are you talking about? I'm not missing. I'm just trapped. In a godforsaken tree *of all things, because Arthurian legend is making a comeback."*

The devastation around them was mounting. And from the

wound in the earth, massive shapes were climbing out, seeking purchase.

"But this is my *dream," Roan insisted, hands now on her hips. "I must just be dreaming you here."*

"No, this dream is mine. I've been having it —"

"— for months now."

The divide in the earth was growing but, with the complete lack of concern of a dreamer, Eli ignored it, moved towards her. Reached out and grabbed her hand.

It was warm. She stiffened and yanked it free.

"This is real." She clutched her hand to her chest, looking around with open terror. "What is this? Is this really happening now? Or is it just another vision from the past?"

"Another?" He opened his mind to hers, to the awareness beyond the dream. She'd blocked him before, but now her mind contained too many images to sort. Invading memories. The stone had begun its work, showing her much more than she could possibly manage.

"Wait . . ." Roan said, recognition dawning as the three massive shapes pulled themselves free of the gash they'd made in the world. "I have *seen this before. Not like this. But on . . . a tapestry." She held her arm up, moving it in a line just above and in front of her. The apocalypse transformed into a stone room, occupied with nothing but a massive embroidered version of the scene they'd just inhabited.*

"Where is this place?" Eli asked, noting the quiet room of weathered stone.

"The Conclave of Fire. I was brought here by the Fox Family. Before . . . it was attacked. That thing, Seela. It came for me. It won't stop."

A voice warm with warning filled the room: This is but

one outcome ahead of us. The stones must not be brought together. They have the power to unmake the world.

Eli looked down at Roan's chest. She looked down at his. Both of them stood before one another, their stones exposed, flashing, painful.

"Do you think our stones are talking to each other?" Roan asked. "Is that why we're both here like this?"

They were back on the beach. Roan stood behind Eli in the shallows, looking at his mother, who stood still on the rocky shore as if she were carved from it, as if she were waiting for the wind and the waves to take her back.

"That's my mother," Eli said. But Roan hadn't asked. "I'm trapped in a tree, and I'm trapped in the stone. It's trying to tell me something. But just as I get close . . ."

A quake to shake the dead.

"Eli?"

They were back on the edge of the dangerous cliff. Now the sea beneath them was gone, having poured itself out into the core of the world. Then the cliff itself cracked, separated, and between them shot a cosmic geyser, separating them, spearing through the stratosphere and out into space. The three black figures took hold of it and vanished into the fathomless sky, to hide amongst the stars as one.

Roan teetered on the edge of the chasm, staring down deep into it.

"Harken! Wait!"

Eli threw himself through the geyser, wings beating through the blazing, boiled sea. He grabbed her outstretched arm just as she slipped over the edge and into the black, his arm with the chain-shaped scars matching hers reaching, and narrowly missing, and the world ruptured from the inside out.

❧

The sirens hooked into the seismograph system were still blaring even as the control room filled and Barton pushed his way through the chattering crowd that blocked every monitor.

"What is it? What's happening?" He found Kita at the head of the group, leaning over a tech's shoulder to glimpse a screen of streaming code.

"That." She pointed to the readout above their heads, peaks and troughs leaping off the chart. She turned her megawatt grin onto Barton, arm coming around him and shaking him off balance. "Time to earn your stripes, soldier. We're going into the field."

❧

I woke to the sound of footsteps in the grass. To the feeling of the morning sun cutting through clouds. The sound of distant thunder. It made my brain burn.

I couldn't help groaning before I opened my eyes. I was moving, prone but jostled with each step. The footsteps weren't mine. Someone was carrying me. We were in the woods, but there weren't any birds. There wasn't a sound.

"Shh," came a voice at my elbow, following close. A little girl, no more than nine, maybe Japanese. Her dark eyes were round with despair. She spoke English, a slight Scots accent there. "You're with us now. You're okay."

I was stiff with pain. My mouth was dry, throat clogged with nagging unease as I noticed the forest around me filling with those red eyes, with shadowy human shapes, following us at a distance. So many children, alert but not threatening. Not coming any nearer than the little girl had. She paced ahead.

I looked up and saw Killian smiling down at me. "There now," he said gently. "I've got ye."

I half shut my eyes against the pain. Something was wrong. Something key was missing. "Where . . ."

"Ye know," he said, in a quiet voice, "I always dreamed of carrying ye like this. When I found out ye were mine. 'Twas the only thing that got me through the long nights, trapped in a cell." The smile faltered to a bleak expression of resolute faith. "Urka showed me a life we might have had. You, yer mother, and me."

No. Something . . . The thunder came nearer. The stone shivered at my breast, insistent, waking, trying to tell me. Something on Killian's shoulder, underneath the torn cotton of his shirt, was glowing. I could barely keep my head up long enough before the Opal's sensory invasion tore my attention away.

I saw too much as it forced me into its cache of stored regrets: Ravenna, hair and cheeks flaming. A fight with words and broken promises. A man who had always been there for her, a friend, then a lover, now a traitor. A man she'd grown up with, who had learned everything he knew from her mother, the Paramount. They were taking him away for good, the scar on his face burning and fresh. Taking him away for an unspeakable act. But now he was just the reason for her to leave and start a new life, to drive another wedge between her and her mother. The new life across the sea, in a city with a river that held a demon. A river that would claim them all.

But not me. No. The stone *needed* me.

The whispers were a fury. *Stonebreaker. Traitor.*

Father.

Suddenly Killian stopped, and I toppled out of his arms into a heap on the ground.

"It will all be clear soon," he was saying, his voice odd, the easy humour gone, but the indulgent grin still there. "You defended me from them. You *chose* me. We chose each other. And now we can be the family we've both always needed."

The ground shook but not like the quakes that had torn a mountain apart. The vibrations of something huge coming closer, out of the dark of the trees. A mountain itself. A mountain with axes for hands, and six yellow eyes, and a furnace in its belly that burned with bruised flame.

"Now we can both choose for ourselves," Killian said, dragging me up by my collar and thrusting me towards Urka like I was nothing more than a weak lamb to be drowned.

"Seela," Urka said to Killian. "Child of my masters."

The demon bowed, and the dark flame lashed out to the Opal like a tongue, holding fast. The screaming hysterical whispers of the past Paramounts went out as I did, and I let the darkness win.

Part III

Fissure

Black Water

Phae had fallen into a miserable sleeping cycle of down for twenty minutes, up again for ten, trying desperately to cling to unconsciousness as the hours ticked by. The trailer was cold and uncomfortable, and there wasn't any relief for her aching back or legs, even when Aivik had pulled into a truck stop three hours into the journey just to check on everyone. But that must have been at least six hours ago, surely? She didn't bother checking the time on her phone screen. It would pass as quickly or not at all, no matter what it took. And Aivik planned to drive the entire way without stopping.

But this was the longest stretch she'd slept now — a little over an hour, her wariness of the polar bears diminished as they, too, seemed just as exhausted as their human caretakers, curled up together in the corner of the trailer. And with this stretch of time came a window to practice, as Phae could generate light in her palm without going full antlers, the small ball of brightness illuminating Siku's head as it came up with every bump in the road, every sound of a screeching car or truck careening by on the other side of the steel walls, as they clipped further down the impossibly long highway to Alberta. She gave up the light after a while, though; tried to rest. Tried to be grateful for the dark and the quiet. It meant they were still safe.

Phae didn't dream now. Not really. It was just dark behind her eyes, though they still moved beneath her eyelids, searching. It was a cold darkness — a harsh one that promised something was hiding the deeper she looked into it.

"Phae . . ."

Had that been Barton's voice?

Suddenly her eyes were open, and the only darkness she perceived was that of the trailer bouncing around them.

Aunty didn't seem to be having any problems sleeping, her snoring the only comforting noise above the rattling of crates and steel. But after checking a few times, it seemed Natti hadn't even bothered shutting her eyes yet. Staying up for long stretches seemed to run in the family.

"I can't stand this," Natti grumbled, and with a gentle ping Phae felt her hair climbing her neck, sparking up, and their corner of the trailer was bright.

"What's up?" Phae asked.

"I'm not hurt. You can put the glowy ball away," Natti said with a grin, but it fell just as quickly as it appeared. "It's the waiting. The not knowing what's going on. It's killing me." Natti looked over at the bears in Phae's light. Maujaq was sleeping but fitfully, and Siku was scenting the air.

"You must be patient, young Seal," the bear rumbled. "The Empress will guide us."

"Again with the damn Empress," Natti barked back. "If she's so mighty, why can't she just come here herself?"

The bear shook his head, unwilling to get into an argument. "Don't allow your anger to cloud what you already know."

Phae frowned Natti. "What's he mean?"

Natti waved her hand at Siku, and the bear put his great head down again. "Ryk, the First Matriarch of the Seals. She can only dwell in the sea. So she can't come on land, which is why she's got the lackey twins here." She folded her hands behind her head, staring at the trailer's rattling ceiling. "All this stuff about the stones, the Matriarchs, this 'coming doom.' There has to be more to it. Apparently bringing all the Calamity Stones together is bad news. But for what? The end of the world?" Then she looked at Aunty. "And it doesn't explain why Aunty is sick. Denizens can't get the Cinder Plague. At least, that's what we thought. So how can Aunty have it?"

"The plague," Siku said, face in his large paws, "did not come from Seela's servants. It has always been here. They are simply able to call it up, to use it, and the more they do the worse it becomes. But this illness was not *caused* by them. It is deep in the earth. It is made manifest by the land's own suffering, brought on by the people that call it home."

Phae felt her skin prickle. "You mean humans caused it? Or they made it?" Maybe it was a biological weapon, after all.

The bear tilted his snout. "Humans carried it with them since they were created. The plague is the pain of the world, manifesting as destruction and death. For every hurt that humanity has heaped on this world, the plague has grown. This was the key role of Denizens. Once, all humanity used to carry the power of Ancient, to use as its steward in the world it so carefully made." Siku seemed to turn inward, shutting his eyes. "But much has changed since then. Fewer Denizens now. Fewer who care to preserve this world over their own ambitions."

Phae didn't know what to make of the speech, nor what to say in response to it. It was so grave, so final. "So the world *itself* is sick?" She glanced round to Natti, who had lowered her arms down to her lap. "How are we supposed to stop it if it's . . . everywhere?"

"The Empress," Siku sighed, air fluttering his huge black mouth.

"What can this Empress do, then?" Phae, as usual, felt behind in the lore. That had become Barton's bag, and she'd absorbed everything he'd discovered in his research. He'd loved sharing it with her. They'd stay up, some nights, almost until sunrise . . . A lump formed suddenly and stiffly in her throat.

"All I know," Natti said, "is that the Seal's stone, the Abyssal Sapphire . . . it's kept at the bottom of the sea. The Seals figured a long time ago that the stones were better left hidden and unused, because even in the 'right' hands with the best intentions, it was a risk. The other Families disagreed, and that's why the Seals are reclusive. Don't get into many conflicts unless absolutely necessary." Natti was squeezing her fists, staring at them. "These stones are the souls of these Matriarchs. When the stones attach themselves to a Denizen, the Denizen takes on the Matriarch's power. Becomes their legs in the world, right? I have a feeling they're gonna want me for it. Or else they wouldn't have come clear across the continent to drag me into this."

Phae edged closer to Natti, which wasn't hard in such a close space. "And? Are you going to say no?"

In the light of her glowing hand, Phae saw Natti's mouth curl. "You don't say no to these things. You have to know that by now. They pick you and that's it. There go your dreams of a normal life, whatever that is."

Natti looked over at Aunty, whose snoring had been exchanged for the wheezing, rattling cough. "But if I can help Aunty . . . maybe stop other people from getting sick or, well, the entire planet getting sick, I guess I have to." Natti looked up at Phae. "I think you know what I mean."

Phae sniffed, nodded. When Roan had dragged her down this road to save a boy she hadn't even met, her already big desire to be of help stretched wider, as if it had been waiting for the space to grow. All it did was make her think of Barton again, so she changed the subject, pulling a stray strand of hair behind her ear, which licked back up to braid around the other glowing prongs.

"I have to ask," she said. "Is she really your aunt? Like . . ." Phae didn't finish because she'd seen something skip across Natti's face. Natti had never mentioned anything about her and Aivik's parents — if they were alive, where they were. But they *had* been Denizens . . .

"We're not related by blood if that's what you're asking." Natti shrugged like it didn't mean anything, like she hardened at Phae's question. "We just always called her Aunty and she always did right by us. I've lived with her my whole life. I thought maybe she was my granny, but I don't think that ever suited her." Natti pulled the emergency blanket Aivik had supplied from the truck's cab up to Aunty's chin. "Our mom went missing when I was seven. She was walking home from her restaurant job. Never made it back. She was *really* strong — a Seal from one of the old tribes. Whoever took her had to be a Denizen, too. Not much could overpower her."

Phae just nodded, listening, afraid if she asked any more questions, Natti's usual prickliness would rise again and the door on these admissions would slam shut.

"I haven't seen her in ten years," Natti went on. "I can still remember what she was wearing when she went to her shift. After she disappeared, Aunty was pretty diligent in our training, our upbringing. She wanted us to know we could all be strong, even when things were at their worst. I still believe that, but . . . how can you be strong when everything you drew on for strength is fading around you?"

Phae brought her arms around her knees. "Yeah," she said. "But you're one of the strongest people I know, Natti. You took that strength and you made it a part of you. For other people to draw from. People like me."

Natti was momentarily speechless. "Oh," she said. "Well . . . you're not as wilty as I keep making you out to be. I still can't believe you're here at all."

Phae shrugged. "Me either. Even though I don't know what I can do to help." She passed a hand over Aunty, who had nearly woken herself up from her choking, but as the prickling blue light left Phae's fingertips and snuck down Aunty's mouth, the older woman breathed easier.

"You've really got a handle on your own power." Natti nodded. "Even if you weren't born with it."

"Yeah . . ." It really was something beautiful, something that went down to Phae's core any time she could lay her hand over pain and make it evaporate, feel the cells themselves multiplying and regaining health. She'd often wondered — could someone live forever with that kind of power?

"I just wish I had someone else to talk to about it. You know, another Deer." She touched a prong of her antler that had let out a spark. "But I haven't met one. I don't know if I ever will. Barton says that the last of them lived like monks in mountain sanctuaries, but even they haven't been heard from in decades. It's like they could sense something was going to happen to the world. That maybe their own power might be sought out or eliminated. In the lore, the Deer were sort of revered and hated for what they could do."

"Lot of wars in those stories," Natti sighed. "Seems like there's always another one coming around the corner."

"War? You really think that's what's coming?"

Natti shrugged. "Nothing would surprise me anymore."

The truck seemed to be braking a lot more the further their conversation had carried. It was moving slowly, taking wide turns — they must be in a city by now. Phae reached for her bag to find her phone, see if maybe the GPS signal would be a little better so she could follow their progress. "Hey, when you mentioned the Sapphire, and all the other stones . . . that got me to thinking. About the Deer's stone. What's it called again?"

"The Horned Quartz," said a voice that wasn't Natti's. It was Maujaq. They hadn't even heard him rise, but he had moved very close to them, sniffing, much more alert.

"Right . . ." Phae dug further in her bag, bringing out the pack of jerky she'd stuffed in there. Maujaq took the entire thing from her open hand and settled in. "So if there aren't any Deer in the world, or very few, do they have a Paramount at all? Who has the stone now?"

"Fia has the stone," Maujaq answered between morsels. "The Deer sent it to the Glen. Because of what it can do."

Phae found her phone, but it was dead. She started checking her bag's side pockets for the charger. "Oh, is it a pretty powerful one? Though I gather they're all equally powerful in their own ways." But it had already planted an idea in her mind — what if the Quartz could cure this illness the world seemed to have? Could stop the Cinder Plague altogether? The Deer, after all, were healers. Surely their stone had the power to heal a darkling curse.

"The stones are all sisters, true." Maujaq licked his great maw. "But the Quartz is more than a power source. It is a key."

"To what?"

Just as Phae plugged her phone into the charger and it booted up, the entire truck jolted and the bears and the girls plus Aunty slammed into each other as if they'd come to a very sudden, unplanned stop. Or they would have, had Phae not encased them all in their own flashing bubbles, bears included.

The forcefields shuddered and vanished when the truck braked completely. Phae held her head, which was throbbing, and lit herself back to rights. The group of them had been contained in another automatic bubble of silver that Phae seemed to have conjured without thinking. "Is everyone okay?"

Aunty groaned, hacking. "I could use a smoke, but an Aspirin would do."

Phae wished she could ease the woman's obvious pain further, but she'd done all she could. Natti helped Aunty up, and the bears swivelled their huge heads.

"You feel it, too?" Natti asked them.

"What?" Phae led them towards the back of the trailer, the sound of Aivik's cab door slamming behind them as he climbed out.

"The water." Something seemed different about Aunty's eyes as she grunted. "Black . . . water."

When the trailer doors swung open, the sunlight was a knife in their eyes, and they all winced.

"Come on," Aivik said, helping Natti down. Aunty stayed behind, leaning up against a crate and taking in the rush of fresh air on her face. Aivik flinched as the bears leapt down, into the side of the road, scenting.

Phae had expected them to be pulled over somewhere bustling, metropolitan — but the blank space surrounding the highway on either side coincided neatly with her phone as she zoomed in on the map.

"We're not even in Fort McMurray —" she started, but the longer she stared, the less it mattered.

They were in the middle of nowhere — one of those prairie spaces along a stretch of highway where only a few trucks passing counted as a population. They were still fairly far from Fort MacMurray's city limits, which was more a company town than a city, made up of those who worked the far-reaching oil sands on what was possibly the last great Canadian frontier. Phae pulled her jacket closer. There was something about this place she didn't like.

The bears didn't like it, either. "Yes," grumbled Siku. "This is the place."

"The place for what?" Phae was confused. "I thought we were just going north. Why was it so important we take this detour?" Aside from the fact that they couldn't move the bears unchecked without the cover of Aivik's delivery run, the bears had seemed, from the beginning, like they thought this route was ideal, however roundabout.

Siku levelled her with a look she couldn't parse. "So you could see it for yourself." He looked to the horizon.

Phae squinted. Natti had shut her eyes, and Aivik was watching her. "We're near a river, aren't we?" Natti said.

Phae nodded, checking her phone. "We're close to the Hangingstone River, which connects up to the Athabasca. *That* flows through Fort McMurray and the tar sands . . ."

That's when Phae heard it. The mad chittering, the hungry, keening wail like laughter and furious clamping teeth. *No. There's no way.*

"Are those . . . river hunters?" Every bone in her body was still, but Natti was already grabbing Aivik by his heavy jacket, dragging him back to the truck. The bears were two rumbling tanks as they leapt back into the trailer.

"Something's happening," she said. "We need to get into the city." Aivik didn't need telling twice; he was already jogging, swinging back into his cab and starting the engine.

"What's happening?" Phae asked as Natti grabbed her hand and helped to haul her back in and shut the doors tight. In the dark, Phae lit up like a nightlight, more out of the rising panic than the need to see Natti's expression.

"There's something in the water. Even this far removed from it, I can feel it." Natti turned to Maujaq and Siku. "Is this what you were talking about?"

The truck moved back onto the highway, speed increasing. Siku pressed his face against the steel, as if he was listening for something. "Tiny cracks in the world. The drills go deep. The oil comes up, gets into the water and the land.

Kills everything in its path. It is the perfect entry point for the slaves of the darklings, making the way clear for their masters."

"Black water . . ." Natti repeated, grasping tight to a steel crate. All Phae could do was cling to her phone, watching the tiny blue dot that was them make a painful crawl to Fort McMurray, and the source of the dread in the polar bears' eyes.

On the other side of the world, the tree did not want Eli awake.

Each time he tried to resurface to consciousness, it fought him. Fought harder to make him a part of it, until flesh and mind were bonded, the soul fled, and the stone squeezed off him like a blister.

The tree knew it would be a trial. But it was a single-minded entity, bent on one thing: takeover. The tree dug deeper into the earth, stretched higher, grew tighter around Eli, but the stone had roots, too, and they went down into the heart of him. It was taking such a great effort, all of the tree's resources, to sever those roots.

Then something happened the tree did not expect: as its bark cinched inward, it felt Eli cry out in his dream, and the tremor went out from his mind and into the soil.

It shook the world.

When the quake subsided, the tree felt something shift. The stone, though awake, was coming loose.

Soon.

Aivik dropped Phae, Natti, and the bears at the edge of town and then took the truck to the depot. He'd decided to keep Aunty with him, so that receiving would unload faster — either out of pity for the woman's ailing health or because Aunty would probably yell at them to speed it up.

"For the love of god, keep out of sight," Aivik begged. "I'll be back to deal with whatever is going down with you. But do *not* go there without me. You got it?" They all stared at him as he drove off.

But Natti wasn't interested in staying put.

"Listen, you two." Natti stood proud and straight, addressing Siku and Maujaq as if they were little kids. "Phae and I are going into that gas station down there." She pointed down the hill towards the big-box plaza beyond their well-treed hiding place. "We'll be right back. But we have to find out what's going on, or if we're all flipping our lids for nothing." They'd all felt a shift in the air, and it had only gotten worse the closer they got to Fort McMurray and the Athabasca tar sands that were just in view. There also seemed to be a suspicious volume of trucks going into the tar pits and not coming back out, and the smoke they headed for seemed a bit more pernicious than the usual environmental blight. Par for the course.

"Do what you must," Maujaq sneered. "We know that to be caught is to fail before we have even reached the north." He was prickly again, the dark stain on the front of him having spread to his shoulder since they'd been out in the open air. "That place down there is cursed."

He meant the tar sands. Natti didn't argue. "Yeah, it's

a horror show. And it's the small towns that suffer from oil spills while the big companies count the money." She scowled, grabbing hold of Phae's forearm. "No time for politics, though. Let's go. I need to pee."

They crossed three massive parking lots to the plaza, and they learned more in that journey than they'd expected. People weren't in the stores — they were crowding around cars, rushing into them, slamming doors, and skidding off. The exits onto the main thoroughfares were bottlenecking. "What the hell?" Natti muttered. There also seemed to be quite a few people rushing into the gas station, which was also a truck-stop restaurant.

When Phae opened the door, she was nearly bowled over by a family hustling to get past her. "Hey!" Natti shouted at them, but they were too intent for their cars.

"There's a TV," Phae motioned, and they took their place at the back of a growing crowd.

"Turn it up!" someone called, and the guy behind the convenience counter jumped to obey, fiddling with the buttons until the sound was blaring from the news anchor on the screen.

"— outbreak of fires at Fort McMurray in the areas surrounding the tar sand. People in the city proper are advised to evacuate, though the cause of the fires is yet to be determined."

"More fires?" a man blurted. "That's just business as usual, ain't it?"

Natti assumed he was a Mundane, because some other people were exchanging glances, pointing for the door, pushing past them. If they were Denizens, they must have felt it, too.

"Forest fires aren't that big of a thing around here," Natti mused to Phae. "There has to be something else."

They went to the washroom, tried to eavesdrop on the agitated conversation floating in the snack aisles as people loaded up and head out. "Something in the water," they heard. "Creatures like . . . I don't know . . . Mundanes can't see them, but Denizens are reporting them everywhere . . ." Hushed tones. Whispered asides. Natti and Phae exchanged looks of their own and headed back outside.

"The fires have to be a cover," Phae guessed, "for whatever is happening on the tar sands site. It'd be the perfect breeding ground for . . . anything. I'm guessing the powers-that-be are just trying to get the Mundanes out. Maybe there are even Owls here right now making it *seem* like a forest fire. But what can we do?" She was twisting the strap of her camera, eyes darting around the parking lot.

"We fight." Natti shrugged. "That's pretty much my autopilot since joining up with you guys." She kept her eyes on the hill and the trees where Siku and Maujaq were hiding. The bears had directed them here for a reason, even though it was off the beaten path to reuniting them with their Empress. This must be why.

"Hey!" A beanpole of a guy came rushing into their path, and Natti came up short, throwing an arm in front of Phae, even though the guy seemed like he could be knocked over by a shockingly bad joke.

"Oh, sorry," he said, holding up his hands and removing his ball cap. "Look, I just wanted to ask — are either of you two a Seal?"

Natti narrowed her eyes, cutting a glance back up the hill, though she didn't see the bears. "Who's asking?"

"Relax," he said, and he conjured a breeze to cool his extremely reddened face. An Owl. "I overheard you two talking. I'm just trying to get some crews together to head into the sands. We need as many water-bearers as we can find, and, well, they're thin on the ground."

Phae stepped forward, hands clasped. "Can you tell us what's really happening?" She was so guileless, there wasn't anyone who could say no to that face.

"Sure," he said, fumbling for his smartphone. "We're trying to get as many vulnerable types out while we can. We don't know what to make of this." He scrolled through his gallery until he clicked on a video. "These are the tailings ponds, where they dump all the muck. Well . . ."

Something had risen, smoking and huge, from the pond. Several somethings that seemed to be splitting up, crawling onto the land, and going after anything with a pulse. There was a lot of screaming. A lot of dark stains left behind. The guy tapped onto another video, showing the things chittering and throwing themselves headlong into the Athabasca River. Someone, a Fox, managed to stop one with its fire, but the creature exploded as if it were filled with kerosene.

"I didn't make this last one," the guy answered, a bit dismayed. "Buddy of mine sent it to me. It's some crazy shit. Puts me to mind what happened in Winnipeg last spring. You hear about that? With Zabor?"

Phae and Natti cringed in unison. "Yeah, we heard of it," Natti said, but she wasn't about to say just how up close and personal they'd been. "But it can't be anything to do with, like, darklings or whatever. Can it?"

The guy scratched his head. "Don't know much about them, but . . . I hear there's a lot of weirdness going on the world over right now. Everyone's spooked. But we have to contain this before they spread. And we need all hands. You two coming?"

People streamed past, seeming to be heading for a group of trucks parked in the next lot over. Natti looked back to the trees, then to Phae.

"They'll be fine," she whispered. "Better they stay out of it."

"And what are you?" the guy quirked an eyebrow at Phae, obviously a bit unsure but happy for any help they could get.

"I'm Natti, and this is Phae," Natti said. "She's damage control."

The guy nodded. "I'm Evan. There's enough damage to go around. Let's header."

"What about Aivik? And Aunty?" Phae asked, hanging back a few steps behind Evan as they made for his truck, others peeling away around them.

"Best they stay out of it, too," Natti answered, flinching as the chittering seemed to get louder, however distant it still was.

❧

As the truck approached the gates, Natti could feel it was ground zero.

The security gate was manned, but after the guard on duty and Evan shared a nod, they drove through without stopping.

"Pays to be an Owl . . ." Natti muttered.

Smoke billowed above the site, and the foul stench this close up was brutal. Phae choked. The landscape was ravaged, trucks and machinery and plants still going at full steam to tear the ground open and extract the oil, continue production, biting away minute by minute until all that was left was a smoking wound.

"You get used to it," Evan sneered, more at the situation than the girls.

Natti scowled. "This place is a breeding ground for bad. Just surprised it took this long for something to crawl back out." The bears had been right; she *could* feel it. The same devastation that haunted Maujaq. The infection that was crawling over the world and spreading. No one was to blame but humans, clearing the way for the demons they were here to blast back.

Natti shut her eyes. "There's something else . . . the river . . ."

"These things are compromising the lines. That tailings pond I mentioned —"

Natti reached for the door. "Let us out here."

"Huh?" Evan slowed down, and Phae pressed up against Natti as the door opened before the truck was put into park, and Natti dragged Phae out with her.

"What is it?" Phae asked, once Natti had brought them down a steep incline where a few other trucks had parked. Their shoes were quickly caked with muck and grime. They were standing at a ledge overlooking a canyon twenty feet below, a conveyor belt passing through it, terminating at a series of platforms where, above, enormous trucks the size of Aivik's rig had been stalled, mid-release, in dumping their black payload.

" — crushing plant," Natti overheard one of the men from the trucks nearby, who glanced over at Natti and Phae. "Hey, what the hell are you girls doing here?"

"There," Natti pointed, ignoring him. "Look."

Black, slithering shadows were darting into the plant, sliding over the rock and seeping into any available crevice they could find. Too many to count. The chittering was aggressive, a horrible buzz behind Natti's eyes. For a painful second she remembered Brother, but there was no use in following that train of thought — because with one last squiggling body writhing into a small crack in the ground, the earth shook violently, and they watched as the land beneath the plant's platform splintered, one leg toppling into it.

And a great, oily black hand shot out, pulling the rest down.

"Shit!" one of the truck men cried, and his arm flared into fire, ready to blast.

"Are you crazy?" It was Evan, skidding down the rise Phae and Natti had just come down. "You'll blow the place sky-high, you idiot! This entire site is leaching oil!"

The ground heaved and Phae slipped. Natti reached out and grabbed her, but she was halfway over the edge. A gust of wind raked rock and soot in a torrent around them, but it also yanked the two of them back up onto solid ground in a heap. Evan pulled them up the rest of the way.

"We have to —" he started, but there was an explosion as the monster heaved its shoulders through the world, screaming with a slanted mouth that bubbled black.

Natti reeled up, saw that great crack get wider, the conveyor and the huge trucks and power poles collapsing into it like a whirlpool. The fissure was a lightning strike, decimating the sands.

"There's another one of those big suckers!" someone was calling from the rise above them. "Coming out of the tailings pond!" And without another thought to it, Natti was racing back up the rise, the noise and the stench and the destruction fading around her. She could feel the water in her blood, hear it, and it needed her.

It was just ahead, but she wasn't even ten feet away before the pond, too, exploded, and the defending Denizens dove for cover.

"Christ!" Evan screamed as the three of them ducked behind a toppled crane, narrowly missing getting doused as the toxic leachings came down in a torrent. But for all their speed and Evan rebuffing the worst of it with a gale, he still caught some on his arm, and he hissed around the pain. "Stuff's lethal . . . What the hell *are* these things?"

Natti risked a look around the crane. It wasn't that the monster was *in* the pond — it *was* the pond, its hulking shape pulling the tainted water to it around a dark core, limbs and a face materializing in the muck. The quake that had thrown them here rocketed back, closer now, and they turned as one to the canyon and the crushing pit they'd just escaped, to see the huge gaping creature that had come up from the ground climbing over, up, and towards them.

Two beasts — one water, one oil, pincer-approaching from both sides.

"Right," Natti said, and she took off towards the pond-beast.

Evan had a hold of Phae, his own panic intermingling with the need to keep her safe. "Listen, you need to stay —"

Her antlers shocked up in a wave, and she grabbed hold of his injured arm, the blue sparks snaking into the burn and righting the flesh. He stared at it in awe, despite the fact the world was coming apart around him.

"*You* need to stay," Phae corrected, and she shot after Natti into the fray.

Natti stood her ground in front of the pale, nasty Pondzilla, its huge mouth cavernous and releasing a wail so vicious her throat tensed, struggling to breathe for the fumes it gave off. She lifted an arm, tuned out the noise, and felt deep only for the water — what little purity there was left — as the creature slithered for her.

It sent out a massive arm, slamming down like a wave, but she twisted, tore the wave from its body, and threw it as far as she could, into the advancing oil beast on the other side. It howled, hissing, but kept coming.

"Dammit," Natti grunted, and when she turned back to the pond-beast it had reared itself on its wavering body, a skyscraper about to topple right onto her.

Natti held up her hands, but the weight was too much to try to manipulate, and in seconds —

But the water smashed and splashed and sizzled off the force field Phae had conjured around them like a bubble, her eyes huge and white with the strain.

Once Natti recovered, she gathered the deluge at her fists, sent it careening to either side of them, and grabbed Phae before the next salvo could knock them both down as the force field guttered.

"Sorry," Phae whispered, once they'd got the air that had been knocked out of them back where it belonged.

"We're still alive," Natti reminded her, surveying the scene. The pond-beast and the oil-beast had switched tacks now that the girls were out of sight, heading for Evan's group of hollering Denizens, which were futilely sending ribbons of wind and fire and huge chunks of rock to no avail at the monsters.

"Those monsters just keep coming," Phae said, leading the way across the open ground as they struggled up another rise, keeping back from the main conflict. "We have to contain them somehow."

"It's a lot of water," Natti said, watching the pond-beast that was bearing down on some Foxes, whose overhand fireballs just seemed to make the water creature angrier, until it deflected one and the knot of flame slammed into the oil-beast with a molten flare that made Natti and Phae duck again.

"And it's not like the Rabbits can just open the world up and put them into some crevice. I have a feeling that's what started this in the first place." Phae's antlers flickered, and she shut her glowing eyes. "There's so much pain here. From them. From this place."

There was a scream. It was Evan, thrown into a pile of discarded shale. Phae dashed over to him, lighting up like a lantern as she composed the shield around her. But by the time she had reached Evan, it was too late. She tripped backward over her own feet, as his entire body was consumed by something black and sickening, his eyes flashing red, and he exploded.

The massive black oil demon that had wrenched itself free of the earth let out a terrifying roar, and when Phae lowered her arms from her face, she saw that all that was left of Evan was a spiking, dead tree — what had been his face twisted in the bark, his branch arms reaching.

"Phae!"

The thing that had climbed out of and become the tailing pond dragged itself across from the black demon, the two of them towering over Phae, reeling back to drop onto her. Natti reached with everything inside her to pull the water to her command, but it was too much, and she wasn't close enough . . .

There was a flash. She felt water then. Too much of it. Pulled up from its moorings a few miles away and rushing the horizon like a tsunami. *Is that the Athabasca River?* The thought skidded across her awareness before it crushed the creatures in its fist, wrenching them into the air and smashing them back into the rock face that had birthed them.

It was a great power, coming from the two figures standing on the precipice of the tar pit they'd all been trapped in. Two figures clad in white, men of the same height, moving in perfect sequence as they lifted the creatures up again with the water, forcing their bodies together as the river crushed them, then froze. The crackling orb split like a seed pod from the rest of the water's mass and smashed home like a meteor into ten thousand pieces.

What was left of the river receded from this toxic place, yet dark bodies separated from it all the same, skittering off to find deeper shadows to hide in before new, more heinous monsters could re-form again.

Natti got to her feet, eyes never leaving the two men on the crest. Even their hair was white, long down their backs. The only thing that distinguished the two was that the man on the left had a dark stain on his chest between the diving collar of his robes, coming up his neck . . .

Then the river washed over them as it retreated, and they were gone.

There would be time to puzzle it out later. Natti rushed to Phae's side. "You okay?" she asked, not bothering to wait for an answer before hauling her up in her arms.

"Yeah . . ." Phae checked out the remaining bewildered Denizens who were slowly coming back to themselves, trying to figure out what had happened. She couldn't look away from the tree that had once been Evan.

"What the hell is happening?" said an older Denizen who picked up a shard of what was left of the creatures. He dropped it just as quickly, as if it had burned his hand.

"Don't!" Phae grabbed his hand, blue sparks shooting down it. But she, too, tore away from him, her hands fizzling.

"It's the Cinder Plague, isn't it?" Natti muttered, surveying both the damage and the people affected, who stared at her with a mix of terror and recognition.

"No, it . . . it can't be," said the man, staring at his hands. "That's not possible. Denizens can't —"

Natti threw up her arms. "Well, what do you call all this, then?" She pointed at the black tree they could all no longer avoid looking at.

The wind tore through the site. The world really was cracking open. And what was crawling out of it wouldn't be satisfied until it was all burned away.

"We need to go," Natti said, glancing back at the rise where the two men had been, the ones who had saved their skins. "North. Now."

United Front

Barton was getting restless. The coalition had been organizing supplies and teams to go out, but all that activity had been called to a halt. They received a distress call, and an inbound flight was imminent. The barracks were buzzing, yet no firm details had come to light. The call had been from the Conclave of Fire. Only a couple of days ago, they'd given everyone a sense of hope — Roan was with them and under their protection. Now all contact with the Conclave had been shut off. No one knew where Roan was or if something horrible had happened. If it had been an accident or an attack.

"I hear it was the compound in Glencoe. You know, the one under the mountain."

"Man, imagine a whole mountain coming down on top of you . . . too bad there weren't any Rabbits there to stop it."

"Maybe there were." Barton had learned a bit more about the people he shared a bunk space with; they'd exchanged names, a few details from home. They'd all been curious about each other — him about their way of life submerged in this world of magic and danger, them about his resurrection, his Mundane existence, his heroics.

"Whaddya mean?" asked Xander, the guy on the bed across from him.

"Well . . ." Barton suddenly regretted speaking up. He'd read and absorbed everything he could on Ancient, on his own Family, since finding out he was a part of it. He didn't want to seem like a know-it-all outsider. He took off his glasses and polished them on his shirt. "The Serenity Emerald is missing, right? Wouldn't the person who had it be able to topple an entire mountain, if that's what happened?"

The bunks went quiet.

"So you think it was that Seela thing the Commander mentioned." Roslyn, the girl on the bunk above him, chewed the ends of her messy blond hair.

"Maybe," Barton said. "Maybe I'm just getting tired of being in the dark." The tremors shifting the earth underneath Eli's crash site had been incredible, the first sign of something happening in days, apparently. Barton worried that they might be missing their chance.

Kita burst into the room, boots slapping against the concrete with her quick strides. "They're here!"

Barton stood, balancing carefully on his carbon-fibre blades. "Who?"

"What's left of the Conclave of Fire. And not only them — but the Council of the Owls as well." Despite panting, her smile was wide and wicked. "Can you imagine the drama?" She hooked onto Barton's arm and virtually dragged him along with her. "C'mon!"

The others followed at a clip to the loading bay. Huge transport trucks were pulling in. On the way, Kita told Barton that the Fox leaders had just been evacuated out of Scotland and landed in Magadan airport. The Owls had been biding their time after being kept in a safe house in Busan. They, too, had suffered an attack. These infected children seemed to be spreading everywhere, tireless and destructive.

"Maybe these kids and their leader wanted to hedge their bets in case Eli made it to Korea, where that tribunal was going to take place. I have no idea how this Seela thing is able to travel across such wide distances so quickly, though . . ." Kita pulled them up short of the loading bay as the trucks parked and the rear doors clapped open. Rabbits rushed to help the members of the Conclave and the Council down from the trucks and onto solid ground.

Barton didn't know what he was expecting — after spending time among the Rabbits in their fatigues, he figured that those at the elder level of the Families would all be Gandalf types. The people getting out of the trucks were battered, injured, and looked more like the teachers he'd had in public school than wise men. One large Black woman with a head wrap looked shaken. She was followed by a man with icy eyes and a beard, his cheek bearing a massive cut recently stitched. This man, in turn, helped down an elderly gentleman with a walking stick, who seemed to be the best put together of the three wearing red and gold tunics, torn trousers. Barton had been told to expect another woman — Mala, the Foxes' de facto leader. But she wasn't there.

Then came the Owls from the second truck. They wore silver and violet. There were four of them. Apart from their colours, the two opposing Families of Fire and Wind did not look any different — just a group of men and women who had seen too much and could do little about it.

Commander Zhou came out of the crowd behind Barton and Kita and the other Rabbits, shaking hands and embracing the Conclave and the Council in kind. They accepted his generosity with stunned looks, as if they didn't expect to find comfort here or anywhere.

"We're so glad to see you're all right," Zhou was saying.

The elderly man with the cane grimaced. "That's a descriptor I'd use lightly, Commander."

"I was sorry to hear about your compound," he replied, turning to the woman with the head wrap. "Madame Fante." Zhou inclined his head. "You were able to get the trainees and acolytes to safety?"

The woman nodded gravely. "Yes. It does not seem the intention of the attack was loss of life this time. Though we suffered it regardless." She lowered her voice as her eyes flicked to the crowd on the dock. "Mala is dead. The attack was a distraction to remove Roan Harken. When Mala tried to bring her back, Seela . . . it took her. We do not know where, or to what end."

Barton felt a knife in his chest. He couldn't breathe. He and Kita exchanged a glance, and she touched his arm.

Commander Zhou barely nodded. "I see." What could it possibly mean now, if this Seela had both the Emerald and the Opal? And what would happen to Roan . . . ?

A sharp-faced woman in hijab stepped forward — one of the Owl Council members. "Please, Commander," she said, "you told us over your message that you have been watching the crash site of our Paramount. Have you . . . ?"

Zhou's momentary stricken look flashed back to the

composure of a seasoned soldier. "Yes, ma'am, we have been monitoring it. And just as we got word of your arrival, we believe that the landscape there has changed. We picked up seismic activity over the site. We are about to dispatch a team now —"

"We will accompany you." The woman nodded, then checked behind her for the approval of the others.

Zhou balked. "But surely you must be exhausted after your journey?" Barton calculated it in his head: from Busan to Magadan had been at least twenty hours in the air, not to mention the overland travel to get to this camp. The Foxes had travelled even farther.

"He is our Paramount," said a rake of a man at the woman's side. "And he bears our stone. We must aide both."

Zhou nodded again. "Understood."

"Me as well," the icy-eyed man put forward. "I want to help. I was there with Mala's party when . . ." but he didn't finish. "I *need* to help."

"As you say, Master Reinhardt."

"Jacob." The woman with the head wrap, Akilah Fante, came towards Reinhardt with a grim look. "Be careful."

He just dipped his head, and she took the elderly man to the side, most likely to find rest for the both of them.

Commander Zhou turned crisply to a group of Rabbits, speaking into a device at his ear. Kita seemed to be buzzing beside Barton, leg jiggling. "Here we go," she said. Barton could see the sun rising higher just outside the loading dock as they started putting the trucks together with whatever supplies and tech they'd need.

Here we go indeed . . . But Barton didn't know if he was

ready, let alone what would be waiting for them out there. And if they stood a chance against it.

❧

Eli slept but dreamt of nothing.

Darkness. Peaceful and devoid of thought. Of the hundred-fold voices. Of the intruding thoughts of those around him that he fought to keep out each difficult day he'd lived.

Of memory, precious or poisonous.

It was as dark inside the tree as in his mind, but something tugged at the edge of that dark, at the barest corner, trying to peel it back.

He heard a rustle.

Opening his eyes, Eli peered out for what he assumed was the last time, watching the grove of the dead. The rustling he'd heard was the wings of moths, gathering and fluttering from one tree to the next.

He couldn't hear Solomon's mind any longer when he cast for it. There would be no turning his head inside this cage, but the tree that had once been the man he'd not yet called father was within eyesight.

And so was the great winged creature beside it.

The Moth Queen turned to Eli with the slight grace her great triangular wings afforded. She came towards him on legs he couldn't quite see, many hands folded before her arching thorax in patient supplication.

Eli's mouth was blocked, still full of the tree's dark matter, seeding his body and separating him from it breath by breath. He knew this confrontation would not have the need for words, anyway. He opened his mind as if it were a closed fist, fingers stiff as claws.

So you've come for me at last. He cast the thought out, a weak tendril, and he saw Mother Death bow her head.

"There are many here who need my tending." Her fathomless black eyes flashed. "But you are not one of them." Her voice was harsh in his mind — nails across slate, yet even that was more comforting than the silence.

He glanced at the tree that bore Solomon. *For him?*

The Moth Queen did not turn. "Soon."

It's only a matter of time. For the both of us.

The Moth Queen came closer to Eli, leaning her head back to take in the full height of his tree. Her thorax stretched and Eli swore he heard a humming between every chinking vertebrae, her entire carapace calloused with age like armour. "You are different now than when last I saw you," she said, "for I have been checking in on you for you a very long time."

Eli didn't directly respond. He thought of the beach, of the little cottage. Of the caer of stone, when he had last seen the Moth Queen come for his mother — and as quickly go.

Different, well. Eli might have been dying, but he couldn't help himself. *I wasn't a tree back then.*

Death does not laugh, but the corner of her puckered mouth lifted. "The tree is cunning. It is trying to remove the stone from you because its master was too weak to. And it is succeeding, because you are letting it." Eli felt her pointed hand, the pressure of it, touching the Moonstone at his breast. "The stones are fickle things. Mortals seek them for power. The stones perceive this and seek mortals to do their bidding. Ancient trusted the stones to this world, and it seems I have been made custodian of the consequences that trust wrought. Always carrying away the innocent who perish in the wake of the conflict the stones continue to wreck."

In his rare moments of waking, all Eli had were his regrets. To remember, vividly, the things he'd done in the service of the Moonstone. In the service of the Narrative, and the things he once thought he wanted. Believed in.

Can you take it from me before the tree does? he asked. Pleaded.

Her great wings shivered. "I can only take you from the stone. And it is not yet your time."

But he was so tired. He had forced himself to live, to carry on. Maybe that was just the stone itself trying to keep connected to a life. Eli's life. He had wanted to survive. But now . . .

I wish to be free.

The Queen bent her head again, considering him. "That will be up to you. And her."

Her?

The Moth Queen's needle-pointed digits ran over the bark that held Eli in its stifling embrace. Eli felt it trying to shy away from her, could feel its coils gripping harder to him, possessive. It was getting tougher to breathe without focusing.

The Moth Queen shut her many eyes. "Help is coming. It is up to you to take it. And to give it back in kind. There is a light in you now, when before there was only darkness. It is faint, but it deserves to be in this world a little while longer. The same light struggles in the heart of another, so much like you. Her light will diminish. The Fox child will need you before the last. Only you can free each other."

Roan. He'd never considered Roan Harken anything like him. She was brash and sarcastic and could never survive on her own. Maybe her stone, the Dragon Opal, really had reached out to him in the dark. So it hadn't been a dream, after all.

The vision we shared. The crack and the sea —

This time the Moth Queen said nothing, gave nothing, just stood still as if she was carved from the earth. Her flickering moth cabal flocked to her and settled like a cloak. "When the time is right, I will come for you. I am the only certainty."

With the last whispered word in Eli's mind, suddenly she was not there at all, may never have been, and the moths faded into the grey.

Then Eli heard a sound he never thought he would again: engines in the distance. Human voices calling to one another through the mist.

But Eli never made out what they were saying, because the tree could hear them, too, and it had worked too hard to fail now. So it squeezed with everything it had, and Eli let go.

The group had spread out, each team leader carrying a handheld seismometer.

"There!" Kita cried, and Barton and the others clamoured close. "A slight one this time. I could feel it before the monitor. But it is coming from here."

Barton looked up to the way in front of them. The mists were still shifting at their feet, the only sound the creaking of the skeletal trees as the barest wind moved through them.

No one seemed very inspired to move forward, even

as Commander Zhou's team drew back from their own reconnaissance.

"Do you recognize any of them?" he asked Barton.

Barton pushed his glasses up the bridge of his nose. He took a step gingerly, then another, the ground hard beneath him and giving nothing away. He forced himself to look, although it was painful, eyes trying to make sense of the gnarled knots and thick bark, trying to find Eli in them. Hadn't this been a game he played when he was a kid, that all kids played? *Find the face* — in trees, in buildings. When played at night it was even more thrilling, letting your imagination conjure demons in your own backyard. But this was in full daylight, and it was no less chilling, because the longer he looked, the clearer the faces pressed to the surface. *Help me*, they seemed to say. *Please, gods, just let me die.*

"Over here!" someone shouted. Barton jumped, staggered away from a trunk he'd leaned into to get a closer look. He spun, inelegant on his blades, and went to find the voice.

One of the Owl Council members was flanked by the other three, and Barton's team closed in on her. She was standing before an enormous tree, its branches spread in twin forks over it. Like bone wings.

"This is him," she said quietly. "This is Eli Rathgar."

Barton didn't need to get any closer to know it. Shining in a black knot that looked like a tumour was a white stone, flecks of gold shimmering along its surface, though faded in the gloam.

"It may be him," said the lanky Owl beside her, "but I cannot hear his thoughts. They're . . . they're silent."

Barton searched the group of Rabbits, looking for the commander. "But what does that mean?"

The Owl woman in hijab who had called them all here served him with a withering look.

"Can't we free them somehow?" This time it was Kita.

Nearby, the commander took a chance, laying his gloved hand over the bark of the demonic tree nearest him. He shut his eyes. "We are connected to all things of the Earth. But these are beyond us. They're not natural. I *can* feel something in them, but . . ." He looked up to the Owl woman.

She nodded. "The trees themselves are giving off thoughts. A single thought, as a parasite might. Total takeover." She swept the grove with another pitying expression. "These people were encased in these things like tombs. The thoughts of most of these victims are either silent or about to be." She looked back to the tree that held Eli. "I'm afraid we are too late."

But Barton wasn't about to accept that or stay silent on the matter. "No," he said, "that can't be it. There has to be a way!"

This time, the Fox Conclave member, Reinhardt, came forward. "I'm sorry, lad." He bowed his head to the stricken Owl Council members. "At least you can perhaps recover the stone."

That made Barton stiffen with shock. What about Eli? Didn't his life matter in all of this?

"That stone is not for you," said a voice behind them, and the crowd turned as one.

A boy with a mat of greasy dark hair stood in the grove. His skin was flocked with the black marks of the plague that the Denizens Barton had talked to seemed all too certain was as unnatural as the trees around them.

"Stand back," Commander Zhou ordered the group. "Don't let him touch you."

Kita frowned, speaking through her teeth. "I thought the Cinder Plague didn't affect Denizens."

"Look around you," Reinhardt said dryly. "Every tree in this grove was a Denizen once."

The boy surveyed them from hollow black eyes ringed with pulsing red. "That stone belongs to my father, Seela." He straightened his spine, like he was completely resolved. "Soon it will be ready, and he will take it, as he took the first one. And when he smashes it, smashes them all, we will *all* be his children. Children of the Bloodlands."

Kita seemed to be humming with fury. So did the other Rabbits around Barton; he could feel it in the ground beneath them. They had gathered in this remote place to be of help in this time of crisis, but Barton hadn't realized until now how deeply the Family mourned their lost Paramount. They wanted revenge.

"There's just one of you, little wretch!" Kita lunged, too fast for Barton to stop her.

She stomped and the ground surged, all the rocks in the radius of her boot separating from the earth and raining down on the boy. He was impossibly fast, weaving between them as if he knew exactly where they'd fall, but other Rabbits went into play, lifting their hands and trying to bury the boy as he dashed out of sight, deeper into the dark trees and the rising mist.

The team rushed after him, Barton bringing up the rear.

"Wait!" he called into the din, his blades devouring the distance as he raced after them, but he pulled himself up short. There were shouts, screams. The mist was a curtain; he couldn't see a foot in front of him. The trees loomed large, and the grove seemed to thicken. The ground quaked as the

Rabbits pulled power from the earth. Kita was right; it'd only been the one boy. How was he getting away?

"Got you," a disembodied voice sang. Barton whirled, but he was too late — the boy leapt out of the trees and caught him around the middle, holding tight to each wrist as he locked on. Barton staggered, tried to shake him off, but the boy was crackling hot, his skin going completely black and popping with bright cinders as he shivered and blackened and burned.

"No!" Barton screamed, but the boy exploded, and Barton became just another gnarled addition to the brutal landscape.

❧

"Barton."

Everything seemed to squeeze tight. Every breath wasn't enough. His glasses had been lost in the chase, but even with them, he knew he wouldn't see anything in the deep darkness that awaited him when he opened his eyes.

"Barton . . ." Someone was calling his name. He couldn't hear it but felt it inside him, and no matter how hard he tried, he couldn't stretch his mouth open to answer.

Help me, he pushed the thought out with everything he had.

"I can't help you now," the voice replied. "Only you can. Remember the power you were given. Remember Heen's gift. *Remember*, karagosh."

Phae? But how —

"I can heal a lot of things," she said — it was something she'd said back in the beginning, when they'd first met, "but there are some things you need to take care of yourself."

Something flickered in the dark, there and gone. Heen's gift . . . Though he couldn't see it before him, he did remember — the Warren. The sacred resting place of the Rabbits and the First Matriarch. The huge hare with ears made of branches, eyes keen and all-seeing. Merciful.

He felt that snout on his outstretched hand again, felt a prickle climbing up his fingers, over his arms . . .

His arms.

The darkness in front of him splintered, just a hair. The tree seemed to be gripping him tighter, but Barton shoved back. Felt his fists tightening, the veins becoming vines, becoming roots. His fingers twitched and they became branches themselves, splitting the bark from the inside.

No! someone cried out. It hadn't been Barton, or Phae, or Heen. It was the tree.

The black split further, cracks like lightning. He pushed harder.

"Yes," Phae said, and he felt her smile against his mouth, just as he let out a guttural scream, and the tree shattered around him like broken shale.

Barton woke to someone turning him, to a face swimming above him. A dark face, with long black hair, crackling into antlers. He cupped it. "Phae . . ."

But Phae was gone as the passing wind took the mist, and it was Kita helping him to sit up. He snatched his hand back, jerking into full awareness. "What —"

"It's not possible." There was a crowd of awestruck faces and mingling voices, and Commander Zhou broke through to help Barton back to his feet. "You're . . ." He padded him down, incredulous. "You're alive."

"Seems that way." Barton coughed.

"But how?" Reinhardt came closer, flanked by the Owl Council, but they froze in their tracks as they stared at Barton, who in turn was staring at his own hands.

The roots that comprised his arms were writhing gently over one another, reknitting into his fingers, his hands.

"Heen's gift," Barton said, wringing his hands to get the tingling out of them. Then he looked over the group, turned back the way he'd come when he'd chased the boy in here in the first place. "Take me back to Eli's tree."

It wasn't far. There was a tense excitement as the Rabbit teams gathered, Barton stepping forward alone. But the Owl Council members were still dubious.

"We can no longer hear his thoughts," the councilwoman repeated. "He is lost."

Barton hesitated, not sure if he should defer to her rank and experience, but he dismissed both as he let the vibrating sensation back into his tendons. "Then it won't hurt to try, either way."

As Barton's hands changed again, hardening and growing outward at a speed no real tree could manage, and he pressed them to either side of the stone lodged in the septic bark, the Moonstone's light fully diminished now.

"You may not be my favourite person," Barton said under his breath, "but you don't deserve to die." And the roots that had been his fingers pierced the thorny bark, going deep.

The ground shook.

Barton was aware of the gathering calling out, but he grunted, hanging on. "C'mon," he muttered, teeth set hard.

He felt fingers brush around his arm, supporting him. For another bleary moment he thought it was Phae, but it was Kita. "Keep going," she said. Barton rooted down into his thighs, into the blades that dug for purchase in the shifting ground as it rippled around them.

Something let out a wail so fierce and ragged that it cut through Barton's concentration. It was the kind of sound he'd heard last spring, when putting everything he had into keeping a Bloodgate open on the other side of the world. The things he'd heard from that dark pit would stay with him forever.

Then the wail became a roaring wind, so high and sudden it took the breath right out of Barton, but he managed to look down in time to see the Moonstone sparking, just before the grove erupted in a hurricane of light.

When the brightness cleared, and the wind died, Barton coughed. He was on the ground again, and he could hear the others behind him coming blearily back into awareness, into motion, as they recovered from the shockwave.

Someone gasped, and Barton jerked as the roots returned into his sore, trembling hands.

Standing before them all was Eli, his ragged eyes mercifully open and gazing out into the gathering like he'd just survived a shell blast.

His wings were bent above him at odd angles, until they snapped down and free from his body altogether, black feathers disintegrating before they touched the ground. The stone at his bare chest thrummed, then dimmed again, but it didn't go out. His clear eyes fell to Barton, and he frowned.

"Took you long enough," he managed to croak, before collapsing to his knees and falling flat on his face.

Barton turned his stiff neck towards a dumbstruck Commander Zhou, and the blank yet relieved Owl Council. Medics rushed towards Eli, turning him over and checking his vitals, confirming that he was alive, though unconscious. "He's severely dehydrated," Barton heard someone say, as Kita helped him back to his blades.

"Our Family owes you a great debt," said the sharp-faced woman, extending her hand. "Alena Jahandar. I've been acting in Eli's stead."

Barton shook her hand stiffly, the feeling coming back in sharp pangs. He watched them take Eli away, then looked back at the utterly still grove of the dead.

Kita nudged him, holding up his glasses, which, miraculously, hadn't been trampled in all the excitement. He put them on, pushing them back up his nose as he settled into the frame of mind to do it all again, however many times it took.

"Okay. Let's see if there's anyone else I can shake loose from the grave."

She Wakes *in* Flames

I don't think I'd ever known what it felt like to burn. Not before Zabor. Not after. The fire was a part of me. *Fire cannot harm a Fox.* I *had* felt cold, of course. There were limits to the human condition, and I was from Winnipeg, after all. Suffering and surviving the harsh winters were a point of pride. But they'd never had an effect on me.

Now if I were thrown headlong into a prairie wind, I'd probably pass out.

I don't remember ever getting a fever, either. Burning from the inside with infection. But that's what this was — like my cells were being sizzled to a crisp one by one. Here, in the dark, in the burning. It's all I could leapfrog between. I was awake, and aware, and I didn't want to be. I curled around myself, shaking. I was sick.

Well, in more ways than one. I rolled over painfully and vomited. I hadn't eaten in so long, so there wasn't much to it, but the bile heaved through me and I quivered with the effort of just holding my head up, keeping my face out of it.

"Here," someone said, a cup manifesting by my face. "Drink."

I snapped my arm up to bat it away, but that took too much effort, and I fell forward on my hands. Rough gravel bit into them as my fingers pressed like claws, as the dizziness subsided.

"You have to drink." The cup was put down next to me by a small hand, blistered with black and enflamed at the edges. I lifted my head. It was that little girl, the one I'd seen in the Meadows, the same one who had been in the woods . . .

Her black eyes caught me off guard — the coal-fire at the centre of them instead of a pupil. Ruo's eyes, before the end. Before she'd killed Mala and turned into . . .

I dry heaved.

"I know it hurts at first. It always does." The little girl sat down beside me, drawing her knees up in her skinny bare arms, splotchy and crackled with black marks. "Eventually your body gets used to it, I think. Eventually you won't have to eat or drink, but . . . maybe you'll be different. Because of the stone."

I sat back on my haunches, willing my head to cease pounding. I'd taken the water, drank it all desperately. I was getting tired of being tired. "The stone?" For a second I had to really process her words. Then I looked down at my chest, at the Dragon Opal that had grown heavier and heavier as the months passed, that had kept me up nights and put me in danger and had made me hurt people.

The stone was dead.

I touched it, and it was as cold as me — cold as any rock

or gem pulled from the earth. Still beautiful, with a lustre of the uncanny. But it was silent. No voices raged to tear me limb from limb. No searing comet of fire blasted out to defend itself. The core of it, bright like the sun, was dim, the corona edges dull.

But my skin around the stone was black, like the markings on the little girl, and the breath I'd tried to catch just now came out in quick, desperate gasps.

"What did you do to it? To me?" I looked at my hands — they, too, had dark splotches, but for now they were like pinprick freckles. Nothing like Ruo's infection had been. Nothing like the spread of it over this little girl in front of me.

Not yet.

"It's all right!" the girl crawled towards me, but I scuttled backward, holding my hands up. "You're with *us* now. You're safe."

"You fucking *infected* me!" I snarled, rubbing my hands on my dirty jeans, as if I could wipe the black off. "No. This isn't . . . It can't hurt me. Can't hurt Denizens." But the black was still there, and I felt younger than the kid in front of me, face contorting under the sob I couldn't control. Most of all, I'd trusted that the stone could protect me, but it hadn't.

The little girl didn't respond right away. She was staring at the ground, kneeling in front of me. There was something different about her; the cinder kids I'd come across had a sort of mania to them, a breathless, mindless loyalty to whatever it was they served. This girl seemed to be considering her words very carefully.

"I think the sickness is getting smarter," she said. "It's feeding off everyone's fear. Off the pain of the world. And the world *should* be afraid. Because Seela and Urka will not stop. Not until they have what they want." Her strange eyes lifted to mine, and they were miserable. "It's okay if you're afraid. I am, too."

I rubbed my eyes hard, then immediately stopped, terrified I'd spread the black by further touching my skin. I couldn't wallow; panic was surging through me like a drug, and I staggered to my feet. "I'm getting out of here," I told her, told myself. I didn't care anymore.

She didn't get up to stop me. "It's no use."

"Where the hell are we?" There was a shaft of light coming down above us, but all around the walls were made of rough rock and stone. The air was slightly damp, like there was water somewhere nearby — and when I quieted my ragged breaths I heard it — rushing. Were we underground? I scaled the jutting rocks as high as I could, but the opening was still too far to reach. I started feeling around for footholds, handholds, anything . . .

This was too familiar. And my spirit-eye was happy to oblige just *how* familiar it was by sending a shocking briar of memory piking through my vision. Suddenly the moisture in the air was replaced by ash, and I was deep in a pit of another kind. A kind where the ground was made of glistening worms.

The scene was clear as if I were there, back in the Bloodlands, and when I looked down to my arm, a thin golden chain bound me to another.

Eli. He was right there, right beside me. We stared at each other.

"Harken?"

I counted heartbeats. "What's happening?"

The hands of our bound arms were close, pressing into

the wall of the pit. His fingers twitched, but they didn't reach for mine.

"Looks like you're at the bottom of another pit," he said, looking up, then back to me. "I suppose you want me to tell you to do it again. But I think I've got my own pit to climb out of."

And then Eli was gone, and so was the ashy chasm of months ago, and I collapsed backward.

"Are you okay?" The little girl had rushed to my side, clinging to my arm. When the daze passed, I flung her off.

"Get away!" I tried to move aside, but I didn't get far. I grabbed my head. What was happening? There was déjà vu, but this was different. A sensory overload. Eli had been here, *here,* and I'd felt him. It had been real . . . but then again, so had most of these visions that had plagued my every moment — conscious or unconscious.

I pushed up the sleeve of my torn hoodie, exposing my pale skin and the chain-shaped scar that wound around it. The black hadn't reached it yet. This part of me was still safe. Ever since that day, Eli and I had been connected. True, we had barely spoken. He wasn't the text-to-see-how-you're-doing type. *Definitely* never the dating type. When the hell did I have time for that, anyway?

But I had thought about him often, even before Phae had suggested I call him. Now it might be too late. He was missing — maybe worse. But he had gone through what I had, with the stone, struggling to stay in control. Somehow he was reaching out to me. Or was I reaching out to him? It didn't matter. I glanced up at the light filtering down on the little girl and me. Yeah, Eli had tried to kill me. But now I understood why. The voices. The demands. Losing yourself entirely. Even if the stone was dead, how far away was I from that?

I wished he was here. I wished any of them were here. I'd pushed them all away . . . Phae, Barton, Natti, my aunt and uncle. And now I was a prisoner. Now I had no one. And it was very likely I wouldn't see any of them ever again.

"It's okay," the little girl said again, drawing away to a distance and taking a seat on a jagged rock, tucking stray uncombed hair behind her ears. "He'll come back for you."

I snapped to face her; she wasn't a Denizen, how could she know what I was thinking? "Who?"

The girl didn't look at me, just the ground. Always the ground. "Your father."

My jaw locked. That knowledge came back all too quickly, and I felt sick again. "Killian is *not* my father."

"Maybe not yet, in your heart. But he will try to be. He will try very hard." The girl shrugged. "Better to have a father you don't like than none at all."

"I sincerely doubt that, and I'd know," I retorted bitterly, pulling myself up on a rock to take stock of things. I didn't know how long I'd been down here or how much longer I'd have to wait for answers. To confront Killian, the real mastermind behind everything that had sent the Five Families scrambling. Killian . . . Seela . . . How could they be the same person?

I was trapped down here with this little girl. That was the only thing I had control over right now. So I best make the most of it.

"What's your name?"

The little girl lifted her head slowly, as if I was the first person to ask her that in a long while. Her face was slack as she searched mine, as if she'd find the answer there. "Saskia."

I nodded. "Roan." *Even though I don't feel like Roan*, I thought. I had too many questions, but I figured I'd get more out of some more personal ones. "What about your parents? Do they know you're out here? Wouldn't you rather be with them than . . . wherever it is we are?" She may be down here with me, but I bet she was no prisoner. Was she here by orders to watch me? Or was it something else?

I didn't know how far I'd get with this, but it didn't matter. I clearly wasn't going anywhere for a while. Saskia dropped her head. "I don't know where my real daddy is now. Maybe he is looking for us. Maybe he gave up and decided to have a different life. Maybe that's for the best." Her mouth twisted, but she didn't cry. "I did this all for Albert, to bring him back. But even he's gone now. For good, I think. You can't bring the trees back. I know that now." She swiped an arm over her eyes. "This is the only family I have. Seela is the only daddy any of us have. And Urka . . ." But she stopped herself, looking around as if maybe she'd said too much.

Then that hadn't been a dream. Urka was really here, in our world, primed to wreak havoc for its masters.

I leapt up and scrabbled over to her so quickly that Saskia jumped. "How did Urka get here? What did it do to me?" I touched the stone, tried to will it to come to life and threaten her, but it was still so cold.

Saskia looked from me to the Opal, touched it herself. "Pretty," she said, her eyes far away, like she was any little girl pining for a treasure. "No wonder Seela wants these stones. They are like magic."

I pulled away. "Seela. You all keep calling Killian that. Why?"

She raised an eyebrow at me. "Because that is his name. Maybe Killian *was* his name, from before. But that man is dead. There is only the creature who is the one true child. And he wants what we all want. His family."

Suddenly something heavy slammed open — or shut — above us. A door? I lurched up, tried to scale the rocks and slipped, landing hard on the jagged edges and cutting my hands, scabbing my knees.

"Careful now," came a soft voice above me — soft and strange. "Wouldn't want to damage the goods."

I jerked back and pressed myself to the wall of the pit, grimacing. The light filtering down on us came through a grate, and I couldn't tell if the thing on the other side of it was a man or woman. But it was *alive*. It looked like a hope tree, gangrenous-seeming flesh all gnarled and nasty and shaped into a *mockery* of a person. It wore ragged clothes, and it hooked a large, blunt limb into the grate, yanking back until the door swung open on rusted, dripping hinges.

I felt Saskia beside me. She frowned up at our monstrous jailer. "Corgan," she said, "you've been gone a long while."

The creature inclined its head. "Master went far afield. There is news on the wind. Our path ahead has changed, the Moonstone reclaimed by our enemies." If the thing had eyes I couldn't see them. But it did have a mouth, working around a crushed palate as if each word was a moist, rotting morsel. It reached its crooked appendages through the grate. "Up now."

"No, don't!" The warning was automatic, but Saskia just served me with a blank expression, held out her arms, and let the monster called Corgan pull her up and out of sight.

For a second I couldn't see them, heard heavy steps of retreat. Panicked, I grabbed for any rock I could, trying to scramble out — maybe this was my chance —

I lost my hold when that massive, eyeless head jerked back into the space. It snapped out for me but I flattened out of the way.

"You next," it said gruffly.

"I'm not going anywhere with you," I snarled, and as fast as I could without splitting my head open, I scrambled back down into the bottom of the pit. I could still hear distant water; maybe there was another way out. It was time to call the fire up, but I was exhausted, weak, so when I tried it was like flicking a lighter low on fluid.

But I didn't get more of a chance to try, because Corgan pushed itself through the opening above, landing heavily in front of me.

"My master bids you to come," it said, rising back to its full height. Its neck was thick and long, the head hanging from it like the tip of a shepherd's hook. "And I will take you to him."

I didn't know if I had it in me to fight, but I'd have to find it. "Come and get me then," I said, feet sliding apart in the practised stance that Sil — Cecelia — had taught me.

Something black shot towards me with the force of a harpoon. I barely dodged with a slide, grunting. It had separated from Corgan's body and stabbed through the stone behind me, shivering with the impact.

"Crap."

Another shot out in quick succession and caught my sleeve, nailing it to the rock. I ripped free just as the monster came at me like a bear; I scampered out of the warpath on all fours.

Corgan growled, but underneath it was a hideous laugh. "Just like vermin, crawling away." I got back up, fists in front of me. This thing was huge but it was fast. I flexed, heaving through my nose. *C'mon, fire.* I tried to build up the pyre within, but there was a pit inside me yawning wider than this one. At the bottom of it were white, spent ashes.

Corgan lunged, this time with its entire arm smashing into the ground where I'd just been moments before. I had been backed into the other side of the pit, and I watched as the monster struggled to remove the arm, a mass of black, shuddering cables.

I had to do something. I shut my eyes, trying to call the fire again. I muttered under my breath, "Deon, Cecelia, Ancient, anyone . . . please. Put your power on my name." I had never felt the need to beg, had always been able to trust myself and my abilities as they grew. But the stone was still quiet, and the power I'd had before seemed gone. Was it exhaustion? Or was it the infection Urka had put on me like a curse?

"You will come in one piece or many." Corgan finally yanked the arm free, and it retracted, almost going *inside* its body, like it was winding up for another strike. "Master did not specify his preference."

I slid along the rock face. Wind whistled through the grate at my back. I didn't dare turn my head to judge the distance. It was far. I'd have to be fast. Corgan was faster. But if I beat him, I could get out. I could run. *Where? To who? Shut up, brain. You're not the voice I need right now.*

Roan.

A whisper. Faint. The last words of several dying someones. Or just one. I squeezed my eyes shut, ground my teeth. "Please." Was that a spark? "*Please.*" I was struggling to flick a lighter to life around its child safety lock, finger bleeding for the effort —

When I opened my eyes again, the cabled arm had let loose like a cannon, and in seconds it would be inside my skull.

But it stopped.

I looked down. *I* had stopped it. Caught it, in fact; my fingers crushing it in my grip, which was clawed, furred, the arm of Deon. But something was wrong. I felt the transformation take hold, but I was still so cold. And the Opal was quiet.

And my fire was black.

"No —" But I felt myself growing, huge, taking up the pit and now towering over the Corgan-beast, which snarled through its croggled jaw. I felt my fist clamp down hard, heard the guttural scream of the creature as I snapped the arm into splinters. It crumpled to the ground, howling.

No, stop! Now I was trapped *inside* myself, helpless as I went after the miserable wretch and couldn't control what my body was doing. I picked Corgan up and smashed it into the rocks like it was a toy. I saw the dark flames licking off it, licking off *me*, and the sick feeling inside took hold, the dark fire climbing. Where was the bright and burning flare, the god-fire that rose of its own accord, the familiar, basking warmth?

Where was *I*?

Roan, the voice whispered. Teasing, mocking. *This is what you wanted, Roan. You* wanted *the power*.

No, I screamed back, pulling the great demon up from the ground, slamming it into the ceiling of the cavern above me. *Who are you? Get out of my head!*

Push me out, it dared, as if it were the easiest thing to do. *Go ahead.*

I felt the demon going limp in my hands. It was over. *Not yet*, the shadow whispered, and the hands, my hands, tightened, bringing the body down carefully and laying it over the rocks in the scant beam of light as I stood back.

It was bleeding, if you could call it that. Dark fluid oozed from the wounds in its head. It cowered, pitiful now. It was only a servant, a lowly prison guard. Even if it was a monster, all I'd wanted was to get out of here.

I felt my nine tails rise, pointing upward like spikes, and I reached behind me — reached for the slate hilt of my blade, and in front of me the empty hilt shuddered, as if in pain.

The black fire consumed it, slow and deliberate. When it peeled back, it revealed only a blade of black, cruel glass, and in it I saw my reflection.

It was not the fox warrior aspect that mirrored Deon. My face was covered in a mask of blood-stained bone, a corroded skull that was a cruel imitation of a fox's head.

I took the blade in both hands and looked at Corgan. It cradled its snapped arm, shivering.

The corrupted blade was hungry. I could feel its need stabbing into my arm. Could see only moments ahead when the blade hacked into the creature grovelling before me, separating it into bloody black pieces.

Do it now, coaxed the voice, as if it was comforting me.

The blade wheeled back and arced down —

— but did not connect.

"No," I said, feeling my blood burn, fighting back for control of my own body. The blade flickered, the black fire giving way to spitting, bright sparks.

DO IT NOW. The voice was a roar, and I threw the blade aside like it was a snapping venomous snake.

I took a step back. It took everything in me, until I was stepping over the mangled creature, my head pushing through the grate it had left open. I shouldered my heavy god-body through and into a wide space, could feel myself being lost again as the dark thing at the back of my mind fought for purchase there.

But I held my ground, and soon the dark fox warrior melted away, the black flames pulling back like cracked lips, as I went down deep and untangled the knots choking the heart of me, one by one.

I let out a gasp, and I was myself again.

"Don't worry," someone at the far end of the space said, not unkindly. "We've plenty of time to work on that."

The room was utterly dark, but then a great flame at the end of it roared to life, split in two, and shot across each wall flanking me, lighting torches on their way before sizzling out.

At the end of the room stood Killian, and with each lit torch, the Cinder-Plagued children peeled from the shadows. Beside Killian stood Saskia, eyes on the ground, holding herself tightly.

I got to my feet, but god did I ever want to collapse.

"I didna ken what I was expecting, girlie. But it wasna that."

The children moved closer, but when I backed up, they stopped. *Weird*. They weren't going to fight me. Not yet.

"What the hell did you *do* to me?"

Killian's bright face fell, hazel eyes flashing in the shadows as he drew closer. "I've helped ye. Can ye not see that?" He levelled a finger to my chest. "That bloody thing. It wants to own ye. To destroy ye. But I silenced it. All those angry voices of the dead, envious of yer beating heart. I put them *down*."

Gone was the man who had become my friend, who I thought had saved my life. Those gleaming eyes burned at the rims. Yet still he looked as human or Denizen as any other.

"Urka put something inside me," I spat back. "Inside the stone." I put my fingers around it, pressing tight, wishing I could turn it back to how it was, however unpredictable it had been. It hadn't made me the thing in the pit. It had been a force for good.

Killian's smile was pitying. "Can't ye see? The stone has been neutralized. Whatever comes out now . . . that's all you."

I felt my heart cratering. The stone was still so cold. *I* was so cold. I know what I was, what I had been, even before the stone. And this dark thing hadn't won. I had called back the fire to me, somehow, from some deep corner at the last . . . *that* had been me, not the skull fox warrior . . .

"Master . . ."

I spun, and out of the hole behind me squirmed what was left of Corgan.

"Ah, there ye are, wretch," Killian sighed, and suddenly he had moved around me, hands behind his back in consideration. "Ye look a bit worse for wear."

The creature bowed its head. "Please, Master. I beg you to kill me. I have failed you."

Killian held up his hand. "Enough of that. I will show ye mercy, same as my daughter has."

That word was a blow in itself, and I staggered as far away from him as I could get. Something was about to happen, and I looked frantically about the room, meeting only the slackened faces of Killian's infected slaves. I couldn't see a way out, and I couldn't blast myself one, either. My eyes met Saskia's, and she shook her head, desperately, and she pointed.

I looked back at Killian. But he was changing, too.

His fire consumed him, then became black, like the rest of him. As it peeled away in dark tendrils, it revealed skin of ash-grey, crackled like scales with the same brimstone glow I'd seen in the children, only now it was intense. He grew tall, and the Emerald on his shoulder pulsed, and I could see from here the dark tinges that corrupted the gem's surface. The ground piked under Corgan and lifted the creature up, assisting it to stand before its master.

Killian bowed his head, and when he lifted it, his eyes were covered in a protruding shard of bone, like a mask. The same kind I'd only just seen in my own reflection.

He laid his hands on Corgan's head, thumbs digging deep into the flesh-bark.

"I place my name on yours," Killian said, though the voice was smooth, accentless, the voice of a viper. "Take power from me and become whole again. Fulfill your dark purpose. Rise." All the breaks in Corgan began healing, stone from the ground shunting into wounds and becoming one with the creature's body, until it stood on its own and bowed its distorted neck.

"Seela," it whispered in reverence. "First Child of the Bloodlands. You do me an honour I do not deserve."

I couldn't help myself and scoffed openly.

Killian — Seela — turned towards me. Slowly. A perfect curve. I saw him fully now: almost seven feet tall, swathed in a robe of ever-changing black, tentacles of living ink curling, seeping. A cloak of oil.

No eyes. Just the mouth, a thin line cut with a knife, crimson. He opened his hands in humble petition. "You doubt my provenance, daughter?"

"Call me that one more time," I spat.

"More's the pity." Seela folded his hands at his elongated waist. He looked like a stretched larva. "You have trouble accepting what is before you. What I am. What you are. Your blood is my blood."

"Shut up!" I shouted back. "Last time I checked, my blood is *Fox*. I dunno what yours is, but there's none of it in me." Biology be damned. I clung to Cecelia's memory, to Ravenna's. Their strength had been mine. It had been enough.

"True," Seela conceded. "But you saw it yourself, I think." He took a step towards me, and I stumbled back. "Can't you see? I have done this all for you."

He spread his hands again, gesturing around the room and at the dead floating in the torchlight.

I was stunned. "For me?"

However evil the thing was before me, its tone was earnest. "I could have done to you what I did to the Rabbit Paramount. Corgan was not always as he is. But once he gave me the Emerald, he submitted to me. He understood what lies ahead." The hulking monster servant drew to Seela's side, and I couldn't connect what he was saying to what I saw.

"That..." I pointed to Corgan, "is the Rabbit Paramount?"

"No longer," Seela said, patting the stone. "But Corgan is much more than that now. He is the future. So are my children. And the trees we make together. We are building a new world. I want you to be a part of that willingly. I want you to make the choice yourself."

I laughed, deeply and loudly and deliberately.

Seela's jaw clenched.

"You should have killed me," I seethed. "I'll never help you."

Seela came closer — not on two legs but many. A spider's legs made of that sick, slick ink sluicing out from under his fathomless cloak.

"You are no good to me dead," he admonished. "The Conclave of Fire would have killed you and cast you aside for that rock you carry. But you are of my blood. And we have been touched by burning shadow. That blood must not be wasted." His body bent at an impossible angle, pushing his face into mine and a long, terrible claw tapped at the dormant Opal in my sternum. "I will free you from your demon, whose name is Deon. I will show you that breaking the stones will free not only you but this world."

He drew away, stalking back down the hall. "We have much work to do, but our works will be great." Then the black flames licked back up his body, to the crown of his head, and he was Killian again. Charming and handsome, pestilence hiding in a human skin suit.

"The second I see the opportunity," I snapped back, no longer bothering to hide my disgust, "I am going to destroy you."

Killian smiled. "Ye can try, girlie. But we have too much on our plate to stop now." Killian's eyes flicked, and my arms were roughly snatched and held in place by Corgan's powerful, creaking limbs.

"Take her to the summoning chamber. See that she is fed. We will be moving again shortly to London. To test a theory." Killian looked straight at me, his hazel eyes a match for the one I had that wasn't touched by the Moth Queen. And the thought made me sick. "The game may have changed, but our purpose is the same."

Flames rose off his skin, until he was consumed by them. In the great light he cast, an enormous shadow appeared on the wall behind him, climbing. But it wasn't his own shadow — it was three. The shadows of his parents, the darklings that started all of this. They were alive, writhing, and I swear I could hear their cries of agony in my head. Impatience. Fury. And yet beyond that, a growing excitement at their impending freedom. As the room filled with the inhuman bellows and ululations, the children had turned towards the ghastly shadow puppet show, their faces raw with longing. The longing of *real* children for their parents. I'd felt it well.

Killian smiled at me from the pyre of his body. The shadows fused together as one black column, growing and growing, consuming the torchlight.

"Welcome to the family," he said, before I was dragged away.

Come *to* Roost

It was still dark when Eli came to, rising to the surface of wakefulness like ballast. No bolting upright, no feeling of falling eternally. No voices screaming at him, invading his senses. Comfort was a strange and foreign sensation. He found himself welcoming it.

He woke, blinked. *Enough rest.* He needed to find out what was happening. Crossing great distances and speaking with Roan in dreams was one thing, but there were too many holes, and too much had happened since he had let the plane crash. Since he had let everyone in that grove down.

Eli pulled himself carefully and painfully into the linen service uniform someone had left out for him, neatly folded on the rolling cart that also held the monitors from which he now unplugged himself. A few months ago, he would have been insulted at wearing another Family's colours. But being rendered barely able to do up his own buttons realigned his priorities. Especially the kind he didn't know if he felt anymore.

But the stone had saved him. Eli never guessed that he would one day be glad for the Moonstone and the space it took up in his heart, in his mind. Or that he'd managed to hold on to it, and himself, this long. He brushed his fingers over it and it felt warm, like it had been touched by fire.

Maybe it had.

His mind flickered back to the dream, where he swore he was back in that miserable worm pit in the Bloodlands, Roan Harken chained arm-to-arm alongside him. But while it was a memory, something that had already happened, it had felt like the present. Felt too real to discount. He could've been looking into a mirror — her mismatched eyes holding the terror he recognized too well. Of knowing that the fate she'd blindly chosen was no longer one over which she had any control.

But something else was growing there. He could feel it. Something dark. Where was she that she was trapped in dreams or moving sideways through time and memory? Were the stones communicating, and was she calling for help?

"You're awake sooner than they predicted."

It took Eli much too long to turn, to take in Barton at the doorway. His mind was also playing catch-up at a devastating snail's pace, barely able to read his thoughts before seeing him. *So this is what it must feel like to be human . . .*

"I'm not one to keep people waiting." Eli tucked the shirt into the pants, yet even touching his own skin seemed to hurt. "I spent most of my time in that tree asleep, anyway."

The Owl Council must have come to check on him and gone, once Eli was found to be stable. However weak and vulnerable he'd been, keeping up a defense around his deeper thoughts was automatic, probably aided by the stone. If they'd tried to look into his mind, they wouldn't have found much. Which was just as well — Eli was still trying to decide whether to tell them all the things the Moonstone had shown him. The warning from the Moth Queen. The visitations with Roan.

Barton came fully into the room, and Eli realized he was standing — walking, in fact, and he took in the running blades with open curiosity. "I see you've upgraded."

Barton eased onto the empty bed across from Eli. "I figured there'd be another horrifying adventure just around the corner, so. Wanted to be prepared."

Eli raised an eyebrow, sending his mind out, feeling around, trying not to make it too obvious. Barton was an incredibly open book, which made it far too easy. Too trusting.

"Thank you," Eli forced himself to say, recoiling from the latent sensations that pinged back from Barton; he'd felt, just now, his momentary experience inside his own divisive tree. "For the record, when you pulled me out of that thing, I *was* dead."

"But you're not now." Barton pointed to Eli's chest. "You probably have that thing to thank."

Eli chilled noticeably. "There's little I'll thank *this thing* for. Though you're probably right . . ."

Barton nodded, though Eli knew he didn't really understand. Never would. And that was fine, because at least he had Roan to . . .

He slammed that thought away, taking a precursory look at the door to the infirmary, which was little more than a workroom, old computers and boxes crammed in the corner between the monitors and beds. The Council could be waiting outside for all he knew, and he threw out a searching mental beacon.

He jolted. "Solomon?" Eli turned back to Barton, who shrugged affably.

"He was almost as far gone as you. Maybe a bit more stubborn, though. He's up now, speaking to the Council."

Relief struck Eli like a wave so hard that he didn't realize, at first, what the pinprick sensation in his eyes was.

"I wouldn't expect anything less." He turned his face away. "And the others? From the grove?"

Barton was quiet.

"I should have expected that, too. You . . . did your best." Eli got up, pouring himself a cup of water from the plastic decanter on the rolling cart. He nodded to himself, sifting through Barton's thoughts, the things they knew so far. "I see."

Barton blinked. "Huh?"

"Sorry," Eli answered after a beat, emptying the cup. "I took the intel I needed from your mind. Sometimes it's a bit automatic when I'm in a hurry . . ." Eli's heart was racing; he could feel himself getting frantic. He had to calm down. "I'm not very good at idle chit-chat. I'm sure you've noticed."

"I'm not going to argue when it comes straight from the horse's mouth."

"Wise." Eli put the cup back down when he noticed it was shaking in his hand. He looked up. "You came a long way to help, not really knowing if you could. And you left . . . that Deer girl behind to do it."

Barton rolled his eyes. "C'mon, man. You know she has a name."

"Sorry," Eli said again, but it was through a scowl.

"Also, stop apologizing. Listen. What happened with the plane. Solomon told us what you did. And you did everything you could, too. And now you're alive, and you've gotta get back to the leadering thing. I get it. Use me as a library for however long you want, but there's still a lot no one knows. What these kids are, what the trees are for, and why they want the stones. Or what's going to happen now that you're free. Since you have what Seela wants, it'll probably come after you again."

"And after anyone who shields me," Eli muttered. "Which means I can't stay here much longer."

"Whoa, whoa, that is *not* what I said." But Eli had already crossed the room, barely making it to the doorway before he caught himself in the frame, blood pressure bottoming out.

Barton lingered beside him, looking unsure if he should lend a hand. "Don't," Eli warned, but it came out sounding pathetic, even to him.

"Where are you gonna go?" Barton leaned up against the other side, but he didn't stand in Eli's way. "People are dying. More people are going to. This Seela thing may be quiet now but it's biding its time for something big. We all have to be ready when the time comes to hit back."

Eli felt himself returning as he straightened. Something of the old razor-thin patience, at least. "If I didn't know any better, which I do, it sounds as if you're trying to make this my problem."

"Isn't it?" Barton's tone was light, but his brow was furrowed. "Yeah, you *do* know better than me about this. Which means you also probably know we can't do this without you. I'm here, at least. I'm here because we all have to step up now. Whatever is going to happen, it's going to affect everyone."

Eli stared down the concrete hall lit by basket-caged lights. Farther down, around a corner, and up a flight of steps he felt his father, the Owl Council — or what was left of it — felt Foxes and Rabbits, and above all that a sting of uncertainty they all gave off. The panic that had risen in him fed off them. *What will we do? When will it happen? Will we be strong enough to make whatever compromises necessary to win a war?*

"And what about Harken?" Eli craned his neck, stretching the stiffness from it. "You see this little coalition as the powers that be gathering to prepare for battle. To assure we are the winning side. At least, that's what you wish it was. I think you're starting to see that in war, the individual doesn't matter. Just the greater good."

Their eyes met, and Barton's dropped to the floor. Eli caught an immediate memory flickering there just in front of him as if Barton had repeated it out loud: *they* were *going to leave Eli to die . . . as long as they got the stone away safely*.

"I thought as much." Of course the Owls wouldn't be interested in saving Eli himself; after all, you can't alter centuries of Narrative-preservation overnight. Perhaps ever. "Which means I owe you double. If it wasn't for you, I *really* wouldn't be here. No one else was moving to get me out of there except you."

Barton got the words out before Eli could snatch them from his thoughts. "So you don't think they'll try to rescue Roan? Wherever she is?"

Eli folded his arms. "They'll try to find Seela. He's the priority. The stones are the only things that matter. And that's what Seela wants from Roan, ultimately. A means to an end. They can thwart him if they get the stones back. Without them . . . well."

"We're fucked," Barton finished for him.

Eli snorted. "Might as well not mince words." He looked back out into the hall. "And might as well save face while I can. It won't take long for the others to realize what I'm about."

He didn't have to turn to feel Barton nodding behind him. Eli took a breath, felt his vertebrae shifting with the phantom weight of his wings, and started down the corridor. Barton went behind him, out of curiosity, it seemed, more than actual support. Eli had to give him credit; he wasn't dumb enough to imagine that he'd go with Eli afterward. Barton knew he had to stay behind to try to do the impossible — convince the coalition that his friends were worth preserving in all of this.

But Barton had been right the first time: Eli knew better.

❧

" . . . a matter of time."

The Fox, Reinhardt, stopped prematurely when he noticed the eyes of the gathering had turned to the doorway, that Solomon, battered as he was, still managed to get up and forget them all completely, limping to meet the ghost of his son across the room.

"Solomon," Eli nodded, extending a hand. Solomon didn't even regard it or stop. He gathered Eli into his arms without a word and pressed him close.

Eli froze. It would be inelegant to push him away now in front of everyone, and for once in his life he didn't feel like he wanted to. He lifted a hand to pat the man weakly on the back, clasping him tight for a nanosecond before releasing him.

"It's good to see you," Solomon muttered, voice low but clear enough to carry through the wide room. He fired the thought from his mind like a sharpened arrow: *This itself will be a tribunal. Tread lightly before you make your grand exit.*

Eli nodded. He and Solomon were of a height, but Eli could feel the man's pain as he fought to stay standing. "I'll join you now," he said and took Solomon's arm to guide him back to the long table the other elders had gathered around. Barton stayed behind. When Solomon was seated once again, Eli elected to stand.

"You're looking well, Eli." The woman in the hijab, Alena, dipped her chin. "We did not expect you to recover so quickly. The Moonstone surely helped with that."

"Surely." Eli set his jaw, surveying the table with a flash of surprise. "Magistrate Park! I have to say you're looking better than I thought you might since we last spoke."

The Korean man at Alena's left gave a grateful if weary nod. "Sir. I can't say the same about the rest of us from the attack. As you can see, we are the only ones from your original tribunal who made it back here. How Seela and his army of misfit orphans could move so swiftly over thousand-mile distances is just further proof our enemy has already outmatched us."

"But we've the upper hand again," put in the Fox, Jacob Reinhardt, cutting a glance to Eli. In that spare instant Eli cast to see what was behind that icy stare: agitation. A soldier's impatience. Apprehension at being suddenly thrust into a position left vacant by his now-deceased leader — a name swam before him . . . Mala? Then he felt a blow that he did everything not to show on his waking face — a man who was a Fox, throttling the earth beneath him, and Roan Harken's devastated scream as she pitched over a fissure —

"Eli?"

Eli felt the blood rising back into his face, but he hadn't moved, eyes narrowed at Reinhardt. "We have one stone," he said quietly. "Seela has two. I'm not sure I'd call that an upper hand."

Reinhardt shared a glance with the rest of the gathering. He didn't have the Owls' perception, and they may have guessed Eli was testing this man. "Your stone was nearly in Seela's grasp. You must realize how close you were."

Eli frowned. "Yes. I was there." He ran his dry tongue over his teeth. "And surely *you* must realize the obvious. Seela could have returned at any moment to strike you down. To stop you from taking me back. But he didn't. Not only that, he left me in the open while his tree did its work. That was a gamble, certainly."

Eli saw Solomon narrow his eyes in thought, before he sat stiffly up, gesturing towards the doorway. "Seela probably didn't imagine we had a means to free you. He couldn't have predicted Barton had such an ability."

Eli turned. Barton was sitting in the shadows by the door, hands folded between his knees as he listened.

"Maybe not," Eli agreed. "But by now, Seela will have noticed I'm missing. And he'll either come soon enough or leave us be to make us think we are safe. If it's as Park says, and this thing can move from one continent to the next in a heartbeat, what's to stop it from coming here now? Ten seconds from now?"

"Enough," Reinhardt growled. "We can speculate all

night, or we can move. Denizen and human lives are at stake, the longer we sit here. Not to mention how this entire sordid affair has now leaked into the Mundane world. We already risked exposure with everything that happened with Zabor." The corner of Reinhardt's eyes twitched, as if he hadn't meant to say all he had. He turned to the Rabbit who had been silent, hands folded on the table in front of him. "Commander Zhou? Has your team yet uncovered anything from the site we can use to track this thing down?"

Zhou clasped and unclasped his fingers as he chose his words carefully. "Whatever materials we recovered disintegrated as soon as we removed them from the site. We know the grounds were shifted using the Emerald. But . . . I fear our stone has been corrupted somehow. We've been cut off from it."

Reinhardt pulled a hand down his face; Eli knew the man hadn't slept in too many hours. Barely any of them had. Too many probable outcomes playing behind their eyes.

"And what about the other stones?" Eli asked. "What have you heard from the Seals?"

Another Fox — *Akilah Fante*, Eli plucked her name up from beneath her wrinkled head wrap — took a breath deep enough to raise her mighty bust as she fidgeted in her seat. "They are moving to bring the Sapphire out of the depths. I say leave it where it is. As long as it's hidden and out of sight, then Seela can't use it against us."

"If they want to join this fight," Reinhardt put in, "then let them." He certainly seemed eager for the inevitable bloodshed to follow.

"And would you say the same about the Quartz?" another Owl, sitting next to Solomon, spoke up — he was the youngest of the four Council members, though at least in his thirties. "It can't bring *all* the stones together, at least. The Quartz is the last contingency against that. Fia will never give it up, and I doubt Seela will be going to the Glen anytime soon to take it from them."

Eli could feel his heartbeat behind his eyes, suddenly overcome with the urge to shut them as the blood rushed to his head. "As we've seen so far, anything is possible, Mr. Gordon."

"This thing will pretty much stop at nothing. I've seen it myself." Reinhardt nodded, picking up Eli's comment to use for his own ends. "It captures and kills to get the stones. It has the power to take them for itself. You Owls may have thought you were high and mighty before, but this thing nearly killed your own Paramount. Let alone what it probably did to Alistair Corgan . . ."

The blood surged higher, louder. Eli winced, the Moonstone getting suddenly hot at the edges. The meeting room was shimmering out of perspective, overlapping with a great hall that stretched before him, lit only by torchlight, by the burning eyes of the children he'd last seen at the plane crash site. The image sharpened closer still, and Eli saw a massive creature with a pendulant head hanging from a hook-bent neck, in its mutated arms a struggling girl —

"The second I see the opportunity," Roan snarled, "I am going to destroy you."

Despite the jarring experience of the meeting room slamming back into place and focus, Eli couldn't help but smile.

"I can't imagine you think this is *funny*, Rathgar —"

"You can call your man back from the mission in Mongolia," Eli addressed Commander Zhou directly. "The

Paramount is as good as dead. Seela has turned him into his servant in exchange for the stone. Something he might well have done to me. But he didn't. Which goes to show there is more at play here."

The gathering was silent, staring. The commander didn't move. Eli had to learn to be more careful with his words; he could feel the commander's sense of betrayal, just now working out that his Paramount had given the stone up willingly in return for his life. Even though now it wasn't much of one.

"And how could you possibly know that?" Alena asked, though it came out more as an accusation. She openly glanced down at Eli's chest, and though he kept the barrier around his thoughts as thick as steel, the Owls were the keepers of Denizen lore and could guess how. He might as well spell it out for the rest.

"Because I just saw him now, as you were all going back and forth in your eternal runaround, trying to commit to whatever path of least resistance gets you what you want the fastest." He gripped the back of Solomon's chair lightly, though it was the only thing keeping him from falling over. "And Roan Harken. She's there, too. And she's alive. For now." Eli shut his eyes again. "It's the Dragon Opal. While I was in that tree, I could hear it. Hear *her*." He undid the cuff of his sleeve, pulled it up, and thrust his arm into the light so they could all see the scars. "However ill-timed the visions are, they seem to be coming to me as they happen. We're connected somehow." He turned to Barton. "It started when she dragged me through the Bloodgate. For better or worse, I think I might be able to communicate with her. To know where she is. Which will help me greatly on my own mission, which no longer concerns any of you."

Eli was surprised that, as the voices at the table rose, the loudest among them was the de facto leader of the Foxes. "You can't be serious," Reinhardt shouted. "After what it cost us to bring you here? You're going to go back out there, for what? *Suicide*?"

Eli lifted an eyebrow. "To bring back your Calamity Stone. Whatever the cost." It was a gamble. Eli would not easily forget the Moth Queen's visitation — that had not been a dream. *You will free one another* — whatever that meant. Maybe it didn't matter. Maybe he and Roan Harken were merely destined to destroy one another, and that could be the only freedom they deserved.

Alena raise her hand. "Wait a moment, Jacob." She turned to Eli. "We may have an upper hand, after all. We may be able to strike when they're vulnerable."

Eli narrowed his eyes at her. It was Solomon's hand covering his that ultimately made him break their warring gazes. He spoke only in thoughts. *I know you think you have to go*, he said. *But you'll have quite a journey ahead to think it over. Killing Roan Harken isn't* always *the answer. Or killing yourself, for that matter.*

Eli would have laughed at that.

"You're needed *here*," Reinhardt scowled. "But if you're able to get the girl to trust you, then you might be our only chance to get the Opal back safely . . ."

The room was silent. Solomon took his hand away. Eli actually felt a heavy clump of dread forming in his stomach. It really had been too easy to convince them that killing Roan was the solution. Déjà vu, definitely. He looked at Barton, whose face was twisted in numb rage. Even the Foxes were agreeing to murder their own. *For the greater good.*

Eli remembered her eyes, glanced down at his arm. *It's a long journey . . .* goddamn empathy.

It took too great an effort to make it look graceful and natural, but Eli rolled his shoulders as his immense, heavy wings burst from them, tearing the linen on his back easily with the force. He flexed his fingers as they lengthened, the black talons shining in the guttering fluorescents that seemed only to deepen the shadows in the faces of the gathering.

"I will try to bring the Opal back, to keep it out of Seela's hands." He cut the rest of them a shining stare, one he knew had turned from grey to amber as he let the Therion's body become his. "I will do what must be done. Whether Roan Harken is still attached to the stone at the end of it or not, I know none of you will stop me out of sentimentality for her."

There was a sound like a thunderclap when his wings stretched wide, and the gathering stiffened as one. Eli could have sworn he saw bloodlust in the Owls' eyes, maybe even Reinhardt's.

"Father," Eli inclined his head to Solomon, "I'll check in." He turned to Barton again, reached into his mind, planted a thought there with as much reassurance as he could muster.

I will try to bring her back alive, he promised, though he scarcely believed it himself.

Barton froze, as if he wasn't sure he'd heard Eli properly, but Eli had already smashed into the rusted-out ventilation shaft and flown out into the forbidding chill of the Russian dark.

West, the stone tugged at him, and the wind took him in her arms, guiding him quicker through the long night ahead.

An Empty Sky

Corgan had virtually dragged me most of the way up the stairs. Which was fine — after the first ten flights I got tired of fighting, so I let the monster do the legwork.

"Where the hell are we going that is *this* high up?" I'd grumbled. All my pent-up tension had turned into sour impatience.

Corgan was more forthcoming with the conversation than I'd anticipated. "Master wants you to be comfortable. His summoning chamber is his sanctuary. Only the best for his true daughter." That last bit came out with a touch of bitterness. Maybe jealousy.

Killian's summoning chamber was above ground? The pit in which I'd originally woken up seemed more like the province of a grotesque shadow demon, not some tower.

I couldn't tell much of where I was, anyway. Sparsely lit, stone hewn. *It'd be way too cliché if this was a castle*, but it seemed to be fitting the bill. Water rushed nearby, and I'd been pulled up into a great hall that might or might not have had windows — it was nighttime and hard to tell, and I'd been yanked out before I had the chance to really get a better look. All I could think of were the huge dark shadows on that back wall, turning their eyes on me.

Suddenly Corgan stopped, throwing me down hard through a narrow open doorway. I caught myself on one hand but the other crumpled at the wrist, and I felt it crack.

"Nng!" I hissed, cradling my wrist.

"Master did not specify if you should be comfortable now or later," the creature croaked nastily.

"Specifics don't seem to be his specialty." I grunted around the pain, looking up, trying to see. But the room was pitch-black, and Corgan blended seamlessly with the murk. There didn't seem to be a way around Corgan, either, as it took up the entire doorway.

Something *splorched* onto the ground between us.

"What the hell was that?"

Shifting footsteps — obviously Corgan backing up. "Master said to feed you."

"Ugh, what!" I recoiled, scampering backward, horrified that whatever he'd dropped could be spreading a sickening puddle towards me. It was already starting to smell. "I am very suddenly *whatever-that-is-intolerant*."

"Suit yourself," Corgan sneered. Then the door slammed, and a massive lock bolted to, and I knew I was alone.

I couldn't tell how many hours ago that had been. I still held my twisted wrist plastered to my chest, pressing it into the stone. I pictured the sharpened edges with geode roots tangled around my ribs, going deeper. *You stupid goddamn bauble. Just when I actually need you, you desert me.* I tried to remember the Opal's vibrant colours — a corona of gold cutting through the centre almost like an eye, the supernova of red and purple and the flashing green I'd first known it by, once upon a time in Winnipeg. But the more I tried to recollect the Opal, tried to call it back to how it had been when I'd first adjusted to life with it — getting out of the shower every day, pulling a shirt over it, tracing it with a fingernail at night . . . even the memory seemed corrupted, the edges going black, spoiling and eclipsing the colour. The cold dark taking hold.

I let my injured hand drop and thought this was as good a place as any to finally lose my mind.

"Come *on*," I snarled, smacking my palm onto the stone. "Wake up!" I needed to move. To get out of here. I had to stop Killian, Seela, *all of them*, before the body count went up. That's all it seemed to do around me. With each impact of my hand on the Opal I saw their faces — Table Five. Every customer in the explosion at Fingal's Pint. Ben. Athika. Victims of Seela's quake at the Conclave of Fire. Ruo. Mala. Then further back — the first of the Red River girls with her eye gouged out. A group of innocent bystanders suspended in the air over the Osborne Bridge. Cecelia —

"Sil." My face was wet — I hadn't noticed I'd been crying, but each memory had transported me, and now I was back in my own body, in the dark, invaded by something that only wanted to kill. *My bones are a haunted house.*

"Sil. Cecelia. Please. I know you're there, somewhere. Help me. The fire, it . . . it's gone."

"The fire is *never* gone," she answered, and my head jerked up so hard I slammed it into the wall behind me.

"Sil?" I got up, looked around, but I didn't move beyond that. There could be an open hole in the ground at any given point, as far as I knew. Nervously, I put my hand out.

"C'mon . . ." I made my hand hard as stone, trying to push the fire out of each knuckle, the flesh.

A spark.

I pushed harder, stopped breathing. "Yes, c'mon!" Harder, straining, the spark was a flicker —

The flame was a blooming flower, perfectly cupped in the palm of my hand. It was normal, a honeyed, splendid glow, and I thought I'd pass out from relief. But in its light was Cecelia's face, and I leapt backward.

"Mother of —" But the flame flared up my arm, licking my skin like it was sweating gasoline.

And it *hurt*.

The darkness peeled back like a sunburn, and Cecelia was still there, but I wasn't. Where I'd been standing was a boy, close to my age, maybe a few years younger. They were in a summoning chamber, clothes light, faces beaded with sweat as though they'd been training. There was no ease to watch this memory as there had been before — it wavered like a mirage, and I was struggling just to keep my eyes open against the roar of the blaze consuming me.

"Yes it does," he spat, petulant. "Maybe not mine or yours. But I've seen it fail in others. Who's to say that one day Ancient won't *just* be asleep — it'll be *dead*, and any powers the Denizens had will die with it?"

Cecelia folded her arms, eyes crawling into the back of her head. "How many times are we going to lapse into this rhetorical debate?"

The boy scuffed the shining gold rings beneath him. "When I'm convinced any of this is worth it . . ."

Cecelia dropped a hand to his arm. "That's enough for today. Are you sure you aren't mine? I'm seeing too much of myself in you lately to think otherwise, Killian."

Killian? No . . . but this was the boy I'd seen back at the stone choosing — the one Cecelia had noted was a trainee of the former Paramount, Chartrand. The one she'd taken on hand-to-hand in the Sun Trial.

But it made sense. Killian had admitted all of this himself, though he hadn't cast himself directly in this role. It was so obvious. It was my fault for missing it the first time.

Nng . . . the heat was so much hotter now, like someone had turned the oven temp up, and the memory shifted, brightened. There was Cecelia, and Ruo, one hand slipped through Cecelia's bent arm as they stood at a gathering. I recognized some of the pillars and the stonework — the Conclave in Glencoe. Before them both stood a girl, her long red hair parted down the centre and draped over her robes of black, red, and gold. *An initiated acolyte* skittered across my understanding. An elder dipped a thumb into a brazier, pulling a streak of ash down from the girl's forehead to her mouth and ending at her chin. Holding the brazier was Killian, and the two shared a glance and a mischievous smirk.

Ravenna.

"I grew up with her." Killian's voice over this memory was more painful still. I felt myself collapse to one knee. Once, Cecelia told me the fire couldn't hurt me. I'd trusted her fully, just as I did now, watching the stone sift through her life. But the fire was doing its damnedest to hurt me now, as if I were the virus. The enemy.

But I had to see.

It was all fire now, and it resolved into a dark alley, the walls close, the ceiling closer. It smelled damp, musty. I'd been down here before — in the memory Ruo had shown me back at the Conclave. The South Bridge Vaults in Edinburgh.

Cecelia slammed a young man against the wall by his shirt. Killian.

"What were you *thinking*?" she hissed. She picked him up again by the scruff, dragging him farther down the corridor. He collapsed in an alcove, groaning. His head was bleeding — no, his face, a gash that I knew would become a neat scar I would admire many years in the future and not understand until now.

"You promised me you'd be careful. You promised for Ravenna's sake, you damn fool."

Killian spat blood, his grin faltering. "I promised I'd do my best to make this a world she'd be proud to live in."

Cecelia cuffed him hard across his bleeding face.

"And how can you do that if you're dead?" She let him go, paced back the way they'd come, casting a flame towards incoming voices. "The others. I didn't think you'd be this stupid to gather in the open like this."

Killian chuckled. "And yet you still came to warn us. Who's the stupid one now?"

Cecelia dragged him back to his feet. "Ravenna would never forgive me if I let you die. And the cause would never forgive me, either." She was older — maybe in her fifties, but still beautiful. Fierce. What had she meant by *the cause*?

"Even if I die," Killian grunted, "it won't have been for

nothing. We're getting closer. Maybe even you will finally be free. You deserve that."

"What I deserve is not to have to be cleaning up after the rest of you damn kids for what little life I have . . ."

"You knew what you were getting into when you decided to join the Stonebreakers." Killian got his feet back under him, but he was limping.

"Yes, well," Cecelia said, but they were getting farther and farther away from me, "I'm still seeing too much of you in me. Maybe I should've joined years ago. And this could've all been avoided."

They faded away down that long dark hall, and when their light diminished so did the memory. I felt myself buckle, slumping bonelessly against the wall at my back with the sigh of a fire going out.

Cecelia had been a Stonebreaker. She and Killian had been allies . . . but to what end?

It was still so dark, yet my eyes were open wide and unblinking. So many lies. Too many secrets. I had trusted everything Cecelia had told me. Had trusted the stone she'd entrusted to me. Had it all been a trap?

I really was alone.

This was a fool's errand, and it only took a couple of hours on wing for Eli to come to that conclusion.

He was strapped and at the limit of what had before been an endless font of energy. Of power. He hadn't let himself recover to any extent — but there wasn't any time. There might not ever be. He knew that going after Roan was impulsive and irrational and made absolutely no sense — even if he pretended it was simply to retrieve the Dragon Opal. He should have left her to her own devices. That's what she'd wanted, wasn't it? To be alone. To carry the burden entirely. That was what it took to be a stonebearer, after all.

But going after her — it was a selfish move, too. Because the Moth Queen's shadow hung over Eli with every stroke of the Therion's wings . . .

There is a light in you now, when before there was only darkness . . . Her light will diminish. Only you can free each other.

Freedom. From the stones? Death dealt in riddles and any offered explanation rarely went deeper than the surface. The phantom chain around Eli's arm, in his chest, tugged hard. *West*, it said. Keep going. But for how long? Eli glanced down, the razored air raking through his thick feathers. Russia stretched tens of thousands of feet below. He couldn't determine where the Moonstone pulled him, but Roan had been in Scotland, before. It would take a commercial airliner at least sixteen hours to cover that distance. And if that's indeed where he was headed, the notion chilled him to the marrow. He hadn't been back to Scotland since he was young. Too young to understand what going after the Moonstone might cost him, even after he'd lost everything.

Don't you dare, he heard his mother say from one of those corners of his mind he thought he immured the memories, hoping they'd suffocate and vanish, *don't you* dare *go looking for it, Eli. No matter what they say, if they come looking for you, telling you it's your destiny. That stone . . . I hear it still. I won't let it hurt* you. *No matter what it says, no matter what they say. Please, Eli, please promise me you won't* —

He extended his will, reached out, and slashed, and the

hysterical pleading died. Too late for that. He felt the stone strobing before him, cutting through cloud.

Help me. The fire, it . . . it's gone. Roan's voice was pitiful, but he heard it all the same as if she'd been beside him in the air. His jaw tightened.

Eli banked higher, latched onto the wind currents at the tip of the earth. *Faster*, he hissed, and the stone took him higher still.

❧

"Rise 'n' shine, girlie."

I involuntarily bunched myself into the fetal position, covering my eyes as light struck them, blazingly bright as if the sun itself were in the room.

I lifted my stiff neck. Huge swaths of black, which I at first took for drapery, fell away from soaring windows. But it wasn't fabric — Killian stood there, pulling the darkness down with a gesture, and the black seemed to seep into the floor, eaten up by his own shadow as he passed.

I sat up. Once he was finished, I could see the room clearly through squinted, flexing pupils. The ceiling was a glass dome, seemingly set in wrought iron like an enormous atrium. The floor beneath me was the familiar obsidian marble with silvery veins of other summoning chambers I'd seen. Killian spun to me with a flourish and a bow.

"Ye look a sight better now than when last I saw ye." His eyes passed over me, then beyond me, and he scowled. "I see Corgan's idea of a joke is still here."

It took too much mental strength to turn, see what he was pointing at, but I shied away, covering my mouth — I'd fallen asleep inches away from what looked (and smelled) like regurgitated entrails . . . possibly Corgan's. I heard Killian laugh, felt a strange heat close to me, and when I turned again all that was left was a dark stain, the offending pile incinerated by black flame.

"Ne'er thought I'd be cleanin' yer room for ye so soon," Killian chided, and then he was hauling me up by my forearm. "Up now. Work to do."

I ripped free and brought the other arm around in a wild haymaker for his ear. He dipped out of the way, caught my already-injured wrist, and twisted it painfully behind me. I thrashed, screaming through my teeth.

"Now, now. No need for that." He let me go and I toppled forward, catching myself against the huge window. My breath fogged the glass — I was panting. God, I was not in any shape to climb a flight of stairs, let alone kill this asshole right now. I pressed my face into the cool clear surface, and as the landscape beyond it materialized, I leaned back.

As far as I could look, a treacherous sea stretched for miles. The day was overcast, not as bright as the stinging daylight impressed on my dark-accustomed eyes, yet the breakers beneath me smashed and left sparkling whitecaps behind. We could've been on any coast in the entire world — there was no way I could even begin telling where on the map I'd been deposited, but it didn't matter; I wasn't getting loose anytime soon. The dome followed the cliffside, as if it had grown out of it, the rocky shore curving inward on either side. An island, maybe. It could be Narnia, for all I knew.

This fortress was impressive, wherever it was. And when I stood back and squinted at the framing of the glass, I realized it wasn't steel. It was charred bones. I recoiled and spun, taking in the rest of the room — gothic spires hung from the ceiling like stalactites, teeth waiting to gnash. The whole building was brick and stone and glass and bone, finely wrought. But the brick was dark, and I'd wager anything it was made from ash, that this entire stronghold was cut from the cliffside and augmented with the material that Killian had at hand in abundance. Bodies. Ruin.

Migraine or not . . . I looked back to the window, tried to judge the distance between the dome tower and the water. The glass couldn't be that thick. But even if I smashed my way out —

"Don't think of it, girlie," Killian said with a sigh. "If I let ye do it, ye'd drown. But I *won't* let ye. I'll bring ye back up and stuff ye back in the hold if ye can't behave. Instead I'm offering you the best view in the house. And my trust."

I levelled him with a dark grimace. "Trust? You think I'll ever *trust* you?" I may have been sick to my stomach, but my spirit eye let me know what he really was beneath his handsome face, his casual stance. A towering mantis shadow on claw legs, spinning a neat web. I spread my feet, dropping a hip and lifting my fists, heavy as hammers. "You're sick."

He puffed out his cheeks. "Not me. Yer fighting it, I see. Though I dunno why yer bothering. The sooner you embrace it, the better ye'll feel."

"Me? I feel fine." I didn't know what I felt. Time was a flat circle, too many lives overlapping mine. I was about to pray inwardly for Cecelia as I had before, but now calling her up felt like a curse. I'd have to summon the fire another way, without her.

"Oh c'mon now. I didna bring ye here to fight. A summoning chamber is a place to learn. And I have much to teach." He started moving towards me round the curve of the room, and I moved away on the opposing axis, willing my fists to stop quivering.

"I'd think something that slithered out of the ground like you would prefer to worship there." Something flashed on my arms, but I didn't look away from him. A spark?

"Oh, yer one to talk!" Killian laughed, wagging his finger. "Fox-girl who trained in a summoning chamber underground thinks she's above me." He turned to the windows as the sun broke through the clouds, arms wide. "My family has been condemned to the dark. In the Bloodlands, all they dream of is the sky."

The flint clicked over inside me and I lunged. Just as it had when I was seeing the stone's memory, it hurt to bear the fire rippling over my skin, but I didn't care. I struck, but Killian was too fast, and my fist impacted the obsidian floor, cratering it.

"Look at ye!" He slow-clapped and laughed again. It only made me hotter, sicker. Angrier.

I ripped my flaming fist free and took another shot, a poorly thrown cross that didn't land anywhere near my target.

"Yer miserable. Ye must know it. But I can show ye relief, if ye want it."

I caught him in the jaw with my elbow, tripping backward just from the impact of it. At least it'd shut him up momentarily, but he was on me just as fast, hammering down hit after hit like I was a speed bag.

He had me by both wrists, crossing them in front of me. The fire still held up, flickering, hurting. I fought back, tried to get loose, get away, but his grip was iron. "Listen to me," he hissed in my face. "Yer in pain. Yer sick. Ye know why."

"Because you fucking *made me sick,*" I spat, trying to jerk away, but he was carefully yanking me back towards the centre of the room.

"I'd ask if ye kiss yer mother with that mouth, but I'm no' such a bastard as ye think." His smirk was unforgivable. "No one made ye sick but yerself. All Urka did was quiet the stone, make way for yer true power. The power I've given ye through my blood. Surely ye've felt it. Ye saw it down in that pit with ol' Corgan, didn't ye?"

No. I couldn't go there. The bright orange flame felt like it was scorching me down to my bones. Maybe I'd see my own skeleton, winking bleached white back up at me if I broke Killian's eye contact, but I hazarded my own hysterical grin.

"You put this thing in me. In the stone. It's just a matter of time before I get it out."

Embrace it, Roan, said that unbidden voice, crawling out of the dark.

"Ye canna eject yer own soul, my wee girl," Killian said, and his gentle voice surprised me. He moved back a step. Then another. *What?* I looked down, and he'd let go.

And the flames licking my arms were dark, purple. Quiet.

"No!" I shouted, and I charged for him, but I didn't get far. Beneath me, three red rings incised in the obsidian began rotating, and I was trapped inside their revolutions.

"Tell me. Are ye hurting now? Are ye in pain?"

"I —" Whatever smart-ass remark was at the back of my throat died. I brought my arms back up, looked at my fingers. The fire acted as it had, once, when I'd first pulled control of it to me. Languid and ribboning, as if it had a mind of its own. My skin felt comfortable. A warmth but a dry one. A wave of nausea crested, abated. The sweat beading down the back of my neck sizzled away.

Killian's face was impassive, calm.

"You did this," I said, but I already knew it wasn't true.

He leaned back against the soaring glass. "I was in a prison for the entire duration of your life. Ye know that?" He surveyed me from under heavy lids. "I'm no stranger to the dark. But eighteen years is long enough. And I didna enjoy a second of it. Yer no' a prisoner here. I'd never do that to ye."

I took my eyes off the black flames and looked down to the ground, made a show of trying to step out of the glowing red rings, foot sparking an invisible barrier. "Oh, so this is your idea of freedom? Maybe you lost the definition of *prison* since then. You don't seem ready to let me just walk out that door." It hadn't been lost on me that this echoed our first conversation in the Conclave, when I'd woken to him. I should have trusted my gut reaction then, that immediate suspicion, but I'd let him convince me he was an ally.

Killian's sardonic smile returned as he sighed. "Ye can go anywhere and do anything ye like. Though I'm not sure where it is you think you'll go. What refuge is there, anywhere, that isn't just another sort of prison? Ye know it just as well. It's not me keeping ye in those rings. Or even here. It's you."

"Stop putting this on me!" I screamed, boiling over, and the black fire jettisoned out from the bottom of me, through my boots, flashing over the floor. "You did this to me! You put this . . . this *thing* in me. You corrupted the stone!"

He shut his eyes as if he was letting a toddler see its tantrum through. "The stone was already corrupt. I'm trying to set ye free."

I couldn't take it anymore. I slammed my fist into the

barrier keeping me from leaving the circles. My arm was a dark comet, a drill, and red jets surged around it. Killian opened his eyes then.

"You think you can make me trust you? You think you'll brainwash me into being your *friend*?" Killian was standing straighter now as I bore down with all my weight onto that fist, a red bolt careening into the floor, a deep crack rising. "I had parents. A mother and a father. They're dead. You're just a goddamn sperm donor. You're nothing to me!"

The rings beneath me juddered, flashing. I let the fury do the work — I needed what I could draw on, and it was the surest thing to hand. It didn't matter what Sil had told me, about not letting anger be my source. Everything she'd told me was a lie.

I needed anger right now. Not just aimed at Killian — for what he'd done to me, for what he'd done to those kids as Seela. Because I could hear that one singular voice again. *Yes. Take this power. With it, you can best the stone. You can best anyone.* It sounded so much like Cecelia, and now how could I doubt it? She wasn't the hero I had been trying to shape myself into, all this time. She was selfish. She was sloppy. She'd broken every rule, even her own. She left Ruo behind. She let Ravenna die. She'd left me.

The black fire climbed higher, and it took hold of me, but this time I could temper it. The barrier of the rings shattered, the floor of the very chamber split, and I allowed myself to feel every bit of grief and betrayal and misery, because while the stone had taken so much from me, I'd come to rely on it. Deep down, Killian was right. All of it, always, had been about power. I felt the mask of bone pressing over my face, growing out of it. Becoming it.

"Harken!"

I staggered, hands up. From behind the screen of boiling flame, I saw the sky. But not the sky outside the windows. A different sky, higher up. The wind screamed past, and the air was filled with black feathers. I felt it whistling through my hair, cutting my skin. Felt his wings over me, pushing the dark fire back down like a damper.

"Eli?"

The flames fell, and Killian was close at hand, catching me as I tipped forward.

"Easy," he said, and I didn't even have anything in me to argue with him as he guided me down to my knees. The summoning chamber was a ruin, but he was sweeping a hand over the floor, and it shivered back into place, a faint glow at his clavicle where the Serenity Emerald flared.

"If you killed me," I offered, "you could just take the Opal. You could be closer to whatever it is you want." I was weak. He'd let go of me, but even the effort of sitting up was too much.

"I want family," Killian said, just as Saskia had in the pit. "I want ye to trust me. I know it's hard for ye to conceive. By now the stone may have shown ye the truth, as ye've been seeking it. Cecelia lied to ye. Kept too many secrets and left her ghost to be the one to reveal them. She was a braw woman, but it was cowardly." He sat back on his haunches, staring up at the sky. "I seek to be open with ye in every regard. Ravenna tried to do the right thing by ye, but she's gone. Cecelia thrust this all on yer head then departed as quick as her daughter. But I was always there. Waiting in the dark. Ye were the only thing that kept me going."

He got to his feet, took a cursory survey of the room.

"We were both abandoned by those we trusted. But I am here now. I mean to create an equal world out of the ashes of this one. But I need your help."

My breath was regular now. I followed his eyes to the dome and felt the ghost of the stratosphere on my face.

"I'm still going to kill you," I said to the sky. But I couldn't help shake that I felt better than I had, even since the Conclave of Fire. Further back, since before the floor of Cecelia's summoning chamber opened up, and I took the stone that promised to bring everything I missed back to me.

"Later," Killian said, extending his hand. "Now up with ye. We're going out."

I slanted my eyes at him. "Out?"

His hand was still there but he wasn't about to give me an answer. I got up on my own steam, squeezing the feeling back into my fingertips. I couldn't fight him — not yet. He'd been toying with me before. I needed to be smarter, to bide my time. I could only do that if he thought I was playing by his rules.

"I told ye. I want a world of equals. An end to this struggle for power between the select few who have it. To do that we need to make this world a bit more aware of that imbalance." He let his hand drop. "The Owl Paramount. He's got free, which was a slight hitch in things. I wasna strong enough to take his stone on my own. Even I have my limits." Why he'd let this slip was beyond me, and I didn't want to imagine it was a show of trust. "But he will come to us, I think. And we can strike while the rest of them are looking the other way."

I was having a hard enough time following him with the accent alone. "What? Strike?" Maybe I was better off throwing myself out the window, but Killian had already grabbed hold of me, yanking me close, his flames spinning their tight web of solid, rippling ink.

"Call it a wee family outing." His insidious grin widened into that horrible crimson slash, body and face contorting into the visage of Seela. "I'll show you the world that I see. And I will show you that this is your family now. We will embrace you. You will be your best self with us."

The black choked us both in its grip, and the summoning chamber in its unholy castle was gone. When the darkness parted again, we were standing underneath the garish, iconic digital screens in the British capital's West End.

London. And not just Killian and me. He'd brought the children with us. The force of the teleportation made me feel like I'd left my guts behind, and they were only just catching up. Suddenly Saskia had her hand around mine, keeping me steady as I clutched my stomach.

She was smiling up at me. "You're okay."

I looked around us. I did not feel okay. I felt like I had a target painted on my back. I felt like something unforgivable was about to happen. "What's . . . how did we — ?"

Her smile was so utterly wretched. "Don't worry. There's nothing you could have done to stop him. There's nothing any of us can do now."

Then I raised my head, and there was Seela standing before us all. And the children were singing, red eyes and flesh glowing.

And I felt the dark thing turn over to its master's call.

The scream nearly ripped Eli out of the sky, tearing the wind from under his wings.

No, he thought, eyes sharpening. Everything was moving so fast — the air around him, the earth beneath him. He'd never flown this high before, and the ice was cleaving in tiny barbs to his feathers. His skull was expanding, the fine bones of it coming apart. *Faster*, he begged anyone listening. The Moonstone, the wind itself, maybe even Phyr. Or Mother Death, if she wanted him any sooner than he was coming.

Eli could feel himself getting closer now. How many hours? He banked, the ground approaching at an alarming speed. *FASTER*. He was a spear, an anvil. A comet. The clouds parted over an enormous, sprawling city. *London*. He was coming down over the West End, and he felt it before he saw it — the heat from the fires. The toppled buses, the car wrecks, and the black shapes stabbing the air with their branches. And the hulking dark mass in the centre of it all, casting black flames of its own. Eli stretched out his claws, and the thing with the skull over the shadow of its head turned as it felt the rush of him, then faltered. Faded.

Eli pulled up short and carried the full force of his descent, smashing headlong through a parking lot mid-evacuation.

There was a person at the core of that hellish thing at ground zero of the carnage, and it wasn't Seela. It had been Roan.

❧

How could this be happening?

The screams were all around me. The screams were mine. Killian had been proselytizing to the children, and people on the sidewalks stopped, gaped, curious about the nut job cosplayer standing in the street, holding up traffic with his gang of orphans. Not only Mundanes but Denizens, too, my spirit eye told me. I tried to shout, warn them away, but I couldn't move. *Roan*, the voice asked gently, *let me do this for you*, and I was too tired to stop it.

I watched Seela's mouth open wide, as I caught my reflection in a boutique window, turning into the dark fox warrior that mirrored him.

Where was Cecelia, my guide and my partner? Where was the line I swore I'd never cross? The Mundanes fled around us, but the Denizens flew into the fray as the cinder children leapt over each other, nails and teeth reaching. Foxes and Rabbits raging, and I realized I didn't know what they were fighting for. What I was fighting for. *The stone was already corrupt*. Killian had been right about that, too. Even if I died, the stone would choose another. No matter who had it, there would just be more death in the name of the Narrative.

Seela upended the roads, cars careening over us and smashing into buildings, power lines coming down in a rain of sparks.

This was my chance to escape, out in the open. But part of me didn't want to. Killian had said it. Where did I have to go? Back to the Conclave, to a different kind of prison? Back to Winnipeg, where the people I loved would die the longer I stuck around?

Memory was a fragile, dying ember — Eli was free, at least. Maybe I was done being the hero. Maybe there was no good side, just the dark in every heart. Maybe I'd worked my way through the versions of me that could do any good, and all I had now was the devil who had always been there.

I looked down at my arm, at the place where the chain scar might still be, beneath the blood-matted fur and the jet-black fire. Then the bone black sword was in my hand, and it was hungry.

A rising wind. A talon scraped along the back of my neck, catching the flesh over my cheekbone and my eye. The dark thing inside snarled and staggered back, and the Opal gained purchase.

An explosion. A storm of feathers, sizzling around my feet. I saw Seela turn.

"The hero of the hour." Seela's harsh bass thrummed in the back of my head, but the rubble parted and a headwind sent him lurching on his scuttling insect legs.

Eli was the massive Owl Therion, barely enough of him there to recognize. But somehow, impossibly, it was him. His golden eyes caught me, but the children were pressing their smouldering bodies to me, keeping me back and screaming in my ears.

Seela struck out, and where I thought he was merely trying to bat Eli away like an insect, he'd grabbed hold of him hard, a gnarled hand latched to the Tradewind Moonstone. Bolts of gold slithered off their dark, thrashing bodies.

In seconds he'd rip it free like a swollen wood tick — like it was nothing. But Seela released him, and Eli curled around himself in pain. A cyclone kicked up around him, and a shockwave that knocked me down blasted through the city. People fell but thankfully they still got up, Denizens coming round to leap back into the fray as the deservedly freaked-out Mundanes took for the hills.

Eli wasn't dead — was barely hurt even, just staring straight ahead as if he'd been stunned to stillness — and our eyes locked across the shattered block, asking each other the same question: *What the hell just happened?*

Then, with a savage reel, that seven-foot monstrosity that called itself my father was in front of me, snatching the breath out of my lungs in those suffocating ribbons that grew out of him, tearing reality and distance apart like tissue paper and taking me down the rabbit hole with him.

The wind rose. A terrible roar, and I saw Eli reaching for me as he had through the geyser tearing a splitting cliff apart —

But I was no longer there. Yet we still felt each other — me now too many miles away, having left him behind in the rubble-strewn street filled with people-shaped trees as the smoke cleared.

The sirens were screaming. The world had seen it all. And it wouldn't be the last they'd see.

The Cold Road

They'd been staring at the map for days before this, but trying to negotiate with two polar bears, one of whom was down with a demon sickness, was proving useless. And they'd been holed up in this house outside of Fort Mac for so long they must have overstayed their welcome before arriving.

"Can't you get how huge this country is?" Natti bristled. "We went in the complete opposite direction of where you wanted to go in the first place. Besides, most of Nunavut isn't passable by road. We'd have to . . . like, fly you there! Last I checked you two are *literally bears*."

Maujaq snarled. "We trusted you to take us to the Empress. And she is *here*." The great paw slammed down on the white space that comprised the territory of Nunavut, which seemed like it was in another solar system.

"If you could only be a bit more specific," Phae urged

gently, drawing a hand up Maujaq's paw, sparking blue, trying to calm him. He pulled back.

They'd been at this for a while, stuck, cut off since the attack at the tar sands. The Denizens there were happy to put Natti and Phae in a safe house, with the bears away from prying eyes, as a thanks for their part — however minuscule — in beating the monsters back that had climbed out of the earth's crust to level them. Siku and Maujaq had their theories of what those monsters were — creatures stirred up by the Gardener of the Bloodlands itself, Urka.

"We have no money," Natti said, watching Aivik slump by, guzzling down a Coke. Phae's phone went off, and after she checked the screen, she left the room. Probably not good news. Natti sighed. "We're at the end of our ropes. We dragged Aunty all the way out here only to get our asses nearly handed to us. Unless you have a way of teleporting there or any other convenient abilities you're hiding . . ."

Siku raised his head, eyes narrowed at Natti. She was certain it had been the two of them, in some other form, that had come to their aid using the river and the ice. Had to be. But neither one seemed interested in imparting that, and after the attack they'd seemed diminished somehow, as if they were more bear than Inua. It had taken days for them to decide to start talking again, and when they did it wasn't at all helpful.

Siku turned away from them, paws crossed. He was the protector, the quiet negotiator. He'd known the risks coming on this journey. "The Ice Road."

Maujaq twisted. "No, brother. We must *both* return to the Empress or not at all. You said this yourself!"

"That tenet is one that you and I have kept to for survival. It was never forced upon us." His smile was wan.

"Has to be another way . . ." Aunty cringed, sitting up. She had been declining, too, refusing to eat, let alone smoke. They were running out of time. "We aren't that desperate yet, are we?"

"Unless you know anyone with a private plane willing to dump us off there for free," Natti said. She glanced up as Phae re-entered the room. Her face was twisted, as it had been lately, in anguish. While they'd been stuck out here, they'd been powerless to affect everything that was happening overseas. And enough had happened. Phae had sent Barton a photo of the tree that had once been the Owl, Evan, and it turned out it wasn't an isolated incident. It'd happened to Eli, but with Barton's help he'd managed to get free. And the thing that had caused it — Seela — had taken Roan. The last they'd heard, Eli had taken off to go after her — at least, to go after the Opal, before it got corrupted as the Rabbit stone had. But this was the first they'd heard from Barton since then.

"What is it?" Natti asked. Phae didn't answer right away, just crossed the room to the television, flicked it on, and passed through channels until she hit on the news.

"The City of London is reeling today after the attack, though it has been twenty-four hours and no known terrorist group has claimed it. Speculation continues as to whether or not this is some kind of film promotion publicity stunt, given the pageantry and perhaps the sophisticated special effects, as there can be no other explanation for what we are about to show you here this evening."

The footage revealed an exploding street, a towering creature scuttling on spidery legs, black flames and burning children, and those trees, those demonic *trees* they left behind, the ones Barton had talked about and now they'd seen firsthand.

Then there were the three leads in this dance — the man with the great black wings and a girl with mismatched eyes. Both were yanked into the abyss in the embrace of the hideous monster that had precipitated the attack in the first place.

The news went on to note the injury count, the damages, but no lives were lost. If only they knew what the trees really were.

"How in the hell," Aivik cried, "is this even on the news? Isn't this, like, the Owls' *one major job*? How many people have seen this?" He whipped his phone out to Google it.

Phae had beat him to it. "Barton says it's everywhere. Facebook. YouTube." Cellphone footage and hashtags and the human world was chattering; the curtain was lifted.

"Seela," Siku shouted, ramming his head so hard into the television that it teetered. Natti swooped in and caught it before it could crash to the floor.

"Easy," she said. "You're not gonna reach him through this thing." Not that she'd want to, after seeing the image of him up close and personal. And they'd had it put right before their eyes: Roan being ripped away back into its fold, and Eli had been too late.

"This is all happening without us," Maujaq moaned. "We are running out of time. We must wake the Empress."

"The Ice Road may be our only way there." Siku looked up at Natti. "Seela is seeking an even playing field. It wants to turn the world against Denizens. What precious anonymity we once enjoyed is unwinding."

"Tagging along with a bunch of bears hasn't done us any favours in that arena." Natti paced, unable to shake what she'd seen.

"What's this Ice Road?" Phae hazarded. "Is it, like, some means of faster travel?"

Siku nodded. "But like all things, it comes at a cost."

Maujaq reared. "I won't let you give up the compass for it. I won't!"

"That is not your choice to make," Siku said.

"Enough!" Natti was at her feet in front of them, tired of the bickering. "No one is dying here. I know what you two are capable of. I saw it at the tar sands. But you came to us asking our help, and we'll give it to you. You just have to ask."

No one in the room spoke or moved — except Aunty.

She had barely contributed even the thinnest sardonic comment in the last few days. She'd spent the long hours staring out windows into the distance, haunted by what was out there. Now she had pulled herself up, waving Aivik away, as she stood in front of the bears.

"I've held onto it long enough," she said. "It's time to use it."

Natti stilled. "What the hell is this now?"

"Hold your tongue, Nattiq," Aunty barked, and she turned back to the bears. "I know where the Shore Clan have gathered. The summoning is going to start soon. Your priestess is ready to bring the glacier back up. I can point you and the Ice Road there."

She opened her hands and showed something Natti hadn't seen in years — the necklace her mother had worn every day except the day she'd gone missing.

Siku pulled himself to his hind legs, proud and strong, and even though he was a bear, he held himself like a man. Maujaq followed suit, though it came with greater effort, and suddenly the room was filled with an icy white gale, and their yellowed fur whipped in the frenzy.

"You have any idea what this is about?" Phae cried over the gust, grabbing hold of Natti to stop from either falling over or being buried in snow.

"Not a damn one," she hollered back, "but I really don't like it."

Siku pressed his head into Maujaq's, his brother's face twisted in grief. Natti felt like a sacrifice was about to be made, and Siku dropped his paw onto the charm that Aunty held aloft.

Somewhere close by, a pipe burst, and the room filled with an impossible volume of water called there by the bears, or by Aunty, and Natti grabbed hold of Phae, who flashed a shield around them all in time for the water around them to shiver into clear, hard-cut ice.

Aunty's hair was cast around her like a great net. The bauble shone, the light engulfing Siku and pulling him away from Maujaq — pulling them all away, through the ice, into the light that the pendant cast, and they were gone.

❧

"But what's it for?"

Natti's small hand wound in the chain, thumb smoothing out the sea glass pendant incised with three gold rings and a jagged pointing arrow.

Her mother's hand eclipsed hers, pressed Natti's fingers to her mouth in a kiss, then tucked the pendant back into her work shirt. "It will bring me back to you. If I ever get lost."

Natti could feel her eyes growing heavy, but something

nagged at the back of her mind. A voice, maybe hers, begging her to stay awake, to hear this clearly. "Are you going somewhere, Ma?"

Back then, little Natti wouldn't have noticed. But through the lens of time she did. Her mother's eyes, still so young, constricting. "Get some sleep," she'd said, then left the room, the door cracked open and spilling light and voices from the hall.

"You need to keep it safe," her mother was saying, voice low.

"It is not meant for me! If you take it off, you know what will happen. The protection will be lost."

"Yes, I know. But it is my time to be tested. The Empress has called me back. I have to complete the journey. I don't know how long . . ." Her mother's voice caught, and she swallowed. "The water is sick. I must go north. I know that whatever happens, you will take care of them." A rustling, as if an embrace, a grunt of knowing.

"Be careful," Aunty said. "There are worse things than darklings on those roads, looking for women like us."

The bedroom of her childhood faded, the last time she'd seen her mother slipping through Natti's fingers, no matter how desperately she tried to hold on.

* * *

Natti groaned. The snow-speckled wind scoured her face. She tried to cover herself but even her windbreaker wasn't going to cut it.

All around her was a whiteout. A blistering blizzard and a flat plain of snow stretching infinitely. Getting to her knees was a trial, for the icy blast wasn't interested in seeing her move.

So she crawled. And, bit by bit, a figure, a shadow, resolved out of the white. A person, sitting upright and calm, spine stiff, staring into the distance.

"Hey!" Natti shouted, and she saw the person incline their head only slightly, and with that dip the air froze, the snow shivering to the ground in a breath, and all around them was clear and silent.

The person stood and turned fully. It was a man, his face lined with dark tattoos stretching from his eyes to his mouth. His long white hair cascaded down his back in a braid, his furs and hide stark yellow. His eyes were a fathomless sea.

Natti got to her shaking legs on her own, since the man didn't seem inclined to help. She grunted. "Where are the others?"

The man lifted an eyebrow. "So you know me, then?"

Natti walked past him, staring out into the tundra. The sky was pink, the sun a caustic jewel ahead. The sounds could have been from an alien world. There was nothing to smell. In the distance, sharp peaks rose, but beyond that Natti felt something she never had — an eternity, filling her blood. The unfettered call of the sea.

The cold was intense, and she rubbed her chest with her fist. "This is all happening so fast, Siku."

"And it must," Siku said, joining her side. "Maujaq is with the others. But I wanted to speak to you, first."

Natti appraised him from the corner of her eye. In this form, Siku still had all the same devastating bearing he had as a polar bear, yet he seemed diminished somehow. "You aren't going with us, are you?"

At that, Siku smiled. "It was canny of Aunty to use the compass. She knew she would have to eventually. But she'd need power to do it. Power she doesn't have any longer. She carries the same corruption that my brother does. We view death differently, and you know that, too. I'm not really going — we will be reunited soon."

The day seemed to pass impossibly fast before them, because it was suddenly dark, and the sky lit with ribbons of dancing green. Natti didn't bother asking where they might be or how this might be happening. This could be the Veil. Some place in between. But it didn't matter. She started when Siku took her hand and placed something in it — a single large bear claw.

"A fight is coming," he said, closing her fingers around it. "You have not just power but a will to help. That is as good a weapon as any. The Empress must be called back up by her messengers. She will lead you all into battle."

Natti stared at the sharp claw, kept on a leather strap. "And what if the Empress —"

"Chooses you?" Siku finished for her. "She already has, in some way. You have come far to deliver us. You have risked much. Even when there has not been much left to risk."

Natti frowned. "So what? You're spent, now? And you're passing the torch to me? What if I can't carry it? Phae and I would've died if you and Maujaq hadn't intervened. I don't have that kind of power. I'm not Roan. I can't lead anyone."

The day was turning again, and the sky was getting so bright it was hard to see. She could feel Siku's hands on her shoulders, becoming the huge paws of the bear, and the sea calling, the glacier looming large in her memory as the wind screamed through her and the blizzard returned.

"You are made strong by the love of your friends. You have already carried so much. And you must be stronger still — if you are to make it back to your mother."

Natti startled. "My —"

But the wind and the tundra took her, and she knew no further promises beyond the cold.

❧

Phae had expected a warmer welcome than this — though she wasn't sure if she'd ever feel warm again, despite the furs and hides they'd been given.

Maujaq had been silent since they'd reappeared in the frozen north with little bearing. Natti was still unconscious, and Siku was gone. Aunty still wore the sea glass around her neck, and she rocked back and forth under Aivik's second blanket, coughing all the while.

"How long do you think they'll keep us here?" Phae asked, sidling up closer to the both of them. They had all come to in a vast emptiness, but there had been the lights of a settlement on the horizon, by the coast. Maujaq had led the way bitterly, and it had been an exhausting journey on foot, in the cold, barely prepared. *The summoning*, Aunty had called it, an impromptu gathering of Seals at this glacial bay to bring the Sapphire, kept hidden at the bottom of the sea, to the surface in order to unleash the tide of war.

They were being kept in a hut with a floor of snow and ice retreating from the central firepit. The wind battered the hides as if scads of monsters were trying to claw their way in, but the structure held firm.

"They'll keep us here as long as they like." Aunty sniffed,

taking a huge breath as Phae pulled her blue-sparking hand away. "These are troubled times. Even coming here with an Inua could be a trap. They've got to take our measure." She glanced towards Natti, who was still prone by the fire, completely still save for her flickering eyelids. "It has been a taxing journey for us all."

Phae's mouth twisted. "Do you think the stone will choose Natti? To lead whatever this . . . onslaught is against Seela."

Aunty shrugged. "Natti is a fighter. So is Ryk. She will want her best on the charge. But the girl is young. Hasn't even had a chance at her own life. Spent it taking care of everyone else's." She glanced up at Phae. "Think you know how that feels."

Phae sniffed — she was too tired to deflect or deny it. In the small space, Maujaq's heaving back, turned on them, was difficult to ignore. "Siku gave up his power, then. To see us here safely." She thought of a Deer, long ago, who had done the same for her.

Aunty sighed. "That he did. But he saw as well as I did that time's running short. For all of us."

All Phae could think about were the tar sands. The monsters that had crawled out of that dark, dead place, that horrible twisted tree that had been a man only moments before. What was happening? And had it been happening all along? Phae watched the tethered entryway, shadows moving past it, voices coming and going. No matter what happened now, there might not be any going back — for her, for Natti, for any of them.

Phae's hands were empty, but beneath her skin the power sizzled. She wanted to be useful. She didn't want to be idle any longer. She wished, most of all, that she could tell Barton he was right.

Natti groaned in her sleep, but before Phae could go to her, the tent flap moved, and Natti bolted upright, eyes wide. She took a bleary look around, a fist clenched in front of her face. She was trembling.

A man had come, flanked by two women, each with similar facial tattoos and fur-drawn hoods. They stared at Natti in silence, then surveyed the rest of them. Maujaq shifted, levelling them all with his dark, miserable stare.

The man nodded. “Come,” he said. “The summoner will see you now. It is time to open the Abyss.”

Natti’s fingers uncurled, one by one, and Maujaq scented the air, coming closer.

Phae helped Aunty up, and Aivik aided her out of the tent, while Phae went to Natti’s side. “Are you okay?”

The two of them stared at the bear claw in Natti’s hand — almost as long as a knife. Natti said nothing, simply slipped the tether over her head and pulled the hair away.

“Guess I have to be,” she muttered, gaze landing on Maujaq, whose sorrow seemed to be edging away when he nodded. “Time to do the hero thing.”

They were led into open ground, into the bright and desolate night. The encampment was on a bay, and the wind off the water was biting. Maujaq walked beside Natti, his progress slow. Natti was in no rush; it could’ve been a death march. She wasn’t ready to take on the burden, but there was no other choice.

“My brother would not bestow his trust idly,” Maujaq finally said. His voice seemed weaker, each word speared on his teeth. “He has given you the blessing of an Inua.”

Natti grunted. “Here’s hoping it was worth it.”

“To say such would besmirch his sacrifice,” Maujaq snarled, but when he looked up at Natti he seemed to balk. He must have seen the dread there. She wasn’t going to hide it.

“It’s not him I’m unsure about,” she said.

Natti tripped and didn’t realize it was Maujaq holding her back until she looked up and saw the man he’d become, so similar to his brother, holding bone-breakingly tight to her wrist. He staggered for the effort of the transformation, the black mark so ugly against the pristine white of his coat, his hair, his eyes.

“Remember,” he said gravely, “you brought us here, and with little knowledge as to what for or why. You are willing to give up your future to see this world has one. You saw what lies ahead, and you did not shy.” Was that a smile at the corner of his mouth? “And I don’t admit such things easily.”

Natti glanced down at Maujaq’s hand, which let her go, and he flexed the fingers, staring at them.

“Not used to a human body?” she hazarded. After all, the Inua were spirits; intervening in human affairs was probably more than an inconvenience.

The fingers made a fist. “Not used to this human world.” He surveyed the scene in front of them; they were being led up a path to a ledge of rock and snow, overlooking the water and lit by the curtained northern lights. If the apocalypse hadn’t been imminent, the sky’s beauty would have stopped them in their tracks.

"Once the Sapphire is brought up," he said, "once the Empress is called, all of us will answer. I will stay by your side, in gratitude for your end of the bargain. And out of loyalty to my brother." He stood aside, and Natti nodded, following the track.

❧

It was a ceremony. It was pageantry. It was nothing that Phae had yet seen. Men and women dancing in cadence to drums. The sky awake and shouting its colours down. A procession of bodies, a prayer, a petition.

"They have been at this for days," Phae heard Aunty whisper, as they all watched from the outskirts of the revels. They were interlopers, yet at least it had been decided they were a part of this, even as spectators. "The fasting, the dancing."

The sea whipped beneath them in time to the drums. Then, beneath the dancers' feet, the three gold rings rose to light, and the drumming stopped.

A woman stepped into the three rings. She wore a costume of delicately hewn blue-dyed trailing fur. Her tattoos cut three lines down her chin, across her brow. Her headdress was mighty, made of fine ivory spikes and threaded with beads. Maybe this was the summoner they'd mentioned?

Natti stood slowly as the woman surveyed them from under heavily lidded eyes, and unbidden, Natti went forward.

"Ma?" she choked out, her face a raw open wound.

The woman did not smile. She looked out at all of them, her voice rising, the voice of the still water behind her. "The world is in pain. The sea itself is choked. The Empress bids we wake her now. Because we have all suffered losses, and the worst is yet to come." This time the woman did look at Natti, her stony expression cracking, only slightly. The recognition was real. Something passed between them. But Natti sat down, face hard, and the ceremony went on.

"Many have travelled far. The road has been a jagged one. But now we call with a united voice to our Empress and her heart. We open the way to the Abyss. We make clear a path for they who will lead us to war."

Maujaq was silent amongst them, yet he went forward to the woman and bowed his head. All around them, the drums and dancing had begun again, rising in a frantic rhythm, louder and faster, and Phae saw the water behind them rising, spreading, separating. The ice parted, and a glacier that had at first been so far away was now rushing towards them, as if it had a hidden engine attached to it.

Phae had been too busy watching the incoming ice to notice that Natti had stood, too, and followed Maujaq. The two stood before the woman, and Natti held up the claw she'd woken with. The woman nodded, and she turned to Maujaq, running a hand over his black-stained pelt. She held them both, and her long hair rose with a flash of water springing from the sea like a wild and tremulous eel darting around her.

Phae didn't know what to do. She was paralyzed, hands so tight at her sides the knuckles cracked. But it was Aunty who stood next and shuffled towards the circle as more darts of water shot forth. She looked to Phae and held out her arm for her support, and Phae was grateful for the prompt to move.

The golden circles shimmered. The drums were deafening, the dancing a frenzied mania. The sky was almost painfully clear as the glacier loomed close, and the sea round it shifted, lifting it, turning it over to its searing blue underbelly.

In the half-moonlight, something flashed, like a just-waking eye. The sea water hung about them in a sheet, and the summoning woman bent back in an ecstatic dance that seemed out of her control. All they could do was watch as with her movements the glacier rose higher and through it shattered a splintering crack that, with one final thrust of the woman's open arms, sent the glacier bursting in a rain of diamond dust that blizzarded around the gathering. When the snow cleared, there was only the stone.

The wind whipped higher, and the sea hung above them, dangerous, forbidding. Phae looked up through the arms she'd raised to protect her face and saw in the waves the shadows of the gliding, mysterious bodies that called the waters home, oblivious to being ripped from their moorings.

Then the sea fell on them, before Phae could take a breath.

All Natti could hear were the voices. Thousands of them, a raging flurry, angry for having been woken. She knew, beyond the water and the waves and the crushing sensation of passing into another realm, that the voices came from the stone. And that it was because of the stone they were still alive.

Phae hadn't been so careless as to think the Sapphire would protect her; she had cast a wide and beautiful net to protect Natti, Aunty, the summoner, and Maujaq. The rest of those who had made this happen, those taking part in the ceremony, were probably back on shore, waiting to see if they would be successful.

To what end, Natti could only guess.

"Are we —" Phae started, her voice sounding distant despite being at Natti's and Maujaq's side. "*Where* are we?"

"The Abyss," Maujaq replied. He didn't hesitate; there was a searing joy in his voice, as if his soul had been returned to rights. And it had. Natti took it in; they were beneath the sea and the waves, an infinity of water. And she, too, felt like she was back where she belonged. Where she needed to be.

The summoner only had eyes for Natti, and when she opened her arms, Natti leapt into them, fierce.

"I thought . . ." She pulled away, not wanting to say it. "You disappeared. Like the others."

Natti's mother tried to banish the despair from her eyes with a smile. "I know, love. I didn't want to leave you. But all of us have to take the Ice Road home, in our way. I was called back here. I didn't know how it'd be, but it was violent."

Whether it was from being in a realm of Ancient or from the power Siku had given her, Natti couldn't say — but just by holding tight to her mother, the water's surface showed her how her ma had come to be here. Coming home from her shift. A car pulling up next to her. Rough hands dragging her in, knocking her out, a fight. Driving for hours and hours north. A river. They hadn't known that the water would be the safest place for her, that you can't drown a Seal. The water spoke to her, desperate. Took her here. She would be the one to call the glacier back up, and the stone in it. This had been her destiny. And she would have to wait, long painful years, until her daughter found her own way back.

"Could've called," Natti sniffed. "Could've told me you were okay."

Her mother's face twisted. "Even Seals have tenets. Everything in its time. We had to trust, you and I. And it wasn't for nothing."

"No," Aunty said. "Really something, all right."

Natti's mother rested a hand on Aunty's upper arm. "Thank you. For seeing her here where she belongs."

"But —" Natti interjected. "I can't . . . it's not —"

A flash, one voice among the deluge. A wave within a wave, and from the Sapphire bloomed a maelstrom in the water. A great body rising, with a long smooth tail. With a crown of fish bones and hair as wild and untamed as any ocean.

Ryk.

She surveyed them all with a gaze as stabbing as a tide. In one hand she held a jagged bone harpoon as if it were an extension of her arm.

"*Long has my heart slept in the waves*," she said, and the sound was all around them and inside, even in Phae's protective bubble. "*Grave must be the tidings to wake me*."

"They are." Natti's mother went forward, flanked by Maujaq, and the two knelt in deference. "First Matriarch, Empress of the Abyss. A child of the Bloodlands has blackened the blood of the world. We need your avatar now more than we ever have."

Ryk seemed to weigh each word of the petition like a pebble in her puckered mouth. Natti hadn't ever seen drawings of Ryk; she had only the vision she'd imagined from Aunty's stories. But not even her imagination could measure up to the powerful woman towering before them, the left hand of Ancient, and the warrior twin to Deon, First

Matriarch of Fire and Foxes. If only Roan could be here to see it . . . Just thinking of her pained Natti. What was her friend possibly going through?

"*Great unrest with my sister stones. I feel it across the current.*" Ryk turned to stare out into her vast kingdom as if to listen. "*Heen's heart corrupted. Deon's faltering. What hope is there for the Sapphire to be sent into the world if these have already fallen?*"

"Fallen?" Natti repeated, dumbstruck, as if Roan's fate had already been decided.

"Surely the Moonstone —" Natti's mother tried, but Ryk silenced her with a glare.

"*The keeper of Phyr's stone moves to reclaim the Opal. But he will fall short. His mortal heart will not be able to do what he must. And he will suffer for it.*" Ryk lowered her harpoon, pointing it at each of them. "*My Inua brought you all here so that I may choose one to bear the stone.*" And as she knew it would, the barbed spear halted before Natti, so she met it with a nod.

But Aunty shuffled in front of it, straightening her back as best she could. "And I choose to bear it, Empress."

Natti faltered. "Aunty, no —"

Aunty held up a shaking hand, and it seemed that even Ryk was considering this.

"*Grandmother*," she admonished, "*long have you been in the world. Truly you have been blessed with power and you have seen much. But you, like my Inua, are corrupted.*" The sharp tip of her mighty weapon touched Aunty's chest, parted her jacket to show the black stain that matched Maujaq's. Her eyes darted to Phae. "*Even a Deer could not heal this.*"

Aunty nodded. "The fight will come soon enough, and I'm dying anyway. Might as well make the most of it, eh?"

Natti didn't know what kind of balls it took to try to pass sarcasm over a Matriarch, but Ryk tilted her head back and let out a laugh to rival a group of barking seals on an open bay.

"*Truly I am spoiled for choice,*" Ryk shot back, and the stone lunged for purchase in Aunty's forehead before Natti could stop any of it. Aunty's body stiffened, was swirled in a violent twist of jagged light, and suddenly Ryk was Aunty, and Aunty was Ryk, and the bone harpoon was in the aged, powerful hand of the woman who had cared for Natti since she was a child.

Natti, her mother, and Maujaq gaped in awe, but the Abyss still twisted and raged around them.

"We have our Matriarch." Natti's mother nodded. "But there's yet another purpose for us here."

"Not us," said Aunty. "Her."

She levelled the harpoon now at Phae, whose antlers glistened in the shadow of the water, brow knit in concentration and fear.

"Me?" she balked.

Aunty nodded, the fish crown and her iron hair a huge and thunderous halo. The currents whipped faster, and when Phae ducked, the forcefield around her quivered.

"It won't be enough to send the Sapphire after Seela. It's only a part of it. But there's another stone, the last stone, that is necessary for all of this to play out," Aunty intoned.

The currents were guided missiles, and they blindsided Phae, pulling her into the waves. Natti leapt forward, tried to catch her, but Maujaq held her back.

"Wait!" she screamed. "What are you —"

"The Horned Quartz," Aunty said, raising the harpoon above her head in both hands and commanding the sea like she was stirring a boiling pot. "Find the heart of the Glen. Find the ruler of that stark land. If Fia finds you worthy of it, finds this world worthy of it, the Horned Quartz would be yours to wield. That is why you came with us. I see it now. As I see far too much . . ."

If lightning could blast beneath the water, it ricocheted off Aunty's long, barbarous spear, making a fist of water that dragged Phae in its furious undertow.

"With this Ancient current I send you there and pray you find your way back again," Aunty said before she jabbed the weapon down like an axe, and Phae was catapulted into another realm.

SON *of the* WIND

"You are losing sight of your purpose, young master."

The darkling summoning tower was filled with ashy smoke, the oily kind from burning tallow. The red rings beneath Killian glowed faintly like plague wounds, Urka's great furnace roiling at his back.

"You question me now?" Killian allowed himself the grin. As Seela, he was sure of himself, but there was a sliver of him that was still human. Even though he'd let most of it go in exchange for his part in all this, Urka wanted it all gone. But a demon would never understand.

"You are the Great Hammer," Urka repeated, as it had every day and night since Killian had been blessed anew in that train station. "You will build the road to the new world. The bridge that our masters can cross. You were given their power and their promise. The Fox-girl. She was not meant to live."

"No. But she will be the one to open the door at my side. You'll see."

Killian heard Urka raise its mighty arms and cut the air with its knife-fingers, agitated. "But the work . . . the work could be in jeopardy."

"Calm yourself, servant." This time Killian's smile dropped, teeth on edge. Seela stirred inside this frail mortal body, growling. "I ken what I'm about. And so should you. Bring me more children. I want cities blanketed with the trees of my homeland. I will make the world ready for my forebears, and no mistake. You do the digging, and I will build the bridge."

The rings stilled. In each of them the smoke hung like gossamer, and shapes took form: before him, a serpent with the body of a woman, her head crested with a cobra's hood that could have been a crown. Another to Killian's right — a beautiful man with four impossibly long arms bent in supplicant gestures, his face obscured by the same mask of bone that Killian carried as Seela. And the third, to his left, the strongest, the one that had not yet spoken and never would until they hung in the heavens with their siblings. They were dual-gendered, their spine on the outside of their body, eyes white, ears wide, mouthless, with the body of a horse.

"Zabor. Kirkald. Balaghast." Their names were an incantation on Killian's tongue. They joined hands around him.

"Our one true child," they said.

A rustling, footsteps. The Darkling Family in the red smoke collapsed with a sigh as if someone had blown them out, and Killian twisted, face contorted. A small gasp as the source dashed for the door, small feet slapping down the stone steps two at a time.

"The little one," Urka said, sharpening its axe-hands, "does not know her place." Urka bore down on itself, grinding deep into the stone and the cliffs and travelling with haste, at Seela's command, to crack the earth from the inside. Urka knew its place. So did Killian. So did Saskia, deep down.

"She knows it right well, in fact." Killian smiled again in the silence, and he let the dark move him.

❧

"And you're safe?"

Eli felt his mouth twitch. "In a manner of speaking." He huddled closer to the roof's air vent, pulling his wings around him like a coat. He'd been up here a while, trying to come back to himself, but he still felt stunned. He was lucky he'd made it up here at all, and unseen.

"It's all over the news —" Barton's voice, cutting in front of Solomon's. "They're just playing it on a loop, everywhere, on every network . . . can't you stop it?"

"I already told you —" Eli bit back a rush of pain "— he touched the stone. Did something to it. It's like it's shorted out. I've never . . ." *Never lost control. Never lost the ability to control anyone* else.

"There were injuries." Solomon came back on the line. "But no deaths. Just those trees. And the destruction. It was —"

"A big show," Eli finished for him. Spectacle. But not just that. He'd seen Roan there, in the midst of it. The core and source of the destruction. Seela had her on the front line — and whether by his will or no, he'd changed her into something else. "Seela wants Mundanes to see Denizens. He got what he wanted. And he wants to divide the world further than it already is."

Eli had tried for hours to reach out to her, the way they'd done when he'd been trapped, stone to stone. It was the only way he'd found her at all. *West*, it'd said so clearly. But either she was too far away now, or he was too out of sorts to do much else but cough up blood and shiver deep into his wings. He couldn't feel the Opal anywhere. And he couldn't feel Roan.

"What are you going to do now?" Barton again, voice low, other voices climbing in the background. "Are you going after her? After Seela?"

"I don't know," Eli lied. "The Moonstone is . . . its power. My power. It's inhibited." *Come on,* he shut his eyes tight, pressing the phone harder into his head as if willing the electromagnetic pulse to charge through him, kickstart the stone like a worn battery. "For all I know she could be dead. Seela could have the Opal. I don't know."

"Come back."

Eli perked up. "What did you say?" He sat up, peered around the air vent towards the sun setting on the western horizon over the city. The roof was empty, the wind a steely howl.

"What?" Barton said. "I didn't say anything. But look, you should get back here, Eli. I don't know how you got *there* so goddamn fast, but you have to return. Charter a plane. We're in damage control. So many people saw it all happen. Regular people. Networks originally tried to spin it as a stunt for a movie, but the buildings, the destruction . . . it's being labelled as terrorism now. Governments are getting involved.

Is there a precedent for Denizens coming under arrest for their powers? Are we all hooped now?"

Eli couldn't stand the panic in Barton's voice. "I have to stay in the field," he insisted quietly. "I'm not coming back. Not without the Opal." He hung up, threw the phone aside, and watched it shatter against a chimney stack.

"Come back."

This time Eli was on his feet, wings raised painfully and ready for flight. The shadows on the roof were vibrating, moving, rising. They took the shape of a body right in front of him, peeling back to reveal a face partially concealed by a mask of bone.

Eli lowered his arms. "Harken?"

There were no eyes, just the mouth. So much like Seela he couldn't bear the comparison. The shadows were peeling back, and there, at the centre, was the Dragon Opal.

Maybe Eli had nodded off in the seconds between tossing the phone and taking a breath. The air stilled, and scattered pigeons were frozen above her head like an augury.

"Where are you?" Eli asked. "I can't . . . reach the stone."

"I don't know," she said. "It's getting crowded in here. Soon there won't be enough room for all of us."

Eli stared. "Us?"

She nodded. "The darkness. Me. You. It's getting harder to breathe."

Maybe she was asleep, too. Was she talking about what he'd seen in the street? The dead, dark fox warrior, who should have been Deon but wasn't. *Corrupted* had been the best word for it. Had Seela infected her, turning her against even herself?

"You have to fight it. You have to keep a part of yourself, however small, however deeply buried, alive."

Her mouth was cruel. "You would know, would you?"

He took a step. "I know better than you." Was this thing that was speaking to him even Roan at all? "The stone. The voices —"

She turned her head aside. Eli could see the mask splintering, sloughing off by half. It cracked to reveal her amber eye. The one that the Moth Queen had given her.

"The voices are quiet now," she said. "The dark even ate them up."

Then whatever this *infection* was had burrowed into the Opal. And the Opal was compromised. The longer Roan stayed anywhere near Seela, the worse it could become. But in this vision she seemed, at least, to be trying to resurface. She was fighting. There might still be a chance.

"The Moth Queen came to me," he said, voice so low he didn't think he'd said it out loud. "She said —"

"Come back," Roan said again, this time looking straight at him. She was now sitting in the woods, beneath the sun, and Eli could see all of her. Could feel the Opal.

"I will," he said, but he was just on the rooftop, awakening from his doze. He took a cursory look around, but there were no woods, no sun. He was alone.

North.

The day had given way to night and, bitter and exhausted, Eli lifted his wings and climbed higher into the dark.

The air was strange. The sun was out, warm on my cheek.

"Is he your boyfriend?"

I blinked. The world came back and I was sitting on the ground surrounded by rock and young, trembling forest. Sitting cross-legged in front of me was Saskia.

"What . . ." I squinted. I didn't bother asking where I was, how I'd gotten here. I was just a passenger in my own body. The stone had had its own plan for me. Now this dark pilot burrowing deeper into it had hijacked even that. Didn't I have a say? Wasn't I the leaseholder around here?

I opened my shirt and looked myself over in the daylight. The black spread all the way up to my throat. I checked the rest of me — my hands looked like I'd dipped them forearm-deep in volcanic ash. Instead of being horrified, as I ought to have been, I just sighed. There was a sort of serenity to accepting shit as it hit the fan.

"You feel better, don't you?" Saskia asked me. She was frowning, though, as if it wasn't the outcome she'd wanted.

"Yes," I said, and even my voice was neutral, relaxed. "I don't even feel hungry anymore." Or like there was anything beyond these woods for me. Staying here could be just fine. I was already forgetting why I'd wanted to leave. "Is who my boyfriend?"

"The beautiful man with the black wings. The angel." Saskia put her own charred finger to the dirt, scrawling, drawing. The grass smoked with each line carved. "He was trying to save you. Trying to take you back from Killian."

"He's not my . . ." Man with the wings? Yes. Hadn't I only just seen him? Hadn't I *just* been seeing him, whenever I closed my eyes? "The last thing I'd want is for him, or anyone, to come looking for me. I can manage on my own.

He's got better things to do." So did all the others. Lives to live. I just wanted to fade away. I think I was getting my wish.

Saskia frowned. "You think you can stop Seela. But you can't beat him. You just join him."

I got up and knelt next to her, eyes narrowed at her crude drawing in the dirt. Stick figures but with defining features — wings for Eli, who was standing on the edge of a hard line she'd drawn, between what could have been me, but my face was scratched out. Around us was a circle, with three black smudges at the edge of it.

Tears splattered the drawing, hissing as they hit the ground. I was so startled that my head snapped up.

Saskia's black eyes with their bright red centres, their flaming edges, were spilling over. "I really thought you would be different. I really thought you could beat him." Her whisper was vicious.

I felt the thing inside me turn over, as if it had heard a noise and its sleep was disturbed. I didn't breathe, and it turned over again, silent.

"Saskia." I grabbed hold of her. "You're not like the other children, are you? Why?" Even just holding her like this, her skin flaked off and danced in the air, underneath that a feverish glowing warmth. I was coming back to myself, breath by wretched breath. She was infected, too, but there was no hunger in her limp shoulders, no desire to do the evil things her dark siblings did.

She didn't look at me; she was staring at the ground, at her drawing. My grip tightened when her huge stare swung back up to me. "I went with Seela to help my brother. The others . . . they did it so they could do things. Have powers. Be part of something. I only ever wanted Albie to be safe.

But he wasn't in the end. He tried to kill your friend Barton, but he failed. Now there's only me. Daddy used to tell us so many stories, about good people doing scary things because they needed to be done. I thought I could be one of the people in his stories. But now I'm the bad guy. I thought you could be the good guy. Maybe you still can be. Maybe that's why I'm not like the others. Because I can still hope." Her tiny burnt arms slid around me, and her small head pressed against the Dragon Opal. "I can hear her in there. The grandma lady. She doesn't want you to be sad. But she can't say it herself. Because there's another you in there. And she is winning."

The grandma lady. Cecelia. Or just her memories. She was too far away to help me now. And maybe she always had been.

I didn't move, my hands hovering over Saskia's back. That's when I realized, in the still unreality of the grove and the trees, that Saskia's body wasn't warm at all, and neither was it rising and falling with regular breaths. Could there be a way to save her? To save any of these children?

To save myself?

"Look at ye two," said that snide voice I'd come to hate for all its saccharine human-mimicry. "What a pair."

Saskia jumped away, crouching behind me as if I'd protect her. It was the first time I'd ever seen Killian level her with a dark look, his eyes pincers. I had thought Saskia was his favourite, because she was always at his side. But it was obvious he could sense something was wrong with her. That maybe her benign loyalty was a put-on.

"Away with ye," he snarled, and before I could stop her she scampered off into the scrub. It was the first time I noticed, too, that in the distance rose the cliffs and the twisted citadel Killian had dragged me to. I could smell the sea.

I twisted back around. "She wasn't doing anything wrong," I said. "Or is that the type of father you are — treat your kids like slaves then cuff them for being obedient?"

Killian took a long breath through his nose, as if he was trying to compose himself. He smiled. "Is that the type of father ye wish me to be to ye?"

"I'm not having this conversation again." That I was echoing Cecelia now wasn't lost on either of us. "Aaron Harken was my father. You would fail literally every parenting course available, if they were open to demon spawn, anyway." I got up, made a show of dusting my hands off when I was actually scuffing Saskia's drawing into obscurity under my shoe. "Besides. Don't you have enough children as it is? You've been busy."

Killian chuckled. "Aye. But there will only ever be one of you."

"That's right. And I'm not the droid you're looking for." I grunted, and the flames, though difficult, came up, ready to go.

"Oh kee-rist," Killian admonished. "Are we doing this again? Thought we were past all that."

"We'll be past it once you're dead and I'm outta here." My pores sparked painfully. "If you want this stone, you'll have to kill me. I'm not going to turn into one of your empty-eyed babies and do anything by your side."

"Kill ye?" Now he looked actually angry. "So you'd die defending that bauble? For a Family that would as soon as do as ye've said, then take the stone and do gods-only-knows to preserve their standing?"

"You're a deluded hypocrite!" I shouted, feeling sweat breaking out on my temples. "You're the one trying to take the stones for yourself!"

Killian was very still. "Ye think I want the stones . . . for power? Ye think I imagine I will live beyond my purpose?" He let out a sharp breath. "Don't ye see? I want to *destroy* the stones. I want all this madness in the name of Ancient to *stop*."

The flames popped off me, my fists shaking as they lowered. "You've *killed* people."

He threw up his hands. "The only ones who've died are those who tried to stop me. The ones who knew that what I was doing wasna so daft, but it went against their precious *code*. And the children, well. They made those sacrifices of their own free will. But you were there in London. You saw it. So we busted up a high street or two. No one died."

"You're lying!" I choked on the accusation, and suddenly I was back in that ruined intersection, the action a frozen tableau around me. The children leaping, Eli reaching, crumbled buildings and fleeing Mundanes and Denizens. There had been hope trees, though. I doubted there was a cure for those. In all it was a stage, a cinematic set-up. But Seela *had* done something with the —

"— Moonstone." I jerked. There had been a flash, a huge aftershock, a buzzing in the air.

Killian looked me over appreciatively, folding his arms. "Ye do know that the Owls' primary part in preserving the Narrative is keeping us Denizens and our powers hidden from the rest of the world? Takes a lot of mental energy, but they've managed it all these centuries. Survival, ye ken. Let's just say I disrupted their main signal to do that."

When Zabor attacked in Winnipeg, when the flood

waters receded and the damage had been tallied, it had all been pinned on a savage storm. I'd known the Owls had been behind that cover-up, and I had been glad of it at the time. But that got me to thinking what other things throughout history had been dismissed as natural occurrences, when they'd really been Denizen activity.

"So what, you . . . you wanted to lift the curtain? Why?"

He snorted. "Denizens think they're above it all. That their actions and deeds and sins are nothing compared to Mundanes, even though we share the world with them. I wanted an equal playing field. I wanted everyone to see that what is about to happen is because of the greed of those who should have been caring for this world. And I will make this world as it's destined to be."

"A wasteland of death," I said, my nose suddenly filled with the scent of the churning waves and raging sulphur of my nightmares.

Killian opened his hand. "Will ye walk with me awhile?"

I stiffened. "Where? Why?"

"Och, away with the twenty questions," he snapped. "Where else have ye to be?" And he started off in the direction he'd come. My first thought was *This could be the chance to nail him while his guard is down*. But the second thought, that wasn't mine, overruled it: *Give him a chance*.

I followed at a distance, so that maybe to my conscience it would seem like I was taking an independent walk of my own. We didn't talk. The scrubby land around us bordered a marsh. I could still hear the ocean, but we were hiking farther inland. I saw movement out of the corner of my eye, but I didn't turn my head. Saskia was small, and careful, but I knew she was following us.

"Did ye know," Killian said all of a sudden, "what would happen to the world if there were no people here?"

Navigating down a burn, I scoffed. "Yeah, there's a History Channel show about that . . ."

"Oh, aye? Didna get much television in prison the past eighteen, me."

He was on the high ground, staring out into the open, wind coming up. I joined him there, keeping my distance. "The world is a bloody mess because of us. Not just the pollution — the wars, the rainforest, all of it. Letting us run the place was by far Ancient's biggest cock-up, yet we think we're entitled to it all. We're not. And we aren't gonna smarten up about it anytime soon, either."

Below us was a beach, craggy and rock-strewn, with plinth boulders set around it like hulking shoulders. Suddenly I was down on that beach, or one very similar, and Eli was beside me.

"Don't move," he said. I didn't. He took one tentative step, then another, his hand out. "It's another vision, I think." Then he looked back to me like an afterthought. "Where are you?"

I frowned at him, carefully moved my head. "I'm here, aren't I?" But that wasn't true. I glanced up to the ridge, which was now empty. I was up there, in some other time or dimension, with Killian.

"It's not a trick question," Eli snapped. "I don't mean here. I mean — there. With Seela."

"This," I glanced about. "When is this?"

"It's already happened. Or it hasn't happened yet. I don't know." He seemed to be getting more annoyed with me the more questions I asked. "I could feel the Opal. I'm close now. But it's hard to keep the signal."

"How do you —"

"He mucked about with the stone. Clever, that. But I've had it longer. I know it better." Eli was within arm's reach of me. He was looking directly at me, eyes intense, and I felt that thing stir inside. It was getting more aggravated than he was.

I narrowed my eyes. "What are you doing?"

His hand stopped at the Opal. Fell. "Something's wrong," he said, checking my face for the solution. "Something's different. Your stone, it . . . it's quiet. I can only hear your voice in it. But that's not possible."

This time it was me who put my hand up, covering the Opal, protective and ashamed. Like it was my fault. "They *mucked about* with it," I mocked. But Eli had recoiled when he saw my hand, black and crackling. So there had been no point in hiding the corruption in the Opal, really.

He was trying to save you, I heard Saskia say in my mind. "I know what you're trying to do. But you shouldn't. I can take Seela down on my own. I don't need you or anyone else risking themselves." I looked harder at Eli, tried to focus. "Unless you just want the Opal. And the Emerald . . . Well, if I kill him, or he and I kill each other, you'll have both then. And you can stop what we saw in that vision before it happens."

"Risk?" Eli's face twisted. He was going to call me stupid or insane. A classic biting ironic quip, of course, to underline how utterly fucked I was, and that I must have known it, too. But his hands clenched and instead he said, "And what will you do when you don't even have yourself to risk?"

I hadn't expected his pained expression to cut the heart of me. And just like that, I was back on the burn with Killian. Eli was gone.

Killian pulled his gaze up from the beach to me — had only seconds passed? There was no recognition on his face that anything had been amiss. "Would you like to know more about her?"

I started like I'd nodded off and dreamt I'd stepped off a pier. "About who?"

Killian dropped to the edge of the outcrop, swung his lanky legs over it, and huffed. "Your mother. Ravenna."

Moments were moving too quickly and sliding over each other like tectonic plates. How had we gotten onto this subject — and anyway, why was I about to indulge in a heart-to-heart with my super-villain enemy? "Does it matter? You're going to just spin some more sentimental garbage regardless of what I want."

"So ye aren't interested in learning what she was like? I might be the last person who can tell you."

"Oh, sure. And how about I tell you what my dad was like? My real dad, I mean. Aaron Harken. You know, the man who raised me?" *However short a period that was*, I bit back from saying out loud.

Killian looked stung, but he was eyeing the water, and he tsked. "A Rabbit, no less."

"Get over yourself. For someone trying to undo Ancient, you're a Family purist now?" Against my better judgment, I sat down, too. "He was a Rabbit and he raised me as his own, and so well that I would have never known I wasn't really his. Until people decided to break the family I knew, without thinking how it'd make me feel."

A drawn silence. Killian nodded. "I should be grateful to him. Yer a pigheaded wee snipe, but that may have been more Ravenna than me." He brought a knee up, rested his arm across it. "I suppose ye turned out all right."

I couldn't help feeling it, embracing it — that big empty part of me that always wanted to belong somewhere, to somebody. I took a chance and watched him while he watched the sea. Killian's eyes were mine. Even the shape of his hands, kind of. Here he looked so at ease, so human. How could he have such a monstrous thing inside him? I knew Saskia was somewhere in the brush behind us listening. This whole campaign was full of people with broken hearts wanting to belong to each other. That was human. Was there a chance I could bring them both back? Could *Killian* be saved?

"They were only around till I was three," I said. "After that it was Arnas and Deedee stepping in for parenting duty. Mostly Deedee. When I didn't go to Zabor as planned, I don't think Arnas knew what to do with himself. But, to be fair, he'd already lost a lot, too."

"What a sorry affair, the lot of it. And Ravenna died for it."

"Yep."

The wind changed — it was subtle, but the hairs on my charred forearms stood up.

"How did it happen?"

I blinked. "Hm?"

"How did she die?"

He was still looking straight ahead, but I'd heard his voice, that cocky brogue, break just a little. And it softened me, goddammit.

"She and Aaron, they were trying to get the targe. To stop

Zabor, once they found out I was marked. Aaron opened the Bloodgate, she went in . . . she didn't come back out again. The Owls found out about the whole thing. It cost Aaron his life." I don't know why I was telling him, why it poured out of me, but I let it.

Killian sniffed, made a show of scratching his cheek. "Damn Owls, eh? Par for the course. Always sticking their beaks where they don't belong. This is what I mean about this sorry world and the Denizens that think they're the masters of it. So much would be different if it weren't for them."

I scoffed. "And maybe you would have never met Ravenna, either, and I wouldn't exist. So maybe it was all just part of the plan."

"We need a new plan." Killian picked up a handful of dirt and scattered it to the wind, like a tithe. "Speaking of Owls, that's why I was right surprised about that Rathgar chap, though it did seem to work to our benefit, him coming after ye. You mixing with the enemy now?"

I threw up my hands. "Why the hell does everyone think we're *dating*? Look around you. You think I have time for anything like that? Jesus."

"All right, no need to bite me head off . . ."

"In fact, now that Eli isn't busy trying to kill me, I'm pretty sure the most he thinks of me is that I'm some inferior, insolent, naïve kid. And he'd be right." Whatever Eli was trying to do, it really couldn't be a rescue mission. I had a Calamity Stone. Maybe the Foxes had sent him to get it, but certainly not with me attached to it as a priority. Eli Rathgar, for what I knew of him, wasn't one to expend time or energy on sentiment. He wanted the Opal. Maybe I wanted to give it to him and be done with all this.

Killian had picked up a leaf and spun it idly between his pinched fingers. He looked up at me. "Naïve about what?"

I can't believe I'd even thought it, but now an idea took hold. Killian had brought me here to try to sway me to his side. Why couldn't I do the opposite and bring him to mine? Naïve wasn't scratching the surface.

"You really loved Ravenna, didn't you?"

He nodded. "Still do."

"Then how could you do this? All of this? She died to save me, to save other Denizens. To put Zabor away for good. And you want to bring Zabor *back*? So Ravenna died for nothing?"

The leaf in his fingers caught fire and incinerated so quickly that what was left behind were its delicate veins, traced with amber cinders.

"You really are her daughter." A shadow passed over his face. "She didn't understand and neither do you. I didn't have the time to convince her, to show her the truth. But you're my second chance." The wind picked up and tousled his chestnut hair into his eyes. "What I'm doing goes deeper than Ravenna's cause. I'm trying to take away the power structure that put Ravenna in that position in the first place. The one that's got us all enslaved, humans and Denizens alike. Without Ancient's influence, we can be free."

He hadn't answered me — not really. But I wasn't about to stop either.

"And without Ancient's influence, your 'masters' will be running rampant out here with whatever other monsters come with them. You're willing to accept the consequences of that, for what?"

But now Killian was on his feet, and the wind had gotten

too high even for him to ignore. I leapt up. "You'll see soon enough," he said. "I loved Ravenna. I will love her to the bitter end. And believe me, girlie, you hold the people you love close while ye can. Even if they look their nose down at ye. I think that Owl was trying to save ye. But he's the naïve one."

His smirk was as oily as the rest of him as his body took on Seela's evil shape, because Killian and I had both seen the massive winged silhouette bearing down on us like an air-strike. I dove just as Eli and Seela collided, the impact shattering the morning as I hit the deck.

Saskia was screaming. I went to her immediately, where she was crouching with her arms over her head in the dirt. "It's going to be okay," I told her as I picked her up. "I'm going to finish this. One and for all."

She clutched tightly to my clothes, but she didn't try to get away. "But he'll find us! He always does!"

"That's the point," I said, and I took off into the trees, back towards Killian's cliffside bastion.

"Son of the Wind!" Seela cried through his split-gourd smirk. "You simply can't stay away, can you?"

Eli threw off every tentacle that tried to smash him down or wrap around his wings and pluck him apart like a Thanksgiving turkey. He was the Therion down to his marrow, and his wings knit close to him when he leapt up, rolled, and drilled himself through Seela's body.

Seela separated into frayed shadow, but when Eli landed

ten feet away on the other side, the pieces came back together, boiling into the huge and sinister monster once more.

He could literally be here all day.

Seela's head cracked upward, and the face that had looked so certain wasn't any longer. Eli followed Seela's gaze and was back in the air like a shot, in the direction in which Roan had fled.

"Bloody . . ." Eli grunted, wings cutting through trees, collapsing, sending him bouncing off the close rock and the jutting burns when he folded them. What the hell was she playing at?

He risked a glance beneath him, saw that Seela had liquefied and was picking up speed like a black sludge torrent, covering more distance on the ground than Eli could muster by air. The trees were alive with the screech and roar of bodies coming for him in a wave — those children, crimson and burning and hungry. He snapped his great wings up, went higher, crashed through the canopy of fir hemming them in.

Below, there was Roan, running to beat hell to a building made of ash and glass, hewn from the cliffside overlooking the sea. She was carrying something in her arms, and when he twisted and banked down closer, he confirmed those arms were black up to the elbows. So it hadn't just been her mind that had been affected. She truly had been touched by Seela's plague. Maybe something more than that.

Something snagged Eli around his foreleg, snapping it back painfully as he was dragged to the earth.

"No!" Saskia screeched, and I risked one look behind me to see Eli's wings sweep up, then freeze as he was torn from the air by one of Seela's tendrils. The ground around Eli cratered with the impact, but he was getting up just as Seela reared back, re-forming.

"Stay down," I told Saskia as I put her onto her own feet, but she grabbed me back.

"There's no use," she persisted, "you can't beat him. Not now."

"Watch me," I said, yanking free and rushing back in. To be the "good guy" Saskia needed. That *I* needed.

I went for the periphery of the fight. Seela had already gotten on top of Eli, dragging him back up. His feathers filled the air as Seela's right hand picked him up by the throat, then encircled it, squeezing.

A flash. I was seeing it from the outside — Eli and I were back on the Osborne Bridge last February in much the same embrace, him dangling me over the jaws of the Assiniboine, telling me it was my destiny to die there and then.

Now he gets what he deserves, the voice crawled up over my nerves.

Goddammit, I snapped, *get out of my head.*

The voice snickered. *Deep down, this is what you want for him. The shame he caused you. The brutality. He deserves to have it given back.*

I shook my head with such force that I was suddenly back in the present. Eli still had his talons, was clawing at the choking hand and stirring the air with his struggling feet.

"You cannot have her," Seela hissed. "Her purpose is not yet fulfilled."

"Hey!" I shouted, and they both looked at me. "Quit talking about me like I'm not standing here!"

Seela sneered, but he ripped his hand back and dropped Eli into a heap, sliding backward.

I held my hand up, shaking, dark. I spread the fingers. "Listen to me, Killian." I said. Had to take the gamble. "Please. Just stand aside, let Eli go. Let me go. Give back the Serenity Emerald. Then we . . . we can do what you wanted. We can be a family."

Seela's face, obscured as it was by the slate of bone, betrayed nothing. Just the mouth, jaw and lips working as if they were chewing something over. I didn't know what hurt more — that Cecelia had made the same empty promise to me, just before we were about to launch into battle or that my spirit eye showed me Killian, deep inside Seela, holding his head. I had to believe he could come back. Or there wasn't a chance for Saskia. Or me.

Seela's mouth stilled, and the gash of a smile broke across it. "Don't you see? It's already begun." And he turned back to Eli, who was losing his Therion shape the longer he lay there, grimacing as he got back up. He stood with all his weight on one leg, the other bent beneath him, blood flowing freely from a gash in his head down his ear. The wind whipped around him but only in small bursts, and his wings sagged.

Seela was shivering with his bruise-coloured inferno. He was moving in to strike again. "You've far outlived your use," he sneered at Eli, hands cutting down. "I could not take the Moonstone when we first met. I wasn't strong enough then. I thought my tree could finish the job, but you are clearly more resilient than I imagined." The inferno rose higher, a long devastating limb reaching for Eli's chest. "But I am stronger now, with my daughter at my side. You won't distract her any—"

I grabbed hold of Seela's limb, crushing it back as I hunkered down between him and Eli.

We were mask-to-mask and I'd let my black flames up, let the dark fox warrior consume me now, because my head was at least clear this time. I had a purpose, and it was to stop him. If this was the only power I could tap into now, so be it.

Eli staggered, shielding his face.

You cannot win, the voice inside me warned, but it was gleeful now that I'd set it free.

"We'll see," I answered, and I threw Seela aside, pulling my bone-blade up and swinging it towards his head. Suddenly his arm was an axe, too, much like Urka's little trick, and it knocked the strike clear away with a sound like teeth shattering.

"Grab Saskia!" I hollered to Eli, going after Seela with blow after blow, until we were one churning mass of spitting fire and muck-black blood that united us.

Eli watched the struggle for a moment before coming back to himself, pain and all.

"Bloody Harken," he hissed, getting his legs back under him and moving towards the place Roan had been only a moment ago. Sure enough, there was a little girl pressed in between the rocks at the base of the fortress.

"Are you Saskia?" Eli asked gruffly, though once his

senses had come back to him, he reached out with his mind to hers. There wasn't much there in that hollow pit, save for the name, for a few sparks of humanity remaining. He didn't bother wondering why Roan wanted her. There weren't enough curses across languages to express how much easier it would be if she'd just . . .

Saskia's red pin eyes were earnest. "You have to save her."

Without another word, Eli scooped the urchin up, wings open as they re-formed, plumage setting anew. He took one last look at the skirmish through the veil of blood on his face. "She's busy doing the saving, apparently."

The children that had chased Eli bled out of the woods, all blazing cinders and blind rage.

Eli snorted. He was in the air when the Moonstone strobed, and he heard a voice. It wasn't coming from his stone. It was the Opal, calling again.

Let it consume you. Let it become you. You are the fire, and the fire is mine.

The voice, whispering and hissing and spitting, had been Roan's.

An explosion shook the air and the ground, and Eli climbed higher.

I am the fire, and the fire is mine. No longer did I burn or sear or question my body as it flowed from one cascading blow to the next. I was enormous, I was Seela's equal. *Yes*, said the voice, *yes, keep going*. I didn't stop to wonder why this thing inside me was so eager to kill Seela, who had put this darkness in me in the first place, but I didn't care. I was the inferno. I was at Omand's Creek, obliterating river hunters. I was the great hero I was meant to be.

The shadows were splitting. Beneath them crawled a human face, pulped and pleading. Killian. He was all bloody teeth as he laughed.

"Yes," he said, "yes, keep going. Ye really are . . . my girl."

I picked him up and threw him into the face of his own fortress, but the tendrils of his shattered cloak caught a spire like webbing, seeping him through a porthole. I roared, went after him. The world was a rush of stone and cliff and shadow, and I perceived the children around me, but I obliterated them with blade and claws and teeth. I wanted Killian. I wanted. To rend. To kill. I burst through the wall and the stairs that took me back to his summoning chamber, pulling myself up short. Killian's Seela form was dripping into the crimson rings, and he was bent on all fours, panting. Bleeding.

He spat. "Can't say it's no' what I wanted . . . Oh, what a sight to behold." Laughter bubbled out of his wounds. "My daughter. Chip off the old."

My blade flashed out. It got him across the eye, but he didn't try to dodge.

No. I felt myself waking — the real me, the one whose hand had slipped from the wheel. *I have to save him. Kill* Seela, *leave Killian!*

He was in my hands, his frail human body. The Seela part of him was stuck to the floor, struggling to keep purchase, trying to suck him back in. The Emerald flickered on Killian's shoulder, and the fortress shifted beneath us.

"Go ahead," Killian said. "Finish what you started. You're almost there. Then you and I will truly be able to do this, together." Something was creeping up my leg, attaching itself to my tails, trying to pull us both down into it. The floor buckled, stone and walls shattering as the stalactite spikes from above came free, impaling the chamber floor.

Inside, I struggled, resisting the urge to open my jaws and crunch down on his skull.

A shockwave. Glass crunching then exploding inward. Beating wings.

"Do it!" Eli screamed — inside and outside of my mind. "Destroy him! Get the Emerald!"

I wanted to. I know I needed to. *I loved Ravenna.* No. *We could be a family.* No! Everything was overlapping, happening at once, and again, and soon.

You have to keep a part of yourself, however small, however deeply buried, alive. The dark thing within me dug its claws into my bones. *Kill. Rip. Destroy. Rend the world. Let them through.*

I took a breath, felt a spark — a bright one. Bright as Deon's solar gaze.

The bone mask fell from my face, shattering like porcelain. I let go of Killian, pushed the dark fox out of me, said, "I won't," and the puddle of Seela held Killian's broken body up as it climbed back onto him like living armour.

The floor cracked between my feet and heaved. I turned in time with the fissure. My legs were pumping to their limit. The sky was huge and open, and I swore I saw Eli there, at least I hoped —

I dove headlong into the sky and the sea, and one of them caught me, and we were gone.

Part IV
Rupture

UNCANNY SHORES

The air was warm on the back of Phae's neck, though it prickled something fierce. She dragged her body up one limb at a time — first her hands, then her knees underneath her. *Cat-cow*, her brain told her, recalling the name for the yoga pose would be useful at a time like this. Her head was last, and the heaviest. She stayed in an almost *heart to earth*, letting her breath come in evenly. Then she raised her head and opened her eyes.

Water lapped at her legs, the tide cresting, trying to gently pull her back in. She crawled up the beach, tempted to collapse again on the silver sand, but she didn't dare — not with the animal calls trilling through the air. The heady heat. The mist.

The jungle before her was thick, sprawling. This beach was but a sliver that managed to escape it. When Phae risked a glance behind her at the water, it spread out into eternity, the horizon unclear. She touched her hands, pressed them into her eyes. She was awake. She wasn't dreaming. This wasn't the Veil and wasn't home by any stretch. Her skin goosepimpled again: this was the otherworld, another realm.

The Glen, Ryk had said, before the current had snatched her and dragged her down, down . . .

"No." She had to say it out loud, had to reaffirm she had the ability to speak. It had happened so fast. She'd barely registered it, hadn't even had a choice. Sent on a mission she didn't understand. Obligated to fulfill it. Roan had done that and more, but Phae wasn't Roan.

The mist shifted. Phae tensed when she got to her feet, because the tendrils of smoke parted and waved and seemed to just reveal deeper shadows. Faces. The beach was small, hemmed in by the jungle . . . or was it getting smaller, the longer she stood here? There was nowhere to go but forward, into the trees, the world in the middle distance cast in golden light and flickering emptiness that itself never seemed to move.

She took a step, and the mist fell to the ground like it'd been struck. Beyond the trees was a mountain — massive and lonely. Nothing stirred, not even the air. And even though all she should have felt was dread, there was a peace, too, that went down to a place Phae hadn't known existed.

Find the ruler of that stark land. Find the heart of the Glen. If Fia finds you worthy of it, finds this world *worthy of it, the Horned Quartz would be yours to wield.*

The Empress — an expression of Aunty now — hadn't even asked Phae if it was what she wanted. To be here, alone, with a task she couldn't quantify heaped on her. *You were asked once before, by Roan, and you made your choice*, her conscience swiftly reminded her. *And you'll get back to the others that much quicker if you just get off this beach.*

One foot in front of the other, despite the howling animal cries, Phae crept off the sand and went into the trees.

❦

"You let her go."

Killian lay, arms akimbo, in the centre of the summoning chamber. It was not active. He had repaired the place using the Emerald, but he was relishing the dark. The only light sources in the room were the pinpricks of flickering flame beneath the skin of his brooding children clutched in the room's corners, watching him.

Urka loomed above, getting restless, eager to dig and tear. "The world is cracking even still. My masters shift against their prisons. They are impatient."

"They've been down there for ages. They can wait a few more days." Killian flexed his fingers, knew that the dark sludge of Seela was working beneath the surface, mending his cuts, subtracting what was left of him and replacing it with darkling. *Good. Faster.*

"I let her go because she is close. This is her test. She will come back and with the Moonstone. You'll see." It was less Killian, and more Seela, who was certain of this.

"If the girl proves unworthy," Urka snarled, its furnace gleaming in time with its rage, "then I should have killed her and that howling bird when first they came upon me in my realm."

Killian sneered. "Wretch," he spat, sitting up with the darkness's assistance, which propped him in its unholy embrace. "Ye knew this has all been as much a part of the Narrative as anything else. It will be carried out to that same plan. I can feel it. This is only a minor setback — she must come to the power of her own choice. She's getting there." He closed his eyes, the pulse of the Emerald insistent; he had nearly had her. He'd held her close and felt her make a quarter turn towards her true self that had woken within. Not close enough to stop them from coming to blows but nearly. Yet in that moment, their stones had connected, too, and now he cast for her, and he knew she floated above the world, dreaming of her part in it.

Soon she would awaken, and they could truly be together. Like she'd wanted. Like she'd promised.

Then the Emerald perceived something else. Another sister, across the same vast sea, rising to the surface.

"The Sapphire." His eyes blazed, his blood seeping back into where it belonged, mingling with the blood of his true parents. The red rings glowed.

"The Seals have gathered then." Urka seemed satisfied by this news. "But we have lost the Opal and the Moonstone . . ."

"Patience," Killian smiled, the bone mask securing itself over his eyes, and he saw all the clearer as he transformed into Seela for the last time, the rest of what had been Killian all but erased. "They will return to us soon enough. But now, we must ready to meet the Emerald's sister. The left hand of Ancient moves to strike. And we must be ready. Once more unto the breach."

The flickering light of the burning children was a unified smile as the chamber went dark and Seela gathered them to him.

⁂

The place may have been bright, may have been beautiful, but Phae took no solace in any of it. She'd been walking for hours; though she didn't tire, or thirst, or hunger (yet), she was still susceptible to the monotony, the tension. The fear.

She had to consciously separate her molars, relax her jaw. Think. *Treat this like a problem that could be solved.* There had to be rules. There always were with these realms in lore. She'd shied away from learning more about it because she was afraid it might all make too much sense. *Think!* Ancient mythos was Barton's territory — so she called up his calm, soothing voice, the feeling of his arm around her as she nestled into his chest, staring at his hands and tracing the lines as he recited whatever particular bit of it he'd been delving into at the time.

Fia. Phae concentrated on the word. *The Glen, the Deer, anything.*

"I read a lot about your Family, you know. The Deer."

His voice was so clear that Phae jerked to a stop and looked around, half expecting Barton to be walking beside her. But she was still alone, and not even a breeze shook the strange trees that seemed to tighten the deeper she travelled. She shook her head, went on, focused.

"Oh do you?" She'd been teasing him. Things were simpler then. Spending time with him was easy, wasn't heavy with the regret she felt now, maybe parted from him forever.

"Yeah. And it would make me happy to share it with you. If you wanted me to."

She had. She did.

"So your Family is pretty interesting, because there aren't

that many of you left. There used to be whole sanctuaries, like monastic dwellings in mountains and deep in the jungles and stuff, of Deer just following the ascetic life. While all the other Families represent some kind of physical element, the Deer represent and follow the intangible. The spirit. The centre of the five. The beating heart. And as healers, they were always drawn into conflicts, expected to bring people back from the dead, and sometimes manipulated into healing wounds when they shouldn't have. They withdrew from the other Families, then realized that the only true way to live Ancient's divinity was to return to the forms they'd forsaken at the beginning of time. Heavy, eh?"

Here in the suffocating rainforest, Phae smiled.

"So anyway . . . at first they were Therions, kind of like what Eli turns into — a sacred animal form. But then they didn't want to turn back, felt more connected to Ancient that way. It's hard to find out from anyone if there are any practising Deer left, really. So you're rare!"

"And alone," Phae said, as she came into a clearing, her voice ringing wretchedly in her head.

Something slithered through the grasses and she spun but saw nothing. Probably the one thing that bothered her the most about this realm was that it had been called the Glen — but it wasn't much of one. She'd pictured a narrow, sun-kissed valley, like the pictures that Roan had sent over of Scotland. That made Phae's heart contract, thinking of her friend now, and it only took that singular moment of distraction for the viper to lunge at her.

Phae screamed, leaping out of the way, but the thing reared back up, jaws wide. It came at her like a taut arrow, a head to kill, but she hadn't come this far to be bitten, of all things, and her antlers snapped into a crown, and rather than generating a shield, she smashed the huge snake aside with a twitch of her neck.

The blood roared in her head, but the snake did not come back. It was as if it had never been there at all. She touched her antlers, her own hair, solid and, for the first time, used as a weapon. Looking at her hands, she felt different, more keyed in, blue sparks crackling over her fingertips. Was it because she truly had a connection to this place? Was she becoming more a Deer now than before?

"Well!" Phae shouted. She was not one to shout or even let her emotions rise to the surface, but she realized she'd reached a limit. She was tired of defending, of healing. She thought of Roan, and she wanted to be like her. She wanted to fight.

The earth rumbled, and the trees rose with the ground. But it wasn't the ground; it was a massive head, a triangle of jagged antlers over the impassive face of an antelope. Phae staggered back, too panicked to hold her own crown of horns as the creature stood tall on its hooved hind legs, like an enormous satyr.

"What does Fia look like?" Phae had asked Barton. Her memory flickered against her present fear, painting the picture before her now.

Barton had shown her, but she hadn't the imagination, at the time, to really fill in the blanks of the crude sketches.

"Fia's sort of strange . . . From my readings she — well, the pronoun used is 'they' — has three faces. Not really gendered, like the other matriarchs are. I think the term is multi-spirited. You know the three gold rings that seem to show up everywhere in Ancient iconography? They represent Fia. The spirit. In fact the number three has a lot to do with Fia, lots of threes associated with them. And Fia is the pivot point of every Denizen's power. Even Ancient's."

"*Ancient's* heart." The antelope's face cracked and turned, like it was operated by a dial, revealing a second face — a woman's, twisted in furious glee. "*We are its beating heart, if it still has one, but not even we are sure.*"

Phae didn't move. There was nowhere else to go, to run. After all, this is why she'd been sent here. To find this fearsome god and challenge it.

The head creaked and clocked aside again, changing to that of a man, with chiselled cheekbones and eyes the blue of an impossible sky. "*It has been so long since we've seen our own blood! And moved to fight, no less! How did you get here? Did our sister send you?*"

Fia was enormous, draped in the woods, and when Phae looked past their body she saw the true Glen, a deep and fertile valley, leading to the vast mountain beyond.

Fia stomped their hoof and Phae jumped. The head swivelled back to the antelope's.

"*There is something in this one's spirit. An intention I don't like.*"

The time to be defensive was now, but Phae tread carefully. "Fia! Matriarch of the Deer! I've come to . . ." But Phae stopped, something else Barton said tickling her memory.

"You'd think that Fia would be some kind of sage, representing the spirit and all. Full of wisdom and understanding. But, uh, how do I put this? Fia is *angry*. Miserable might be a better way to put it. They feel that the world was Ancient's precious gift to humanity, and we kind of spoiled it, and they would be in absolutely no rush to save it from itself."

The head swivelled three more painful times, sorting through the woman, the man, and back again to the antelope. Every face was unimaginably enraged.

"*She was not* born *a Deer,*" the three voices overlapped. "*Someone else gave their power to her. And for what! To be misused in the world again!*"

Phae felt her blood go cold. "Please," she started. "There's . . . The world is in danger. It's in pain —"

The woman's face: "*Oh, she thinks we haven't* seen*! That we don't know the world's pain!*" Their laughter was a howl dimmed only when the man's grave face swung back to the forefront.

"*We know that pain too well, false-daughter. Because we bore it ourselves.*"

"What does that mean?" Phae blurted.

Beneath Phae, the three gold rings flashed, searing. Then they were crimson.

The antelope swivelled back, deep eyes liquid. "*Because the source of the world's pain is the darklings. And it was we who gave birth to them, long ago, before the Narrative even began.*"

There was a sound like a heart, like trampling hooves, and Fia bore down on Phae.

"*She wants the Quartz,*" Fia shrilled, but Phae darted between their legs, heading straight for the Glen, before they could stop her.

Barton lay awake in his bunk, numb.

His knees tingled as if he'd been running. He looked at his hands. He'd woken in the middle of the night, absolutely certain Phae had been curled against him, and she was asking him questions about Ancient, about the lore, and he was faithfully helping her solve some kind of puzzle.

This had been a welcome relief since, just hours before, he felt like the bottom had been ripped out of him like a bathtub drain. He'd sworn up and down to anyone who would listen that something had snapped. A cord, a ribbon. The tenuous connection to Phae.

He knew, without a doubt, that she wasn't in this world anymore. And he was sick with it.

"You are just tired, stressed," Kita had offered, trying to be comforting. "We all are. You more than the rest! You have been fighting hard, trying to undo all of those tree things. I am sure she is fine. You can try calling her . . ." She'd put a hand on Barton's forearm, but he ripped it away, angry at the suggestion of the touch, as if that could erase Phae. As if anything could — though maybe something had.

"You don't understand." Even Barton barely had. He should've held on to Phae tighter when he'd had the chance. Should have kept her close to him. Should never have left her behind.

He stared at his hands, covered in blisters and still-healing cracks. For days he'd been sent from site to site — too many cropping up, and not enough Denizens stepping up to develop an early warning system to prevent the attacks that were ravaging cities, small towns. For every hope tree he'd undone (even the name sounded insipid when he thought of them), three more had appeared that he couldn't undo, couldn't save. And most of the Denizens he pulled free succumbed to Seela's dark plague. Those who didn't seemed unable to shake that they couldn't outrun the Moth Queen for long. That the more darkness the world allowed through, the more it just seemed inevitable.

Phae. He reached out to her, not knowing if it'd get there. Not knowing if she could hear him. But he willed his heart to swell with the hope it'd lost, to help him find her across this terrible void, and to run alongside her if she needed him.

Phae ran forever. She still didn't tire. It was such a blissful, strange feeling, even when she was fleeing for her life from a ferocious god that ruled the place where she'd trespassed.

She ran on, even though back in her own world she'd never been athletic. Yoga was one thing, a means of grounding her chaotic thoughts, but this was exhilarating. Now she understood why Barton loved it so. The air rushing against her skin, the delight in it. *Don't get carried away*, she chided, losing herself down into a steep canyon, leaping, as her powersake would.

Soon, she realized, she was not running alone. Alongside her, what she at first took for shadows, were the lithe and streaking shapes of deer. Shades. Their eyes, regarding her with both gravity and curiosity, were steel-white, their strides far outstripping hers, but all the same her chest swelled with a sensation that they were running *together*. That these shades, likely the spirits of Denizens long passed, took her for one of their herd. She flicked the tears forming at the corners of her eyes and ran on.

She ran until she'd outstripped the hysterical bellowing of Fia at her heels. Until the shades dispersed back into the trees and the hills. She ran until she ended up on the other side of the mountain, where it was night. Strange to imagine that the otherworld had a divided day, but she didn't wonder for long what use eternity might have for counting time.

Phae slowed down when she came to a great tree. She needed to think and to be still. False-daughter, they'd called her. That had hurt more than she'd thought it would. She hadn't realized how much of her wanted Fia's approval before coming here, that while she was here to get the stone and get out as quickly as she could, she also wanted to be told *you're doing fine*. She'd felt that running among the Deer shades, but that seemed so far away now. She took a quick look behind her at the shuddering jungle. She was definitely not going to get that angry god's approval anytime soon.

Phae looked up the tree. It was old and its bole spread wide. She felt calm here, so she found a foothold and climbed as high as she could until she pulled herself over a branch thick as her body and let out a ragged breath.

Despite the threat on her life, she did still feel something like belonging as she surveyed the island from the base of the mountain. Shades galloped and darted here and there, in clusters or on their own. She had so many questions — is there where she'd end up after her own life ran its course? And what was on the other side of the mountain? Would it be daylight, the inverse of where she'd planted herself now? That the Glen was really an island made her a bit sad — such an isolated place, cut off from the other realms. But Fia probably liked it that way. Easier to protect themselves from any pain that could be inflicted on them.

Phae.

Someone had called her name — someone inside. From

far away. Across a floating thread. She shut her eyes and tugged back.

It's so good to hear your voice. If her thoughts could weep, they surely were now, because she felt some part of Barton clasp her close.

I thought you were — He cut himself off.

How? she asked. *How are we doing this?*

You'd know better than me, he replied, but she knew he wasn't wrapped up in the how. *Where are you?*

Phae opened her eyes. Nothing had changed. It was still night. *Far away. The Glen. It's nothing like your stories.*

She felt Barton smile, almost rejoice. *The book's always better.* His grin lit her up inside. Then his voice flashed to concern. *Are you okay? Are you hurt? Why the hell are you in another realm? Can't I leave for five seconds without you ending up in danger?*

She frowned. *Now you know what it feels like.* She'd been his protector, after all, since last winter, since before his power came back to him.

He cooled. *Why are you there and not here with me?*

Now she really was crying. *It's like you said. I have to figure out my part in all of this. I think I'm close. For once I feel useful.* Failing spectacularly was, at least, progress.

They held tight to their connection to each other. But Phae was still in this tree, at the base of a mountain in another dimension. And Barton couldn't be here. With that thought, he faded away, and she leaned her head back into the thick bark behind her.

"Curious," said a sibilant jeer, and Phae nearly fell out of the tree.

The snake hung from the branch above her, enormous

and slightly injured from their earlier encounter. But it wasn't dead nor nearly as angry as Fia had been — more amused than anything.

"What is?" Barton may have been well read in Ancient folklore, but Phae still did know a thing or two about snakes popping up in fables or parables. And if there was one common thread between Ancient and those stories, it was the riddles.

"You are not borne of Deer, yet you are in their realm. Your spirit is bright despite your Mundane flesh, so radiant it can speak across a universe to the one its heart holds precious." The snake wound itself down, raising its head and slanted eyes at Phae. "Perhaps you *are* strong. Perhaps you should not be suffered to live."

Phae was still scared, but curiosity overpowered that in the moment. "And what," she asked, "is a snake doing in the Glen?"

The snake's head split into three as they laughed, its tail winding around Phae's leg. A threat.

"*We are everywhere and anything in this place,*" Fia said with the snake's many mouths. "*Why should we allow you to live?*"

Ryk had warned Phae would have to prove herself and defend the world's very right to continue turning if she were to get Fia's help. She struggled against Fia's grip, but the coils only squeezed harder.

"I've come to learn about the Family of which I wasn't born." This was an honest answer, and Fia's three faces seemed intrigued. "I know your power is a lonely one. I know you think you have a lot to lose. But I just want to talk. To learn. Don't you want the company?"

The coils squeezed as hard as they could, before relaxing, receding, and the snake became a part of the tree, and Phae was alone.

"*Company,*" said a voice from the ground. It was Fia, with their triple face and enormous horns, yet shrunk down to human size.

Phae climbed down, dropping beside the diminished god, their three faces considering.

"*Talk,*" said the man's face.

"*Listen,*" said the woman's.

"*Learn,*" said the antelope's, but its face was bleakest of all.

"I'm not here to steal the Quartz," Phae insisted. "I know that the world has to be worthy of it. If I don't prove to be . . . then I suppose you can kill me." After all, if she went back, what else but death would be waiting for her and the rest of the world? She thought of the tar pits, thought of the whole world swallowed up and clear-cut. She wanted to be like Roan. She wanted to be strong and fierce and above all brave.

Fia nodded their great head. "*Then let us walk to the mountain, and you will see what we have seen. And you can determine for yourself if the world is worthy of being saved.*"

The DEVIL YOU KNOW

I woke up with the crushing cold wind pressing into my face, an arm tightly braced around my middle. I opened my eyes just as we cut through a cloudbank, but the air was stolen right out of my lungs when I dropped my jaw in a screech. Someone close by hollered — maybe a bit too joyfully for my taste. I saw Saskia's ash-pale face braced against the wind, smiling as I'd never seen her, like she was on a roller coaster.

I looked down and, through the clouds skittering beneath us and past the shifting shadow of Eli's wings, it was only sea.

I was going to barf.

"Down!" I screamed, yanking on Eli's collar, which was half-feather and half-linen. His sharp face looked about ready to bite off my hand, but I was not one for caring. *"I said down, right the fuck now!"*

We banked hard, which did not help matters, the waves

approaching alarmingly fast. Was he just going to dump me into the sea?

Then, as if conjured out of the mist and the white caps, there was a crust of land peppered with bare mountains that looked so unreal as the descent quickened, and trees reached for us, that we narrowly missed them as Eli pulled us up, the downdraft of his wings ripping my hair up as they snapped. Our feet touched terra firma. He basically dumped me, and I fell to my knees, dry heaving. I hadn't seen him put Saskia down, but I hoped it was with more care.

"God you're heavy," Eli grunted, massaging the arm that had been wrapped firmly around me. "Both of you."

Saskia whooped, giggling as she basically cartwheeled next to me, until she realized I was staring straight ahead. "You don't like heights, do you?"

"Don't give him any more material," I said, cringing, then as Eli got nearer I sprang up, remembering to be furious. "What the hell is the matter with you!"

He jerked, and his gold eyes faded back to grey as the Therion form receded. "What —"

I reeled back and punched him hard enough in the arm to half spin him. He tripped over driftwood and I kept coming.

"I was handling it! I had everything under control!" I kicked up sand, picked up a rock, and he ducked.

"Are you seriou—" He caught my next hook and held firm, squeezing so hard the knuckles cracked. "What the hell are you raving about?"

"*I didn't need saving*!" I screamed, ripping the hand free, heaving as the adrenaline spiked. "Why are you really here, huh? You want the Opal, don't you? Goddammit, Eli, I had him, and if you hadn't —"

He knocked my legs out from under me and I landed in a painful, breathless heap on my back. I spluttered.

He panted. "Are you legitimately going off your nut at me for saving your life? And *that one's* life, no less?" He swung his finger at Saskia, who had been watching the proceedings with amusement. "I'm here because *you asked me to come*, dammit!"

I willed the air back into my vocal cords as I rolled onto my side. I didn't like the way he was looking at me. "I didn't . . . I have no idea what you're talking about."

But by then Eli was pacing down the beach, snatches of his muttering carried back to me on the sea breeze. "Come back, she says, across the goddamn planet, so I can tear you a new one —" He twisted back around and came at me fast enough to make me scuttle back.

"Have you looked in the mirror lately? You look like you lost a fight with a tar pit. You're more far gone than I thought. And you thought you could take Seela down? In this state?"

I grit my teeth, standing. "I was close, you abominable twat. I had him —"

"Oh, you *had him*?" Eli was essentially spitting in my face now. "Seela had *you*. I should *rip that thing right* —" His fingers were talons, snatching at the air in front of my chest, and I took a step into them. His body shivered.

"Go ahead!" I yelled. "Try! Take it! That's what you want, isn't it? That's what they all want! Do what you do best and try to kill me! I won't stop you!"

"You — !" Eli lunged, but he didn't get far. His arms froze, his frantic eyes wide, then his mouth slackened, and I took a step back just in time to avoid him face-planting onto me.

He was out cold.

"Just goddamn perfect!" I whirled on Saskia, who was staring out at the steely water. "Now what? And just where the hell *are we*?"

A big wind came up that seemed to come from Eli's comatose body. It pulled his wings apart and sent the scattered feathers out to sea. His clothes were shredded, and his face was turned. I'd been too intent on yelling at him to realize what a sight *he* was. *He couldn't kill me if he wanted to.* My stomach dropped. Had he wanted to?

I came because you asked me to!

It only just occurred to me that he'd been *missing* before this point, and I really didn't know what he'd been through since then.

But he was here. And he'd made that call on his own.

"Dammit . . ." I got down, turned him over gently. He let out a noise of discomfort, but when I smacked his cheek experimentally, he didn't move. My hand came away bloody from the wound at his ear.

"I know this place." I looked up as Saskia spoke, the wind messing her already snarled, burnt-at-the-tips hair. "Daddy used to bring us here on holiday."

I really needed to stop passing out at every available opportunity. I hadn't known how long we'd been in the air, let alone where Killian's hideout was. Saskia had a bit of an accent — subtler than Killian's, closer to Eli's. On holiday . . .

"Are we back in Scotland?" I'd been tossed around the map with too much frequency. We could be on another planet.

"The Isle of Skye," she said, then something caught her eye, and she was staring down the beach. "Someone's coming."

I swung back up to my feet with surprising dexterity.

Would I ever feel like myself again? Would I ever get over this constant requirement to tense for a fight?

The figure walking towards us was bent, a wool shawl wrapped around her. I loosened — but I wasn't about to let my guard down. When she got closer, my spirit eye showed me that she was an Owl, maybe in her fifties. My heart clenched as I thought of Cecelia, then brushed the thought away just as quick. She stopped short of us by a few feet, head tilted.

"So," she said. Then she smiled at me. "He's come back, has he?"

I bent my ear towards her like I hadn't heard properly. "Uh . . . you mean Eli?" I stepped gingerly away from his prone body, since I'd been standing directly over him. "I really have no idea where —"

"The croft is just a ways up the hill, up a track. You can follow me there. Solomon rang ahead so I've opened it up for ye."

I felt a spray on my face that wasn't the sea. It'd started raining, and the woman had turned to go again. "Wait! He needs help. I can't —"

"Ye look a hale lass," the woman said, pausing to wave. "It's just a ways to carry him."

I looked helplessly to Saskia, who seemed to be waiting for me to make a decision.

"He did carry *us* all this way." Saskia said.

I looked down. Eli was more than six feet tall and, though lean, probably almost two hundred pounds.

I sighed, opening myself up to the dark fox warrior for just a little while longer as I scooped him up, and I followed Saskia and the woman up the hill.

❧

Eli felt a shadow pass over him. He opened his eyes to wings, but they weren't his own.

Though he'd only seen her likeness in the books, in the training ground of his isolated childhood among other acolytes, none of those depictions even came close to Phyr's actual image. She was huge, as all of her god-sisters were. Her eyes were bright, pupils moving and reshaping like energized mercury as they assessed Eli. Her nine wings were three times the size of her, and in their midnight sea winked stars and unfathomable galaxies.

He could only manage to slide up to his knees before her. At her side was the Pendulum Rod, which she used to keep and manage time.

"My lady." Eli inclined his head. If he was in a vision, in the Veil, he couldn't tell. He seemed to be on a floating rock, somewhere in the heavens, separate from reality. The dreamlike atmosphere of this moment felt like the stone choosing he'd endured and now regretted, when Phyr's great gaze swung to him instead of his father.

But really being here was something else.

"*What have you done*," Phyr levelled, "*to my stone?*" Her voice was the harshest north wind.

Eli tucked his chin and looked. The Moonstone, its white surface with gold flecks, had something dark at the centre. Dark and growing.

A great talon came down to Eli's eye, close enough to push through to the other side of his skull. *"My sister's stone, too, has been poisoned. You have been linking to it. And now the Moonstone is corrupted."*

Eli stilled. Nodded. Whatever realm he'd found himself in — maybe the Roost itself? — he had to tread lightly. "I beseech you, my lady. All I want is to reform the balance of the Narrative. Is there any way —"

"*No*," she said. "*The only way you will rid yourself of this poison is to rid yourself of my sister's stonebearer. She is moving beyond the pale. Soon, she will be one with the demon inside her. And not even the Moth Queen can bear her hence. You know what must be done.*"

Then Eli felt a cosmic wind push against him, push him right off the rock and into space, his body falling through the stars.

"His . . . cousin."

Watching the woman preparing tea set my teeth on edge. The scene, with Saskia sitting with her knees pulled up to her mouth, hiding behind them, was too unreal. I'd laid Eli down on a bed down the hall a few hours ago, and since then I'd stayed close to the sitting room window. Watching. Waiting. The dark fox hadn't put up a fight when I sent it back down. Whatever it — she — was, she was biding her time. Trying to make me feel like I was in control. I knew better.

"That's right," the woman answered, pulling the hot kettle off the electric stove. "My mother and me, Phyr rest her, used to look in on Eli's mum, Demelza. She was touched, ye ken." Sound seemed dialled to eleven. Even her pouring the hot water was loud, like it was right next to me, even though the small kitchen was at least ten feet off. "Eli was made to grow up too fast. Still taking the world on his shoulders, I see."

"Yeah, he's a real saint." I wasn't about to rehash the complicated allyship — if you could call it that — we seemed to have going. "So he lived here?"

"Aye," the woman, Agathe, came round with a tray that had tea and biscuits, setting it on the low table in front of Saskia, who hadn't yet moved an inch. "But after the sorry affair with his mum, his father came back for him. None too happy about that man, but he did his best for Eli after the fact. Bought the land up here and gifted it to Eli in trust, should he ever need a place to come back to." She leaned back, hands on her hips. I recognized something in her, something that was maybe a dream or maybe a memory I hadn't meant to see. Eli, me, a woman with long whipping hair on a beach. *That's my mother*, he'd said.

Agathe was looking at Saskia. "And why did you bring one of them here, then?" Saskia seemed to fold tighter. "She's an ill omen."

"So am I," I snapped. Agathe glanced up at me with the wry patience of a caregiver.

"Aye," she said. "You are a sight, and no mistake. But you're still a Paramount. A stonebearer. Which means ye have it in ye to bite it back. None so sure about this one." She sighed, bending down to pour a mug and pass it to Saskia. "But if young master Eli brought her here, she must have a purpose."

I left the window, satisfied for now that nothing was coming after us. Yet. "I asked him to bring her." I'd had to. I didn't want her getting swept up in that fight. Or getting left behind, forced to turn her fragile body into a tool for Seela, as I was slowly becoming.

"Oh, aye? Well, that there is a wonder in itself. That he

listened to ye, I mean." She had picked up her shawl from the electric fire, was flapping the remaining damp out of it before draping it back over herself. "Boy's always had a thick skull. Only ever sought his own counsel. Surprised anyone could make him do a whit."

I felt my face flush. "I'm loud and persistent enough, I guess."

"Ye'd have to be to get through that." She tapped her head. "In any case, I'm off."

Like a feral cat, Saskia snatched a biscuit from the tray, wrapping herself around it but not taking a bite.

"Off?" I said.

"Aye. Ye've got yerselves to sort out here. Trouble's coming. Don't need to read minds to know that." She pulled a hat down from the rack near the door, fastened the flaps under her chin. "The Owls here will try to keep you lot hidden until ye make yer move. We trust that the Paramount of our Family will know what to do. Phyr ever guides us, even if Ancient does not." She stopped me with one last appraising stare, nodding. "And two Paramounts are better than one."

I didn't bother correcting her. She didn't know the half of what I wasn't capable of, despite everyone's blind belief. I stood up and caught her at the door. "Listen. I . . . Thank you. For this."

Her smile was crooked — how Eli's might look if I ever got more than a caustic smirk from him. "Don't thank me. Thank him." Then she was out in the rain, and I let the door close behind her.

"Tea?" Saskia asked, and when I turned back, Eli was standing in the sitting room, surly.

"Black," he said, and when he came around to one of the sofas, he lowered himself gingerly onto the cushions as if his joints needed a bad oiling. He'd changed his clothes into, presumably, whatever had been left behind in the small cabin's musty closets. He wore a fisherman's cable-knit sweater and cargo pants, feet bare. Blood was still crusted in his skin and hair, despite having obviously tried to scrub most of it off. He glanced around. "Still the same damn furniture, I see."

I huffed. "The prodigal son et cetera." I came back to where I'd been near Saskia, to begrudgingly make small talk. "How you feeling?"

His eyes were mean, annoyed I'd even ask. "Better than either of us look," he rasped, coughing. "But anything is better than being slowly squeezed to death inside a tree."

I blanched. "Is that . . . Wait, how did you get free?" Maybe this interlude would be good for something, after all. Now that I'd seen the cinder kids in action, seen what they were capable of, the relief that Seela's wake of destruction could be mended was welcome.

"Your Rabbit friend. Barton." Eli winced at the tea, put it back down. "Egh. Not even steeped."

"Barton? He's here? I mean. Well, wherever *you* were."

"Russia," he said.

I pushed myself deeper into the armchair, letting my head loll back. "Russia? God . . ." Toto, we were not in Winnipeg anymore. "I'm not even gonna ask how you got all the way from there to London to . . . wherever I was. To here."

"I believe the place Seela holed up is somewhere in Newfoundland. And I'm not going to waste either of our time alleviating your guilt about me or any of it. I obviously should've just let things play out and made off with your stone. Less trouble." I was too tired to sort through any of that statement to separate the sarcasm, if there was any.

"He's lying," Saskia translated for me. "He wanted to save you."

Eli was still when I lifted my head, glaring at Saskia. Was his face colouring? "And please remind me why *that* is still here, and why she hasn't been exterminated like the rest of her vermin siblings ought to be?"

I let my head drop again, shut my eyes. "Saskia isn't like them. And I figured you'd want a two-for-one deal on the rescue."

"I didn't. Also, weren't you biting off my head earlier about this? I thought you didn't *need* rescuing."

I waved my hand at him, hoping he'd just go away.

When I opened my eyes, he was standing over me. I jerked.

"There's no time for sleep," he said, yanking me out of the chair by my shirt. "We need to come up with some kind of plan."

I kicked him in the shin with little force, but it was enough to make him buckle.

"Says the guy who's been sleeping for the past few hours." But the truth was, I didn't feel tired in the way that I should. I felt . . . separate. From my body, from its needs for rest or recuperation or healing. I was alert. I knew I wouldn't sleep even if I tried, but I needed time to sort things out. I needed to at least pretend I was still human. "And anyway, I thought you were the one with the plan? You found me easily enough, got past Seela's guard. You wouldn't have gone to the trouble if you didn't have an endgame."

Eli took a seat again on the edge of the sofa. "I can only improvise so far. It's your turn now, because we're running out of time."

He unbuttoned the front of his sweater.

"Wh— Hey," I warned, turning away and holding up a hand. "What are you —"

Eli glanced at my face, then recoiled. "Did you . . . oh, get your mind out of the gutter, Harken, this isn't a bodice-ripper!" He opened his sweater enough to show me the Moonstone, but his cheeks were definitely purpling, and he couldn't look me in the eye. "I need you to tell me what's going to happen to me next."

Saskia had been crumbling the biscuit into the carpet, sifting through the crumbs. "Just like the Emerald."

Eli threw another withering glance at Saskia. "Ignore her," I told him as I sat down beside him, muttering, "bodice-ripper . . ."

Where the stone met his skin was only slightly grey. Comparing it to the Opal, which I'd had for only a few months now, the Moonstone looked genuinely like it was a part of Eli. Like he'd been born with it. He didn't carry it with the heavy submission I did, and its geode spread was much wider. It was a pale white thing with equal parts edge and curve, flecked with gold. In the middle of it was something like a black inky stain.

I sighed. "I don't know . . ." Our eyes met and I quickly looked away. "You hearing any voices? The Paramounts' voices, I mean."

Eli inhaled as he mulled it over. "No. I'd managed to get them under some semblance of control and they were quieter. But . . . you're right. They're completely gone." I didn't want to revel in it, but his expression looked a bit relieved, despite what this meant.

"Any other voices?" I pressed. "Like one villainous one, telling you . . ." There was a fist suddenly around my heart, squeezing, keeping me from going on.

"No," Eli confirmed. "Not yet, anyway. Nothing like the one you've got in you."

"How did —"

"Just when I think you can't possibly be that dense you confirm it," Eli grunted, fastening his buttons again. "Have you really not felt it? Don't you remember any of the visions over the last week?"

Damn his patience was thin. I looked back to Saskia, who had now covered the carpet around her in crumbs, arranging them into symbols and shapes I didn't want to interpret.

I shrugged weakly. "They were dreams, I thought."

I felt the back of my neck prickle. I'd already forgotten there wasn't much point in lying to a telepath. "Idiot," he confirmed.

"Twat," I volleyed back. "All right, maybe not dreams. The Opal has been showing me so many things. Too many. Memories, flashes, projections into things that couldn't have happened. *Your* memories. It's all jumbled up. And yeah, just one too many crises. How did you expect me to sort out what's real?"

Eli moved farther away from me. He really didn't do well with even the *chance* of human contact. "You're untrained. I suppose I shouldn't have expected an amateur to grasp the sheer magnitude of what these stones can do. Or undo."

"You're the one who said we didn't have time, so stop lecturing me on shit I already know." I bristled. "So the stones are linked, somehow, and we were able to . . . I don't know. Communicate. Which explains how you found me, unconscious or not." I gripped the cushions, sorting through what I'd seen. "So I somehow . . . passed this infection on to you when we were linked, I guess? Or else Seela did. Or this 'voice' I keep hearing."

"A demon," Eli said, and I looked up.

"Maybe." Whatever it was, it was overriding my ability to make my own calls. It was stronger than me. I lifted my arm — the skin was peeling back, burning beneath. Fire rose from the core of my palm, the flame as purple-dark as my flesh was becoming. "You're right. I still don't know what I'm doing. Or what's going to happen. I'm sorry you've been dragged into it, too."

Eli grabbed my wrist so hard and so roughly that the fire guttered out. I looked down, saw that he'd rolled up his sleeve. His chain-shaped scar was clear as mine, which still somehow showed through my darkened skin. "Stop being so Canadian with the sorries and *think*." He threw my hand aside. "Whatever is infecting us is secondary. Seela has to be stopped, and with us on the lam he'll be coming sooner than later. We have what he wants."

That reminded me, and I suddenly thought of Corgan. "The Rabbit Paramount. I've seen him. Seen what Seela turned him into before taking the Emerald." I glanced at Saskia. "So maybe that's what's at the end of this for both of us. Death, though, would probably be preferable."

"I wouldn't have come all this way and carried your sorry hide here if I was looking for either of us to die." Eli stood, rubbing his hands in thought. "We aren't meant to die. Not yet."

"What does that mean?"

"The Moth Queen paid me a visit," he grumbled. "I tried to tell you — or your subconscious — that. Not a lot sticks with that unfortunate lemming brain of yours." He bent down to turn the electric heater up, but I felt nothing. Temperature, or even my comfort, seemed to matter less and less. "At any rate. She said that . . . ugh . . ."

He stretched, hands on the small of his back, face contorted in disgust.

"Out with it," I snapped.

"She said that we have to *free* each other. Whatever that means. Saying it out loud sounds even more saccharine than the thought of it . . ." He sighed. "No specifics, though. But I learned long ago to trust Death when she gives you a get-out-of-jail-free card, and to figure the rest out later. I'm sure you know what I mean."

I opened my mouth to say something smart, but I thought better of it. "Why is the Denizen auto-reply always some goddamn riddle?"

Eli snorted. I couldn't help it; I felt proud that he was amused. "The gods like to see us squirm. More entertaining for them."

"You're beginning to sound like my fa—"

I choked on the word, but Eli perked, and despite trying to freeze him out of my thoughts, he snatched it from me and turned slowly to face me.

"Seela," he said slowly, "is your —"

"I don't want to talk about it," I cut him off. "Anyway, it doesn't —"

His face was a gallery of fury. "That's why you didn't

want me to intervene. You wanted to *save the bastard*." Now his laugh was really something else. "Unbelievable."

"And what if it had been your father? Your mother?" I was on my feet, in his face despite him being a head taller. "No matter what either of them did, and you saw the chance to bring them back, would you have killed them?"

"Then maybe there is hope," Saskia said from the floor. We turned as one to look at her, and from this angle we could see she'd smeared biscuit into the carpet into the shape of three rings.

Eli looked back at me, almost . . . softened. "I don't know if there is any coming back from this, Harken." He was tired again, the words losing all their bite.

I felt the corner of my eyes prickle, but I moved away from him to the unlikely cinder kid we'd saved. "What are you talking about, Saskia?"

She raised a bony finger, dark eyes wide. "Your stones. They're what's killing you. Why can't you just take the stones off, like Killian did with the Emerald?"

In all of this I'd forgotten Saskia wasn't a Denizen. *Lucky her*. And it'd been a hell of a — week? Month? — for a crash course in a lot of history and lore and their consequences for me, but at least I had the answer. "We can't remove them," I said with a sigh. "We're stuck with them. Unless we die."

"That's not true." Eli's hand was up, finger in the air like he was testing the wind direction in the stuffy room.

I frowned. "That's not what the Conclave —"

"You have a brain in there somewhere, Harken, otherwise I'd just be reading empty air." Eli's mouth twitched into something that may have been a grin. "There's one person we both know who managed to separate herself from her stone. And go on living."

Another four bad names jockeyed for priority on my tongue, but I bit them back as it dawned on me. "Cecelia." My eyes dropped to the floor as I tried to compose myself. "It's her memories I've been seeing in the stone. I thought she was . . . guiding me. But she's not the person I thought she was."

"Oh, who cares." My head snapped up at Eli, appalled but not surprised by his complete lack of tact. "Whatever she was, she's left the answer behind, at least. Because somewhere in there —" he'd come closer, pointing at the space above my chest where the Opal was, and realizing it was probably inappropriate in a vastly different context, his finger dropped. "Somewhere in there is the way that she did it."

"But it took her *fourteen years,* Eli. She went looking for the way, and by the time she got back up, I was nearly fed to Zabor and my mother, whom she was trying to save, was long dead."

Eli grabbed my sleeve and hauled me out of the living room. "Then we'll have to do better."

The COST *of* FREEDOM

They'd left the Abyss behind. The bottom of the ocean was an Abyss unto itself, in that way. It was hard to tell where one ended and the other began in this dark and infinite place. Natti had spent days walking across it at Aunty's side — but not fully Aunty, entirely. Ryk. Some aspect of her.

"Why did you do it?" she'd asked at first, still trying to deal with Phae's absence, hoping that she could handle her own mission. Natti wished she could be there to help her but also here at the same time.

Aunty shrugged. The Sapphire gleamed so bright between her eyes, eyes that knew what she needed before Natti did. "You are young. There is enough fight to go around for everyone. You'll need your humanity by the end of it."

Back at the glacial bay, Natti had parted with her mother with a tense hug, still full of questions.

"I have to stay here as a guide for those who cannot fight," she said. "My duty was to the Sapphire. And it is still to the Empress. I'll see you again after this. I promise."

Natti frowned. "Better not make promises you can't keep." But she knew what her mother really meant. Whatever happened, in whatever plane or realm their souls went, they could find one another in the end. And things seemed keen on ending soon.

Here at the bottom of the sea, there were cracks slowly spreading over the sea floor, splintering trenches in the rock. Dark places, dark mouths, where darker things could emerge at any time. Nowhere was safe.

The world is in pain. The depths weren't all beautiful dark blue expanses — there was garbage suspended around them the further they travelled through the world's oceans. They hitched to a current to spell them away from a terrain as devastated as the tar sands miles behind them now.

As they travelled, they encountered Seals from the world over. Natti lost her orientation somewhere past the Bering Sea. With Ryk's influence they could move from the Atlantic Ocean to the Indian with a whisper, gathering their forces. The islanders from Polynesia, the Maori from New Zealand. Natti had spent her life feeling landlocked and like she and Aivik were the only Seals. Now they were surrounded. And as their numbers grew, a slight hope swelled.

"The Empress is with us," Maujaq had said, but as they travelled, as the sea life seemed to be swimming ever faster to escape an incoming tide of shadow, Natti didn't know if it could be enough.

The current buoyed them closer to that horizon, and Natti thought of Phae.

"Tell us what you know of the Quartz."

They had walked round the mountain so many times now that Phae could recognize its varied landmarks and details. And they'd done these circuits in contemplative silence, all the while Phae pinged to Barton that she was okay, while he pinged back that he wasn't, that the world wasn't. But she couldn't rush this conversation, and when Fia spoke after such a long quiet, the words rang in her skull, and Phae didn't know how to answer.

"*While you think,*" said the antelope, "*let us tell you something else. Denizens are divided into Families. But the Matriarchs are a part of a family of our own. We love our sisters, however different we may be. We had our own clashes and conflicts before the humans came, but we never dreamed that we would fade as we have, especially from each other. If we could speak to our sisters again we would, but it is not to be. We cannot be anywhere near them. It is too painful.*"

Phae just nodded. "It's the same in most families, I think."

The woman's face was twisted in a grin. "*It is painful because we have failed even our sisters. We brought the darklings into being for balance between creation and destruction. Now the scale has tipped to that dark end, and we feel it is a just reward for humans' damage to the world for which our sisters sacrificed so much.*"

Phae didn't bother arguing with that circular logic since, after all, it was Fia who had put the darklings into the universe in the first place.

"*Each sister represents part of Ancient's body,*" said the man, and though his eyes seemed full of longing, he sounded calm reciting this knowledge. "*Deon and Ryk are Ancient's hands, the left and right, two forces using their great powers to fight and defend. Phyr is Ancient's great fathomless mind that never sleeps. Heen is Ancient's womb and legs, and we are Ancient's heart. Spirit. Soul.*" The comfort fled when he was finished. "*We are all parts of a whole. A whole that will not stir, not matter how much we try to shake Ancient awake. The Quartz was entrusted to us when Ancient fell silent. It is the bell that will awaken Ancient. It is the key to the Brilliant Dark.*"

Phae stopped. Fia went on walking, but when they noticed she wasn't following, they turned.

"That name," Phae said, clutching her forearms. "The Brilliant Dark. What does it mean?"

They stood at the base of the mountain, staring up at it, then Fia beckoned. "*The Brilliant Dark is the edge of all things. The last realm where Ancient sleeps. Only we can open the way there. Only Ancient can stop our dark children.*"

There seemed to be a double meaning in every word the god had spoken. Surely they were speaking about the darklings. *Surely* they were pointing to a way to stop all of this mad destruction before it started. Phae noticed a twitch at the corner of the antelope's mouth. Or were they?

"And only the Quartz can open this door?" she asked, ignoring her mounting doubt.

"*Come,*" they said. "*We will show you our pain. What is to come. Because it is not your fate that will determine this, but hers.*"

Fia climbed. Phae only hesitated a moment longer before following. *Hers*. She knew, without asking, that Fia had meant Roan.

❧

"Couldn't we have waited till the rain let up?"

I don't know why I was complaining. The rain plastered my hair to my face, but I was numb to it — the damp I should've felt, the bone chill. Even the refreshment the rain promised, considering I couldn't remember the last time I'd showered. But nothing seemed able to penetrate the dark shell I was growing, inch by inch.

It was tough to see for the mist and the whipping wind, and I didn't like us being out in the open, despite Eli's claims that we were hidden behind some invisible brain force field he and the other Owls on the island were putting up.

"The rain lets up for three days in August, thereabouts. In Scotland that's called 'summer.' Get used to it." We'd elected to walk from the town, called Uig, up the highway that curved high along the seashore. I wasn't about to let Eli take me back up under those wings — I needed a break, however minor, from the proximity. "Besides, aren't you from a place that's colder than Mars? It's just up here."

"Owls," I muttered, "can't have a summoning chamber indoors like civilized people."

"Don't get me started on you Foxes with your claustrophobic burrow holes."

Up the road rose hills like the cone spires of a Seussian sandcastle, dusted in grass in the fading daylight. But I had to admit, the wind up here was something fierce and perfect for Eli's uses, probably.

"It's called the Fairy Glen," Eli called over the din as we scaled the face of a hill, leading up to a giant crest of red sandy rock. "But don't expect any of the wee folk to be interested in a sorry lot like us."

Saskia gripped my hand as I helped her up. "Do fairies really live here?" she asked.

Eli rolled his eyes so hard he shut them. "No," he snapped, "but I'm certain there are other things that could snatch you away and relieve us from babysitting duty."

"The only person who needs babysitting is you," I spat back, watching as Saskia went running to the next hill, sending a group of errant sheep scattering. There certainly couldn't be anything up here more fearsome than a cinder kid.

"You should've left her behind," Eli said. He didn't mean at his croft.

"Get over it already. She's here. I couldn't just leave her. If you were in my position you wouldn't have, either, you feckless crankshaft."

"Your mastery of the English language never ceases to amaze," he muttered, long legs eating up the distance between him and the ring of rocks he was headed for.

The wind was so hard that it pushed me after him. "Bloody —" I cringed, following with the gust at my back. At least I was still able to feel some things, like exasperation. And Eli could deliver that in spades.

He led us to a sheltered space where the rocks seemed to rise and curve. The rain had let up and, remarkably, the sun was creaking through. The hills shone bright despite the dark clouds above us.

I let out a long, ragged sigh. "This place is beautiful. Can't say you don't have taste." I now faced a jutting rock pile that bore a striking resemblance to a tower, and I leaned back to take in the top.

"Up here." Eli had climbed another rise, which had some small switchbacks that seemed to lead directly to that tower. I scrambled after him but obviously not fast enough, since I felt his fingers gripping my forearm and basically dragging me behind him.

"Jesus!" I staggered, and he shoved me lightly to keep me upright. "All right! I'm going." Maybe killing him at the end of this wouldn't be *such* a bad call . . .

After a bit of a climb and a struggle, we made it to the top. Eli brushed past me impatiently, then scuffed his shoe on the ground and crouched down to smooth it with his palm. I looked down at a sheep bleating across the verdant green, joining the group that seemed to be gathering curiously around Saskia. We were at least twenty feet . . . well, high enough off the ground to bring up the vertigo. I pulled away from the edge.

"Come here."

I turned. Eli was seated with his body facing the wind, his hand out towards me but his eyes elsewhere. When I didn't come, he waved like he was calling a dog. "Stop gawking. Let's get going while we still can."

"You really have zero people skills. Can't you be nice?"

"Not to you," he seethed as I came closer, and he pointed to the space in front of him, at the edge of the landing with my back to the sharp air. "Sit there, facing me."

"Ugh . . ." I lowered myself carefully onto the dirt, bringing my legs awkwardly underneath me as he had. I glanced over the crest again, felt the sharp air at my back. How had I managed to get to the top of the Golden Boy last spring without hurling? I recalled, too late, that Eli had been there. "There, Captain. Now what?"

"If it's at all possible, shut your howling screamer."

"Hey —"

He pinched the bridge of his nose. "I need to focus. *You* need to focus. For the love of any god that is listening, just be quiet."

"Fine." I took a breath. The dark passenger riding stiffly in the coach of my soul hadn't moved yet. I was getting anxious that if we started poking around in the Opal, it'd come back to bite me hard enough that neither of us could recover.

But at least some part of the real me was still alive? I couldn't help blurting, "So you really think this will work?"

Eli's eyes popped open, the hands he'd been holding in front of him stiffening into claws. "It will if you let me —"

"I mean, even if we get into the Veil, and link our stones, and try to sort through Cecelia's memories, this thing inside me could notice. It could come after both of us."

I was trembling, and it wasn't because of the cold. I still couldn't feel that, but I could feel uncertainty. Eli tilted his head, staring, his grey eyes changing over to gold.

Now I was getting riled up, and my mouth quirked. "Stop looking at me like that. You should take a picture. You like doing that, don't you?"

As the feathers bloomed at his neck, they prickled. "Are you seriously going to bring that up n—"

I slapped his hands down, even as the gold rings shimmered beneath us. I couldn't take it anymore. "Look, before we go any further, I really have to know. What are we?"

I'd never seen him look so downright terrified. "What . . . ?"

"I mean, are we friends? Are we enemies on a truce?" I sidestepped the implication on purpose, despite how everyone around us had been making it. I certainly didn't want to get into that. Not right now, anyway. Maybe not ever, smug bastard. He seemed to relax but barely.

"You're just a really unpleasant human at your base function, you're always quipping inappropriately, you bring me out here but you say it's not a rescue, but it *clearly was*, but maybe it's just because you want to secure the Opal, or the Moth Queen sent you —"

Eli covered his changing face with his talon-tipped hands, and the groan he let out was definitely otherworldly. "Why in the gods' names does any of that matter *right this second*?"

I don't know who was more shocked — him or me — when I reached out and touched those feathered hands, and they lowered slowly, reservedly. I pulled back, frowning.

"Because this will go easier if you cut the crap and try to be authentic with me. I'd rather be doing this with a friend than whatever you're putting on right now." I bit the inside of my cheek. "I miss Phae. I miss Deedee. I tried doing this alone but I obviously can't. So I know I need your help, but —" I looked straight at him "— you're being a dick."

His blink was slow. *Owlish.* Like I'd been speaking in another language. The rings beneath us rotated, and he folded his hands in his lap. Hands that had hurt me. Hands that had pulled me out of hell — twice.

"All right," he said.

I made a show of cupping my ear. "What was that?"

"I'm *sorry*," he hissed, definitely nonplussed I'd yanked it out of him. "A lot has . . . happened. Not just lately. Since we were both in the Bloodlands. Since Zabor. Shifting priorities . . . and I'm still not very good at this."

My chest constricted. I cleared my throat. "Obviously."

"I'm not sure if I'm your 'friend.' Or if I want to be." His eyes cut to me with less malice and more amusement. "But I'm not the enemy. For better or worse we are connected. And I suppose I'd best come to terms with that if either of us is going to make it through to the other side."

The rings flashed, and the wind picked us up in a torrent, pulling the Fairy Glen, and the world, away beneath us.

"Okay," I managed, before our spirits crossed over.

Eli felt his spirit come away from his body, re-form in this space — this dark, hollow vacuum of in-between. The Veil. The place where only spirit existed. Memory and heartbreak, altered senses, the awareness of a dream. He could not see, only feel, insinuate, and draw images from that. Roan was somewhere nearby but getting farther away, as if they were both boats being carried across a windless sea.

"Wake up," he said into the nothing, trying to direct it to her. The Moonstone lit the way for him, kept him grounded. He knew she might need help with staying grounded herself, as well as managing the corrupted Opal, so he cast out his mind, and his stone, with a tether of light.

It hooked onto something.

"I'm scared," she said, grasping the line.

"Of what?"

A flicker. A spark. "Of what I might do with the Opal."

Eli thought he'd just feel the same ruthless impatience as before, but all he could feel was Roan's terror and sadness coming back to him along the cable. He grasped with his mind, as if it were his hand, and pulled.

"You're stronger than you give yourself credit for," he said, something bright on the other end of the line clarifying, along with his sense of sight, of tangibility, as it came closer. "And you know I'm loathe to admit that."

He had been reeling in a flame. It was orange and white and purple and black. A twisted, confused shape trying to coalesce. Then a hand came into view, holding the line for dear life, and attached to it was Roan.

"I'll help you as best I can," Eli said, and the Moonstone and the Opal heard each other, and the space was bright.

Roan opened her eyes, wincing against the glare. "Thanks." She peered around. The Veil shifted, trying to interpret their thoughts, their needs. It was a cacophony of sound and images and intent. A liminal space for the spirit to pass through any of the planes or the Realms of Ancient.

"And what realm are we going to, then?" Roan asked. Eli jerked; they were now truly riding the same wavelength, so his thoughts and hers were overlapping.

"We're not going far," Eli said, letting himself take shape with finer detail. Roan still looked like a smudge of fire and brimstone, but her face was becoming more recognizable. "The answers are in the Opal. So we will go inside it. Together."

Eli knew they'd have to be careful. He could feel the vibration coming from Roan up the line, pinging back from him. They were an even match — capable, slightly foolhardy. And above all, vulnerable. There would be things that Roan would be privy to, inside him, that he didn't want her to see, and vice versa. He put up walls around these secrets, and around his unvoiced intentions, but she couldn't protect herself like that. She was trusting him, and he knew it.

She knew, too. She hesitated, drawing away.

Roan . . .

They both turned towards the voice, but it was smoke in the ether, gone as quickly as it'd been conjured.

"She's awake," Roan said.

"She?" Eli cast his mind further into the mire of images skirting past their awareness; the voice had been familiar. He'd heard it before. It was similar to Roan's, and he'd mistaken it for hers.

"It doesn't matter," she said. "We came here for a reason." Then she reached out for Eli and drew him down into the fire.

On the other side, their spirits' impressions of their bodies were sharper, more defined. More like they had been when things were simpler. *Were they ever?* Roan thought, and Eli mentally echoed her sentiments. Roan's image rippled with a flickering overlay of her ashen skin. Her eyes, however, remained the same — one hazel, one amber, piercing to the quick of Eli when they looked at him.

"Well?" she asked.

He honed his concentration, like a weapon. "You have to lead the way," he said. "You're the only one who can navigate the Opal's memory. I'm only here to help direct your focus."

She shut her eyes. "But how do I know what we're looking —"

Suddenly they were falling. Fast. Smashing through space like the storeys of a skyscraper.

"Harken!" Eli shouted. "Focus!" He threw his mind into hers, tried to extinguish the growing panic.

They hit the ground; a jolt of pain went through both their minds. It was still dark all around them, like the rabbit hole Alice fell down, until, in smatterings of colour and sensation, it wasn't dark at all. A woman with short-cropped hair was sitting in a beam of sunlight cascading through a window. It was cracked open slightly, letting in fresh air, the sounds of the road. She was bent over something, absorbed. When Eli got a closer look at her, he saw she was working at a huge mass of clay with her hands. And that she was blind.

"Ruo." The name shot across his awareness like an arrow, splitting open a cask of the rest of what made this woman.

"Cecelia's partner." Eli nodded. And as if he'd conjured her by name, Cecelia came up behind Ruo, kissing her on the cheek.

"They're beautiful," Cecelia said. "You really can do anything."

Ruo smiled, easing back and rubbing her knuckles. "It's just memory in my hands, that's all."

Eli glanced at Roan. She was standing close enough to the women to be able to touch them. They did not notice her, nor would they. The pain in her face was a prism as she looked around the studio. The other sculptures were just as large and finely crafted — a seal, a rabbit, an owl, a deer. Delicate. Intense. The sculpture she had been working on was a fox.

Eli felt the shudder across their connection as something inside Roan clicked.

"A wedding gift, I think," Ruo said, stretching. "I'm sure it'll be soon. Don't you?"

Cecelia moved to the window, arms folded, giving away nothing.

"You don't think he's good for her, is that it?" Ruo guessed.

Cecelia grinned. "You sure you're not secretly an Owl now?"

But Ruo's face wasn't amused. "What has Killian done, Sil? And what did you have to get him out of this time?"

Cecelia's smile dropped and she was grave. "He hasn't done it yet. I don't know. The Stonebreakers are getting more desperate. I joined them because I do agree with them in principle, but . . . the rituals they're considering. Turning to darklings for aid? I'm afraid Killian's going to do something stupid. Something he'll regret. And Ravenna won't think so highly of him for it."

Ruo stood, fingers trailing around the edge of her worktable to join Cecelia at the window. "So why don't you talk to Ravenna about it first?"

The pain Eli had seen on Roan's face was now on her grandmother's. "You know I can't. We argue enough as it is. And she loves him. And . . . I'm trying to have faith that Killian will do the right thing and steer clear of the extremists if he really wants a future with her."

"And you think you can convince him?" Ruo seemed dubious, but she slid an arm around Cecelia's waist, and Cecelia put her arm around her in turn, drawing her close.

Roan grabbed hold of Eli, pulling him back, away, and the memory faded when Cecelia said, "I can only do so much."

Eli and Roan fell backward through something fluttering — ink and paper. Letters. Roan seemed more mindful of herself now, her direction, and Eli twisted, trying to keep up. "Wait!" he called after her, and he reached out and grabbed her, but it wasn't her panic he was feeling now — it was his own, and they went into a memory that didn't belong to the Opal but to Eli.

"Why is she like this?"

They were back in the croft, in the narrow hallway that led to the small bedrooms. A boy sat on the floor, wrapped in a cabled fisherman's sweater that was much too big for him, pulling it closer and closer as if he could disappear into it.

Roan looked up at Eli, concerned. "Is that you?"

Agathe, a much younger version, knelt down beside him, trying to get him to stand up. Behind the door were fitful cries. Little Eli wouldn't move.

"Yer mum," Agathe said, "was the smartest, bravest girl I knew. One day, she found a treasure she ought not to have, and when she refused to take it, it cursed her. But she made sure it stayed hidden, because it was a dangerous, precious thing, and she didn't want anyone else to experience the pain it brought. So she has taken all the pain into herself. To protect everyone. Including you."

Little Eli's face twisted. "That's just a story you made up. There's no such thing as curses or treasure."

Just misery, the thought escaped Eli's mind before he could take it back, and Roan looked stunned.

"We need to focus," Eli said gruffly, and he grabbed hold of Roan and steered them away, from one dark place to another.

When they touched down again, raised voices cut through like daggers, slicing away the croft and repurposing the jumbled images when the Opal took hold.

"— and you were there! You were involved! You *knew*."

A woman with long red hair — Roan's hair. And maybe her nose, twisted in fury. Cecelia was pressed into the room's corner — a kitchen — her face in her hands, which were covered in blood.

"Please, Ravenna —"

"No. I don't want to hear any more about it!" Ravenna was crying, face red and tears streaming. "You — you knew he was going to do this, and you didn't stop him. I bet you were there to *help him*! You've been one of *them*, those fanatics, all along! My own *mother*!" Then she whirled, finger pointing, to the other woman in the doorway even though she couldn't see the gesture. Ruo. "And you still stand by her! After everything she's done to you!"

Ruo's head dipped, her milky eyes flickering as if they could see. "Ravy. I'm sorry —"

"Sorry?" she screamed. "Killian's under tribunal review now. They'll put him away for good, I'm sure. In one of those, those . . . Denizen vaults. And they'll keep him there forever. And he *deserves* it! And what about me? He wasn't thinking about me. No one ever does, I guess! And not just me but *us*." She clutched her belly, and Eli realized that beneath it was Roan — the tiny spark of her. Roan watched this go on, expression dark.

The women were silent. Then Ravenna said, "I'm leaving."

"Where?" Ruo took a step forward.

"Winnipeg," Ravenna said, clutching her waist in her arms. "I have a few friends there still. They'll put me up. And it's far enough away from *you*." She spat this afterthought at Cecelia, who still couldn't look her daughter in the eye. Cecelia, who, for all her great height and bearing, seemed shrunken. Ravenna crossed the room and took Ruo's hands. "Come with me, Mama Ruo. Then she can't hurt either of us anymore. She's just going to try to get you involved in whatever scheme —"

Ruo touched her daughter's face. "I love you so dearly, Ravy. But my place is with Sil. And it always will be."

Ravenna ripped herself away. "Fine." And when she stormed out of the room, no one tried to stop her.

"*My* mother," Roan said, the memory dissolving, leaving only the two of them behind. She looked at Eli. "I guess we've both got issues there."

Eli held her gaze for a little while longer, then said, "We're getting close, I think."

Roan nodded. They ducked underneath a panel of shadow and came through over a bleak horizon. Beneath them, memories shifted like sand: Roan born, Ravenna trying to build herself a life, meeting Aaron Harken. Beneath that still, on a crimson layer, was the impression of Zabor, her mouth open. A moth drew itself across the image like it was water, scattering it. Roan was marked, and Ravenna stood on the Allens' doorstep, beseeching them for help, but none was coming.

Then they went through a door into another fully formed memory. It was in a place underground — the vaults under South Bridge — in a summoning chamber not unlike the one Eli had seen when he'd brought Roan back from Seela's fortress. A dark and dismal place where the air prickled. Yet the two figures occupying the space were Cecelia and Ruo.

"I may not be a Denizen any longer, but this place . . . this feels wrong," Ruo shivered.

Cecelia stood in the centre of the room. The Opal shone bright and proud from beneath her long neck, and her cascade of dark hair, though marked with streaks of white, was as proud a mane as any. "I have to do this, Ruo. Ravenna is my blood. Which means she's bound to do something rash.

And as the Paramount, I can't intervene or stop our granddaughter from being marked. But in another form, maybe I can skirt the tenet . . . and I can't do that with the Opal attached to me."

"This is exactly the ritual that got Killian put away. It's too dangerous. And you could *die*," Ruo hissed, as if saying it might make it real.

Cecelia closed her eyes. "Ravenna could die. Roan could die. I've lived my life. And Deon herself told me my purpose was to keep Roan safe." When she opened her eyes, they were flashing discs of sunlight. "And to keep that promise, I have to do this."

The rings in the floor shone scarlet. Cecelia's body changed into the fox warrior. Her garnet blade flashed, and she cut her mighty hand, spilling a wash of otherwordly blood onto the flecked granite beneath her feet.

"If this is the ritual Killian was attempting . . ." Roan started, then she turned to Eli. "What exactly are they going to summon?"

Eli was watching intently. "Surely —"

The black that seeped up from the rings was impenetrable. Ruo shrank against the wall, and Cecelia stood firm and proud as the creature emerged, a mask of bone over its eyes.

"I sleep in the dark of the Bloodlands," spoke the creature, its mouth an unforgiving hollow. "Call my name so I may hear your petition."

The creature was beautiful — its near-humanoid proportions perfectly formed, four hands bent in supplicant poses, arms extending from a long, mantis torso. Two hands clasped flat together in front, one with the thumb and middle finger touching, and the last with the thumb and index finger in an

o. These mudras shifted, indicating the elements that bound them all and that identified this darkling. Zabor's brother. One of the mighty three bent on removing the world.

"Kirkald," Cecelia said, "most beautiful and wretched. I am a daughter of Deon. Your prison walls beneath the world are thick. You are bound by a targe of Ancient, and so you can only speak the truth to me."

Kirkald was quiet for a moment, then his smile was cruel. "Oh yes. I will speak to you only truth. But it will serve me well, it seems." Kirkald reared up. "I have seen you before. In my vision of the far past, a vision of my sister."

Cecelia growled, "You break your oath so soon? I have never seen you before, world-shaker. I have come to ask you — can you truly separate a Paramount from their Calamity Stone, without a cost?"

Kirkald laughed. "There is always a cost, daughter of Deon. And I cannot speak an untruth to you. You said so yourself." One of the four hands reached up and opened its palm to her, revealing a jade green targe incised with three gold circles. "I am bound by the same tenets you are. I can separate your stone for you. But you must complete a task for me in return."

Cecelia tightened her bloody hand on the bone hilt of the garnet blade. "What sort of task?"

The four hands wheeled, dancing in the air and cutting crimson sigils into it. "A task you have already done. A task completed hundreds of years ago. For I can send you into the past to do it, as even your Matriarchs cannot."

"Hundreds of years ago?"

"For it was you, daughter of Deon, who broke the targe of Zabor. It was you who allowed her to return to the Uplands, to wreck her havoc. It is because of you she has chosen your blood for her feast."

Eli felt Roan stiffen, as if she were going to try to leap into the memory and try to change it herself. He held her back; this was, after all, what they'd been searching for.

"Time," Cecelia said. "You're going to send me back in *time*? To release my enemy? If I refuse you, then she'll never be here in the first place, and I won't have to bother with you at all."

"Sound reasoning," Kirkald agreed, nodding. "But Zabor is already here. And your granddaughter is already in peril. It has already happened. And you will do this so that you can stop Zabor regardless, to send her back to her noble brothers who have so greatly missed her." When Kirkald smiled again, his teeth seemed to lengthen. "The choice has already been made."

Cecelia turned to Ruo, who was still plastered against the wall in the dark. "Will you take the stone and hide it for me?" Cecelia asked her wife, her own voice overlapped by Deon's great flaming roar. "Until I return?"

"What?" Ruo hissed. "What have you done?"

Cecelia turned back to Kirkald. "How long will this task take? Will I be back in time to save my granddaughter?"

Kirkald's grin was too ecstatic. "Oh yes. Plenty of time. And once you have achieved this and your soul returns from its journey, you will take on a form that will keep you safe. But remember — once I've removed the stone, you cannot return to your body, except before its death. Do you understand?"

Cecelia nodded. There hadn't been any time to consider

what any of this meant. And she had always been a creature of action.

"*Enough time*," Roan thundered. "Fourteen years."

But suddenly the four hands of Kirkald held Cecelia in their death-grip, and a fifth emerged from beneath its mask of bone, clasping the stone. It wrenched, and Cecelia cried out.

"Remember your promise," Kirkald said. "Break Zabor's targe. Set it all in motion. This is your place in the Narrative, after all."

As Cecelia's nine tails fell, the fox head dipped, and what could have been hot tears sizzled away between flaming locks of fur. "I promise."

"Then I will see you again. And again," Kirkald said. The stone came free, and Cecelia's body collapsed in an empty heap, the beautiful and terrible Dragon Opal caught in Ruo's open hands. Cecelia's spirit had fled through time.

Roan reached, but the dark took the moment away in a fist, and they were inside a memory of Roan's. There she was, so small, rubbing her eye. Aaron Harken bent down, scooped her up. He was tall, hair and glasses askew, hands covered to the wrist in dirt, as if he'd been in the garden. The memory smelled of well-turned earth. Of some semblance of happiness, despite the dread hanging over the house.

"Don't do that, love," Aaron said, taking Roan's small fist in his and kissing it. "It'll only make it worse."

He carried her away, but they passed Ravenna, standing in the hall, a phone receiver pressed to her ear, the other hand grasping a table that burned as she held onto it.

"I don't want them!" she shouted. "Send them back!

I know she's trying to tell me to accept it. That's why she won't talk to me, isn't it?"

The room split, and the line of the phone was held by Ruo, thousands of miles away. "No, love. She just . . . she just wouldn't be able to talk now if she wanted to. They're a gift from me. So you remember. That you are a part of a family, of something greater, and we love you." Ruo did not tell her that the Opal had been set inside the fox's head, that it could be freed again once Cecelia returned. "She's going to make it right. You just have to trust her. Just wait a little while longer."

"Make it right?" Ravenna laughed coldly. "You know how she could make it right? She could fall off the face of the planet." And she smashed the phone down.

The Veil began to rumble.

"What's happening?" Eli whirled on Roan, and she was staring at her hands. The heat coming off her was harsh, a torrential wave.

"I can't . . ." she started, then she held herself as tightly as Ravenna had, as if she were trying to stop herself from disappearing. Or exploding. "It's getting stronger. And I . . ."

The world shattered, and Eli and Roan were ripped apart in the flaming black gale.

❧

"Time is different there," Eli was saying from the other side of the bathroom door. "You could go in and an hour can pass but it's really years and years."

I had pulled the door shut but he didn't seem to care. Trouncing around with our souls tied together had made him completely oblivious to personal space, I guess. Ever since we walked in the door, he couldn't stop his mouth.

"Right." I stared deeper into the mirror, wondering, hoping I could will away what I was seeing. "She also went back in time, didn't she? Hundreds of years back . . . then she got spat out again fourteen years too late. Though nothing surprises me now." *I saw something terrible deep down where I'd gone*, Sil the fox had said. Had she just seen the same vision Eli and I had, of the world burning? A vision that would come about because of her own actions? Or was she just haunted by too many regrets that couldn't be mended, even after her physical death? I didn't think I had the will to go back into the Opal to go hunting for that answer.

Eli grunted. "I've never heard of a darkling having the ability to remove a Calamity Stone. In everything I've studied . . . I suppose that knowledge was hidden, to keep people from doing terrible things to rid themselves of the stone. Too late for that, though." I could hear the gears of his brain grinding even from in here. He seemed a bit too giddy after everything we'd seen. "Still. It's a method. Though Cecelia wasn't able to return to her body. Maybe we can get around that . . ."

"I doubt it." I blinked. Blinked harder. The eye that had been truly mine, was half-black, and the pupil had turned red. I opened my shirt, and the dark stain climbed up to my jawline.

This was happening too fast. And when I pressed my face closer to the glass, I saw the black bleed over, into the amber eye that Death had left behind. Déjà vu. Again and again.

The thing inside me was eager to get out.

An impatient knock at the door. "What are you doing? You've been in there for twenty minutes."

"Am I to have zero privacy before the apocalypse?" I snapped. My reflection hadn't changed, and it wasn't going to. Not tonight, anyway. I needed to lie down and shut my eyes, shut all this away for a while.

"We'll need to tread carefully. The game has changed," Eli was saying as I pulled the sweater I'd found in a bedroom drawer over my head. "The Stonebreakers just wanted the stones to destroy them, and that was that. Seela wants the stones to unmake the world before he gets rid of them — if he intends to. We can't ask the Celestial Darklings for aid because they'll use us to their own ends, as they are doing with Seela. So we need a different darkling to do it . . ."

My hand was hovering over the doorknob. I couldn't hide my face any longer. And I could definitely hide less from Eli, who sensed I was there, suddenly ripping the door open before I got the chance to.

His face was bleak, looking down at me, but he didn't turn away. I tensed. "A different darkling?"

"Yes," he said, grim. "You."

❧

There were two beds in the croft — in rooms that seemed virtually unchanged from Eli's memory that I'd accidentally stumbled into. He'd been what — ten? A decade and a half ago, and this place a time capsule as much as a mortuary. I lay across one of these beds, staring at the ceiling. Saskia was curled beside me. She was like me and wouldn't sleep, but she said she wanted to pretend. To try to remember what it was like to dream. I couldn't blame her.

The other bedroom was empty. It had been Eli's mother's. I'd recognized the doorway, almost as if that little boy were still frozen outside it. I was trapped on the carousel of my thoughts, thinking of families; that you could have none and feel like no one, or have one and still be separated by a phone line or by regret. I thought of Phae and Barton and Natti and, yes, even Eli, and maybe Saskia, and how family could be what you made of it. Blood or not. Powers or not. You could have all the power in the world, in fact, and you could still feel as vulnerable as a child.

Eli had elected to sleep on the sofa, if he could sleep. He was as tightly wound as me, but he needed rest. This whole thing had taken a considerable chunk out of what little he had left. When I had the time to sit back and think about the distance he'd travelled, the sheer breadth of what he'd done, I was surprised he was still in one cranky-ass piece.

But he was here. That had seemed a stretch. And we were on an even keel, careful territory. We'd both lost much. We were both running headlong towards an uncertain ending. Mutt and Jeff at the brink of certain doom, trapped by our shared griefs.

Being together in the stones had been . . . a trial. And a dangerous one. But without him we would have faltered far sooner, wouldn't have come out the other side with what we now knew, even if the truth was painful. I was grateful for that. For him. Even though he'd seen into parts of me I didn't even want to face myself. I'd seen into him, and for a guy who could read minds, could completely wall up his own, that must have been hard.

Painful truths. Here was one: Cecelia wasn't perfect. I already knew that. Everything she did, everything she gave up. It was out of love. I knew that, too. But so many lies piled on top of one another can suffocate even the brightest love. Lying here, still alive despite everything, I didn't know if it had been worth it.

Saskia suddenly sat up beside me, swinging her legs over the edge of the bed.

I sat up on my elbows. "What is it?"

But she slid off without answering me, going across the room to the door and ducking out of sight. I was about to go after her, but Eli suddenly appeared in the doorway, and I froze.

"Hm," he said, looking in the direction she'd fled.

I didn't bother asking. Saskia had known he was there, maybe, in the strange way she seemed to know too many things, and now I was alone with him.

"May I?" Eli asked, lingering there. The bed was small, and now suddenly the whole room seemed *way* too small if he was going to come in. Too many things railroaded in my head, and I just stared at him.

He put up a hand, obviously reading this. "Or not —"

"No, no." I shifted over, patting the bed awkwardly. "I mean, also, it's your house . . ."

He took his damn time thinking about it, which made it more unbearable. Then he dipped his head down, crossed the room, and sat on the edge of the bed, looking around the space as if it were an alien planet. "Yes. I suppose it is. Though I've never felt at home anywhere. Not really."

My body was changing right under me, but I could still feel surprise. An unfamiliar breed of anxiety. I pulled my legs up, knees under my chin. "You scared Saskia away. How long were you lurking out there?"

"Not long," he said. "But she asked me to come in. With her mind. I'm not going to ask how she could do that. I've decided to just let things play out since she isn't interested in killing us. It's a nice change of pace."

"Right." My jaw was working, teeth grinding. What was that kid up to?

"Saw a lot today," he said. He was perched so precariously, shoulders hunched, probably in case he had to flee from his own discomfort. Though he was just his normal jaded self, it was almost like his wings were there, a heavy shadow holding him down.

I turned my face away. I didn't know if I had it in me for whatever this was — an oncoming argument, a pep talk turned berating. I didn't *want* to bicker with him anymore. But I never expected Eli to be anything less than coarse with me. "Yeah? And?"

Eli looked at me strangely, and I became very still.

"The thing about grief," he started, and his voice was very quiet, "is that it doesn't go away. You don't 'get over' anything. It gets packed away, and you learn to live with it. You heal *around* it. If you can call it healing." He crossed a leg, leaned over it. "Really you rebuild but you aren't the same as you were. And that's fine. You can't stay the same forever. You can't be a child forever." He hadn't moved closer, but I turned my face aside, a stinging coming up under my nose. "Whatever it is that's inside you, that dark thing trying to take control. It feeds on grief. It makes you vulnerable if you ignore it, too. You have to remember you're not just holding on to your own grief. The loss of your parents, your grandparents. You are holding the grief of too many people who had their chance at life and have passed from it. Their choices weren't your responsibility. You have to know that."

The room got even smaller, and so did whatever room was left inside of me. Why was he saying all this now? "It doesn't matter," I muttered. "They're all gone, and we're the only ones left to clean up the mess."

I could tell his hackles were going up. "Your grief is what kicked us out of the Veil today. If you don't master it —"

"You just said I can't 'get over it' just like that. So why are you asking me to?"

"That's not . . ." He let out an exhalation so big I thought it'd conjure a windstorm. "I'm just trying to do as you asked and . . . not be such a *dick*."

Spoken in his cultured accent and with deadpan exhaustion, I couldn't help but laugh. He did, too — I could see him smile in the dark.

After a beat, after remembering what was at stake, the mounting dread came back. "Eli. If I try to remove our stones, using this dark power, there's nothing that can stop it from taking over once I let it in. It's been hard enough keeping it down, keeping it buried. And you heard what that thing Kirkald said. There's always a cost. What if —"

The bed shifted and Eli was pulling himself up beside me. Extremely close. He stretched his long legs out in front of him, folded his hands over his stomach, and leaned his head back against the wall, shutting his eyes. The porch light outside the window was set on a timer, and it suddenly clicked on, sending a slanted beam into the room, and I saw his passive face in profile. Really looked at it for probably the first time.

Definitely getting crowded. If I scooted any farther over, I'd be sitting on the nightstand. So I gave up, stretched my own legs out, and tried to get comfortable . . . despite the fact that I didn't know *what* I was feeling right now, if there was any *room* for that, anyway —

"I can leave," he offered, his eyes still shut.

I frowned, more annoyed than embarrassed. "Stop doing that."

"Doing what?"

"Doesn't it get tiring, the mind reading?"

"I wasn't," he claimed. "You're just exceedingly obvious."

I tried to push the growing grin down and turned away again, even though his eyes were still closed.

"Roan?"

I prickled at his sudden, careful use of my first name. "Hm?"

"I said I'd help you the best I can," Eli said. "Now close your eyes. I'll try to help you now. If you like."

I should've rebuffed him, gone to the living room myself, spent the night in turmoil like I deserved, as if marinating in all the possible disasters scratching at the door would do me any favours. Instead, I did as he asked, because he *had* asked nicely, and behind the dark of my eyes there was an almost-relief from the pain in my heart, a gold tether reaching out, wrapping around my withered senses, and pulling them into a state of peace I never imagined I'd feel again, when I grabbed hold.

Enemy *of* Ancient

They had reached the summit of the mountain long ago, but this still wasn't what Phae had expected. She knew that something was wrong as they'd climbed, a creeping doom growing in the pit of her stomach. She knew that the closer they got to the top, the sooner she hoped she would see Roan, catch a glimpse of her dear friend — but it wouldn't be anywhere approaching pleasant. And she would be unable to act, since her own task was still not done.

"*This is what you wanted,*" Fia said, standing over Phae with their hands pressing her shoulders. "*This is your test. You must watch but you cannot intervene. You will know what it has been for us, with these children we made. You will try to change the Narrative, even from here, but you can't. No one can.*"

Phae stiffened, biting her tongue, because by now she knew better than to talk back to a god. She heard the great neck creak, saw the shadow of the enormous triple rack of horns shift as their faces changed. But Phae knew, without looking, that each face would have the same expression; that all three held a sort of bitter contempt and maybe even a sadness, however reluctantly felt.

Fia's three rings glowed beneath them, and Phae saw Roan and Eli in one, sitting side by side on a bed, her head tipped on his shoulder, his eyes wide open as she slept. Images of Barton and the coalition occupied another, preparing to board a plane.

The third ring was dark, set between the other two. It was this ring she watched, trembling.

"*If you still think the world is worth saving after this,*" Fia sneered, "*then the Quartz is still not for you.*"

More riddles. Phae shut her eyes, felt her spirit grow, and reached for Barton.

⁂

The plane dipped. Barton held on, cringing.

It's happening too fast. It's happening now. *Barton, please. You have to help Roan. Do it for me.* Even in another realm, on the upside-down of reality, Phae was looking out for her best friend. And here he was, desperate to help Phae.

Across the aisle of the military plane, Solomon sweated through his fatigues despite being strapped securely in place.

Barton didn't comment, but the man smiled bitterly. "The last time I was on a plane, things didn't go as planned." He cleared his throat. "And what's your excuse?"

Barton raised an eyebrow. This man was definitely not like his son; his demeanour was too pleasant. "You could just read my mind, I guess."

"I could," he conceded, "but what's on your mind is one thing. How you communicate it and interpret that is entirely another."

Barton sucked on his teeth as they banked, the Broadford Aerodrome coming into view through the small window by his head. He and Solomon had had many conversations in the days leading up to this, the man eager, almost, to be a teacher and a father to anyone who needed it, maybe to distract him from his fears for Eli's safety. And he'd been the only one Barton had told about Phae — in fact, Solomon had been helping him hone his focus to take in Phae's desperate messages from the other side, using the neutralizer's skills that Arnas had passed on to him. If only he could open a passage that might allow Phae back through . . . but he knew he couldn't be so selfish, not when she had her own tasks to complete.

"I'm just . . . I hope we aren't too late."

Solomon did not hesitate. "We just have to trust," he said. "Trust that they'll be all right. Eli has more than just the power of the stone to rely on. He feels a strong pull for this girl. And he wouldn't trust her lightly, either."

Barton shut his eyes. "We can trust Roan all we want," he said, "but she has to trust herself." They weren't his words but Phae's, and though he'd kept his voice even, across the tether she'd cast to him, there was more doom and desperation than blind faith underneath them.

❧

I'd been dreaming. Something I hadn't done, really, in so long my brain and body forgot the way of it. I had been dreamed into the lives of others so often that mine had become forfeit. Cecelia. Ravenna. Ruo. Eli. I'd faded behind the weight of them all. What was left for me, anyway? What kind of life or future? School or a job or a career? No — they were fairy tales. And the monstrous reality was, I might not live long enough to remember I once cared about any of those things, anyway.

I'd been dreaming of kindness. Of a world unburdened. Of vast, empty spaces, populated by no one. I dreamed of a room, with a woman sitting next to a hospital bed that held another woman, silent for years. Ruo shuffled a handful of postcards she could not see — postcards she will send to her almost-granddaughter, in Cecelia's stead. She will send one out whenever she remembers, but her mind has been failing her lately, and no one is there to hold her hand through it. Just ghosts, closing in.

And then the room, and all those blissful vast spaces before it, turned to ash, and death, and I was still alone. But still serene.

In the middle distance, separated by gnarled trees, a woman with long dark hair striped with grey approached. She wore armour that made her look like a fox god, long legs set in leather bracers depicting battles and triumphs. She removed the helm with the pointed ears, the cape that was split nine ways, and she discarded them, along with her sword, in the dirt at my feet.

"Well," I said.

"I know," Cecelia sighed, ragged and bloody. She surveyed the land as I did.

"You made a mess of things," I told her, but she didn't need to be told. She knew it better than me.

“All we can do,” she said, “is try to make things right while we still have the chance.”

“Not much of a chance now. And you could’ve made it right when you were alive, instead of leaving it to me.” I was bitter, true, but the apathy was fast taking over. “At the end of this, how much of it will have mattered? The mistakes. The fixing of the mistakes.”

“Come with me,” she said. And we walked the path across the Bloodlands that she had taken, to a place the thing inside me called *the Darkling Hold*, and I heard grave singing.

The hold was at the bottom of a canyon, it seemed, stretching on into infinity. It had cracked. Would keep cracking as the great bodies of its prisoners rallied.

“Look into the fissure,” she said. “What do you see?”

I didn’t want to. “I already have. I’ve already tried looking.” The sea, the chasm. Eli. I had tried to see . . .

“Look again.” And when she pointed, I couldn’t help it. I saw what could have been the very edge of the universe. A web of dark, and in the centre of it, I saw —

— me.

“Just tell me what it means. I don’t have time for riddles.”

When I looked at Cecelia again, she was Ruo, young and still able to see her future. She touched my face. “It’s not a riddle,” she promised. “It’s the cost of freedom. It’s love that brought us all here. Love can consume you or set you free. But at least there’s a promise in it, however fragile, of the continuation of life. You just have to hold on.”

“I can’t.” I felt the dark fire stoking higher on the pyre of my good intentions, and it was climbing up my feet, consuming. “I’m not strong enough. I’m not either of you.” Ruo’s eyes turned black with pin-dot red centres, as if stained by black acid rain. Her skin hissed away, revealing something underneath, and then it wasn't Ruo at all.

Ruo was now me. The dark copy. The thing with the voice that had staked me as its territory.

"You keep treating me like I'm an invader," this duplicate me, this *dark* me, said, a finger pressing into the Opal. "But I've always been here. I'm nothing more than you. What you were meant to become. Not long now."

"You're not me," I said, but she grabbed hold of my hands, pulling me close, and the fire ate us both up, and I could really feel us smouldering, fusing, like burnt acrylic.

"We are all the children of the Bloodlands," the dark me said, "and it's time we embraced our family."

Down on the beach where we'd first crash-landed, Saskia asked the question I couldn't.

"Once you take the stones off," she said, skipping a flat rock across the expanse of the water, "what will you do with them?"

Another stone skipped after hers. Eli had thrown it. "We'll destroy them." He said it as if it had been obvious, so easy, and when he saw my face, he frowned. "What? We can't hide them. If we do, this will just keep going on until Seela finds them. He needs all of them to succeed. Destroy them and they won't fall into the wrong hands. It's simple."

"Simple," I muttered. "Why don't we just try to take the Serenity Emerald back instead? And just destroy that one? Or the other stones that aren't currently attached to anyone that we know of." I had only the barest details about the

Horned Quartz or the Abyssal Sapphire, and I was reaching. Of course, Eli knew it.

"This is what we have to do, Harken. It's the only option available to us." He shielded his eyes from the harsh wind, looking out to the water. "There are no guarantees, anyway, whatever we do."

He was right, but I wanted to change the subject. We'd come outside to chill, not do this dance again, and it'd been me steering us back into it.

We'd allowed ourselves the one day. Eli was starting to come down as I had, his stone losing some of its potency as the dark virus took it over. We were running out of time. Neither of us could sleep anymore, but we still tried to bolster each other.

"And what about you, Saskia?" Eli swung in and changed the subject for me, and this time I didn't call him out for the psychic thing. "What will you do, once this is over?"

It was an odd question, coming from him. He was making an effort not to look at me. He didn't believe there was something on the other side for any of us — he'd already said as much.

But there was more skin in the game than just Eli's and mine. There was always so much more at stake than just our own lives. He was a Paramount, after all, even if I'd only seen the dictator-ish side of that until lately. But even the few Owls here in Uig we came across — they respected him. Trusted him as they would a true leader. The kind I'd only played at.

Saskia was considering Eli's question carefully, and I wondered if she had always been such a serious child. "I will find my true daddy, so he isn't alone anymore," she finally replied. "I'll tell him what happened to Albert. And then," her eyes were narrowed, "we will go to Disney World. You guys can come, too."

"Never been," Eli and I said in unison, and he smiled.

"If there is still a Disney World," Saskia corrected. "If the sea hasn't eaten it by then."

The three of us looked across the water, at the shapes in the distance, an insinuation of land. I felt something stir in the water as it lapped at our shoes.

"What . . . is that?" I asked Eli, the most likely of any of us to know what was going on.

He shut his eyes, casting his mind out. The Moonstone guttered with the effort, and his face strained. "The wind has changed." He tipped his face up to the sky, as if he were up there, looking down at us. "And the sea, well . . . it's not my area. But it's changed, too."

I blew out my cheeks. "You sound more and more like a D&D DM as time goes on. Roll initiative already."

Eli rolled his eyes instead. "Whatever that means." And he checked the horizon once again. "I think the Sapphire has been brought up. I can't tell for sure. But it's a presence that hasn't been in the world for a while, and the stones react to their sisters."

I almost envied him; I hadn't felt anything from my stone in so long, I'd almost forgotten it was there.

And now it was time to pry it out, before . . .

"Then we better do this now," I said suddenly, glancing at Saskia, whose eyes were raw, wide wounds. "While we still can."

Barton fastened his flak vest, tightened and secured the running blades. Commander Zhou had gathered them in the hangar, the vehicles waiting just outside on the runway dock.

"Spar Cave is where we're headed." His finger was on the map of the Isle of Skye, but his eyes were up at Barton, who nodded. "Tough to get to, but nothing we can't handle. We have to time this right. The tide will go out but only stay out for a short time. We go in and grab the two, whatever state they're in. And the stones, if they're still intact." His mouth was twisted. "Don't think the Owl Council or the Conclave of Fire will be too pleased that our priority isn't extraction of the stones. But there it is. I'm making the calls out here, and I agree with Eli's plan. If they are successful in removing their stones, then we have to destroy them. Don't get any ideas into your heads, any of you, that we're here to do any less."

The assembled Rabbits, Foxes, and the odd Owl, decked out for whatever was to come, just nodded. The coalition had one purpose, and it was to stop Seela, without direct conflict if they could manage it. Too many had died already. The attacks of things seeping out of the cracks in the world had gone up, even in the past twenty-four hours. The world was watching. This needed to be stopped before there was no one *left* to watch.

Hurry, Barton felt Phae insisting, her voice breaking.

Solomon sat on a steel crate, knowing he'd only be in the way, trusting Barton to be his eyes for this. He'd had only one request: "No matter what happens . . . please bring my son back. If you can."

Hurry!

"We have to go," Barton said. The Commander nodded, and they fell out.

❧

I knew we'd have to cross into the Veil, and that this time it would have to be me leading us there. I'd only done this once before, when Sil had been compromised and needed me to take the wheel when reconnecting Barton to his power-sake. Thinking about it now, despite how high the stakes had been, compared to this it was a bit of whimsy — *if I believe hard enough in myself, it'll all be okay!* This time there was no room for Hallmark card affirmations. I had to be certain.

The dark thing — the dark me — stirred.

"I don't even know if this will work," I muttered, carving the lines in the dirt with the garnet — now obsidian — blade. I'd been reluctant to even take it out, but it was the only Ancient tool we had to work with if I was going to make a convincing, or even potent, summoning circle. A *darkling* summoning circle. The blade stained the ground with my blood, spilled from a cut I hadn't felt at all.

"Here." Eli took the blade from my hand, marked the points of certain sigils I didn't know. "I saw these in Seela's chamber. And one in Cecelia's memory." When I raised my eyebrow at him he shrugged. "Eidetic memory. Made studying almost comical."

"That and the mind reading, which probably allowed you to cheat on a few tests."

"Now, now, Harken, that was, of course, frowned upon," he chided. It almost felt nice, normal.

That was about to end, too.

We'd driven out here in a small car Agathe had lent us. For the entire ride, I pretended we were just a little family going on a day trip. The sun was out, the sky was clear and infuriatingly beautiful. Eli drove, and he did it with a strange, one-handed ease. We could've easily flown here, but he'd insisted we do it this way. I had a feeling he was pretending like I was. Playing a nice game of make believe to make the pill easier to swallow.

"So I figure . . ." He looked at me, and if I could feel it under my breast anymore, maybe my heart was breaking just a bit. "That I'll have to . . . do you, first."

Eli's cheeks, pale from exhaustion and the sickness, coloured just a bit. If I had anything left in me, I'd have laughed at him. With him. But he wanted to get this over with, whatever would happen. "Yes. I figured the same. You're the one who's going to have to separate us from the stones. You can't very well do that if you remove your stone first."

Like a suicide pact. Two bullets, one gun. Someone had to fire first. I was very, very still. "You trust me?" I asked quietly.

Eli stabbed the blade into the ground, leaning forward on it, considering me. He could have been King Arthur — or any other sad, doomed fairy tale knight trying to negotiate with the dragon that was really the princess, the one he'd tried to save now about to open its jaws to thank him for it.

"When we first got here," he admitted, "Phyr herself told me it would be best to kill you, take your Opal, and leave."

Not like I hadn't accused him of this a hundred times. "Why didn't you?"

I wanted him to talk to me the way he always had with snide disbelief. Blunt arrogance. Mistrust. That way I could have walked away and said it was because I wasn't ready. I trusted his opinion, I realized, more than mine; he'd spent a huge chunk of his life preparing to be a Paramount. Flawed or not, it should have been him, not me, taking the lead.

"You're not so bad," was all he said.

I looked past him to Saskia, who sat outside the circle. She was a glowing coal from underneath, and I thought of the man from table five, when this had all started. It was so long ago. I'd been cocky then. Now I was paying for it.

The bone hilt was in my face and I snapped out of it. My hand gripped it and slowly drew it away from Eli, the charred bloody tip pointed directly at his chest, where his own heart was.

The Moonstone awoke, sputtering a shine through the dull, darkening patina over it. His wings slid out from his back, wide and open, the tips brushing against the close space of the sea cave we'd trekked deep into, as far away from people as we could manage. I suddenly realized that after this, I might not see him again.

"You're not such a bad guy either," I said, throat thick. I was grateful that he could figure out what I meant without me having to spell it out. That might have been too much.

The space around his eyes tightened. He didn't try to hide it.

When the blood from my hand dripped down the hilt, I squeezed it harder. Eli's hands twitched at his sides, his eyes turning to molten gold. He opened his arms, and the wind in the cave picked up.

"I call upon the wind that has shaped this stone down from the moon itself," Eli intoned, and the circles and the sigils we had incised together lit with a flash.

"I call upon the fire at the heart of me and the dark that is a part of me still." I squeezed back my tears until they were just hot mist, never there at all.

"To the stones that we two bear, spirit to spirit, dark to dark, we make this appeal."

Now our voices were one, the same, and if Eli was putting the words into my mouth with his mind I didn't care. I was as desperate as him to see this right.

But then his mouth was still. *He* was still — frozen, shivering, eyes wide. I looked down, tried to move my feet, but the three crimson rings were overlapping now, and what came up from them was that dark oozing black, climbing up my legs, taking over what flesh I had left. And I let it. I looked back up at Eli. I grit my teeth, my hands still out in front of me — one holding the blade, and the other tight around the Moonstone. I saw my freckled, imperfect skin was no longer there; the dark was even eating up the chain-shaped scar I'd come to almost admire, and it was crackling like scales. Burning scales. Except not scales at all — sigils, symbols, matching the ones Eli had written beneath us both. Messages from hell.

"Speak my name," I whispered, still looking at him, voice trembling. "So that I may hear your petition."

Eli's eyes constricted one last time, and then they shut, his wings raised, the wind higher still.

"Daughter of Deon," he breathed. "Stonebearer. Child of the Bloodlands. Roan Harken." He choked on the last word: "Friend."

And the world fell away.

"It's here!" Barton called to the others once they'd found the car abandoned at the footpath. Kita drew up beside him.

"How can you be sure?" The only people he'd told about this certainty of where Eli and Roan would be had been the Council, the Conclave, and Solomon. He wanted to protect Phae as much as any of them, but he couldn't bear to tell even Kita. He'd already told too many people, and what if he'd been wrong, all this time?

There hadn't been any fissures or tremors like last time, in the grove of the dead trees. Nothing to tell save for Barton's dire stare down the beach. The rain came down harsh and sudden, drenching the lot of them, while he stared at what could have just been another cleft in the cliffside. They'd have to be quick about it; the tide was coming back in and might drown them all.

Hurry, Phae's voice insisted again across a distance he couldn't determine. "I'm just sure," he said, even though he didn't want to be. Kita took his arm and helped him navigate the huge, sea-strewn boulders, and the other Rabbits fell in before them in a rush.

Across Barton's mind, from the island's east coast, it was Solomon. *I can see what you see*, came the thought. *Be careful.* Barton nodded; he'd let the old man tag along inside his mind as a courtesy. *I can feel Eli there. It's —*

A fizzle of uncertainty shivered under Barton's synapses. Had that been Phae reaching out to him again? Or Solomon? "Wait!" Barton screamed, and he yanked Kita down to the ground, covering her just as the cliff exploded and cut off the first wave that had gone in ahead of them.

Barton's hand trembled overhead, then cut aside the rubble that had nearly crushed them. The dust cleared, and what had been the cliff and the sea cave, still floating in the air, went out to sea at his and Kita's command, the face of the land scythed aside to reveal just one person left standing.

"... Roan?"

But ... it wasn't. And it was. And not standing — she was floating inches from the ground, black flames ribboning off her. When the dust fully settled, she was holding the hand of a struggling little girl — a cinder child — and instead of eyes there was just a cruelly made mask of bone, like a fox's skull. In the heart of the shadow blaze he glimpsed the Opal and something else bright, keen, on her shoulder.

The Moonstone.

Oh gods. Solomon's thoughts crackled to silence since there were no other words to say, yet Barton could feel the heavy despair from the connection he'd allowed him. Beneath Roan's feet was Eli, and he wasn't moving.

"Fall back!" It was the Commander — suddenly Kita and Barton were up, and they were running, because the air was crackling with lightning and impossible, greasy heat.

They rounded the bend, narrowly missing another corona of furious black flame eating up the space they'd only just occupied.

"But it ... it was Roan!" Barton choked as what was left of the contingent stumbled back to their vehicles. "We have to go back!" His promise to Solomon hung heavy, now impossible.

"Don't you understand?" Kita whirled on him, yanking him down into his seat as the engine roared to life, and behind them the beach was just a sonic flare of brimstone and a rising, terrible storm. "She has taken the Moonstone. The Paramount is dead!"

It couldn't be. It just *couldn't*. They'd failed before they even tried. There was a grief there — as strong as the supernova that blasted across the sea, taking Roan and the stones with it. Solomon's grief. Phae's. Barton was sick with it.

"She is Seela's now," breathed Kita. "An enemy of Ancient."

The beach shrank behind them, and so did Barton's wretched, faltering hope.

Three stones gone of five. The chasm widened.

Part V

Calamity

A Shattered Sea

Aunty's body shifted, changing into Ryk's, her great, scaled face and crown of fish bones tipped towards the sea's surface.

Maujaq, half of his white robes now black with Seela's plague, was still beside her. "Will we rise, Empress?"

Ryk rested her hand, manacled in furs of her own, on the Inua's head. He would soon turn into one of Seela's spawn. Ryk perceived deeper trenches stretching wide across her vast ocean, and she longed for her sister Heen to close them up again. But her sister's soulstone was lost, and Ryk was glad that Heen herself could not hear the earth cry out. Deon's light in the world had, too, gone dark, and so had Phyr's. She shut her eyes. Fia would stand by and watch them blink out like stars. The Deer child may not have had a chance, after all.

Ryk was alone. Her fury was great, the core of it a stinging grain of grief.

But there was no use for grief in war.

Maujaq stiffened, then relaxed, and shut his eyes at last.

"*We* will rise," Ryk turned to Natti, who emerged to take Maujaq's place, his white furs clasping her body like a prayer. "You will lead the charge now. As you were meant to."

Natti dipped her head. "We're going to fight?"

"Yes," said Ryk, who was Aunty and who wasn't. "A fight to the last. A fight with our friend."

⁂

Seela stood at the cliff, waiting, a statue of bone and flame and darkness. He could feel her approaching, could feel the stones she bore. Yet he could no longer feel the burden of her spirit, which had held her back so long and had also brought her to him.

She crested the horizon, moving in a torrent of ash and wind, travelling quickly, *learning* even quicker than Killian had when the darkness took hold of him, before there was something other than Seela.

She made landfall but didn't stop. The tendrils of her body and its mass dragged itself like a lightning strike up the cliff, and Seela scuttled backward to allow her space to re-form. To rise.

The children fell in behind him, burning, longing, for their sister.

Saskia burst from the black mass into the grass, tumbling onto her wretched knees. Dark tears streamed down her crackling face. Seela clicked his tongue. "I could beat you for running away," he snarled, "yet one shouldn't harm the dog that has returned. And it's a better punishment, I think, to see that I was right, and to kill that hope that has kept you alive all this time."

Saskia looked up at him through her tears, and Seela dragged her to her feet, throwing her to the other children. Roan's form materialized before him, standing tall. There, on her shoulder, he saw it for himself through the mask of bone: the Tradewind Moonstone.

Seela dipped his head in deference. "You've returned to us, Daughter."

Roan's face, obscured by the helm that was the fox's skull, was blank; the mouth showed no joy, but she would learn that quickly, too. The Opal at her breast was alive once again, a shining beacon of painful dark light.

Her nine tails were spears. "Father," she said. And the word made him soar.

"We must go back out to sea, child. Though you have felt it, too." She nodded. "The Sapphire is at hand. And with us both, it will be easily taken."

"Easily," she echoed, drawing up beside him, facing the howling water. "And the Quartz?"

Seela's smile was as sharp as the rest of him. "It will come to us."

She took his hand. This must be what pride was. Then the black consumed them in one howling mass, and they split from the cliff, careening headlong for the sea.

"*Your despair,*" Fia sneered, "*makes you weak.*"

Phae pressed her hands into the rings, which were now quiet here on the summit of Fia's great realm. She pressed and whispered and must have said inside herself too many times, *No, no, no.*

"*Your Fox friend made her choice. She let the darkness in, and it was stronger than her. Your trust was for nothing. Now what will you and your allies do? How will they stand?*"

Phae sat up stiffly. How could Roan have done it? There was so much Phae hadn't been able to see — the fire, the black. Just Eli's and Roan's voices, the red rings, then nothing. Roan had taken the Moonstone. If there was anything left of Roan. What Phae had seen there couldn't be the girl she grew up with. The girl she trusted.

There was no wind up here, just a sorrowful wind passing through the jungle below. What would happen to her if she flung herself off? Would the laws of physics also be wrong? How can you die when you're already in an underworld?

"Your sister is going to fight," Phae turned, and Fia's face was the impassive antelope, nostrils flaring. "Ryk."

Fia nodded, now with the woman's twisted, gleeful face. "*Oh yes. Another great battle on the calamitous sea. Yet another mistake that my sisters keep making — trust the humans with their very soulstones. Let them handle their own wretched destinies and leave us out of it. The Sapphire is as good as gone. And then what?*"

Phae felt herself sharpening. "You tell me."

Fia's antlers flashed, and so did Phae's, a high and heavy crown weighing her down, the tines growing too fast, too long, encasing her in a cage of bone and hair. She was pinned to the summit.

"*In all of this,*" Fia's male face said with a sigh, "*did you not stop to ask why the Families are divided? Because they must be. They are stewards for different causes. There is a balance.*

The stones represent that balance. That requirement of separation. You all think unity is what will save you. But it won't. Unity will cave the world in and devour whatever is left."

Only Phae's finger was outside of the cage in which Fia had crushed her. Fia had to be wrong. There had to be something good from unity. *We are stronger as one*. If only she could master herself, her own crushing doubt . . .

"*When the stones come together, their unity creates a vibrance. A power unparalleled. But it needs to be directed — pointing it through a prism will make a frequency that can shatter the targes from beyond the Bloodlands. Open the way for the darklings to rise.*"

Phae's neck quivered. She hadn't yet felt pain, not really, but the image Fia painted was bleak, as if it were carved on the inside of her skull, inevitable. And that truly hurt.

Prism. She held onto the word, the feel of it in her mouth. "But there's another prism. A prism of light. The . . . Quartz."

Her finger found purchase in the ground. She felt a sensation, a crackling blue spark that came from Fia themself, a bald curiosity at the challenge.

Her head became lighter, inch by inch, as the flickering tines wound back down, until they were only hair, and Phae was breathless in the dirt.

"The Quartz can open a different door," Phae said, tilting her eyes up to face Fia, their faces ticking around in turn, as if they didn't want her to see their expressions, to guess anything else. "And if it can awaken Ancient, then that is the only hope we have."

Their neck clicked to a stop between faces. Fia's antlers glowed once, then the leaves in the tines shifted and were still.

"*Ancient will not rise.*" There was no doubt, just misery, in this admission.

"We need to try," Phae pressed. "My despair makes me human. What does yours make you?"

Fia brought their hands around their body, pressing tight. As if it wanted to disappear.

"*We will not give you the Quartz,*" they said, and Phae was alone on the mountain.

The rings flashed beneath her. Her antlers rose. *Please*, she begged. *Let me see. Let the whole realm see what happens next.*

A world of waves and water. A bleak iron sky. A cataract of heaven cleaving open as the storm whipped up, and the force tore the air currents out of the stratosphere.

A tsunami. A hurricane. A monsoon. In the heart of the southern Atlantic, where no promise of landfall could be seen, Seela and Roan emerged from the dark heart that their intentions had stirred.

Rising from the waves was the army of Ryk, Empress of the Sea, and in her battle crown she bore the Abyssal Sapphire.

Once more into the breach. But only one side would come out again.

The thing that had been Roan Harken felt something creep across its face, beneath its death mask. A smile.

She and her father were fluid fire. But that fire had been augmented by its sister elements. Her father, Seela, had not only the command of fire but the earth. The Emerald saw to that. And while the sea may be vast and formidable, the earth was beneath the sea, buried in the dark. And it would shift for them.

Seela worked on the tectonic plates. Trenches opened like gashes. The sea raged. Deep in the water, where the Seals banded together, preparing to fight back, the water warriors were not prepared for the earth beneath the waves to break. They fell back behind Ryk and her new Inua. These Seals had gathered from every ocean, throwing themselves into this last salvo. Tribes from the North, from the South Pacific, from the hidden places on coasts with weapons of rock and souls that hadn't known the cities or industrial world that had brought them all here in the first place. The cities that would flood and burn, soon enough. And the thing that had been Roan Harken grew stronger just thinking about it.

But she had the wind, too. The Moonstone. Her wide wings gaped. There were no feathers, no galaxies of Phyr set in them; they were bone wings, but they ripped air from lungs, currents from skies, stirred up spirits that could not beat back against her. The earth heaved below. The sky fell above. And in between the sea, full of brave and doomed warriors shattering and dying. The cinder kids, alive and dead all the same, poured into the water, ready to fight until they were ash and nothingness. The Seals cried out, full of battle rage. They, too, were ready to die for their cause.

Above the roiling water, Seela and Roan physically intertwined, two strands of the same DNA. The sky cracked wide with black lightning. The sea pulled back like the moon had dropped out of the sky, waves now a curtain. And in the middle of it was Ryk, her huge jaws wide, her massive harpoon twice her size and covered in the black blood of the cinder kid army that had ripped their forces apart. She was lacquered with gore, fevered with the fight. She was flanked by her last fighter, her Inua in polar bear furs. The Sapphire in her crown gleamed with a threat.

Seela and Roan split apart, two darts of smoke and ash and burning, always burning, rocketing towards the Seal Paramount. Roan held back, watched as Seela and Ryk clashed in the raging seas, the water that had split apart now crashing down on them. Roan fell before the last Inua, and there was a twinge of horror, and recognition, on the girl's face.

"Roan?"

Roan pulled the bone mask back as her body and form changed, spine-wings and spear-tail buoying her up. She tilted her head at the squat girl in the armour of fur — armour that reeked of death from its last inhabitant. Roan smiled.

"Natti." The word was foreign in her stretching mouth. It had meant something to other-Roan, weak Roan. Friend and ally. Now it meant nothing.

"What have you . . ." Roan watched the girl's eyes, cutting to the Moonstone she wore proudly. She relished that grimace — a comedic smear of fury. "You killed Eli."

A twinge. *Eli.* Another wretched foreign word on her tongue. Roan spat it out. She didn't want to consider it. Not just what it meant, but what sat underneath it. A question she couldn't answer. Something she was forgetting.

"None of that matters," Roan said, letting it come out in the voice this Natti Seal knew, all the better to hurt her with. "Nothing matters but the end."

Roan's bone blade, black and furious, was hungry in her hand. Natti raised her fists, and they collided.

“This is where it’s happening.” Commander Zhou winced for his broken arm as he hit a keystroke that enlarged a map. They retreated by air to a compound in Newfoundland, and Barton still felt a twinge from being back in Canada, after everything. *I’m home, and since leaving it’s all gone to hell.*

Zhou moved the cursor to the Atlantic. “We can’t get a visual. No equipment could break through the atmospheric disturbance. They’re on their own.”

The Council of the Owls and the last of the Conclave of Fire had joined them through a shuddering video feed. They could have been ghosts. The Owls’ Paramount and their stone were lost. The Fire Conclave’s Paramount had turned against Ancient. They were running out of things to say.

“So we do nothing,” Barton said.

Zhou exhaled. “There is something we can do.” Another map came up, populated by red dots. Too many red dots, so many more than the last time they’d checked.

Winnipeg was one of them.

“The breadth of these creature-risings has expanded. Again. It’s at the point now where there’s one almost every three hours, at random. There are Denizens on the ground, of course, trying to fight back. They’re the ones who need us now.”

“— Mundane interference,” Alena said, voice cutting in and out of the feed. “Now that the Moonstone’s influence has been lost, our ability to hide Denizens has been compromised. Governments have mobilized their own militaries. Denizens are rounded up now as the culprits for these attacks.”

Barton stood for the first time in several hours. He hadn't had the heart to do so, not after seeing Eli back there on Skye, and Roan above him, the last person he'd ever thought to have given up, given in. There didn't seem to be anything left to stand for. But from across the void he'd felt Phae. She was still hanging on. He could, too.

"Then that makes all Denizens fugitives," he said, "but we're the only ones who can beat Seela's children back. So we'll do what we have to do."

The Conclave and the Council exchanged glances. All the Denizens on land could do was defend now, try to plug as many holes as possible while the ship went down, drowning them all in blood. And they would have to defy the human laws they'd tried so hard to live with. The world had already changed. There would be no going back.

"Very well," said the Jacob Reinhardt. "Word will be sent out. The Fox Family will fight to the end, since it's come to that."

Alena nodded, too. "The Owls, too. To the end."

Zhou straightened. Nodded. The feed went dead, and the ground shook.

He turned to Barton. Nothing left to say. No sense in hoping. One foot in front of the other.

Barton's arms stiffened, cording with the roots of Heen — the only sign that the gods, however weakened, were still with them.

⁂

The sea bloated with the bodies of its defenders. The fight

was bloody and terrible. And over far too soon for the thing that had been Roan Harken.

Seela had beaten Ryk and her last contingent to land — a barren one of cliffs and rocks and the touchstone of history. *Newfoundland?* What use did this creature have for the names of countries given by the animals that had no right to it? Territory claim had shifted. The age for land and sanctuary and home had come to a bitter end.

She dragged Natti onto the rocks, slammed her forward. Broken and bruised but still alive. The thing that had been Roan wanted that. Killing was a simple thing — but this girl was special. There would be those who needed to bear witness.

Roan's head snapped up to a shuddering bellow, Ryk fighting to the final breath. Natti hadn't moved, and Roan yanked her back up, held her aloft so Natti could get a clearer view through the screen of blood in her eyes.

Seela stood over Ryk, his body crushing. Then Ryk was still, just an old, spent woman, spirit fled. Natti screamed. Roan's wings flexed, and in a teleported flicker they were now behind Seela. His great body was bent, and his blood hissed into the ground, onto the stonebearer's body, as he tried to pry the Sapphire loose. His grip was slippery. He couldn't hang on. Roan watched him struggle a while longer, his face contorted.

Then he jerked and saw her — his mouth twisted in joy. Relief. Then a twinge of fear.

"Daughter," he said. "We have done it."

Roan dropped Natti in a heap at her feet, moving to her father's side, dropping a heavy black-blazing hand on his shoulders, which heaved from the effort. He had been weakened. Too weak to take the Sapphire, just as he'd been too weak to take the Moonstone the first time.

"Yes," she said. "At last."

He tried to reach for the Sapphire but Roan held him back. She had become stronger than him. His smile faltered.

"If you'll lend me your strength," he said, trying to sound convincing, "we can summon them. Our family. Together."

The ground shivered. Seela looked down at the bald rock beneath them, shaking apart for the three red rings, and the black that seeped from Roan and took hold of him, climbing.

"What —"

Roan's fingers bit into Seela, and she felt him knowing, felt his terror. "You are tired, Father," she said, the brutality of her voice not attempting to offer comfort. "Your work is complete. It was never meant to be you. Surely you felt it before this." She smiled again, and this time it felt right. "The child is always meant to surpass the parent."

Urka split the ground behind Roan, pulling itself up, smashing its axe-hands together to make sparks. Its six eyes gleamed.

Seela peeled away from the human vessel it had inhabited, until Roan looked into the spent and stricken face of Killian for the last time.

"No!" he moaned, free too late of his curse as Roan took it from him. "Roan! Don't do this! Stop!"

"Don't worry," she said. "You still have a purpose. You always did."

Natti managed to raise herself up on one weakened arm. She lifted a hand, tried to call the sea to her, to strike one last time as the monster that had taken her friend and her Family from her had its back turned. But nothing came. Her hand dropped. All she could do was watch as the black reared back, a trap of razor teeth, and Roan devoured what was left of the man that had been Seela, bones, stones, and all.

The air was still. Roan turned fully to face Natti.

The Emerald was now on her right shoulder, the Moonstone on her left. The Opal at her heart, and the Sapphire in her skull.

The blades of her wings flexed. Natti's head dropped, and the last hope she'd been carrying went as dark as her vision.

The HORNED QUARTZ

The beach had been silent when Agathe climbed down it. Even the wind had left, the wind that had sung this very island into being. *You can hear her sing the best from up here*, her cousin had said. Demelza, Eli's mother. That bright and beautiful gem of a woman.

Carefully, now. Agathe climbed over the rocks, one by one, counting them. Demelza had twisted her ankle down here once, but even then she had borne the pain. *Do you think that the rocks were hurt, too?* she had asked. She was not a child then — sixteen, maybe. Still in her right mind. But what a question to ask.

That strange, encompassing empathy had only made her vulnerable.

Agathe picked carefully around the bend. The tide had come in; though the wind had gone, the moon still had authority. It hung over the beach, a slender crescent, keeping vigil. Phyr's symbol. Her seat of power. Her soulstone may have been gone, but her eye was still turned to them.

Its light seemed to be directed between the cleft megaliths to a figure in the rocks. Caught there like flotsam or rubbish, abandoned by the sea. Kept watch over by the moon.

He's down here, Agathe called out with her mind, sending up a psychic flare. The others weren't far. They'd be here just as she reached him.

A man came to the island, Demelza had said. *He's one of* them, *a magistrate. A keeper of the knowledge. He's looking for the stone, the one I dreamed about.* Agathe was not an Owl particularly blessed with strong power — but she could read a bad wind when it came in. She warned sailors and boatsmen off the water when she knew something ill was on the air. She warned Demelza of the same when Solomon Rathgar made landfall and made her feel more than just empathy for the rocks.

Agathe stood over Eli's body, her hand over her mouth. She sucked in a breath, shut her eyes, but that was all she allowed herself to feel. His dark hair around his sharp cheekbones that had been Demelza's. She bent down and moved his mottled sweater aside, which had been charred in the centre, leaving only an empty jagged scar behind where the Moonstone had been.

She touched his chest. It rose, weakly. But she knew it was just a body. The true part of Eli, the part that made him himself, was elsewhere.

When the others arrived, they bore his body up and took it back to land. Agathe knew she hadn't imagined the night bird screech in the distance.

Phae ran through the Glen, to every aching corner of it. The light was going dull. The trees were coming down. The fabric keeping it together was unravelling. And Fia still had not shown any of their faces.

"Fia!" Phae screamed, circling the mountain, the valley, the jungle. No snakes, no bird calls, no mist. Even the water at the silver beach had peeled back and away. The horizon was a bleak black smear, bleaching white, crumbling inward, and the island fell away into it, devoured.

There was no way home. No one to send her back.

Barton! Her heart was in pieces. *Are you there? Please!*

A prayer. Phae had known, after what she'd seen, to pray. Should have prayed sooner. Only silence replied.

Natti? But that, too, was desperation talking. Something worse was wrong. This realm was breaking apart. Maybe its mooring to the universe was battered. Maybe the universe *itself* was shifting. There were no answers, only a deep and terrible knowing: everything had fallen. Everything *would* fall, just as every turn had predicted. But she hadn't wanted to listen. There had always been another way.

Phae finally collapsed in the clearing. The trees shrank back from her, and she felt their terror. She slammed her fists into the ground, insensible, and her head, too, until the ground beneath her cracked with each impact, her antlers heavy and gorging the delicate, dying flesh of this other-world she was trapped in. Would die in. And she thought of the precious world she'd been born to, the people that she loved, and she was raw with the impending loss of them.

Roan. Eli. Natti. Barton. Her parents. Winnipeg. Any future. The world.

Her antlers were immense. Her protective shield was a

battering ram. She smashed straight through the crust of the island, as if it were just a thin ceramic layer and fell through to the heart of the Glen.

⁂

They laid Eli's body in the cleft of the caer — the castle of rock at the Fairy Glen, where the wind might reach him, however little of it was left.

The Owls of Skye turned their faces to the setting sun. To the place the wind once came from. *Phyr*, they prayed, *Mother of Skies*. *Please*. There wasn't much else to the prayer. How could there be? But these Owls knew that they would keep vigil over this body of their Paramount. The last Paramount of the wind. Whatever happened to it.

Agathe only watched the skies as they dimmed. A night of lasts. She shut her eyes and knew it wasn't enough to pray just to Phyr any longer. The other Owls — men and women and youths — knew this, too, and linked minds, linked petitions. They called out to every realm of Ancient, and whispered those names like a spell.

Deon in the Den.
Ryk in the Abyss.
Heen in the Warren.
Fia in the Glen.

They all thought of Ancient. They all wished the impossible. They couldn't fathom the breadth of that fell place, but they whispered it just the same. *Ancient in the Brilliant Dark*, they begged. *Please do not let the world go dim.*

Agathe turned. Eli's body was gone. There was nothing left to do but to pray. And wait.

❧

Phae opened her eyes to a splintered realm. Trees still held fast to the earth that once kept them, huge chunks of rock, literally the last of what had been Fia's great mountain. Down here, in the depths, they floated like tiny islands unto themselves, the last of the Glen. And the thing at the centre of it all was great Fia themselves — body all cords and tendons, antlers hanging over them like branches, the eyes of all three heads shut. It hummed.

Phae got up to her knees. She didn't have any fight left in her. Beneath them hung the world in Fia's three shining rings.

"So that's it then?" Phae said. Her voice was raw. "You're gonna just stay here and watch?"

The antelope's mouth quirked. "*Our eyes are shut. We will not watch.*"

But Phae wasn't beneath that. She stared into those rings. She saw a city go dark with hope trees. She saw the sea go absolutely still. She saw Seela fall but Roan rise. She saw the Denizen Coalition, the last sign of union, preparing themselves. Somewhere in there was Barton, but she hadn't the heart to try to find him.

They had come to the end.

"Have you ever been in the world?" Phae asked, voice echoing in the emptiness.

Fia's six eyes moved beneath the lids as if they were dreaming, but they did not open.

"Have you ever experienced life? Not just transiently,

through your Denizens. Not through that thin cable of power that connects you to them all and to Ancient and back again. You're eternal. You haven't ever left this place. Maybe you were in the world once, but you never lived. You'd never know what that means, because you can never end, can you? You can't see beyond your immortality. And that's why you don't care."

The eyes slid open slowly, dangerously. The rock that Phae perched on orbited close to those huge eyes, each one as big as a house.

"*How sad*," said the woman. "*She still thinks she can save it.*"

"Even if I can't," Phae replied, "I'd rather be down there, dying alongside my friends, than trapped here with you forever, doing nothing."

The antelope's eyes narrowed. "*And what would you do?*"

Phae closed her eyes. She was back in the Assiniboine Forest. The air was muggy, and the mosquitoes were out, and her DSLR battery was low, but she didn't care. She watched the deer scatter across the open field. Felt the true wind bristle through the trees. She knew she would go home and walk on eggshells to her room to avoid another argument with her parents. But she would appreciate that tomorrow the sun would rise, and there might be another chance to grasp that fleeting time left.

"Live," she said, "however much longer that is. And count myself thankful I had the chance to."

Then something came up from the rings, from that fading reflection of the world. A hymn. Something terrible. But it was the same melody Fia had been carrying in the back of their throat. And the sound reached even up here — out here — and Fia couldn't look away now.

They leaned forward, creaking and breaking, this god twined hard around the core of its world, of itself. Their ribcage cracked and swung open. Their beating heart was amber, harled, with too many facets to count. It was a prism. It was the Quartz.

"*This is our heart*," the three faces said, clicking and switching with each word. "*This is the heart of everything*."

"*No!*" screamed the woman, mouth a ruin. "*Don't take it! There are variables we cannot see. There is a balance. The inevitabilities run aground on each other as far as we can look. There are no guarantees*."

"*There never are*," said the man, who no longer seemed pale with misery. His blue eyes flashed.

Hands of corded stone reached up, plucked the Quartz free like it was a fruit. It was too big. Too unwieldy. Something felt wrong. Then Phae remembered — there was always a test.

"No," Phae said. "Don't give it to me unless you're certain. You can just send me back, and you can keep it here."

Fia faltered. "*You refuse it when we give it willingly?*"

Too many questions. "Why do you give it to me now when you've refused all this time?"

The three faces took one last revolution, eyes askance, as if each set of eyes were trying to meet the glance of the other two.

The faces softened when they looked down at Phae.

"*Even if there is only one of you there on that wide and fragile world who would think of it as precious, then we would save it just for you, dear daughter*."

The hands compressed the Quartz until it was a mist of fine stardust. The hands parted, and there was nothing there but the dust filling Phae's lungs as they took in precious, mortal air.

"*It's time you left this place,*" said the sad, doomed god. And Phae couldn't reply, for her throat was hard as crystal, and the rest of her body was changing, hardening, into a shell. A tool. An instrument.

"*Tell our sisters we miss them,*" Fia called, as Phae fell to the fragile world she'd been born on, with a power she had chosen, to live or die as she pleased.

❧

The black owl stretched its wings, golden eyes roving. The size of a large house cat, this owl belonged in the woods with its nesting fellows, not flying through the abandoned ruin of Halifax-Dartmouth. It wove between the quivering branches of fresh victims, past the leafless charred boles, and fluttered to the top of the still-standing bridge connecting the cities to get a better view.

The darkness had been busy.

The owl turned its small face to the spare, faltering wind. The wind whispered the path that the darkness had gone in — back to its stronghold on a hidden coast of cliffs and ash not too far away now. The owl knew the darkness would rest awhile there, confident in the next step, and the owl would relish breaking that confidence.

The owl's head swivelled as a moth fluttered past. At its side was a hulking woman, great triangular wings wide, hundreds of needle-pointed hands folded as it surveyed the trampled city below the bridge.

"This has been a busy day," the Moth Queen said with a sigh. She had seen it all before.

The owl, being an owl, said nothing.

The moths fluttered around its head, and it snapped its beak, impatient, snatching one and swallowing it whole.

If the Moth Queen could laugh, she would have. "You're right. Not just yet. You're still waiting for her to walk the path you put her on. But she is buried deep. What if she doesn't rise?"

The owl levelled the mother of death with a hard golden stare that brooked no doubt.

Her shivering wings flexed, and she opened her hands, and she was gone.

Black Bastion

Natti sprawled at the bottom of the dark rock pit. She heard rushing water beyond the walls. It made the pain harder to bear.

There must have been other pits close by. She heard moans, voices crying out. Other Seals, maybe. Every tissue in her body was on the way to giving up. There was no saving her, and there'd be no saving the others.

The horrors were too many to count. She knew that however much longer she had left, there wasn't much point in cataloguing them.

Everyone was gone. Was there some solace that her mother was, maybe, still safe on land? For however much longer that was. She'd lost sight of Aivik. The Seals were smashed to pieces. She was just happy he hadn't been there to see Aunty. See Roan. See it all, as it played back, endlessly, on the wet walls of the pit.

"The Horned Quartz," said the thing that had been Roan, her friend, with a voice like a jagged piece of metal dragging across rock. Natti and the other survivors had been dragged before this abomination, kept alive for what knowledge they had left. This was before the pit.

"What of it?" Natti had spat.

The thing that had been Roan was massive, all joints and sharp points and knife blades and sludge. No eyes, just that terrible mask. Worse to look at even than Zabor. "I have seen into the memory of the Sapphire. It sent one to the Glen to negotiate for the Quartz. But she's fallen out of sight."

"Phae," Natti said. "Your best fucking friend, Roan. If there's any of you left in there."

The mouth was a gash, working methodically, like it was considering the answer. "No," said the mouth. "Nothing left."

Natti squeezed her eyes shut, the blood roaring in her ears as dizziness ricocheted. "I don't know," she said. And there was no lie. "She could be dead, for all I know." When Natti opened her eyes again, the thing that had been Roan didn't move. "Are you gonna kill us now, or what?"

The mouth widened into a terrible mimic of a grin. "I think I will put you away." Little pinpricks of light filled the dark space — the burning eyes of those sick and twisted kids. "I want you to feel like you can still survive this. If the Bloodlands has taught me anything, it's that nothing tortures more than hope."

Some of the Seals had tried to kill themselves, then and there. Natti hadn't fought when they put her down in the pit. She just lay still and waited for the pain to stop for good.

Something grated — like a door opening. Shutting.

"Natti!"

A hiss from above her. Only her eyes moved. It could have been a trick, the face pressing into the crack of light from above. Aivik.

The grate smashed open, but though it was only a few feet away, it could've been miles. Natti wouldn't climb up there — couldn't. She shut her eyes.

"And I thought I was lazy!" She cracked a lid. Aivik's face was a mire of muddy bruises, and he smiled, though he was missing a few teeth.

"Go away," Natti croaked. Her bones relaxed.

Aivik's head whipped back, as if he was checking the space behind him. "Natti, please." Any trace of humour, however hard-won, was gone. "We have to get out of here. Now."

"Why?" Natti's voice broke, and she let herself cry, after all the tedious work spent on keeping it in. "Where will we go? There's nothing left. Nothing."

"That's not true."

Her head rolled. Climbing down from the grate was a cinder kid, a little girl, burning from the inside with a terrible fierceness. Natti was a dead weight as the little girl made her sit up with an impossible strength in her thin, twiggy arms.

"You're one of them," Natti said, the little girl wavering in her bleary vision.

"I'm still me," said the little girl. "And I'm going to do what I should've done at the beginning."

Suddenly Aivik had slid down into the pit, and though limping with all his massive girth, he picked his little sister up as if she weighed nothing, got her to her feet, and let her lean on him for every step.

"And what's that?" Natti had given up much but not her bald curiosity. Aunty would be pleased.

"Be brave." And the little girl scuttled up the rock in front of them, holding the grate open, leading them and the other battered Seals they'd brought with them out of the dark.

❧

The fortress was an anthill of narrow passages, big halls, dead ends. Saskia navigated them with certainty.

"Why are you helping us?" Natti asked as the tight group of them limped along, constantly checking behind them any time they heard a rustling or saw a flicker in the shadows.

Saskia's fists shook at her sides as she paced ahead. Ever since that night in the woods, she could feel the burns of the ropes as she dragged Albert towards the beginning of the end. "Because it's what Roan wanted. She told me to do it, before she went away."

Saskia heard Natti scoff. "You think the real Roan is going to come back and save us all? There's nothing left to save." But Saskia had promised: *Get out as many as you can while we're gone, Saskia. I know you can do it.*

Roan had believed in her. Saskia had to return the favour.

Saskia stopped so quickly that Aivik nearly tripped over her, and she turned and looked Natti in the eye. "You're wrong."

The ground shook when they came to an impasse of corridors. At the end of one was light. The main knot of the fleeing Seals took off for it, but before Natti, Aivik, and Saskia could follow, the ground heaved, and Urka smashed through it.

"This way!" Saskia screamed, and she ran in the other direction. Helpless, Aivik and Natti followed, leaping over crumbling stone and dodging as it fell in their path.

"Little girl," Urka bellowed from behind them, gaining ground, "your time has come."

The three of them burst out of the corridor into a huge antechamber made of glass that faced the sea. When Saskia checked back the way they'd come, Urka was gone — there was nothing left of the huge rock monster save a deep crater.

"You have to get out of here!" she said. "Go down to the water! The others will be down at the rocks — there are others like you, ones with powers. They need you —"

The floor shattered with a thunderclap and Urka reared in front of them like a shark, its hands serrated blades coming up before the dark furnace gaped in the belly beneath those six terrible eyes. The way was blocked.

Aivik helped Natti stay standing, sweat pouring from his battered face. "Any other ideas, small fry?"

Saskia stepped in front of them. "Remember what I said," she repeated, jaw set. "People need you to keep fighting."

Natti jerked. "What —"

But the chamber was filled with Urka's sick, jagged cackle. "My masters are rising. There is no place left for you to run. I have tilled the soil for them. I have helped make it ready."

Saskia felt herself getting hotter. Glowing. She shook all over. "And you won't get to see it," she said. "Not ever."

Then she felt her bones separating. Her thin paper skin erupted in black and hardened as she grew, but her legs pumped, and she threw herself into Urka's great furnace, growing faster, and as her branches pierced the monster's body like a spear, she felt its rage, splitting it in half, until all that was left was the horrible tree where Saskia had once been. Urka's last guttering wail shattered the glass and opened the way to the sea, to Natti and Aivik diving headlong into the tide.

❧

The sound carried across the water, to the place where the thing that had been Roan Harken was waiting. She perceived the dark furnace going out. *Urka has fallen.* Her mouth twisted. His purpose was fulfilled. Hers had just begun.

But the sound carried something else with it. A word, in a little girl's voice, almost snatched away on the wind but carried here all the same. The little girl's call echoed into the Calamity Stones, into places that even the thing that had been Roan Harken couldn't stop it from reaching. And once the sound died, the creature flicked away the thoughts like an irritating insect and turned to the task at hand.

❧

Deep in the dark, buried alive in a tightly packed, terrible grave of my own making, I heard someone.

Wake up! Saskia cried.

I opened my eyes. Took a breath. And screamed.

The dark thing inside me had put me here. Put me away like a toy won at a grimy mall bowling alley that you hold onto for years but you're not sure why. Sentimentality? Shame? Then it gets buried at the bottom of your closet until one day it's rediscovered and, likely, thrown in the trash.

I pushed and slapped against the walls, inches from my

face, pressing on my body — my *spirit's* body. Then I stilled, realizing something else.

I was still here. I was *alive*. Whatever that meant.

I shut my eyes, steadied my breathing. *Think*. Where could I possibly be? This was metaphysical — it's not like I was hiding in the corner of my own mind. I had been locked tight *in* somewhere. Something?

I felt a flash of warmth beneath me, like a beating heart. Like maybe, possibly, a flame.

Was I inside the Dragon Opal?

Suddenly the bottom cracked beneath me, and I went down. Not far — more like I'd stumbled onto faulty ground, into an abandoned mine shaft. The walls were still close. I'd had nightmares like this before, of getting stuck in tight spaces, no way to move or turn around. Nothing to do but to screw my eyes shut and force myself to wake up. But there'd be no waking up — not yet, anyway. That's when I remembered that the dark thing hadn't put me down here; *I had*.

Which meant tucked somewhere else in my memory was an idea. Maybe not my idea. Maybe an idea that had been put there by someone else. A distant name I couldn't remember. The name of a friend.

I really wanted to wake up, but there wasn't any time for that. So I grit my teeth — even though here I really didn't have any — and I hunkered down, pulling myself through the muck, one twist of my shoulders at a time, not knowing what was ahead on the other side.

In the Bloodlands, the Darkling Hold split.

"*We have been here so long*," Kirkald said, pressing his four hands to the ash-blood rock of his prison. "*I am almost reluctant to leave it.*"

Zabor tipped her scaly head up, narrow pupils the width of threads. Grey light crept in through the breach as it widened. "*I have tasted free air*," she snapped. "*I would have it all one last time*."

Balaghast said nothing. They sat still and listened, as they always had. The prison wasn't the only thing splitting. The targe that bound them here, that small piece of green and gold, had cracked. And Balaghast thought of their mother, Fia, as they did every day, and they shut their eyes.

❧

The narrow passageway widened after a while. Hours? Weeks? And by now I was at a crawl, the space above me mercifully higher. I could almost stand. Almost — but any hard-won victory down here was a small one.

I was following the voices.

They were voices I definitely recognized. A long time ago, in a lifetime far away, I'd hated every single one of them. They'd hurt me. They'd made me feel insignificant, like I was less important than what they were trying to tell me. I could pick out each one because the scars they'd left were still raw. The voices of the Opal. The voices that Seela had shut out, as if it had done me a courtesy.

Now they weren't the panicked wall of blazing hysteria that had cut me down. I caught snatches, here and there

— different languages, yes, but the tone was the same. *Help us*, they said, wary of me the closer I got to them. *Help us, Deon.*

The voices were praying. I joined them.

By the time I was able to stand, there was a light, too. Many lights. Foxfire. Fireflies. Little globs of incandescence floating close to me, so small, but I could pick out the shapes they showed, and the farther I went, the clearer they became. It was a gallery of statues, of the fox warriors — the Paramounts — that had come before. In that weak light I saw the mouths of the stonework move in those hushed prayers: I walked on.

I came to the end of the hall, that led to another, to the last statue there. She blocked the way forward. She was tall, and her hair went down to her waist. She was not wearing the armour. She did not have the blade. She was not a statue at all.

"Hello, Roan," Cecelia said.

I stood there only for a minute, looking at her. Then I tried to dart around her. "I can't," I muttered, "have to keep going."

She caught me by the arms, bending down, wavering. Then she gathered me close to her, and I felt her shaking. She was crying.

"No," I struggled. "I have to *keep going*." The urgency was manic. Where I was going still wasn't apparent or even possible. I just knew I couldn't stop.

She pulled away from me. She had blood on her face, and she wiped her eyes. "Can I walk with you, then?"

I jerked out of her grasp. "Fine. But we have to hurry."

We walked on in silence. The statues went on, but there were more lights here, and I saw that the statues weren't as freshly hewn as the others. They seemed older, eroded by time. We were going backward.

"I know I hurt you," Cecelia started, "and that I hurt Ravenna . . ."

"That's enough," I cut her off. "I've seen it all. I know it all. I don't need to hear it again."

She was different from the last time I'd seen her in that bizarro dream. This wasn't some portent of doom. I felt, deep in whatever was at the core of me right here and now, that this was the real, last remaining scrap of Cecelia, my grandmother.

"Then you see now. All the sins —"

"Yeah, yeah," I sighed. "Every single one of them."

There were wider and wider gaps between the statues. "Is there going to be one down here for me?" I realized maybe I was rushing for nothing, and I was heading for my own rocky platform. I'd climb up and turn to stone, adding my voice to the fading cacophony inside the Opal, repeating my past regrets for no one to hear.

"No," Cecelia said. "We're going to see Deon."

Something prickled behind my nose. A suggestion of a memory. Déjà vu. *You have to hide inside the stone,* a man had told me. *Deep deep down, where even the demon can't feel you. And you'll have to wait.* That voice, too, I recognized, but it wasn't a voice from the Opal. It had been outside it once. Just a voice on the wind.

"And what is Deon going to do to help us?"

Cecelia exhaled. "It's not Deon whose help we need, Roan. It's yours. Not far now," she said, and we walked on.

The thing that was no longer Roan enjoyed this world as it was. Feeling the fresh air against its rotting flesh, sending out its tendrils of flame, its sickness. It had become what it was meant to be. It followed the red trail of its beginnings in an egg, sung to life, and it even remembered the slick feel of its mother's womb, and her name, the monster that started it all. *Zabor*. It remembered the ashy ground that the Gardener had buried it in. So much promise. What a journey to get here now. What a trial. It had come to pass so nicely.

The sea beneath the creature that had been Roan boiled. It enjoyed the sea. The empty rage of it. What a strange sensation, all of these stones here as one, inside her — it — the dark with no name. The Great Hammer — that's what they had called Seela. Seela was now a part of her. A hammer, yes, to drive the wedge that would crack the world and build the bridge and open the door and so on, and so on. So tedious. No more of that. It was time to go home. To come home. To *be home*.

The thing that had once been Roan Harken opened its arms, rearing back on its broken spine of needles, the flat planes of its empty wings. It opened its mouth and sang back the song that had made it, and the four stones awoke and resonated.

The END *of the* NARRATIVE

The little black owl soared over land. It was getting close. It remembered the last time it had flown over the sea, where it was heading now, back then carrying two precious packages when it still had arms.

It remembered. As it got closer to the Moonstone, it remembered more than that. A cave safe from the tide. A hand around the stone when it had still been a part of him.

"It has to think it's won," Eli had said quickly, feeling time unwinding thread by thread as the darkness rose. "Show me into the Opal, and I'll hide you there. With everything I have left. Got it?"

Roan's broken face had twitched. One last sarcastic grin. "So damn bossy."

It had been only an instant — but Phyr had perceived and dropped her pendulum, and for a moment time slowed. Eli's mind splintered and wrapped around Roan with what little light was left. They shot down, down, into the dark, into a honeycomb. She was just a flame beneath him; he was just a snatch of wind. And the Opal and the Moonstone quivered with the effort, moment by moment the darkness pulling him back.

I am with you, Phyr had said.

She is strong, Deon had whispered. *She will rise.*

Eli hadn't wanted to let her go. He was glad Roan was in a state where she wouldn't know that. But he did, and Phyr pulled him out of that accursed place as the pendulum swung again, the dark closing the connection up like an infected wound as the Moonstone pulled free of Eli's body, and his spirit was thrown out, and away, into a great sky of galaxies kept safe in the wings of his god.

The owl's black wings grew.

His old body was near. So was the girl.

Roan, thought the owl, as the red song reached him across the void. *Hold on.*

❧

"I know why you did it," I said. "All of it."

Cecelia had been slowing down. The statues around us were so old and corroded that their voices were the barest whisper, nothing much left of their carved mouths. We walked on, in tense silence, and I kept my head down. Anger boiled in me as Cecelia diminished.

When I finally looked up, the statues were gone, the last one fading behind us into the dark as I glanced over my shoulder. Ahead of us, firefly lights were joining together in one great comet.

"It's the same reason you did all this," Cecelia finally answered. Looking up at her, I saw that her great head of dark hair, almost the same as Ruo's but more chestnut than black, had gone entirely white. "For love."

"Yeah." The comet expanded, releasing corona tendrils experimentally, like it was stretching old, stiff limbs. "I just didn't want it all to be for nothing. Your sacrifices. Everyone else's." I frowned. "Even Killian acted out of love. Even if it was twisted. So did Saskia. So did Eli." They'd all traded the purest parts of themselves for something higher, something outside of them, for the hope that the sun would rise and the chance it could change everything.

Cecelia staggered and I caught her, and she leaned on me as we walked the last part of the way. "I used to wish I wasn't a Denizen. I used to wish them all away. I used to think that they all deserved whatever was coming to them, and that I had to be outside of it all if I was to preserve my family. The people I loved." She shut her eyes. "Even I couldn't outrun myself."

We'd come to the end. The ground in front of us was now a path suspended high above a molten sea. The comet in front of us was revolving, speeding up.

"She's here," Cecelia managed, just as the comet collapsed inward like a dying star and grew into the Deon I'd seen in Cecelia's memory of the Arbitration so long ago.

"*You brought her the rest of the way.*" Deon bowed her great head. "*And now you, too, can rest.*"

Cecelia turned to me, standing as straight and tall as she could manage. She held onto my arms tightly, and I realized I'd held onto her long enough.

"I forgive you," I said. "I can go the rest of the way alone."

"Never alone," she said, and she bent down and kissed me, and in a rush of heat she was gone.

The whispers rose, the air filled with the petitions of the past Paramounts, Cecelia's voice now among them. I turned to Deon.

"So," I said.

Deon looked weary, too, but she grinned.

"*You hid yourself well*," she said. "*You needed the help to do it, and you were canny enough to take it when offered.*"

I hardly knew where to start unpacking that, and I tilted my head. "But I figure that now's not the time for hiding any longer."

Deon flickered, faltered, just a bit, and in that tiny shift there was only darkness, and I panicked.

"*The child of the Bloodlands has still corrupted this stone*," she sneered. "*I have called you here to ask your help. You must burn it out.*"

If I was panicked before, I was hysterical now. "Me? Burn it out? You're a god! Why do you need me?"

Black lips peeled over shining, frustrated teeth. "*Because this thing has wound itself around* you, *stonebearer*. You *must cast it out*. You *must take control. My sisters and I are fading*."

Three other voices — resonant, older than anything kept here in the Opal — and calling from outside of it. Heen. Phyr. Ryk.

This was worse than I thought, and I was almost too late. "Seela has the other Calamity Stones?"

Deon dipped her head. "*It's only because of you I can awaken now, as this memory here. You are now the last living Paramount in this world. And a ghost like me cannot awaken Ancient.*"

A deep song rose from the dark. The cavern walls flexed around us. Like it was going to collapse.

Deon flickered again. "*The song has been sung. The targes are broken.*" There was an immense seismic shift when Deon looked to me, imploring. "*This is the task you must do.*"

I threw up my hands. "I don't know what you expect me to do now! Every time I've got to pull a rabbit out of a damn hat, climb back up out of hell, perform, yield, bow. I'm tired! I don't have anything left. And even if I do this — what then? You want me to wake Ancient? How the hell am I gonna do that?"

Deon shut her eyes. "*Fia has sent us the Quartz. Phae is coming.*"

Phae? My heart hammered. But I still couldn't move.

"I just —" I suddenly felt like my chest was going to cave in. "I can't do it. I can't do it alone."

"You won't be."

I turned. The sound of wings, the feeling of a golden light outside of the Opal, tethering into it. A thin chain reaching across the vast hopelessness.

❧

"They're not here."

The first site the coalition had headed for was near their landing site at Newfoundland. It was the last place they'd felt the fissures, the same kind that always came before a city-wide attack. "I think it's Urka," Barton said. Zhao agreed that if that huge servant was so close by, it might be a chance to mount a surprise attack and stop any others before they started. Or, at least, find any survivors of the battle at sea.

When they arrived at the cliffs, there was no one there. Just a huge ruin of crumbled stone, ash, and glass. *Always one step behind*, Barton thought drearily.

But there was something in the rubble — a tree.

"It's different than the others," Zhao said when he met Kita and Barton there, as they were about to head back to St. John's, which was still reeling from an attack of its own and was desperate for aid — Denizen or otherwise, despite the panic that revealing them had caused. Barton figured there'd be more time in the aftermath to go after Denizens, but the Mundanes had to survive first.

The tree was almost a storey high. At the base of its great, sprawling roots was a boulder, like it had very suddenly split it in two. Barton couldn't shake the feeling that the boulder had once been alive, somehow, and was not from this world.

When he touched the tree's bark, it was warm. It sent a shockwave into his heart, and he remembered something he hadn't thought of in months. It was an image of him running a track, and Phae had been there, and a child. *Their* child. It filled him with longing. It was something he'd seen when he, Phae, Natti, Eli, and Roan had sealed Zabor away last spring. A tremulous connection. A promise of the future. But how could such a thing exist now? How could something so precious ever take root again in a world where he was always too late?

Don't let go, he heard Phae say, and it cleaved him in two.

The roots in his arms shot out without warning, wrapping firmly around the giant black tree. Kita and Zhao leapt back, and Barton's eyes went into the back of his head, and there was a thunderclap —

When Barton opened his eyes, and the air came back into

his leaden stomach, there was something heavy in his arms. A body. A little girl. She raised her head, her hair cropped close to her pale face. Her brown slanted eyes cleared when they looked around, looked up at him. She was warm, and she took a breath.

She was alive.

"Hi," Barton managed.

The little girl smiled. Something above them let out an ear-splitting screech, and they both looked up. An owl with black wings wheeled overhead and headed out towards a rocky chain of islands in the sea.

Margot had never heard so many evacuation sirens going off at once. Had forgotten all about them, really, since they'd always been silent and had just become part of the rusted landscape. *They were originally put in for storm warnings*, she'd overheard someone say at the Quik Stop down the street, where she'd been buying milk when the first wave went off.

Cell towers had gone down in the last attack. Major ones. The phones that everyone had become dependent on had been rendered useless. People were running out into the streets, threading through neighbourhoods, trying to make sense of what was happening. "Something went down out in the middle of the goddamn ocean," was the word in Stella's on Sherbrook, people communing there, needing community more than to run to their basements as the sirens blared louder.

"That thing was spotted in New York. They're saying it's the work of terrorists with abilities. Abilities! Like some goddamn movie! What the fuck do they take us for? Is this just global warfare dressed up as a stunt with wizards and shit?"

Margot would have been the last person anyone would have asked to weigh in on things. She'd been there, though, last week when that six-eyed mountain monster, burning from the inside, had split apart Portage and Main. Had seen it burning black from the inside out, wailing and calling its zombie children to it. She was on her lunch hour, just coming up from the underground pedestrian pass for some fresh air. For a cigarette.

Some goddamn smoke break.

Now those twisted trees littered sidewalks and made the roads impassable. The Canadian government mobilized the military, but more attacks crept up across the country. The world. Winnipeg had enjoyed its landlocked isolation, but it could no longer boast it was safe from anything. Nowhere was. And no help was coming. Margot had gone through as many smokes as she'd wanted. She'd earned it.

But Margot was pragmatic. She went back to her apartment, shut the blinds. The world had been spun on its fucking head. What else was there to do except go home and wait? People were reporting the resurgence of strange memories from last winter — from the major flood that hadn't been just a storm or a fast melt. A shared dream of a demon in a river with thousands of angry, chittering children. And now they all had the horrible dreaded certainty that the monster was about to come back. Anything was possible.

She knew there was no point in turning on the TV. Cable was out, too. The prairie wind was high today, battering the windows. The potheads below turned up their music to drown it out, drown out the world ending, the images of people with magical goddamn powers ripping cities apart all over the news and YouTube, of children with that fucked-up plague tearing and transfiguring people into burnt husks. Into an urban forest of the dead.

The sirens suddenly died and the wind stilled. Margot got up from behind her couch and peeked out her third-storey window, down into Westminster Avenue.

The birds were frozen, mid-flight. The sky was red.

The world had stopped.

And then the earthquake hit.

❧

When the targes broke from the resonance of their song sung back to the Bloodlands, it was like they hadn't been there at all.

The walls of the Darkling Hold came down so suddenly, that in that deep canyon of ash, the three forgotten titans blinked like newborns. Out here, the song was a red, devastating call.

Zabor and Kirkald turned to their third sibling. It had no mouth, and yet it sang back the first chord. The red rings beneath each of them flashed. Above them, the Bloodlands were opening.

❧

When the song had ended, and the crack across the sea went from shore to shore, the thing that had been Roan Harken opened its eyes behind its mask of bone.

The one thing Natti hadn't lost in all of this, as she held tight to Aivik, was Maujaq's bear claw and the power in it. It was pulling the sea around her and sending her into the fastest current. She was weak, but the water buoyed her up, made her stronger. Even in the Sapphire's absence, the water was still telling her something.

It was telling her to turn around.

When she stopped, pulling Aivik back, his huge eyes were a single question.

It hadn't been the water telling her to stop. It had been Phae.

The bear claw stung in her hand. She sent a message piercing through the water: *We have to open the Abyss*. But Aivik shook his head. *We can't! Not without the Sapphire!*

Natti turned again, hearing Phae's voice getting closer, and Natti grabbed hold of Aivik, and she swam in the direction of her friend's call.

Beneath them a red trench was tearing at the sea. Fast as lightning. They would have to be faster. She put everything she had left into bending the water to her will, the will that Aunty had told her would get her into trouble one day. Maybe one day had finally come.

Something bright was coming through the darkness, and Natti heard Phae say *hurry!* The bear claw broke as she thought one last time of Aunty and the water admitted an amber silver light that swallowed them all.

So far from who I was, from who I loved. From who I wanted to be. Eli pulled my spirit up with the golden tether he'd cast around it, but even with that I didn't know if it'd be enough. And I faltered.

I knew I was still inside the Opal, but it felt absolutely bottomless, like I still had so many miles to climb before I could surface. Any clear visual of it fell away. There were only sensations, a rush of brightness. I felt like I was being simultaneously crushed to death and pulled apart. *You're almost there*, Phae said, her voice and her presence so close in this strange plane that I could touch it. An amber light . . . With the line of Phae's voice came a sense of Barton's spirit, grasping hold of her for dear life, and maybe even holding on to Saskia, with the ghost of the promise that Natti had survived and was out in the water, the water that swelled around my invaded body's ankles as I pushed my way through.

Eli's tether was firm, but I felt myself slipping free of it. I knew I'd still need him for the last part of this.

You'll have to stick around a bit longer, I thought in his direction, still knowing there was no way I could finish this alone. *If you're still offering*.

I could sense his wings opening wide — he was that close to me now — and finally the darkness parted.

❧

The sea separated. The thing that had been Roan saw the huge crimson crack that her host's visions had promised. She could smell the burning ash of the Bloodlands across time and memory. She felt these dark parents rising to meet the light and the sky they had dreamed of making their own since they'd been made.

But standing over the crack was that Seal girl, and she had been the one to push the water aside. And with her a figure of crystalline, amber light.

The Quartz.

"I knew you would come," the wretched darkling beast creature that was just the Hammer cried. "But the song has been sung, and the work has been done, and I will be reunited with my true family!" The pale blades of its wings snapped open, and it felt itself expand, ready to take and unmake this last shard of the one thing that could stop it.

You're damn right about that, a voice said, and for the first time in its short, cursed existence, the thing that had been Roan Harken froze.

"No," it said.

"Yep," said the voice. Bright and chipper. Coming out of its own mouth.

The bone mask cracked. The darkling demon essence peeled away by inches. Wheeling in the sky above them was a black owl, which grew larger the closer it came, roaring more than wailing, and when the last of the demon didn't yield, talons grabbed hold and pulled.

❧

I took a breath when I reached the surface. It was cold out here, damp. I felt awake. I *felt*. Tired and beaten and fragile. But I was human. My eyes opened — a hazel eye given by a man who I had seen fleetingly in memory, his mouth forming an apology before his spirit fled for the last time. And an amber eye, given by Death, whose shadow hovered somewhere closer.

The black thing sucked off my body with a painful tear, but there was life in the old girl yet. The sludge-shadow tried to take down the owl, and they fought in the air for a while, and just as the dark thing and me dropped to the rocky exposed bottom of the sea by a trench between worlds, the wings came back for me and caught me in arms I hadn't seen hidden there. The beak stretched aside, and Eli looked down at me.

"Damn," he muttered. "Still heavy."

On the other side of the crack, Natti was on her knees, struggling to keep the onslaught of water from crushing us all. The dark thing that had been Seela, straddled that chasm, but it had been snared in a ribbon of amber light between the antlers of my best friend, who had travelled farther than I had.

The world was coming apart beneath us, and that canyon yawned huge and red and hungry. It was time to end this thing.

The three gold rings flashed beneath Phae. Eli held me up, and three more rings came up under me. Six. Then twelve. Each stone had echoed the call of its sister. And I felt it resonate, and I pushed that sound out of me and towards Phae, catching it in the tines of her sparking blue antlers.

The darkness shrank until there was nothing, and the chasm beneath us shone. I said one last prayer — *Ancient, hear this call.* A prayer and a last desperate plea to wake the only thing that could close Seela's handiwork and —

The Dragon Opal shattered.

Then the Emerald, the Moonstone, the Sapphire. Each

cracked under the pressure of the last fissure. The world was silent. And between us a geyser of darkness shot up from the Bloodlands, throwing us all aside into the raging tempest of the sea.

❧

"Did you see that?"

From the mainland, it was almost as if the entire world saw it. A jagged black line fissuring out of the sea, a black mass tearing through the red sky and disappearing into the vacuum of space.

Satellites were shattered in the mass's wake — but it didn't get far. When the dust cleared and what was left of the world's shaken technology came back to life, they'd know it wasn't all some fever dream. The world was populated by people with powers. Soon enough they'd learn that there had once been a precious balance these people maintained, under the influence and guidance of gods.

And soon enough they'd learn to blame them, too, for the break of that balance, which may have been intended all along.

Hanging in the sky was a second moon. A dark one, made of three beings luxuriating in their newfound freedom. The darkling moon kissed the heavens. Someday soon it would fall back to earth. But for now, the single entity that had been three would bide its time and enjoy the chaos below, making no promises.

It was where it belonged.

❧

Phae had done all she could. So had Natti. The sea had borne them back to the shore. And, impossibly, Phae felt warmth on her face from a clearing sky.

The world was still there. But so was the dark moon above.

Barton was somewhere near. Close now. The tether between them was growing shorter. She shut her eyes. So much had changed. But, at least, there might be a tomorrow to consider it.

❧

"It . . . didn't work."

The crack in the world hadn't closed. Eli and I looked down into it from the clifftop he'd carried us to. There was something at the bottom of the chasm, a glimpse of something, a place that I had seen in a distant nightmare. Another realm. The last realm.

Eli's wings swept down, though remained taut, ready for flight just in case. "So now what?"

I scowled. "That's my line."

He grunted. "The stones are broken. Ancient didn't wake up. The world has shifted." His golden gaze traced behind us to land. "Denizens are exposed. And that —" he pointed to the black smear in the sky "— is not going anywhere anytime soon."

I squinted at it, that faraway threat. Then I looked back down into the trench, understanding vaguely where, and to whom, it led.

"It should be me," I said, trying to be the brave one, one

last time. "Ancient is down there, and even though it slept through its alarm, it's the only thing that can —"

"You really need to come up with some new material," Eli said. "You went alone last time. Look where that got you."

I exhaled. "Good point."

"Besides," he said, "the stones may be broken for their use in the world. But I'm still here. Which means there isn't much else for me to do except trail after you to pick up the pieces. And I could use a change of scenery."

It was something in the way of humour. We'd need that, I was sure. Wherever it was we were headed.

"And what if we go so far down we can't get back out again?"

But I knew the answer before he said it. "You don't go down into something like that expecting to come out again."

Ever the pragmatist. I took one last look at the precious world. Thought of the people I loved in it. Said goodbye.

I felt a flicker inside me. The barest light. And it was a spark. A glowing ember. I looked down at my pale hands, at the chain-shaped scar on my arm. The wind rose. The heat rose. *There's life in the old girl yet.*

Our feet left the cliff's edge, and we dropped through the Quartz, into the chasm, together as we knew how to, down into the Brilliant Dark.

Answer

The world had stopped.

At the edge of the universe, Ancient awoke.

Tethered by creation, set as firmly as a keystone at the pivot point of life and destruction. The place, the feeling, the breath and notion from which all things come and return. Ancient felt the world grind to a halt, strung delicately in the heavens it had wrought, on a line that strummed directly into its enormous heart.

The darklings were gone. The stones were broken. But they had returned. Closer now than they had been for ages unmeasured. Ancient felt it — the wheel it had cast into motion, not quite making that last revolution, before it moved widdershins. Turning towards the inevitable.

And Ancient perceived. Which meant, after so long, it was awake. Awake to make that last revolution. To bring it all full circle.

It felt her there — the one who had once carried the stones. A pinprick in the vast eternal black. The one it had been waiting for. She had a long journey ahead. Ancient blinked, saw it all happening as it had before. As if it had never happened. All at once, these parallel narratives. But the end was always the same. As it had to be. And yet the girl was not alone. Ancient was, for once in its existence, surprised. Curious. *At long last*, Ancient thought. *The end has finally begun.*

Acknowledgements

There's a special tidbit I'm about to reveal about *Children of the Bloodlands* that I waffled about sharing. It either makes me look like a speed-writing adept (definitely not) or slightly psychotic (well . . .). But here it is: I wrote the book you are holding in under thirty days, start to finish, in April 2017. This seems slightly crazy (slightly?) considering it's nearly five hundred pages and the first draft was 130,000 words. Also considering that *Scion of the Fox* hadn't even launched yet (it did in October), and I was in a flurry of preparing for that and travelling monthly to promote it.

But that's how it goes in publishing, and I learned a lot about myself as a writer that month. I also realized, even harder than before, that you don't really write books alone.

So, once again, thank you from the bottom of my heart to so many people who made this book happen. To my lead editor, Jen Hale, whose comments are a lot of fist-pumping in the margins but also so much support and great constructive work on the narrative. To Jen Knoch, copy editor extraordinaire, who caught so many things and really brought this maddening book home. To the rest of the team at ECW — from typesetting to packaging to marketing to publicity — thank you for making another beautiful book I am ecstatic to share with the world, and for letting me do so much with this world.

Obviously, I could not have done this without my family, namely my parents, who stopped by my house every once in a while during that month to make sure I hadn't died, and dropped off copious volumes of vegan cake. And always, to my long-suffering husband, Peter, a.k.a. Dr. Bear, who stood back in patient wonder while I hammered away throughout many nights on this book. My rescue dog, Sophie, put up with a lot that month, I'm sure, but if it wasn't for her daily two-hour walks, I wouldn't have been able to so vividly brainstorm all the terrible things I put Roan and the gang through (again). A good doggo indeed.

And once more, thank you to the readers. Really, what would be the point without you? All the people I've met and spoken to about *Scion* since it entered the world have been so wonderfully kind. Thanks for joining me on this epic quest.

To be concluded in

THE BRILLIANT DARK

THE REALMS OF ANCIENT, BOOK III

We Are the Flame

Stick the landing.

That's the only phrase — a dumb one, a desperate one — that clung to Saskia's brain. She didn't know who exactly she was talking to in her head, since only stupid people gave themselves advice (so said Phae). But what she was doing tonight was plenty stupid, so she'd take what she could get.

No one knew she was out here, either. Not the curfew wardens. Not the neighbours. Not even Phae. Saskia was quiet, knew when to watch, when to listen. And you had to be stupid not to know that any authority would be otherwise occupied with what was going down at the Old Legislature. They wouldn't be for long, and she couldn't hesitate any longer.

Ultimately, Saskia didn't trust that she'd stick the landing, but as she scampered between buildings up Broadway, under flickering street lights, her canvas bag smashing heavily across her chest, she figured she had nothing else to do but jump.

It was dark. But the dark wasn't much of a threat to her — and hadn't been, for a long time. Sometimes it felt safer in the dark, considering what the world looked like during the day. Saskia kept her hood up. It wasn't the dark that worried her, but the cameras. The constant feeds. In the 4,067 scenarios she'd run in her stress-addled brain, she didn't dare consider anything other than success. There was no alternative.

Saskia flattened against the wall and turned her face away, stiffening — members of the Task Force Guard rushed past, grunting under their heavy packs, their full-helm visors cartoonish and faceless. Her heart sped up when she flicked her head back to see where they'd gone — towards Memorial, which was now called Reclamation Street. She focused on her breath, forcing her pulse to slow, but those cracks of burning doubt crept in. *This is so stupid. Why are you out here risking your neck for them, anyway? They wouldn't do the same for you.*

She shook her head, hands diving into the pack at her hip and pulling out the battered tablet. Plastic and steel, the weight of it slightly more reassuring. It made her feel in control. Stick to the facts — and the facts were that she was already out here. If she went back now, she'd just pace in her room until sunrise, knowing she could've done something and that she'd chosen to be afraid. No more of that, no matter what they said.

Saskia pressed the power button, checked the time against her wristwatch. Fifteen minutes. A few keystrokes and swipes and the app was up. So were her firewalls, old code that would do better in a pinch than nothing. Her pulse was back up, eyes darting, and when she zeroed in on exactly what — and where — she had to go to make this work, it played out in her head as cinematically as it had when she'd programmed this weeks ago.

Now all she had to do was not get caught.

"I don't know why you think this is, like, the best idea you could possibly come up with to *pass the time*."

Ella's bottom lip had curled at Saskia's comment, but she still kept stuffing her bag. "This isn't some game, Saskia. You wouldn't understand. You're not one of us."

With Ella's words, Saskia felt the stab between her ribs just as acutely as she always did over the last seven years. Anger roiled up in place of the shame, no matter how she tried to shove it down. "I think I know more about any of this shit than you do!"

"Shut up!" Ella whirled, but this time Saskia could see on her best friend's face how torn she was. "You don't get it, do you? You can leave this crummy apartment and be, like, normal. Have a future. You can have all those things that Mundanes want. But I can't. My Family *can't*."

The two girls jerked at the sound of something crashing in the apartment hallway, Ella's bedroom close to the fire escape and the walls always so thin. A woman yelling. A baby crying. The electricity flickered and went out, but it wasn't dark for long. The palm of Ella's hand lit her stricken brown eyes with bright Denizen flame.

"I just . . ." Saskia's jaw was tight, eyes bone dry. She was upset, but she hadn't cried in years, not really. "I don't want anything to happen to you. I don't want to lose you."

Once, Ella might have put her arms around Saskia, and they would have hugged fiercely, feeling each other's bones move with their love, but they were older now and knew better, and these days, Denizens should stick together, trust only each other. Mundanes were the enemy.

"If you want to help me," Ella said, focusing now on her little flame, which was growing wider and wider, "you won't get in my way."

Instead of heading back out into the street, Saskia shuffled along the building she'd hidden against, farther into the back lanes of houses and small apartment buildings crushed against Young Street. Even before the Reclamation Project, coming down here after midnight would have been dangerous, but with the Task Guard posted everywhere, especially downtown, *especially* by the Old Leg, no one dared come out here. Not even errant *Mundane* drug dealers. A cat yowled, darting out of the shadows. Saskia froze when it threw her a withering stare before scampering back to the much-safer hole from whence it came.

It's just a cat, she told herself, twice for good measure. It wasn't a f . . . well. It couldn't have been *that*. Not anymore.

But the line from the story leapt up like a familiar friend whispering in her ear. *Once upon a time, a girl was followed home by a fox . . .*

Saskia shook it off. *Pull it together*. Across the back lane, she rushed a collapsing fence and vaulted over it, landing shy of one of many huge piles of trash crammed between houses, against chain-link. A quick survey with her watch's flashlight showed it to be more of the same — charred old tech, probably seized from a Denizen house, decommissioned and flung out here to be collected for precious metals and scrapped. The Task Guard didn't want Denizens to be connected in the ways the Mundanes got to enjoy. Wouldn't want them to assemble, to think twice about putting their powers to use. It was in these many junk piles that Saskia scavenged often and whose contents filled her bedroom nearly floor-to-ceiling. It kept her hands and brain busy. It kept the quickly tumbling world on some kind of keel.

It kept the shadows quiet.

. . . and after the fox followed the girl home, Death came for both of them . . .

Saskia bent over, digging the heels of her hands — callused from soldering wires and pinching receivers — into her eyes. *Stop. Not now.* Her heartbeat was picking up. *Please, not now.* This was what she wanted, she reminded herself. To be the damned hero for a change. She wasn't going to freeze up. Not this time.

She took a breath. She counted. She straightened her spine and dropped her shoulders. *Not this time.*

The cat was long gone, and Saskia was alone in the back alleys of a city she'd never known except under the rule of anxiety. Of caution. Of an undercurrent of fear that she carried everywhere with her. She took another sharp breath and darted from light post to light post, feet quick and legs strong. Just like Barton had taught her, each stride like she was pulling against a current, and somehow, the stronger the bursts, the more her heart evened out. It was in running that she felt him most with her, and though she desperately wished he was here now, wishes were no good to the logical mind even at the best of times.

She'd have to cross Reclamation Street eventually, be out in the open with little protection. Saskia had known the risks, made all the calculations. But she was still more human than all the half-finished devices strewn across her workbench. Machines that had been her closest friends . . . apart from the one she was stupidly trying to save tonight.

Saskia dashed up another side street when she heard nearby bootfalls, more shouts. She crouched, gripping her black hood tightly. She squinted at her watch and then at the app. Not yet. She still had time to stop this.

Saskia's head jerked up. Quick-checking the map, she was ten feet from the outskirts of the building's side lanes, the perimeter of cameras waiting for any opportunity to catch her. She ran through the probabilities. The former was becoming the likeliest. *Stupid brain.* She didn't condemn it long — she'd need every neuron to make this work.

Keystroke. Flick. She realized she was close enough to deploy the code. A sudden rush — she could pull this off from the *shadows*, be home before Phae noticed she was gone. A flush of premature triumph. She —

The explosion rattled the windows of the rundown apartment block she hid beside, hammered the ground. Saskia went flying into a dumpster at her back, though she didn't land hard enough to do more than knock the wind out of her. Screams and shouting, the heavy, horrible noise of weapons charging up to fire the first sonic salvo. Saskia winced, looking up at the wall in front of her, emblazoned with an icon that was seared into her eyelids whenever she shut them and tried to sleep.

The fox head wreathed in flame, the red spray paint shining bloody in the luminous dark. The face of a girl. A face Saskia knew once, though briefly.

Beneath the icon: *WE ARE THE FLAME.*

Saskia's jaw set, and she leapt up on shaking legs, racing into the open street.

⁂

It wasn't a bomb, per se.

Besides that, explosives weren't Saskia's style. She wasn't that desperate. Not yet. The Elemental Task Guard may have been at the forefront of the changing world, may have had the right Denizens on their side, and all the tech the nation could muster to keep the *weirdos* in line, but like people, every machine had a weakness. Every gear or line of code could be outmatched. All it took was one person who stepped back and saw things from a different angle to pull the wires apart and expose the throbbing core.

That was Saskia's superpower, negligible as it was. But she'd relied on it for the past seven years as if it were a gift from whatever had touched her when she was small and more desperate than she'd even been. That little darkness that had crept out of the earth and stayed with her — it made her see things more keenly, especially in the dark.

The Task Guard cast its own shadow, especially over school. And after they got what they wanted, their perceived peace after Denizens were outed, they liked to gloat. That was their first mistake. There were so many ETG presentations at school, talking about their fancy tech, their one-up techniques to keep the enemy down.

Even though her classmates often slept through these presentations, Saskia had always listened.

Each guard is equipped with state-of-the-art optical enhancements, utilizing government-sanctioned augmented reality programming, helping them to identify those Denizens who don't wish to take part in our peace. There had been a sad irony to that. This new regime had invented a Spirit Eye. Death's patent had been robbed.

But now these devices, little more than contact lenses, could suss out any Denizen wishing to hide their identity. Their *power*. It fed information back to the guard through the optic nerve. It made things easier for them.

And it certainly would for Saskia.

She made it to the range road — the ring of high-security fencing and military-vehicle access roads around what was once the provincial parliamentary building of Manitoba. Now it was an army palace for Federal Task Guard only and hiding gods-knew-what beneath the sprawling complex.

There was still some kind of commotion going on towards the front of the building, likely where the blast had originated, and Saskia threw herself down into the cold, wet grass as another explosion went off. A siren was sounding. She had to act fast.

Her bag was already on the ground beside her, and she yanked out the heavy spikes, their cords trailing, thick as her thumbs. She hooked the clamps at the end of them to the posts on the enormous control box, then shoved the spikes into the ground. Atop these were the caged speakers. She turned every dial up, and though the buzzing was low it vibrated harshly in her shivering stomach. She hesitated only another second before hitting the main button on the huge device.

The sound that the device emitted was like the weapon the Elemental Task Guard favoured — a hand-held baton, shaped almost like a spear, that gave off a terrible smell of ozone before it was slammed into the belly of anyone not cooperating, shocking them to a crumpled pile. *Set phasers to stun.* Except Saskia's version put out a high-pitched sonic wave that temporarily shorted out the electricity functioning on the perimeter fence, including all spotlights directed on blind spots and the sirens.

It also left a gap in their digital fence, something Saskia was about to burst through.

Body low, she rushed towards the part of the fence that had been taken out in the blast. The Task Guard soldiers were otherwise occupied at the front steps of the building, and she'd have the element of surprise on her side now that they were shouting, scrambling. She took out the VR visor, slid her finger across the banged-up tablet, and shoved it into the back of her jeans. The firewall was down. Her code was doing its parasitic work in their periphery system and would provide ample distraction for those in the Old Leg's control centre in the massive dome Saskia stared up at.

The Dome was once the eye of the Owl's authority, but no longer the story went on. A lot had changed. But that wasn't going to stop her now.

Saskia dropped the VR visor over her eyes, slid her micro-sensored gloves on, and lowered into the stance she'd seen her real hero, first-hand, drop into before rushing in.

"Showtime," she muttered.

"Get away!" Ella screamed, arms and fists flaring bright with fire, and every time she lobbed one at an advancing guard, her elbow felt the kickback like a sawed-off shotgun.

She wasn't the only Fox still standing, but there weren't many left after the first bluff. The Guard had known they were coming. That was the risk they always took. She hadn't wanted it to escalate like this, or so quickly. They hadn't even gotten inside, to the general. They were still within the main courtyard. They hadn't made it very far before the sonic clubs were out, before Denizens had gone down.

Now Ella was trapped, cornered on the huge limestone steps that she'd only ever seen through industrial fencing. She'd gone on a tour of the building, once, when she was very small and the world had been different. Damien was on her right, but he was coughing up blood, and Ella wasn't exactly the strongest of the lot of them that had rushed in here in the first place. Clare, on her left, was cradling her shoulder, and when her crisp eyes met Ella's, they were wet with tears. Ella had never felt more like a kid than at this moment. And she was definitely no Roan Harken.

She wished Saskia were here. To tell Ella one more time that she was an idiot, so that Ella could tell her she was right. And though she knew it would fall on deaf ears, Ella prayed, stupidly, to anyone who would hear: To Deon. To Ancient. To Roan Harken herself. Prayer was the last futile thing she'd try for liberty as the guards charged up their weapons and advanced.

Then the sirens and the lights died. And the Task Guard wasn't looking at Ella anymore. There were surprised shouts, the blue sparking light of the sonic batons fizzling along with the certainty of their trigger-happy owners.

"What the hell is that?" she heard a guard cry, pointing towards the ruined fence in the murky dark. He dropped his weapon and fled, screaming.

Ella lowered her fists, squinted. They were all looking towards the gates now, the ones she'd blown apart to barely make it past the first wave, and the guards were scattering now, terrified. Some staggered, as if struck, and with each blow of this invisible monster chasing them out of their own turf, there was the sound of an awful roar, like a house fire, like a howl, and Damien nearly fell down the stairs when they all caught a glimpse of what was on one fleeing guard's visor monitor.

"Deon?" Clare hissed, and Ella caught Damien, and the three of them decided that, divine intervention or not, it was time to go.

❧

The problem with any bit of tech that is worn to augment reality is that *anyone* can augment it. So reality itself is easily manipulated. Saskia knew that better than anyone, code or not.

She'd spent foundational weeks, probably more like months, sculpting and designing and building the enormous image of Deon now burned into the retinas of the fleeing guards. Her research had been thorough. She'd interviewed a lot of older Foxes who had been more than happy to describe the god their Family had taught them to revere. An enormous warrior woman, with a head — or a helm, some people said — of a fox, with a mantle of white flames on her wide shoulders, nine tails, like the Japanese myth, wagging behind her, arms and legs braced in the leathery hide of primordial beasts she'd slaughtered with her blade of flickering purple garnet.

A world like this could still use a few heroes. And Saskia was more than happy to provide one.

The second problem with tech wired into an optic nerve is that seeing was believing — physically. Tangibly. It meant that, whatever the poor viewer was seeing, their brain registered it as real. Corporeal. So if that manufactured semi-hologram took a swipe at you, your eyes told your brain which told your body that you were, in more pointed terms, screwed.

These were problems Saskia had planned for. But she had her own crosses to bear. To get the best range, she had to move in order to make her digital Deon maquette move. She picked up an errant bit of fence from what was probably Ella's first foray into criminal terrorism, and that bit of fence became Deon's garnet blade. And many of the Task Guard weren't sticking around long enough to figure out they were being bested by a ghost in their well-oiled machine.

It was anarchy, to say the least. And those without the faux–Spirit Eye tech caught on to the fleeing guards' hysteria. She hoped Ella had dropped the stupid risk-taking bravado and seen this turn for what it was — a way out. Saskia lifted her visor, and her enormous, flickering mirage of Deon stood over her body like a skin, waiting for her next physical command. There was a flare of fire somewhere near the huge stone steps of the legislature, and in that flash Saskia swore she saw a girl, grinning, as she ushered two others past the still-dead fence and into the safety of the dark.

Saskia laughed out loud, pumped her tense fist. She

imagined that her VR Deon cracked its wide fox jaws in an unsettling smirk of its own.

Then her chest tightened, because in that same dark she'd only just thought safe, something else climbed out into the gloaming and was staring right at Saskia.

She stopped breathing. *No. Not now. Not again.*

There was a second of pregnant silence, then a bang like a thunderclap in her skull, and the lights and the sirens were back on, the doors of the Old Leg bursting open before her, with the Task Guard in their cruel grey service-issue uniforms pouring out.

"No," she hissed. She slammed the visor down, ripped the tablet out from her pants as she backed up, back towards the busted fence she'd only just brazenly come through, certain and unafraid. But when she whirled she was knocked over by the butt of something made of steel, and the tablet and the visor went flying. They didn't matter now. Both were useless. Dead. Her head rang with pain, and she tried to get up, to run like Barton had taught her, but her hands were being pinned behind her, a zip tie tightening as a knee pressed her into the cold pavement.

She didn't close her eyes, though, still staring at the place where Ella had gotten away. Where the Moth Queen stood, as she had moments ago, clear as the illusion of Deon Saskia had conjured. She knew this was no illusion. Death's many eyes were full of their terrible knowing. Her enormous wings gaped wide, many needle fingers folded, patient.

"Follow the moth," the great old Mother Death whispered. "The choice must be yours."

The words cut the last shrinking bit of fight out of her. As Saskia was hauled to her feet like a quivering fawn in a sprung snare, as she was taken up the steps and inside, all that was left behind were a few brown moths, fluttering around the floodlights of the city's Denizen prison.

This time, unlike all the dreams she'd suffered in the years since Roan Harken had changed her life forever, Saskia was wide awake.